THE CRACK IN THE TEA-CUP

By the same author:
A Responsible Man

THE CRACK IN THE TEA-CUP

Cynthia Kee

Published by NLJ

Published in 1998 by NLJ, 35 Goodge Street, London W1P 1FD.

A CIP catalogue record for this book is available from the British Library.

ISBN 0 9531642 0 9

The lines from 'As I Walked Out One Evening' by W.H. Auden are reproduced by permission of Faber & Faber Ltd.

Cover design by Alan Fletcher
Cover photograph by Denis Doran/Network
Typeset by Richard Reeve in Adobe Garamond
Printed and bound in Great Britain by Antony Rowe Ltd. Chippenham

To Bill and Rosemary

The glacier knocks in the cupboard,
The desert sighs in the bed,
And the crack in the tea-cup opens
A lane to the land of the dead.

W. H. Auden

1

James Potterton presses his nose against the wall. It's one of the bits of himself he can move. There's a jelly bit at the end that wobbles as if it were on a spring. If he crosses his eyes he can see it like a shadowy blob. He wishes he could finger it but his hands have to be kept behind him. They feel hot and bored there. He can't even scratch up underneath his shorts.

Ever so sneakily he shifts his weight and lifts a foot to push his sock further down his leg. If his mother were here, she would punch Mr Lovejoy on the jaw and they would drive off to Tesco's with the roof open. She would be wearing her stripey jeans and he, James, would be allowed to carry her purse.

An unknown voice comes down the corridor talking with Mrs Upjohn. They pass his back. He swivels his eyes as far round as they'll go and catches the merest glimmer of blue – a flash, a swish, a whiff like sweet orange peel. Blue's his favourite colour. He fidgets with his sock.

'James Potterton! Stand still.' Mrs Upjohn's voice makes him jump. He hates Mrs Upjohn. She's not even a proper teacher. As soon as they let him out, he'll cannonball round the playground, crashing into the little ones and making the girls cry.

Oh, Superman! Oh, Terminator! Oh, 007!

Rose saw a boy about nine, face to the wall, by the Headmaster's door. He looked chubby and mutinous. His grey shorts were very short, his shirt awry, his tie half undone, his round-toed sandals scuffed and his socks round his ankles. He was fidgeting from foot to foot.

The scourge of the school, she thought. Probably a non-reader. One for me. She did not dare smile. Instead, 'It's very nice of you to take me round,' she said to the white-coated woman in front of her. She knew those welfare ladies, tyrants of propriety and convention. It was important not to antagonise them.

Mrs Upjohn ignores her and knocks. 'Miss Pitt to see you, Headmaster,' she says as she walks in.

'Mrs ...' murmurs Rose.

The man behind the desk is stout and sandy – eyes, eyebrows, hair, skin all the same colour. He rises: 'Thank you Joyce,' and shakes Rose's hand. 'Please wait a moment while I go and see to this young man.' He moves out, propelling Mrs Upjohn before him and closes the door.

Rose sits on the edge of what she knows is called a fireside chair. It has wooden arms and the seat and back are upholstered in knobbly, colourless material. Cries, shouts and the hard ring of rubber balls bouncing on asphalt, homogenised into general hubbub, come juddering in through the Crittall windows. Mr Lovejoy's pipe lies in a metal ashtray on the desk, a box of Swan Vestas beside it. A whistle shrills and stillness falls on the playground. A male voice bellows.

'Line up fifth years!'

Rose twiddles the pearl button at the neck of her silk shirt. Across the years, a recurrent dream from childhood swims back to her.

She sat on the floor of the classroom, plump and puzzled, while a circle of girls round her threw a netball at her head. The girls were laughing and Rose was trying to laugh too.

She clears her throat and the upper part of her body contracts with the faintest of shudders. It's all right. I'm on the other side of the classroom now, she tells herself.

On Monday, Rose starts working in the school. She wears a grey silk shirt this time and a grey denim skirt with a pink belt round her waist. Her brown curls are held back behind her ears with a velvet-covered band.

'Playground duty for you today, Mrs Pitt,' says the Deputy Head in the staffroom before Assembly. He hands her a whistle, hurries on ticking off lists, handing out notices, sipping from his mug. He is called Mr Foster.

'Give it a lot of breath, dear,' says a grey-haired woman near by in a low voice. She sits down on one of the fireside chairs arranged, backs to the wall, in a formation at odds with the wishful cosiness of their function. She starts talking Welsh to the woman on the next-door chair.

'Thank you,' says Rose.

The Deputy Head is on the far side of the room now.

'Excuse me, Mr Foster, but what does one have to do for playground duty?'

Mr Foster sighs.

Rose smiles at him. He has a sharp, lined face but he wears a good grey flannel suit with a light tie.

Without looking up, he says, 'No large balls, no fighting, no shouting. Blow the whistle three minutes before time, line them up in years, march them in. No talking after the whistle.' He speaks as though he has no time to spare for raising voice or eyes, in a fast monotone. He purses his lips and leaves the room, taking small busy steps.

A bell rings. The room empties.

Line them up in what ...?

She steps out of the room and into a muffled stream shuffling slowly through the corridor.

Teachers are filing at the front of their classes. Some hold children's hands. Others march at the head of their troop.

Rose sees the boy who had been in trouble outside the Headmaster's room. His shirt is already hanging out of his shorts and he's trying to hook his feet round the legs of the girl in front. The girl has red cheeks and long golden hair. She's holding hands with another girl. She turns round and pushes. The boy punches her. She squawks.

'Miss! James Potterton's hit me,' she wails.

The teacher points a long arm: 'James, go to the end of the line and be quiet or else you'll be in trouble again.'

Dragging his feet, James Potterton goes to the end of the line. He walks alone, shadow boxing and muttering all the way to the hall.

Rose sits on a chair at the side in front of the parallel bars. Other teachers are sitting there too. There are climbing ropes looped overhead and the children, cross-legged on the floor, fill the body of the hall. Mr Lovejoy stands on a platform by a piano and more teachers sit on chairs alongside. He plays some chords with a heavy hand.

'Good morning boys and girls.'

'G'morning Headmaster. G'morning teachers,' shout back the children in pile-driver rhythm.

Faintly averse, Rose watches.

By her feet a white-faced shrimp, an urchin with enormous eyes, scratches his eczema and rocks. An Asian child, brightly clothed, sits absolutely still in the second row. A stocky boy with freckles mouths words in time with the Headmaster, a serious expression on his face. He scrambles to his feet and sits just out of sync with the crowd. Two girls point at Rose and whisper. A boy in the back row takes a car from his pocket and runs it up and down the floor in front of him. A teacher slaps him sharply on the hand. The boy drops the car and goes to put it back in his pocket. The teacher thrusts an open palm and the boy, eyes on the floor, places the car upon it. A fat boy sucks the thumb of one hand and holds on to his crotch with the other. And the girl with the long golden hair opens her mouth and sings to the song of the piano as if releasing a flock of birds into heaven.

Afterwards, Mr Lovejoy leads Rose round the classrooms.

He explains her to the teachers.

'Mrs Pitt will be taking your six worst for remedial. I've arranged a space on the landing. Please work out a timetable with her. Very good.'

Rose smiles at the teachers and smiles at the children.

Few smile back.

As the first bell rings he leaves her on the landing where a small space facing the window has been fenced off with bookcases. Inside are three interlockable tables, knee-high and seven small chairs.

'You'll find we're a very happy family here at Meadowbrook. Let me have a copy of your timetable in due course.' He inclines his head and moves away.

Blimey! Folding her legs up small, Rose sits down on a chair.

Mr Lovejoy's head and shoulders appear above the bookcases. 'By the way, Mrs Pitt, seats down the side of the Hall are reserved for class teachers at Assembly,' he says.

'Oh, dear. I'm so sorry. Where should ...?'

But Mr Lovejoy has gone.

Oh dear. And her hand in the pocket of her grey denim skirt closes on the hard surface of a whistle.

She looks at her watch. Five to ten. From her bag she takes a loose-leaf file and on a clean sheet writes 'Timetable'. She takes out a ruler and underlines it.

'Miss. Mi-iss!'

A line of children, four boys and two girls are standing at the level of her eyes a few feet away. Each holds a reading book. A girl with pink plastic bows in her hair is speaking. 'Miss. Mr Foster says we're to come to you now for reading.'

She looks at Rose and giggles.

Rose stares. Then, 'Hullo!' She smiles. 'Sit down. What's your name?'

'Please Miss. Wendy, Miss.' The girl sits next to Rose. She wriggles on her bottom and reaches down to pull up her pink socks.

'Do I have to come?'

It's a wiry boy with scarred knees. He looks straight at Rose and kicks the leg of the table nearest him.

At a loss for a truthful answer, Rose looks him in the eye.

'We can talk about that. Please come and sit down. What's your name?' she says.

'Simon.'

He hurls his reading book into the air. Stained and dog-eared, it falls with a splat and lies crumpled on its face. He turns his back and starts kicking the bookcase.

Wendy's mouth purses into a tight rosebud: 'Stoppit Simon. I'll tell Mr Foster.'

Two boys are fighting. One, the eczema-covered urchin, has his thin arms gripped round the waist of a taller boy. He is butting him in the stomach. The taller boy seizes his shirt and punches him. A sound of material ripping comes through the dull thump of blows on flesh.

Beyond, a small hairy Indian girl is standing. Her mouth is open and there is a vacant expression on her face. She seems completely passive.

At the end of the line with his back to the others, James Potterton makes faces at himself in the window.

Rose turns to Wendy with a piece of paper. She does not smile. 'Write down your name, Wendy. And your age and the people in your family. Then make a picture of you all together in action.'

'Mr Foster says we're to read to you, Miss. What's action?'

'Action means doing something.'

'Haven't got a pencil.'

Rose gives Wendy a pencil and puts a packet of felt-tips in front of her. 'You can use colours ...'

She stands up. Books are falling out of the bookcase faster and faster in response to Simon's kicks.

The two boys are rolling on the floor among the chairs, which make harsh scraping sounds on the wooden floor.

James Potterton has started hitting the window with his fists.

She goes over to the little Indian girl and takes her hand. It lies limply in hers. She leads her to the table, sits her down, puts a pencil in her hand and paper before her.

'What's your name?'

No reply.

'Write it down,' says Rose, 'And your age and your brothers and sisters and make a picture of your family all together doing something.' She wants to shake her.

Stepping over the bodies writhing on the floor, she takes paper across to Simon and puts it on top of the bookcase. She tells him what to do.

'Why can't I go back to my class?' he says angrily.

From behind comes Wendy's voice.

'Can I go to the toilet, Miss?'

'Must you?'

'Oh, oh, oh. I really need to go.'

'All right.'

Wendy slides off her chair and runs, pink socks flashing down the passage like a rabbit's scut.

Should she be running?

'James Potterton!' To her surprise her voice comes out with an accusatory ring. She modifies it. 'James. Please come over here and write down your name.'

'Can't' says James, stagily breathless.

'Why not?'

'I'm busy.'

'Okay. When you're ready, then.'

He stops the dialogue with his reflection and comes over. 'Can I use colours too?'

'Yes. Write down —'

'I know. Don't nag.' Sitting down, he grabs a fistful of felt tips and starts to draw, using both hands alternately.

Rose runs her fingers through her hair, tugging at the roots. She feels as though she's driving into a vortex of snowflakes.

A whine from the floor: 'It's boring here. There's nothing to do.'

The taller of the two boys is lying on his back drumming his heels.

He looks worryingly dishevelled and covered in dust – clinging grey grime, well-matured from years undisturbed under pipes and radiators. The white-faced urchin is scratching. Though startlingly thin, his face is beautiful and his uncut hair curls in smelly Carolean tendrils round his grubby neck. Before Rose can think of anything, the taller one, like a tight coiled spring, jumps up.

'Come on Sam! Let's play gorillas!'

He bounds on to a table and leaps for the next one.

'Great idea!' Sam shouts back. Batting his hand in front of his mouth, he makes a jump. 'Come on, Si. This is good fun.'

His voice is husky from shouting.

Rose is drowning. Panic tightens her stomach and rises to grip her throat. She want to hit out. Scream. Shout … Nothing she has learned in her select band of 'mature' students at College has covered this – nor has her imagination. Her principles prevent her from the use of force or coercion. And she knows she would suppress valuable signals and openings if she did.

She notices that the little hairy Indian girl is crying. She notices too that she feels no compassion.

'Which of you two boys is best at football?' she calls.

'Me, Miss. Me!' The taller one jumps up and down on a table top.

'And which of you runs faster?'

'Me, Miss. Me. I'm the best!' He bangs his chest.

'What's your name then?'

'Gary. Gary the King,' he says with an evil leer.

Sam, the urchin, sits on a table. 'Ask him who's the sexiest, Miss.'

Rose ploughs on. 'Which of you has the most letters in his name?'

'Me, Miss. Me. Sa-am.'

'Gar-ry! Ga-ary.'

Rose seizes paper and thrusts a pencil in each boy's hand. 'Write it down and we'll count …'

A quarter of an hour later when the bell rings, Simon, still standing at the bookcase, has covered his paper with disconnected black pin-figures and written '2 9 ½ 1d 1 2.' Every now and then he bends with a jerk, picks up a book and hurls it overhead with a mad yodel.

James has filled his sheet with a bold drawing, brightly coloured in, of a woman and a boy in an open car, scarves and long hair flying. The boy is larger than the woman and he has written 'James P' in firm, rounded, jumping letters.

Sam and Gary have folded their paper into aeroplanes. They are throwing them around the room. Rose, keeping her voice low and even, tries to persuade them to write their names on the wings.

'Nah,' says Gary, drawing swastikas on his, 'Never. It'll spoil it.'

Sam throws his aeroplane at Rose. 'There you are, Miss.' He runs away. The wings are covered with smudges and thumb marks. But on the body he has written 'sAm 10'.

The little Indian sits mute and impassive, a pencil drooping in her hand where Rose put it. She has stopped crying and has rolled her eyes so the pupils have almost disappeared and a lot of white shows.

As Rose wonders what to do with them, doors begin to open and a movement of teachers and children takes place between them.

A sudden disturbance, as if of tides meeting, stirs on the edge of her patch. More children, larger ones, jostle on its periphery. They too hold battered reading books in their hands.

A histrionic boom: 'Miss. Miss,' wails James, 'He's taken my picture. Tell him to give it back!'

Two large boys are passing his drawing above their heads. James turns on the little Indian girl and punches her. The little Indian gives an animal grunt. With a swift dreamlike movement she buries her fingers in his hair and clings. Tethered, he thrashes and flails.

Rose closes her eyes.

'Who are you?' she shouts at the newcomers.

'Please Miss, we're sixth years, Miss,' those still standing chorus in reply. 'Mr Foster says we're to come to you now for reading.'

9

2

'How did you get on?' said her lover after they had made love in bed that night. 'It was your first day, wasn't it?' His fingertips felt damp scalp; his palm, matted fuzz. She never flagged. Whatever he called for, she gave. He pulled her in to him closer.

'It was rather ghastly,' said Rose. 'Hell, in fact. The children seem desperate. Doomed. And nobody's interested. In the staffroom they sit round the edge in terrible uncongenial chairs and talk about the best kind of rounders bat to buy. There seem to be an awful lot of hidden rules. I used the wrong mug ...'

'Poor Rosebud,' said her lover. 'I hate schools. They unman me to this day.' He put his hand to her breast and fingered the neat little nipple under it. The textural contrast never failed to move him. He squeezed. 'You looked very pretty tonight. Was that a new dress?'

'No,' said Rose, 'You've seen it before.' She reached for his penis but he laughed and rolled away. His first meeting was at nine.

'So what else?' he said and felt for her leg to grip between his own.

Rose settled the soft parts of her front into the concavity of his back and laid her arm on the long curve of his flank. She loved his flanks and she thought their shape, like the pale belly of a salmon, one of the most perfect on earth. 'There's one boy who seems so terribly way out that I can't think how ever I'll get in touch with him,' she said into the nape of his neck. 'He's white and skinny, whiter than paper, whiter than air, and tough and smelly with huge eyes and straggly hair and he's covered all over with eczema. He's scratching all the time. He seems unattainable. Unreachable. And then there's another, oh God, called Simon. He seems accident-prone to a suicidal degree and his drawings are all black and disconnected …'

'Disconnected – how d'you mean?'

'Not joined,' said Rose. 'Heads, bodies, arms, legs. It really means he's very disturbed. Well, you can see can't you? But at least he made some marks on paper. There were others who didn't do anything at all.'

'Black and disconnected …' His voice was low and sleepy. 'Oh, Rosie, hold me tight.' He felt for her arm and wound it round his chest. 'At least we're all joined up.'

'And rainbow-coloured,' said Rose.

'Dove grey. The breast of a dove,' and he fell asleep.

Rose lay beside him, her cheek against the flat space between his shoulder blades. She thought of James Potterton's nose and her mind filled up, not with dove grey feathers, but with hard-edged dissonant shapes in harsh colours that jostled and jockeyed in an uncomfortable tangle of racket and clatter. Several times during the day, teachers had flung open their classroom doors on to the landing, shouting for quiet. Once it had been Mr Foster who gave Rose a look of such scorn as he settled her group to copying from their books that she had felt weak at the knees.

Her performance in the playground had been far from satisfactory. As she wandered round its asphalt surface, little girls came up to hold her hand or swing on her arm. Plastic footballs flew around, but she succeeded in tracing only one to its source. She confiscated it and the owner burst, unexpectedly, into tears. He was escorted aside by a knot of consoling and, it seemed to Rose, accusing peers.

'I'm afraid you're not allowed large balls in the playground,' she said to a group of girls jumping and shooting at a netball post.

'Oh, but we're practising, Miss,' said a girl she'd seen before, golden-haired with red cheeks.

Everywhere she looked boys were punching and scuffling on the ground.

Did that count as fighting?

At four minutes to eleven she took the whistle from her pocket, filled her chest with air and blew.'

A piffling squeak emerged. A few nearby children giggled.

'Let me do it, Miss!'

'Oh, I know how to do it!'

'Give it to me! Give it to me! I always do it for Mr Foster when he's busy!'

Rose wavered. Then she put the whistle to her lips and blew again, a long piercing blast. Slowly, like a ragged blanket, partial silence descended on the playground and Rose experienced a tiny sweet trill of power.

Three or four children came and stood behind one another by the entrance. Others watched and soon began to shift and scuffle. The few lined up bumped and fidgeted.

'Line up fifth years!' shouted Rose. It was like picking up mercury: the globules, uncontrollable, split into ever diminishing particles at the least touch until even the tiniest speck rolled away and disappeared into the vicinity.

A flat explosive thud. A football flew into the air. Rose ran to pick it up, felt her rear exposed, backed into a corner. Few children were standing still any more. Most were talking openly. She'd lost them.

'Do you just go in now or does everybody line up first?' she asked a nearby boy in spectacles.

'Usually we wait, Miss. But can I go in now? I'm books monitor.'

He ran off. Three girls jumped up and down: 'Can we go in? Oh, Miss. Oh, please. We've got to feed the gerbil.'

'You can *all* go in,' said Rose and the ragged line broke up, halted, retreated before an oncoming figure in a white overall.

It was Mrs Upjohn.

'Whatever is going on?'

She approached Rose, her face button-tight. 'I've got the doctor in the welfare room. It's medical inspection for the first years ...'

'Oh dear ...'

Mrs Upjohn looked at Rose and her nostrils flared. She took a whistle from her pocket, blew and stillness fell on the playground.

'Line up fifth years!' she called in a voice of vinegar and sandpaper.

Clamped close to her lover's back in the quiet night, Rose shivered and closed her eyes.

Rose's lover was a married man. A farmer by profession and a Labour lord, his name was Wetherby. Frank. They'd been to the opera that evening. Invited each in their own right, both had said yes – an indulgence Frank seldom permitted for, practical considerations apart, the pleasure, the pain, the danger involved so heightened his sensibilities that he felt almost skinless. While Rose ... Well, Rose sparkled happy-to-delirious wherever Frank pleased. They had their own playground in the parks and riverside walks of the city, in the pizza places and kebab houses of the outer suburbs, in the open country and in Rose's white attic so much closer to the stars than to the metropolis.

As she'd flown round it that evening earlier, piling books and papers into stacks and putting clean sheets on the bed, she'd battened down the memories of the day inside her. She fastened herself into the narrowest black strapless tube she owned and pinned her hair up on the top of her head. As she put on scent – Bluebell, for him – his key turned in the lock and tiny prickles of pleasure went off, pop, like soundless sparklers inside the stiff fabric of the dress.

He came into the room in his dinner jacket.

'Evening, Rose,' he said in an elongated baritone. Excitement slowed him down (a tactic he'd learned long-since in the nursery). He advanced to kiss her and the tickly feeling in his cock almost took him over. They looked at each other, wavering.

'Darling,' he said.

'Darling,' said Rose.

Then they both laughed. He took her hand, 'We'll be late,' and helter-skelter pulled her down the stairs to the street where they ran for his car.

At the top of Bow Street, he leaned across her and opened the door. 'We're going to have such fun,' he said as she slid out.

'I love you,' said Rose. She moved off towards the Opera House to make her own entrance.

At the side door into the Box, the doorman smiled at her with delightful informality like an old friend: 'Good evening, madam. Professor Vane is upstairs. We've still got six minutes.'

'Hullo,' said Rose. Her eyes danced as she smiled back at him. Low overhead the big chandelier flashed and twinkled. Life at this level was so easy to slip back into.

At the anteroom door another liveried man smiled at her. 'Good evening, madam. Five minutes – and there's one other gentleman still to come.'

Inside, six people, formally clothed, were standing with glasses in their hands.

'Rose, my dear,' called Professor Vane, 'How good to see you. You look ravishing. As always. Ravishing.' High-glossed and beaming, he came over, took her arm and brushed her cheek with his bland ruddy one. 'Your father will be so pleased. Dear man. So pleased. We'll be seeing one another at the club tomorrow.'

Rose let herself be led round the room. An unknown gentleman bent to kiss her hand. She could see the fine comb marks in the shiny carapace of his hair.

'My dear,' said Max Vane, 'this is our new Ambassador – we're so lucky – Jean-Baptiste de la Vigne. Old friends. They've just arrived. Ambassador, this is Rose Pitt; Rose Hardy, she was. You may remember ... ?' Chuckling as if presenting a trump card he moved his hand to her upper arm which he squeezed in a proprietary way.

'But of course,' said the Ambassador and he could not help smiling as he looked at Rose, so beguiling was the sparkle in her eye, 'the Brigadier Hardy. A most distinguished friend of France. I remember him well. And you also, maybe? With your sisters – three little girls in white, like dolls, handing round the titbits at the evening cocktail. A charming touch.'

'Oh dear, was I drunk?' said Rose. 'Did you notice? I used to gulp everything I could find on the trays in the corridor. But you won't tell my father, will you?'

'I promise,' said the Ambassador, joining in the game. He turned to the taller lady at his side, seriously ravishing, dressed entirely in navy blue with a single glass jewel flashing at the end of a long ribbon and no make-up on her bony face from which the hair was pulled back into a flawless chignon.

'Chloë,' he said, 'here is Madame Pitt, the daughter of Brigadier Hardy. You remember him no doubt when he was *en poste* in Paris ...'

'Come along,' said Professor Vane. He led Rose a little further across the carpet, past the Home Secretary's wife who raised her chin and smiled an unhopeful smile, to where his own wife stood with the Home Secretary himself. Their heads were close together:

'For the chop,' the Home Secretary was saying *sotto voce*, 'the new appointment will be one of those loyal troopers from the back benches – or', his voice dropped to a mutter, 'or a *woman.*'

Millie Vane, sharp as iron filings in her pink chiffon raised vestigial eyebrows. 'No!' she said. 'What a lark.'

With a genial boom, Max Vane interrupted, 'Millie, I've got Rose,' he said.

Millie Vane took in Rose's presence. Her face stiffened and she started to prattle: 'You know the Home Secretary. We all know the Home Secretary,' she said in her high, childish voice. 'He's invented a new way of cooking scallops – with *Pernod* and Morello cherries. Perhaps he'll tell you ...' and she shot an appraising look over the black curves, the upswept tumbling curls and the bright lips of the young woman facing her.

Rose had her doubts about the Home Secretary. He bobbed altogether too easily along the smooth surface of social life.

'Does it work with *Ricard*?' she asked brightly and the grey shades of unkempt children, illiterate and unconsidered, swarmed behind her eyes.

The door opened and Frank was there, slightly out of breath, his dinner jacket, a little too short for his long body, slipping sideways on his sloping shoulders. 'I'm so sorry,' he said in his unhurried fashion, 'Millie, Max, do forgive me. This city is impossible ...'

'My dear fellow!' said Professor Vane. He hurried over. 'So good of you to make it. I had quite a struggle getting away from the laboratory myself. Let me get you a drink. May I introduce you to our new Ambassadress from France? Chloë de la Vigne ...'

'Two minutes, sir,' said the footman. He stood beside Frank with a single glass on a silver tray.

'Oh, but we 'ave met!' cried Madame de la Vigne, making a trill out of the last word. 'Last week. At the opening of French Cheese Week.' She held out her hand.

Damn the Wetherbys, thought Millie Vane furiously. How typical of them to get in first. How unfair.

From the corner of his eye, Max saw his wife's expression tauten and her mouth turn down. He reached for her hand. 'Delightful, delightful,' he said vaguely, 'we're all going to have such fun now you're here.' He gave it a squeeze and a little pull in the direction of the Ambassador. 'You must let Millie tell you about her years at the Beaux Arts. She's rather a spiffing painter, you know.' He spoke with inextinguishable bonhomie.

The Ambassador bowed. 'I have great admiration for your Turner,' he said.

'One minute, sir,' said the footman.

'Come along,' called Professor Vane. He placed his guests, giving himself the Home Secretary's wife. His own undirected conviviality, now in gear, would carry him through no matter whom he sat next to. They moved into the half light of the Box. Rose felt Frank's long fingers play against her buttock as he passed. As the music began and glorious sound swelled up from the pit, she breathed in with it. She was in love, her love was close at hand, and music was the food – no less – of love. She found she was holding her breath. As the overture died away and the curtain rose, she let it go.

Next morning at half past six Frank fumbled for his glasses and rolled out of bed. Bereft of the sticky contact between them, Rose felt for a pillow and held it close. She doubled another under her head and watched as he clothed his body in the colourless light of early morning. It was an improbable body to love, long and shoulderless like a Brancusi bird with very white skin. But love it she did as she had never loved anything before. Its planes and contours filled up her mind investing the world about her with new meaning, and she marvelled at this sensibility that had fallen on her like light from the sky.

He rolled up his bow tie and put it in his pocket. The top of his vest showed above the open collar of his shirt and his neck looked infinitely defenceless within it. When he sat on the bed to pull on his socks, Rose slithered out and knelt to put them on for him. He put out a foot and rubbed the woolly toes between her breasts. 'Get back so I can hug you goodbye,' he said.

'Rapist,' said Rose as he came, in his black suit, towards her.

'Whore,' said Frank as he took her in his arms.

'Stay,' said Rose with her lips in his ear.

'Don't look,' said Frank. He pressed her eyelids down over her eyes and she heard the door close as he stole away down the stairs and let himself out into the waking city.

3

'I don't think I'll wear my tie today, Mother,' announces James Potterton in his plummiest voice. He stands on the vinyl-tiled floor of the kitchen, cream, orange, green and knobbly-surfaced, in his grey school shirt and underpants, holding a long stringy object of faded blue striped with green.

'Oh, yes you will,' says his mother from the draining board, 'I don't want another of those nasty notes from Mrs Upjohn.'

James plants his feet apart, taking care for them to be on the orange bits. 'Oh no, I won't. I'm the boss in this house, and Mrs Upjohn's a whore.'

His mother, still in her dressing-gown, whirls round and the garment flaps open showing her plump legs up to the thigh in her shortie nightdress. She has the bread knife in one hand. 'You're *not* to use those words. I don't know where you get them from. You do as I say. Put on that tie.'

'Won't.'

She comes at him, all flying blonde hair and pink legs and when she's nearly upon him, James makes a leap for the cat basket. The cat jumps out with a growl and James curls tight inside it. 'Meeiouw,' he says fiercely.

His mother kicks off her fluffy mules and bends down. She drops the bread knife. Picks up the basket, using all her force. Tips her son out.

'Get out,' she screams and slaps his face. 'Get up. Get dressed. I

18

don't know what to do with you. You'll be the death of me. What have I done to deserve all this?'

Hunched on the floor, holding his cheek, James shouts back: 'You're not like a proper mother. I hate you. I wish I was dead.'

His mother gives a loud wail. Her face is white. Her uncombed hair stands out in permed ringlets round her head. She sits heavily down and slumps forward on to the Formica-topped table which shudders on its spindly legs. She begins to sob.

'Why aren't you like other children? I work myself to the bone for you. I give you everything a child could want ... Oh. Oh. Oh.'

James crawls hurriedly towards her.

'Meeiouw!' He nips her sharply on the leg.

She yells. 'Ow!' Jerks up her head. Shrieks, 'What have you done James? Oh, James!'

From the cat basket to the kitchen table lies a gleaming trail of blood, smeared flat into the tiles where James's knees have dragged. Startled, he sits back. Looks at his hands. Blood pours from a cut in one of them. He makes a loud roaring sound and starts to cry. His mother seizes his hand and, holding it above his head, pulls him to the sink. She lifts him against her body, turns on the tap, holds his hand under the cold water.

'I'm in agony,' wails James. 'I want to be sick.'

But he feels quite comfortable there, held between the hard edge of the sink and the familiar softness of her unbound bosom. He wriggles himself further into it.

'Oh my baby,' whispers his mother into his hair. She hooks her foot round a chair and draws it towards them. 'Stand on that.' She runs to the bathroom. Deprived of her enclosing warmth, James gives a howl, 'Mother, don't leave me,' and watches the water turn pink.

'Look at the lovely colour I'm making.'

'Brave boy,' says his mother, returning with antiseptic and sticking plaster. 'Isn't it lovely! Just like gargle.'

'Strawberry juice and snail's blood,' says James. He snuggles into her.

'Keep it up!' says his mother sharply as blood drips on to her nightdress.

James holds one hand above his head, his right hand. There's a deep cut, white at the edges, on the ball of the thumb. He puts the thumb of his other hand in his mouth and sits, sucking and swinging his legs. He feels like a d – or is it a b? His mother reaches for the sticking plaster.

'No!'

He takes the thumb out of his mouth. 'I want a bandage and a sling.'

'James Potterton ...' begins his mother. She sighs. 'All right.'

She starts bandaging. Beneath his breath, James is humming. She's the prettiest person he knows. He's going to be an artist as well when he grows up. But most of the time, his mother works in a restaurant. He might have a restaurant too ...'

His mother finishes bandaging. 'What can we use for a sling?' Their eyes meet. 'Oh, all right ...' She picks his tie up off the floor, knots it behind his neck under the grey shirt collar and puts his wrist gently through the loop. James groans. It sounds good. He groans again.

Sam's mother did not get out of bed at all. She was a graduate and she had married beneath her. Her husband was a plumber, a good man but useless to her now. She was on her own, cut off from her family, removed from former friends, too far from shore to try any more. The weight of lethargy bearing down was so great she was unable to move. She lay under the thin sheet and the only sensation that penetrated her senses was the faint unwashed smell of her own body. It brought with it the vestige of a thought too weak to be translated into action. In the sludge of her brain, it flickered and died away. She minimised her breathing. The least movement of mind brought conflict, causing intolerable anguish, and her sole motive was the avoidance of pain.

Downstairs, the children moved silently in the kitchen. Stained teacups, greasy plates and the old blackened frying pan filled the sink on which floated tea-leaves, potato peelings and nameless scum. Sam cleared a way through and stood on a chair. He lifted the kettle, filled it with water and carried it carefully to the cooker. He found the matches and, holding his breath, lit the gas. Once, the gas had leaped out of the oven and bitten him. The fright had been so unsettling he did not wish the experience to be repeated. It was over now and he scratched the scabs on his arms.

Maggie sat at the table in her vest and knickers. She was waiting for Sam to give her some breakfast. She caught his eye as he turned from the stove and he flashed her a smile, luminous and full of love. It was her second day at school.

'Marge or jam, Mags?' he said.

'Jam,' said Maggie.

The jam pot was sticky and the dulled surface of the substance inside was studded with crumbs and yellow fragments of margarine. Sam took a piece of bread, floppy and white, from the packet and spread it with a wet knife from the sink. He was immensely proud of his sister. He was proud of his Dad too, and his Mum. When the kettle boiled, he would take her up a cup of tea. Maybe she would get up and look after them again soon. Maggie had got jam in her hair so he wet a corner of dish-cloth and wiped it away. He would deliver her at Infants before he went to his own class in Juniors. It was good in Infants.

Scratching, he went to get his boots from the back door. They were damp and hard but they were good kickers. He forced his feet inside and took a couple of flying kicks at the scarred and pitted door jamb. Boots were not allowed at school. He would start with trouble before he had done anything else. Maggie had plimsolls, not allowed either except for P.E. He told her to put them on and tied the laces for her. She sat very still and the only sound in the dim back room as he laboured at her feet was the small sound of wheezing breath and the whistling of the kettle, now on the boil.

He found the teapot, listing and half drowned in the waters of the sink, groping further into their clammy depth for the lid. He made tea. He was tough; stringy, but tough as they come. Nevertheless, it took both hands and all the strength in his skinny arms for someone of his height to manoeuvre the kettle from the cooker to the draining-board and direct the boiling water from its spout into the smallish hole intended for it. He gave Maggie a punch in the middle of her vest when he had finished and she squealed and flung her arms round his neck. He lifted her off the chair.

'Put your clothes on, Mags.'

Her dark hair fizzed round her white face in wild corkscrews. She looked up at Sam through them. 'Can I have a bow?'

Sam did not answer. He poured tea into three cups. His mother had a special cup, see-through thin, with a curly handle and pictures of Chinamen and ladies all round it. He began the trek up the steep stairs.

In the bedroom, his mother in the half-light lay motionless under the covers.

'Mum. Tea.'

He made a space among the bottles of pills on the floor by the bed and put the cup down.

'Mum.'

He climbed on to the bed and lay beside the slow-breathing hump in it. He wished he could stay there all day.

Elaine met Tracy at the garden gate. Her garden had a pond with gnomes fishing and a crazy-paving path leading to the front door. Tracy's garden had weeds and long straggly grass.

'Swimming today. Have you got your things?' said Elaine with a hop. Her long fair hair, brushed daily by her mother till it fuzzed, fell down her back to her waist though sometimes she had it in plaits. Later, she would pull it back into a rubber band and push it under the white cap that was rolled up with her swimming costume in a towel in her school bag. Now that she had little bumps on her chest, she had implored her mother for a bikini but her mother had said, 'Not for school.'

Tracy clapped a hand to her mouth. She looked wildly back in the direction of her own empty house. A door key hung round her neck on a shoelace, but she knew she would never find a costume even if she still had one. She shrugged her shoulders.

'Oh, Trace,' said Elaine, 'what are you going to say? Have you got a note?'

Tracy shook her head and droopy mouse-coloured hair fell across her face. She picked up a stone and threw it, overarm, towards the next lamp post. It hit the concrete and clattered on to the pavement. Elaine could only throw underarm. She longed to throw overarm like her friend. Not many girls could do it.

'Mrs Upjohn'll kill you,' she said, rather primly.

'Don't care,' said Tracy.

'I wish you'd find a nice girl to play with,' Elaine's mother said sometimes as she smoothed lemon handcream round her nails after the washing-up. But Elaine, devoted and awed, hung on to her friend. She was fascinated by her house too, where nobody ever hoovered or made the beds and people drank cups of tea and watched the telly all day. It was another country next door.

'Don't care,' said Tracy again.

Elaine put her hand in Tracy's. 'I'll tell you a secret,' she said. Tracy bent her head and Elaine whispered under her hair in her ear. It smelled like candle grease in there in the half-dark with the long strands of hair falling over her nose, and Elaine felt tickly with excitement. She loved making secrets. Now she and Tracy would be special all day long, at least until break. They could give each other knowing looks, whisper, giggle and drive the other girls in the class mad with envy. Maybe she would tell Wendy, then there would be three in the know but for the moment, two was perfect.

'NO!' said Tracy. 'No! She never!' She held her hand in front of her mouth and made her eyes big and round. Elaine nodded her head up and down vigorously. 'Don't tell,' she said.

Giggles overcame them, wave after irrepressible wave. Now, every time they looked at each other for the rest of the morning, their private tickle would sweep them away into their own no-man's-land on the border between naughtiness and virtue. They put their heads together and whispered as they walked, hand-in-hand, through the girls' entrance into school. As they did so, Rose, in her Morris Minor, drove through the main gate and parked alongside Mr Lovejoy's Escort at the side of the school.

'Look, there's the new teacher,' said Elaine.

'She's pretty,' said Tracy.

'She's putting her car in the wrong place,' said Elaine. She started to skip. Tracy took a worn tennis ball from her pocket and threw it at the wall. 'Let's play willies,' she said. They threw the ball and caught it, alternately, inserting an increasingly complicated series of movements between each throw and catch.

> 'My friend Billie
> Had a ten-foot willie
> Showed it to the girl next door
> She thought it was a snake
> Hit it with a rake – an'
> Now it's only five foot four'

they chanted.

4

Sam sits across the table from Rose. He drums his heels fiercely against the legs of his chair. Otherwise his body is immobile, his face impassive. Rose wonders that such skinny legs can support the monolithic weight of his boots, hard as wood and raw with wear. She pulls her mind back and tries to keep it fixed, where her eyes are, on the child before her.

Without change of expression Sam bends and scratches both legs with both his hands. The movement brings a whiff of unwashed hair on to the air that hangs between them. The silence is tangible. Rose's eyes slip involuntarily to her watch: she sees the fine hairs on her wrist and the veins on the back of her hand. A quarter of an hour has passed since she asked him to write down or make a picture of something he likes. She's asked him twice. Not a word has passed between them since. She longs for the bell to release them but interminable minutes stretch into unforeseeable future between now and then.

Sam waits for the blow to fall: a cuff on the back of his neck, a reprimand, a plea, and he can dig his heels in deeper. An image of his mother crosses his mind. Is she still in bed? Maybe he'll see Maggie as the Infants come in and the Juniors go out at break. What does this woman want to make him do? He won't do it. It's the only thing he can do. When he gets out he'll fight with Gary. Kick. Punch. Shout. Over they'll go, flailing and scuffling in the comfortable dirt of the playground. In trouble again. The teacher is still looking at him. She doesn't say anything. He scratches and sits it out. Suddenly, a funny feeling is coming up his throat and making it hard to breathe.

Rose feels a shift in the atmosphere. She pricks up her senses. She recognises it as sadness and restrains herself from putting out a hand. Instead, she makes a conscious effort to relax both where they lie in her lap. She doesn't know what to do, so she too does nothing, hoping that no member of staff will pass by and disturb whatever it is that's going on. Sam is the farthest out of all the children she has to deal with and she's decided to give him half an hour twice a week on his own. Today is the first of their sessions. She wants to scream, shake, reason, plead. The tension is unbearable.

Sitting in his chair, Sam feels an unaccustomed sense of ease creep up on him. The charge drains out of the air and he begins to feel at home. Perhaps this woman's not going to make him do anything. It must be nearly time for the bell. He almost whistles. 'What's the time, Miss?' he says.

'Eighteen minutes to eleven,' says Rose. She does not smile at him.

Sam drums his heels harder. His boots will never let him down. He feels like a king.

With a horrible shrill clamour the bell goes off. Sam grins at Rose. He pulls in the new writing book and writes on the cover 'sAm'. Then he opens it and, pressing hard with his pencil, writes 'futBOL' near the top of the first page. The black marks look okay on the white paper. 'See you, Miss,' he says and flees.

Rose watches him go. She's smiling and her heart feels free, as though she's stepped through an archway from a dungeon into the light – and then, damn. On his trajectory to the stairs, Sam collides with a slow-moving adult figure. It's Mr Lovejoy. Sam strikes at groin level.

'Sam Clark,' booms Mr Lovejoy. He seizes the boy by his thin shoulders and holds him. 'How dare you run in the corridor? Where do you think you're going?'

Sam looks at the floor.

'Answer me, boy.'

Oh hell, thinks Rose.

Sam says nothing.

'Go to my study,' commands Mr Lovejoy. He flings out an arm and with inappropriate grandeur, as on a field of battle, points a finger. 'Wait outside until I come. And why are you wearing boots on school premises?' Sam makes a desperate feint to sidestep and dash for the stairs but Mr Lovejoy catches him by the shirt tail and shakes him, thrashing, like a rag. 'Do as you're told, boy,' he thunders. 'I will have obedience in my school.' He turns Sam round and pushes him in the direction of the school offices on the other side of Rose's enclave. 'Mrs Upjohn,' he calls.

'Yes, Headmaster?' Mrs Upjohn pops out from an alcove.

'See that this young man waits outside the office for me.'

'Tzt, tzt.' Mrs Upjohn takes Sam's hand and pulls him off. 'Come along now,' Rose hears her say, 'you're a very naughty boy.'

Mr Lovejoy proceeds on his way towards the classrooms down the corridor. 'Good morning, Mrs Pitt,' he calls. 'Settling in nicely?'

'Good morning,' says Rose. She stares at him with all the dignity she can summon and feels her regard slither down the hard shell of his righteousness like a spider in the bath. Oh, bloody hell, she thinks again and begins to tidy up the tables. She looks at the word Sam has written of his own free will and closes the book. She puts it in a folder, writes 'Sam Clark' on the outside and places it on the stack in the shelves behind her. Then she walks to the staffroom, slowly, to queue for the kettle and put her fourpence by the jumbo tin of coffee powder on the shelf by the sink.

In the staffroom, everyone is sitting in silence round the edges of the room, mugs in hand, in their customary chairs. Mr Foster is addressing them from his. He speaks in an urgent monotone:

'The noise level at dinner-time is getting out of hand. There'll have to be a no talking rule.'

What's going on? Rose looks round. She has not got a customary

27

chair. She generally sits on whoever's is on playground duty.

'Staff meeting,' whispers one of the younger men teachers by the door.

'Oh, sorry,' whispers Rose. She sits on the floor in the space next to him, her long black legs loosely deployed alongside her short skirt. Several pairs of eyes turn on her – and turn away.

'Quite right, Mr Foster,' says one of the white-haired Welsh speakers. 'At home we keep our voices low at table. Any shouting and they're not allowed television.'

There's a murmur of agreement.

But eating's meant to be a pleasure, thinks Rose. She says nothing.

Mr Lovejoy comes in. He goes to the table in the corner and sits in the upright armchair behind it where no one ever sits.

'We were discussing the noise level at dinner-time, Headmaster.'

'Carry on, Derek.' Mr Lovejoy glances at Rose in her little space and frowns. 'I wonder if you'd fetch Mrs Pitt a chair, Mr Woolf,' he says to the man next to her. Mr Woolf squeezes his way out and comes back with a child-size chair. There's a hush. Red-faced, Rose takes the chair and sits on it.

'Thank you.'

Mr Woolf gives her a bare wink.

'Carry on, Derek,' says Mr Lovejoy, again.

Taut on the edge of his chair, clipboard on his knees, fountain pen at attention in one hand, Mr Foster says: 'Dinner-time. Noise. Unacceptably high. *We must put a stop to it before it gets out of hand.*'

'There's a terrible echo in there,' says a woman teacher.

'Can't hear oneself think,' says another.

Everyone laughs. Teachers who eat school dinners – and most do – sit with their legs hunched sideways among the children at low tables in the hall at midday.

'Indeed,' says Mr Lovejoy.

'It's not nearly as noisy as most restaurants,' says Rose out loud but not, apparently, loudly enough for anyone to have heard her.

'Perhaps they could talk quietly with the sweet,' says a teacher in a pink blouse.

'An excellent suggestion,' says Mr Lovejoy. 'Silence in the dinner hall until half-time. As each table gets its sweet, permission to talk quietly. I'll give it out in Assembly tomorrow. I take it you're all agreed. And now, I'd like to discuss arrangements for Harvest Festival. As you know, Meadowbrook has quite a reputation in the borough for putting on a good show ...'

Rose closes her eyes. How could they? How could I sit here and let something like that be passed into law? She wonders what's happening to Sam. No wonder he has eczema. She feels like scratching herself all over. She opens her eyes and lets them stray over to the window. A discussion of muted animation is taking place around her. *We plough the fields and scatter* ... Harvest murals for the hall. A major yoghurt-pot sculpture of Plenty at the main entrance. The relative merits of *Ski* and *Eden Vale*.

Outside, there's blue sky in the window pane. A very small cloud drifts into one of them, shifts slowly into another and falls into wisps. The movement is slow as a heartbeat. The agitation in her body quietens. Her mind, weak as water, floats out on to the surface of the blue. She feels too floppy to recall it.

Last weekend in Grassdale she had watched just such a sky from an open hillside, in Frank's arms.

'I love you,' he said as he drove his penis into her.

'My love,' said Rose.

Like little bits of blue glass from a mosaic, the sky was coming down in showers round her ears. She laughed and, welded, they slithered until their heads were lower than their legs. Rose clung on. Frank laughed. 'Western readers should not expect to achieve full orgasm in such advanced positions,' he said and rolled over so she was on top of him. He dug his heels into a grassy hump and heaved them both so they rested against it. Rose looked down into his dear, creased face. His eyes, pink and undefended without their thick glasses, were half closed and crinkled at the edges, his thin hair was matted into occasional stooks like an untidy schoolboy.

'Where on earth can your specs be?'

'Dunno. Don't care.' He put up a hand and pushed Rose's head down into the warm viyella-covered dip between his collar-bone and his neck. 'Darling,' he said now and again.

Skylarks tossed unseen in the firmament above and, below, on the track, a man in a cap walked past with his dog and averted his eyes. A little wind, got up from nowhere, played on their backs. 'Has anyone ever been closer?' said Frank in a husky, halting voice in her ear. Tears moistened the corners of his eyes. Happiness took him that way. The intensity of his feeling for her sometimes shook Rose; hers in contrast seemed merely plebeian. She kissed his eyes and licked the tears away. Then she fluttered them with her eyelashes. Frank began to laugh. 'Helpless,' he said, 'quite helpless.'

Back round the curve of the hill on the thin track, walking briskly, came the man in a cap accompanied by a black Labrador. 'There's someone,' said Rose. Frank adjusted his trousers. Rose hid her face in his armpit. 'Good morning,' said Frank in his official squire's voice. The man stared.

'Afternoon,' he said and walked on.

'Is it?' said Rose.

'Can it be?' said Frank. He sighed. 'I suppose we'd better look at the time.' He groped on the slope above and peered at the face of his watch, obscured by many years of dust gathered in little hairy balls beneath the glass. 'Half past thirteen!'

'Your specs,' said Rose.

'Four o'clock, my God,' said Frank.

Rose grinned at him. They sat back to back and, pushing against each other, levered themselves to their feet. Then they put their arms round each other and held on fast as they launched themselves downhill towards the track. They went at speed, on through woods, over a stream, under barbed wire, past a flock of sheep who gazed and ran, woolly bodies wobbling on spindly legs. They gained the fields below and swung along, hip to hip.

The car was in a lane at the outskirts of the village. Frank put on his old jacket and patted at his hair. 'I've got to telephone,' he said, 'I'd better do it from the box.' Rose turned away and looked out of the window. He laid a hand on her leg, high up against the inside of her thigh. Driving one-handed he threw the car with a flourish round a curve, towards the centre of the village. Alongside, low walls enclosed brown stone cottages; dahlias, Michaelmas daisies in the gardens, a few roses still climbing, some bright red berries already. Ahead, the village green opened up, a sloping triangle in the quiet sunlight.

The telephone box was by the church. Frank got out. He smiled at her. Rose smiled back. She watched as, inside, he picked up the black Bakelite receiver, put in his coins and dialled. Behind the red-framed panes he pressed the button and started to speak. 'Darling,' he would be saying, languid and rueful, 'so sorry. Terrible traffic. Such a bore. How's your poor back?'

In his old stone farmhouse on the moor that night, they ate boiled eggs and toast before an open fire. Entwined on the hearth-rug, skin to skin, they settled into the curves and hollows of each other's bodies, made love, made love again and drifted inviolable and complete. Outside, the cold steady light of the moon threw black shadows on the bleached ground. The underside of leaves, the flanks of trees showed white in the white radiance and the line of the hills flowed dark against the night sky. It was all Rose had ever wanted.

5

Rose wrote, 'Monday night came like a flash of lightning. Rain poured down. Thunder hit the ground like cats and dogs all frightened ...' She stayed very still. Elaine was dictating a story: her voice, high and toneless, had stopped. Rose's thoughts strayed. She held her pencil ready. Frank, was he thinking of her? She must telephone her father. Her dress for the evening – should it be backless black or silver jeans? Frank. Would he be there and his – his wife? Elaine stared, apparently, out of the window. There was silence. Rose pulled back her thoughts. Confusion seethed in her mind. She tightened her lips, then made a deliberate effort to relax; forehead, chin, throat, shoulders. After many minutes, Elaine spoke. 'People ran to their houses,' she said in a flat voice, 'switched off their lights and went to bed. Billy came and put them all to sleep. The End.'

Carefully, Rose put down her pencil. She looked at Elaine. 'The end,' she repeated. She kept her voice and her face free of innuendo. Elaine nodded. She was wearing a neatly knotted school tie, and her long fair hair, held back from her face by a tartan ribbon on a piece of elastic, was in thick sheeny plaits.

'Would you like us to read it back?'

Elaine shook her head.

'Would you like me to type it out so you can read it next time?' She wondered whether to say anything about the story.

Elaine nodded.

'Right. And would you like to do a picture to go with it?'

Elaine fiddled with the felt-tips on the table and took an orange one. Rose held her breath. Elaine had never drawn anything before. Law-abiding and lovable, 'a little pet', she had round clear writing but could read and write nothing except her own name, though she copied beautifully. She put the felt-tip down and picked up a pencil. Very slowly she drew two pointed ears on the blank page that faced the lined one in her book. She stopped.

'Can you tell me about them?' said Rose.

Under the ears, Elaine wrote 'c a t'. She put the pencil down again and without warning sat herself on Rose's lap. Her firmly packed little body felt quite solid. Rose waited. Elaine said, 'Why are you sad, Mrs Pitt?'

'Sad?'

'You're not smiling.'

'People aren't always happy when they're smiling,' said Rose, and hoped she had not gone too far.

'Are you angry?'

'No.' They sat silently for a minute or two. 'It'll be time to go soon,' said Rose.

'When do I come again?'

'The day after tomorrow, Thursday.'

The bell went. Elaine got up and took her plastic pencil case and a small, purple-haired troll she sometimes brought to sessions.

'It's a good story,' said Rose, as Elaine turned to go. 'Well done.'

Elaine looked her in the eye. 'It's the end because they're all dead.'

She turned, walked demurely across the landing and away down the corridor back to her classroom, pink-cheeked and undemanding in her pleated grey polyester flannel and her stout pink legs in their clean socks.

'What a poppet,' said Mr Lovejoy, passing by with measured tread. He paused and an almost benign expression overcame his face. He inclined the upper half of his body over the bookcase. 'Everything in order, Mrs Pitt?'

'Fine, thanks,' said Rose and then, beguiled by the warmth in his eye, 'but I'm a bit worried about Elaine. I feel she's rather a disturbed child with a lot of problems ...'

'Disturbed? Problems? That poppet!' said Mr Lovejoy. He drew himself upright again. 'Why, her father's a security guard. We know the family well. Most respectable people. We had her sister here ...' He frowned and walked away.

Rose laid her head on the desk. Her eyelids felt heavier than she could manage and her mind slid away from the manifold complexities spewed into the little exercise book before her. On the other side of the plate glass, leaves the colour of ginger biscuits and thin slices of mango, were piling up in the playground and a few, unfallen, still wavered on the branches above. They were infinitely melancholy. A sense of longing overtook her and some lines of verse came into her mind:

> Margaret are you grieving
> Over golden grove unleaving ...?

They were from a poem she herself had learned at school. She struggled for the rest:

> Leaves, like the things of man, you
> With your fresh thoughts care for, can you ...?

Next day there's a staff meeting again. This time, Rose has picked up the news in advance. She is sitting in a chair well before one o'clock with an annotated list of the children she teaches. She badly needs to discuss them. Simon has fallen twice on his head in the last weeks and been taken to hospital once, his drawings are black and dislocated as ever, she's sure he's accident prone to a suicidal degree. The little Indian girl, Selma, has still not spoken – surely her hairiness, her speechlessness, her strange underwater movements are linked and there's a developmental flaw of a physical kind that someone knows more about. James Potterton seems unhealthily enmeshed with his mother; Sam, so neglected he might fall to pieces at any moment; Gary, unnaturally preoccupied, at nine, with sex;

Elaine, so split as to be approaching schizophrenia. Every child on her list, bar one or two she feels should not be on at all, is desperate. And so is she.

'What happens about playground duty?' she whispers to Mr Woolf as he sits next to her.

'Welfare,' whispers Mr Woolf.

He teaches the six- and seven-year-olds. Rose often sees him, surrounded by small boys, running football games after school. She wonders if he means Mrs Upjohn. Welfare, as a notion, sits oddly with her narrow withholding person. She looks uncertainly at Mr Woolf and he raises an eyebrow. He's wearing a patterned V-neck pullover with a tie and under the rolled-up sleeves his arms are hairy right down to the backs of his hands. He looks more like a sailor or a builder … She can see hair through the spaces between his upper shirt buttons and there's a dark shadow round his chin already.

Mr Lovejoy enters. 'Good afternoon.' He picks up a ruler and, absentmindedly, lets it snap on the table in front of him. Down in their easy chairs the staff recross their legs, direct their gaze upward, rearrange their expressions into ones of businesslike expectation. Mr Woolf rolls his eyeballs heavenwards for the fraction of a second before he too drops his features into neutral. Rose's heartbeat quickens. In the next half hour she has to make herself heard. It's a daunting imperative.

Mr Lovejoy begins: 'I would like you all to know that the DoE has accepted my invitation to attend our Harvest Festival here at Meadowbrook. I am sure you appreciate that this is a mark of the regard in which we are held at the Office …'

What on earth's he going on about? thinks Rose.

'… displays of leaves and berries … allocation for extra art materials … special periods for singing …'

Straight-backed at the Headmaster's side, Mr Foster leans forward, 'Shoes, Headmaster,' he whispers.

'Thank you, Derek.' Mr Lovejoy raises his voice. 'Mr Foster

reminds me that suitable footwear *must* be worn indoors. Mrs Upjohn has a small reserve of second-hand items for cases of proven hardship but notes must be brought.' He lowers his head and looks out from under his sandy eyebrows at the men and women sitting tight round the room. A few nod. No one speaks.

In the silence, Rose's mind which has been occupied with the composition of a sentence, wanders back. She tries to place a construction made up of visual clues and half-heard words on the faces round her. A nudge causes her to glance left. Mr Woolf is looking steadily at his trouser leg. On the paper fixed to his clipboard he has written: DoE = Director of Education' and 'Local Education *Office*.'

'Thanks' she writes in her own loose-leaf file and politely returns the nudge.

But Mr Lovejoy is addressing the elderly teacher whose classroom is closest to Rose's corner on the landing: 'Mrs Jenkins, I take it the subject for Home Economics in the week leading up to the Harvest Festival will be cheese straws. I shall be serving sherry in my room to the Director and the Governors before the service.' His tone is grave.

'I think we can manage that, George,' says Mrs Jenkins brightly, 'but I shall need some airtight tins ...'

There are murmurs from round the room. Rose finds herself thinking of the old shortbread tin in her flat; if she empties everything out of it, she can join in.

Aspects and dimensions are explored. Round and round goes the discussion in ever tightening circles. A young woman teacher pipes up:

'What about doilies? My class has been doing symmetry. Some of them have got quite good at paper and scissor work.'

Everyone bends towards her.

'An excellent idea, Miss Bunting!'

Miss Bunting, new from College, purses her lips and a slow blush spreads across her cheeks and reaches the lobes of her ears from which her fine hair is pulled up into a short topknot. She begins writing in the book on her lap.

Teachers turn and begin talking and, 'Thwack' goes the Head-master's ruler on the table before him.

'May I have your attention? Mrs Upjohn will be ringing the bell in five minutes. We have urgently to consider what to purchase ...'

Oh no, thinks Rose. A scarlet ribbon of thought waves in her mind. She swallows and sits upright:

'Plasticine. Could I possibly have some Plasticine?'

Her voice appears to have gone unheard. She leans forward. Her heart is thumping. She thinks of Selma's small incompetent claw in which writing implements flop tonelessly. She looks directly at Mr Lovejoy.

'Please. I'd like some Plasticine. I know it would help some of the blocked ones express themselves. Could I have some Plasticine? Please.'

Silence falls. She sees that no one is looking at her but at the books on their laps or the haircord beneath their feet. One or two pick up their handbags. The bell rings.

'Plasticine comes under sundries. I'm afraid we have no money at all left in sundries, Mrs Pitt.' Mr Lovejoy clasps his hands and rubs them in front of his chest. He congratulates the staff and wishes them all good afternoon.

What enormous feet, thinks Rose as she watches his giant snub toecaps cross the haircord and pause at the door. She feels too foolish to raise her eyes and she flicks over the pages of her file: Simon, Sam, James, Selma, Elaine, Gary, Wendy; Darrel, Lee ... one for each child, while the metronomic double-beat of the Headmaster's steps knocks in her ears and fades in the corridor outside.

6

Frank also had had an awkward day. To-oo boring, he said to himself
as he drove away from it. None the less, the hairs in his armpits prickled uncomfortably at the roots and he gave a little languid laugh to
suppress them. Rage was an emotion he disliked and his humorous
regard, as he looked quizzically over the top of his spectacles on the
many meetings over which he presided, had an invariably civilising
effect. He was a fun chairman, much in demand. People left his com-
mittees laughing instead of seething. All the same, it was not fair. He
loved his country. Its quiet contours were in his bones and their
destruction before the megalithic advance of development was more
than he could bear. Mindless greed, he thought angrily. He parked
and reached over to the glove compartment for the tin of fruit drops.
He felt around in the powdery glucose but the red ones were all gone.
He took an acid drop. All is vanity, he thought, as he placed it on his
tongue and sucked.

Across the river, the softened outlines of cranes and towers haunt
the skyline and the sun, a moon-coloured disc, hangs glinting
behind a mist which, in this still stretch of riverside city, has failed to
lift since dawn. The wide sky above him, the grey streets around him
– small houses, corner shops, dark pubs – loop, uninterrupted
monochrome, into infinity. He finds the prospect quite perfect in its
own quiet way. How redundant the innuendo of colour introduced
by Impressionist painters from France. What cheek to breeze across
the Channel and plop dots of flesh pink and mauve all over someone

else's river. He laughs at himself, and then sighs. Whatever's happening to England, his England, gripped by worship of the Golden Calf. He must not allow himself to be carried away by emotion but must stand, steadfast, against the tide of vulgarity and commercialisation. It'll turn, by and by, and some peerless features will remain intact. But they'll have to be fought for.

He looks at his watch. His next appointment is at half past six. He has two hours, two and a half at a pinch, in which to recoup. His cock tingles at the thought and a shiver goes through the sides of his body, right up to the thinning hair on the top of his scalp.

'Hullo,' says Rose, out of breath, and there's her bright face at the window. Frank's heart lurches and starts knocking on his ribs. He reaches over to open the passenger door and she tumbles in, all softness and orchard smells, like a waterfall of light on his senses.

'I'm dazzled,' he says. 'Give me my sunglasses.' For a second they look, almost shyly, at one another and then lunge with a single violent movement across the gear lever. The car steams up, the constrictions of the day drop away and their clothes hang undone around them.

'Half-time,' says Frank when the air has quietened down. He feels for his briefcase on the back seat. 'I've got us some tea today, rum and ginger biscuits.'

Rose sighs with happiness. 'Let's have a picnic.'

They set off, entwined, down the quiet streets towards the river. Through an alley between empty warehouses they find a way and there before them is the Thames; a slow brown ribbon in a glistening waste of mud.

'Ecstasy,' says Frank. He squeezes Rose closer. The river-bed with its skin of black slime is pocked with intermittent pools, dully gleaming, and much debris whose forms, half buried and coated with mud, conceal their identity of origin. Before them, blackened stone steps streaked with strings of thin weed, virulent green, lead downwards and from them rise a wet watery smell of tin, rust and river.

'Come on,' says Rose, tugging. A fleeting image of the official reception ahead passes across Frank's mind. 'Darling,' he says, 'let's sit on that bit of wall and have our picnic.' He lets go of her and, with his arms out, wobbles along the embankment edge towards a patch of public garden. Putting her arms out too, Rose follows.

'That was too long without you,' he says when she reaches the end. 'I feel deprived. I'm never going to let go of you again.'

'I'm always there,' says Rose. 'Always.' There's an ache in her throat.

Leaning close, legs dangling, they bounce pebbles at the nearest puddles and eat their ginger biscuits through mouthfuls of rum.

Rose throws a piece of biscuit at a seagull stalking on the waste. Three more swoop down on it and fight, squawking and fluttering. 'What did you do today?' she asks.

'My day was like that. Blind acquisitiveness, ugly jockeyings for power. I'm afraid I nearly lost my rag.'

Rose puts both arms round his waist and lays her head against his chest. 'Tell me.'

'Wait.' Frank puts a hand under her sweater and finds her breast. 'Now. Well. The morning wasn't too bad. I spent most of it at the Ministry trying to save the precious hedgerows. And I managed. In some places. But others are going, shaved away, wantonly, in the name of more and bigger. By the way – you may be interested in this – there's going to be a new Min. of Ed ... old Lady Jolly-good-all. She's not a bad old stick. I had her next to me at dinner the other night. She can still laugh if you prod hard.'

'Her! How extraordinary. I thought she was dead. Then what?'

'Well, then I had a conference.'

'What did you have for lunch?'

'That was all right. I managed to get out of the official do and I had a bacon sandwich in a caff. But then comes the horrible part; the conference about the new museum, a plenary affair, and I broached my version. They were all hell-bent on putting up a hideous new building. Concrete of course. And I'm determined to use those old train sheds behind King's Cross. You can see, can't you? The Englishman and agriculture. Heritage. Mechanisation. The great age of the railways. Cathedrals of the industrial age. Aesthetically, economically, it makes sense in every way.' There was a plaintive note in his voice.

'There, there. My crusader. Of *course* you're right.' Rose pats comfortingly and can just feel spine through the material of his jacket.

'It was ghastly,' says Frank, and Rose, her ear to his chest, feels the sound of his swallowing. 'I was boiling. Had to use all my powers. Flattery, toadying, teasing ... And all we got was nowhere. There's to be another meeting in a fortnight. It's hellish, and it means a lot more work for me because they'll all be networking like crazy. It's too much.' He gives an exasperated growl and the sound vibrates, rolling round his ribcage.

'Do that again!' cries Rose.

'Growl,' says Frank. He presses her head into the tiny-patterned suiting of his waistcoat and Rose clings. 'I love you.' She looks up into his face. 'But you'll do it. One smile, a single irresistible ray, and they'll be at your feet.'

Frank moves his fingers through her hair. 'Darling! But it's worse than that. I'm going to have to do a lot of beastly sums. And, oh, I did so want to get up to Grassdale.'

A little cold hammer strikes at Rose in the pit of her stomach. *Their* weekend, two from now? Or had he planned to go up this one too with ...? She burrows her head closer. His fingers tighten under her breast and he moves his thumb down towards the nipple, making it stand up like a pink radish. The icicle reaches Rose's mind. She must not permit prosaic preoccupations to infiltrate their own perfect paradise. She gasps as Frank catches her to him and covers her mouth with his.

On the cement surface of the wall that divides the scrap of park from the river-bed, they rock backwards and forwards. A small boy on his way to the corner shop stops and peers. As Rose cries out he turns and flees. But he returns a few minutes later with a bigger boy. Together they edge closer.

'Hey, mister,' says the elder, 'give us a fiver an' we won't tell.' They take a step nearer. Frank raises his head. 'Scram,' he says in the voice of command and they scurry away. He turns back to Rose's face, so close to his own. It has an undressed look and she stares back at him, her gaze blurry with love. Waves of tenderness overcome him. He cradles her, swaying gently while a tear trickles down his lined cheeks and disappears in the folds round his chin.

'Oh, darling. And you haven't even taken off your specs.' Rose puts up a hand to stroke the skin under his eyes.

'Damn.' Frank has just seen the sun, unrelenting orange now, and slipping quite low in the sky. He nudges her upright. 'How prettily you dress,' he says and holds her face between his hands.

'Is it time?' says Rose.

He nods. 'But I can't bear it.'

'You don't have to.' Rose puts her arms round him. 'Just take my hand, hold fast and we'll stroll along the strand and catch the next boat and sail overseas into the sunset. And there'll be starlight and the moon and we'll sail on through days and nights until we come to an isle that takes our fancy and we'll jump into the warm blue sea and swim to where the waves break in little white frills on the coral sand. And we'll make our bed and lie on it for ever and ever. Come on.'

'I can't wait,' says Frank.

They straighten their numb and buzzing limbs and walk through the darkening streets to the car.

'All aboard!' Frank starts to sing.

Rose lays her head on his shoulder. 'More,' she says.

Threading their way through the rush-hour traffic, they come to Battersea Bridge.

By the gardens on the north bank he stops under the tall plane trees. Above, the birds chattering like film going backwards, fuss in swarms on the branches 'Darling,' he says, reaching across to open the door, 'you know how windy I get in this neck of the woods – too many pinstripes and briefcases.'

With one foot already on the kerb, Rose clings to him. Then, in response to some obedient pilot within, she put the other foot beside it and steps on to the pavement.

'Darling.' Frank closes the door. He speeds towards St James's and Green Park. Rose waves gaily. Then she stands still watching the red tail lights in the dusk. When she can see them no more she turns away and walks across the bridge to where her car is parked.

Despite the fascination of the scene to her right hand and to her left, the buildings greying in the dark living again in reflection; the fragmentation of lights on the water; the slow curves and steady flow of the river, she feels strangely unmoved.

7

Constance Goodall looked at herself in the glass over the drawing-room fireplace and tugged at her bow-tied blouse. 'God's teeth, I can't. I simply can't,' she muttered to her reflection. 'They've got the wrong person for this part of the job. One of the private secretaries should go to the receptions while I get on with the paperwork. I should never have left Oxford, dammit.' She poured a tot of whisky into a tumbler. Brace up, she told herself, it'll all be over in an hour.

She felt the slow burn deep in her oesophagus and put the empty glass down beside the clock. As it struck the quarter the front door bell rang. That would be her car. She squared her shoulders: Cheerio, old girl, she said to herself in the mirror and walked purposefully out of the room, down the dark stairway, to the front door.

'Evening, Tomlinson,' she said as she threw it open.

'Good Evening, Secretary of State,' said Tomlinson. His peaked cap was tucked under his arm and his young ears, pink-scrubbed, stood out under the hard curve of his short back and sides. He ran down the steps and held the door of the heavy green Rover. 'What's the traffic like?' she said as she settled herself, bottom tucked well into the angle, on the upholstered leather of the seat beside him. 'Not too bad, Secretary of State. We should be all right,' said Tomlinson and swung the car soundlessly on to the roadway.

By the time the car reached Carlton House Terrace, Constance Goodall's composure was more or less restored. The bow still bothered her: its absurd floppiness just beneath the chin took her, willy-nilly, back to the hateful party frocks she had been buttoned into as a girl. She swung her legs out of the car before Tomlinson could get to the door.

Mind over matter.

'Pardon?' said Tomlinson.

'Her Majesty's Secretary of State for Education and Science,' called the major-domo.

'Constance, how splendid,' said the Foreign Secretary at the head of the receiving line. 'General, may I present Lady Goodall, our new Secretary of State for Education?'

A heavy man in an epauletted uniform took her hand in a limp clasp. He bowed and rattled off some sentences in Spanish. At his elbow the interpreter murmured, 'The President says that the democratic government of the Republic of Oronada is initiating many reforms for the good of its people. Education is the key to development. He looks forward to co-operation with your department. Long live freedom and democracy.' Beside him, a middle-aged Englishman of meek appearance stood with downcast eyes. He raised them briefly to nod at the words 'freedom and democracy'.

'Hear, hear,' said Constance and she passed on down the line, wiping her right hand against her skirt.

At the end, she found Max Vane. 'My dear Connie,' he said, grasping her hand in both of his. 'Congratulations. The Prime Minister couldn't have made a better choice. I'm delighted.' He lowered his voice. 'It's about time we had a minister capable of understanding the importance of scientific research.' He bobbed back and forth on his polished toes taking the hand with him as if it were an oar.

'You must put me in the picture, Max,' said Connie, withdrawing it. 'We've been drifting far too long on post-graduate education and research. I'm thinking of setting up a commission. How would you feel about taking it on?'

Max's heart, ever ready, expanded like a crimson peony into flower. A royal commission would suit him splendidly just at the moment – and Millie would adore it. Sensible woman, he thought … 'But you must have a drink. Let me get you one!' He flagged down a passing waitress. 'Whisky for the Minister,' he said, and Connie took a warm draught. Sensible chap, she thought, looking round her.

The great Wyatt ballroom was full of familiar faces, a sprinkling of representatives from overseas spread rather thinly among them. They were conversing among themselves, apart from one she noticed talking to the grey little man who had been at the President's side in the receiving line. The two of them had their heads together at the far end of the room where the gathering was at its sparsest. 'Who's that?' she asked. She was still standing beside Max Vane, though people were coming up to her in droves to shake her hand. It was rather jolly and quite unlike her customary experience of social gatherings.

Careful to respond, Max shed the person he was talking to in mid-sentence and looked. Out of the corner of his mouth he said, 'Ainsworth, Ted. Old family business – agricultural machinery, tractors, tanks, electronics. Vast empire. Very clever man.' He depressed the lid of the eye on her side of his face and resumed his sentence.

'Hmmph,' said Connie and a fleeting memory of Clause Four and the stirring days of unilateralism at Blackpool gave an admonitory flicker in the back of her mind. She would have to update her principles now she was in government. She spotted an old Somerville chum, now headmistress of a high-profile girls' school, and began to make her way towards her. Then she caught herself. A good natter was too expensive a luxury for someone in her position. Just such an establishment had been the making of her. But it would be as well, for her first week in office, not to be seen too patently in cahoots with one side or the other, so she signalled with her eyebrows and received, in reply, a glass uplifted in salutation. She nodded and turned away to find herself face to face with Frank Wetherby. He looked, even to her eye, more than usually rumpled.

'My favourite Lady,' he said, squeezing her arm. 'I'm going to have to treat you with great respect from now on. If you get your hands on my old school reports I'll be ruined.' He bent to kiss her cheek, such a delightful smile illuminating his lopsided face, such a conspiratorial twinkle dancing behind his thick spectacles that Connie almost giggled. 'Idiot,' she said gruffly.

Keeping his head close to hers, he said in her ear, 'I've been having the most appalling time with the darling dagoes and our own ghastly people at Ag 'n Fish. They want me to use my powers of persuasion' – and he dropped his tone making the phrase, somehow, comic out of all proportion to its content – 'to soften up our chaps here so that they can bring in God only knows how many thousand tons of tiny garden vegetables so that their rich landowners can get richer and their nasty generals can order more Uzis from Israel plus the latest hardware from Ted Ainsworth over there, while our poor dear farmers get lumped with all our own honest-to-God carrots and spuds – and all in the name of freedom and democracy. Honestly, Constance, you must say, it's not fair. I do get landed with the most fearful chores. I mean, how can I?', and he took off his spectacles to wipe beneath his eyes with a spotted cotton handkerchief.

'Tut tut,' said Connie. She patted his hand. 'But we've all got to pull together. I'm sure you'll find a way.' She felt slightly shocked at his indiscretion but also privileged and curiously touched.

'What a brick you are,' said Frank, blowing on his spectacles and wiping them before putting them back . 'Nothing can go too far wrong with people like you on the bridge.' He smiled down on her, so close, they almost touched. 'You have cheered me up,' he said. 'But I must go and rescue Tamarisk and you must come to dinner soon. That is, if you can find time for us any more.' He pressed the top of her arm affectionately and set off, with his giraffe gait, for the other side of the room.

Connie, whose limbs felt warm and relaxed in a way that was

unfamiliar to her, gazed after him for a moment. She saw Tamarisk Wetherby, her back to the painted wallpaper, bare shoulders meringue-white above the white cotton frills of her blouse, chattering at the industrialist – what was it, Ainsworth? – from up north. At Frank's approach, she saw him raise his eyes and shoot a peculiarly sharp glance in his direction. The piercing quality of the stare for that single moment startled Connie. She turned and prepared to depart. A mountain of documents awaited her and more would have been delivered in her absence. She had done her bit. She would get into her pyjamas and down to her paperwork with a couple of boiled eggs on a tray. Once engaged, her well-disciplined mind would swing through the memoranda and the minutes. She would show them a thing or two in the Department when she got there next morning on the stroke of eight-thirty.

As Tomlinson drove her back along the Mall, she looked across to the Houses of Parliament. Those illuminated towers, that square half mile of Whitehall surrounding it was not unlike Oxford. She tucked her bottom into the angle of the seat again. Dear old Oxford, she thought with contentment and just a touch of condescension.

8

That morning, Sam's father got back from his first job in time to take the kids to school. They were waiting for him at the back door, which was really down the side in the thin pebbled wall by the dustbin. Maggie let go her brother's hand and ran when she saw him and he swung her, squealing and thin as a sparrow, off the ground and into the air above his head. Then he set her down and she stood, watching him. Maggie seldom spoke.

'Come on kids,' he said.

Sam met his father's eye and grinned. 'Mum's upstairs,' he said and took a flying kick at the garden fence. His legs felt fine and free and the fence made a good squeaking crack and listed a foot or so further into next door. 'Good lad,' said Sam's father, 'get into the van, you two, and I'll pop upstairs and see how Mum's doing.' He was thin and wiry like Sam, only his white face was veiled with stubble and black in the lines round his mouth and on his forehead. He ran up the stairs and pushed open the bedroom door. 'Samantha,' he said, 'Sammy, love, how're you feelin'?'

The room was dank and strewn with clothes. Light straggled in through the drooping curtain. He put out a hand to draw it back and his wife, on the bed, moaned. He sat beside her. 'Sammy,' he said and waited. What could he say? There was no bright side. The prancing teenager he had married, tossing back her shiny hair, flying in the face of her family's opposition, laughing on his arm outside the register office in her red shoes and short skirt; crying with pain as her breasts leaked and the new baby fought, shrieking, against the nipple; pushing the pram, counting the pennies, slipping down the slope, she was here for him and all he could promise her was toil. He stroked away a matted strand of hair and laid a finger against her cheek. She opened an eye and he was shocked at its dullness. 'There, love,' he said, 'there. Take your tablets now. Get some rest and I'll try to look in later.' He patted the blanket up round her shoulder and the rough surface of his hand caught, like sandpaper, on its woolly surface. 'Don't leave me,' he thought he heard her say as he left the room.

Downstairs, the kids were in the van, sitting on the brown rexine front seat through which black springs and pubic curls of horsehair leaked, banging their heels against the scarred tin of the plinth beneath. At least Sam was. Maggie sat watchful and silent close up to him, her small feet in their dirty white gym shoes dangling by the gear lever. The van had some words written on the back: Phil Clark, Sanitary Engineer. Hounslow, and a telephone number. Sam's father had painted them himself when the van, bought with the last of his wife's money, was new. But they were barely decipherable now and the telephone had been disconnected for some time past.

He hopped up into the driving seat, slammed the door and turned on the ignition. The slam set up a shuddering rattle and the turned-on ignition made an empty tocking sound. 'Hell's bells,' said Sam's father. He pulled out the choke and depressed the accelerator, then he slid out of the cab and disappeared under the bonnet which wavered on its prop. Sam clambered over Maggie and balanced on the edge of the driver's seat, one foot stretched out to the pedals and one hand on the choke. Eyes big and round, Maggie held herself tight beside him.

'Choke out!' shouted her father. 'More ... Accelerator ... Ignition off!' He struggled and fiddled at the engine, concealed from view, while Sam pushed and pulled. His father's face appeared round the bonnet. 'Give us a hand, lad,' he called.

'Here Mags, you take this,' said Sam. He put his sister's hand on the choke and made a leap for the pavement where he landed with a thud and dashed, all skinny legs and arms, to stand beside his father.

'Dad?' he said, looking up at him.

'Hold this,' said his father and ran round to the back for the petrol can. There was a little left in the bottom. He poured it into the pump and the two of them began rocking the van.

'Choke right out, Mags.'

Inside, Maggie, eyes screwed shut, pulled with both hands. A preposterous splutter, a mighty hiccup, an explosion and the engine lurched into juddering life. Sam's father threw down the bonnet and they both raced for their seats and hurled themselves in. Popping and spluttering the van moved off. 'Good lad,' said Sam's father. Sam patted Maggie's hand and she bounced ever so slightly on her bottom. You could tell she was excited because of the way her eyes shone. They grinned at one another and the three of them all in a row settled down for the short journey through back streets, under the motorway, past the front gardens and the gathering affluence, to the school gates.

The playground was deserted. 'Run kids,' said Sam's father. He kept the engine going as they slid out and ran, hand in hand, across the empty asphalt, dead-quiet in the soft sun. Maggie peeled off to the right and the entrance marked 'Infants'. Sam disappeared into 'Juniors'. Phil Clark accelerated, jerking, away towards his day's work.

When Maggie got inside the door there was no one around the high arched hallway to tell her what to do. She could hear sounds; scufflings, murmurs and the thumping of teachers' voices coming, muffled, from behind closed doors along the corridor and, from round the corner where the hall was, a disunited tinkle of triangles, a trailing shiver of tambourines and the despairing cries of Mrs Jones as she struck chords from the piano and shouted: '*One*, two, three, four ... all *together*, triangles.'

Maggie stood still. Her presence displaced as much space as a feather, less than the loud celebrations of harvest – yellow corn, orange apples, red tractors, white clouds – bluetacked to the walls farther down the corridor. The Infant Head's room was at the end of it. She came out, by and by, with Mr Lovejoy and a man in a raincoat. They were talking in that long flattened way grown-ups did. They passed by Maggie and out into the playground without taking her in. She bent down and scratched her leg: there was a scab on her shin and a bruise where a boy from Juniors had cannoned into her as he charged round the playground. She had not cried. A wasp cruised down the hall making crazy zinging darts as though the air was full of unseen solids. The zinging stopped and it settled on a brick quite close to Maggie's head. She could see its fat pointed tail pulsing in and out and she inched away, silently, without lifting her rubber-soled feet off the floor. On the other side of the hall was a bench. Children sat on it when they were waiting to see the Head or to have their eyes tested. If you were very late being fetched, you were brought in from outside and told to sit there too and Mrs Darrell sometimes gave you a Polo. The wasp took off veering madly up into the arches and then zoomed back and crawled across a pane of glass above the door. Every now and then it took off with a whirring jerk before alighting again more or less at the same spot. Maggie wished it would go away.

Suddenly, all at once, doors started banging and the hall was full of raw sound. Teachers stood at classroom doors shouting at children to stand in line and be quiet. Some of the children were shoeless, in socks; the girls in their knickers, the boys in underpants. The hall and the corridor beyond filled with milling jagged lines going in all directions at once. Two little girls from Maggie's class, hand in hand, caught sight of her. 'Come on,' one of them mouthed. But Maggie could not move. The other one ran to the teacher. 'Please Miss,' she said, 'there's Maggie.' The teacher looked over to where Maggie stood and called above the clatter, 'Margaret Clark, come over here. Where have you been? I've marked you absent on the register. Have you brought a note?' Maggie's eyes widened and she stood as still as she could. Her breath would have left a cobweb undisturbed. The teacher sighed and came over. She took hold of Maggie's hand and pulled and Maggie came, unresistant as water. The teacher looked down at the matted head of fizzing brown curls and the dead-white face below. She saw blue rings under the child's eyes and smelled the smell of unwashed hair. She sighed again. 'Come along, dear,' she said, 'I'll change the register at dinner time. We're going to do PE. Your plimsolls'll be just the thing. But you must bring a note tomorrow.'

Caught up on the tide now, and going with it, Maggie merged and felt herself being coloured in like a picture in a magic painting book.

Mrs Upjohn fell on Sam the moment he slid through the entrance. It was as though she had been waiting there behind the door with a butterfly net. She gave him a terrible fright. The events of his morning so far possessed him and, the general wariness that overtook him on school territory apart, he had not yet considered what he was going to do when he got there.

'Whatever do you think you're doing coming into school at this hour?' she demanded. 'Answer me this instant. And what are you doing in those boots?'

He froze, and the manly satisfactions of the past hour shrivelled to a tight nut at the back of his head. He focused his eyes unseeingly on the wall behind her where a giant frieze of red apples in green trees and stooks of corn, yellow in yellow fields, was fixed to the wall.

'Look at me,' said Mrs Upjohn, 'where's your note? Your family's quite impossible. No wonder you're such a mess.'

Autonomously activated, Sam's foot shot out and landed hard on Mrs Upjohn's ankle. 'Don't you say nuffink about my Mum,' he muttered without shifting his gaze.

Mrs Upjohn staggered, clutched her ankle and howled, twice: the first time from pain and shock; the second, with outrage. She clamped a hand on Sam's neck and shoved him violently forward. 'You're coming to see the Headmaster, young man,' she said through her teeth. Sam forced his head back against the pressure and braced his legs. Mrs Upjohn pushed, Sam pushed back and for a few moments they battled in wordless stasis like stags with locked horns. Then Sam found himself giving ground and Mrs Upjohn, breathless with fury, marched him, feet dragging, across the hall, up the stairs to the Headmaster's door. There was no one within.

'Right, young man,' she said and pushed his face against the wall of the corridor outside, 'just you stay there. Don't you dare move. You're in big trouble already.' She gave him another shove in the small of his back and hurried away to seek out Mr Lovejoy.

As soon as she had gone, Sam peeled himself away from the wall and sauntered down the corridor, pausing now and then to look out of the windows on to the silent playground. And there, Rose found him.

'Why, Sam,' she said, 'I've been looking for you. It's your time with me now. What's happened?' Sam said nothing, so Rose waited. She leaned against the wall facing him and waited for a signal. She felt oppressed and acutely aware of stormy weather. Five minutes passed thus, slowly and in complete silence and then the air between them lightened.

'Shall we go and sit down?' she said.

'Don't mind,' said Sam after a bit, still looking out of the window.

Uncertain whether he would follow, Rose turned and walked to her corner. She sat down in her chair and got Sam's folder from the shelf behind her. When she looked up she found he was sitting opposite. On the table between them were five packets of Plasticine; blue, green, red, yellow and white. She had found them there when she came in that morning and Elaine had already made a series of blobs and squirls which she said were noses. Rose put Sam's folder in front of him and took his writing book out of it. 'Would you like to write anything down?' she said, 'Or make a picture?' Sam slid to the edge of his chair and leaned back. He started drumming with his heels against the floor. He went on and on. Rose took a deep breath and sat it out. His hand, thin, bitten and black with grime, went out towards one of the packets of Plasticine.

'What's that, Miss?' he said.

'Plasticine,' said Rose. Sam said nothing but his hand stayed on the table. 'You can use it if you want to,' she added and bit her lip because Sam's hand withdrew to the edge. Oh God, you've done it now, she thought to herself, and brought her feelings, on the verge of breaking out, under control. Quite soon Sam put both hands on the blue packet, shook out the contents and unwrapped the block of sticks from their cellophane. He broke off a quarter, horizontally, and started mashing at it with his left hand. Rose glanced at her watch: there were five minutes of the session to go. Sam sprawled right forward from his chair, laid his smelly curls on the table and made a rough bowl out of the lump in his hand. Praying that no one would come by, Rose said, as flatly as she could: 'There's two minutes left before the bell.' Sam reached out and broke off another piece of Plasticine. He rolled it into a short worm and set it into the bowl. Then he broke off another fragment and fixed it to the top of the worm. The bell went and he stood up.

'Can you tell me what it is?' said Rose.

'A boot,' said Sam.

'A boot?' said Rose. 'And what's inside?'

'It's a bear,' said Sam. 'A li'le bear.' He gave a hop. 'Cheers, Miss,' he said and ran.

Rose sat on for some time considering the enigmatic object on the table before her. Then she selected a piece of cardboard from the store she saved from stocking packets and manoeuvred it underneath. She put it on top of the bookshelves. Next time she would ask him to label it, maybe. There were dozens of openings but she doubted he would take up any of them. She gathered her things and made, without enthusiasm, for the staffroom and coffee. She must find a way of thanking nice Mr Woolf – it was surely he – for the Plasticine without being observed. As she moved off she noticed, from out of the window, Sam being apprehended in the playground and hauled off by Mrs Upjohn. She shook her head and sighed.

Like a ship delineated through fog a memory from long ago surfaced in her mind.

9

She was walking down the stairs slowly, one hand shoulder-high on the banister, the other firmly clutched round the soft body of the playroom kitten. Conditions under Chantal had become intolerable. She had decided, not for the first time, to run away. With this resolve furiously in mind she had emptied the penny jar and put on her red shoes which were strictly for receptions when the children were allowed down to hand round baby sausages and bits of bacon on sticks. As she descended into the hall she watched their beautiful shiny round toes appearing directly below but some way off from the school-striped body of her frock, one at a time. They went slower and slower as she reached the bottom stairs.

Around her the house, three floors down from the bright rooms where she, her sisters and the hated *au pair* were quartered, was still, almost alarmingly so. From behind the big doors into the dining-room she could just hear sounds of the table being laid. Her mother must be having people and, thought Rose bitterly, proper grown-up food, chicken and ice-cream, probably.

The door opened and Ela came out carrying an empty tray. Ela was Polish and had been with them since Bonn which was as long as Rose knew. '*Dzien dobry pani* Rosebud,' she said and pinched Rose's cheek. Cheek-pinching was what people abroad always did to children, who were supposed to like it. The Hardy sisters had been schooled not to flinch and to smile back. Rose bit her lips together and stretched them so that her cheeks felt tight. Ela's eyes fell on her shoes. 'You are going to see the Queen, I suppose?' she said. 'Hurry, please. I have lunch for you already in the lift.'

'What is it?' said Rose. But Ela would not tell. She simply shrugged her shoulders, raised her eyebrows and said, 'Wait to see.'

Leftovers, thought Rose, cold ham, yoghurt and apples. Her eyes filled with tears of ill-use. Ela's expression softened. 'Rosebud,' she said, in a stroking voice, 'tzt-tzt.' She felt in the pocket of her overall and brought out a toffee of the cheapest sort, forbidden to the children. She unwrapped it and popped it into Rose's opened mouth. Then she put a finger up to her own, shook her head and hurried down the basement stairs to the kitchen.

Strong, powerfully scented, synthetic pink savours filled Rose's mouth, mingled with her saliva and slipped like sugared Gloy down her throat. She was good at sucking and almost always won slow races with her sisters, but she decided to bite in case anyone found her first. A long way off across the black and white marble squares she could see the front door. She made for it and the kitten under her arm gave a convulsive squirm, but Rose clamped it tighter into her stomach. She opened the front door, a thing she never did on her own, pulled it back a crack and manoeuvred herself through. She gave a jerk and, her spine prickling with fear and excitement, heard it shut behind her. There was no going back now.

Outside it looked bigger than usual. In the square there was blossom on the cherry trees and the main trees, too smooth for climbing, were still bare but pricked all over with green. Inside the railings a Filipino maid, holding two dogs on a lead, walked round and round the gravelly paths. As she neared the gate nearest the Hardy's house, Rose pressed herself into their own railings and shut her eyes. The kitten gave another iron wriggle and dug her claws into Rose's shoulder. Its tail started twitching and Rose put up the other hand to hold her down. The maid in the gardens had her back turned now on the far side of the square and Rose took the three steps down from their own front door and was on the pavement. Up the area steps of next-door but one a delivery man came, two steps at a time. Rose turned her back and frowned down at the pavement. Three pigeons pecked at a crack, their sheeny heads jerking in and out. The man jumped into a Harrods van and drove away. Rose started walking, stumping determinedly. She was going to cross the road on her own and later on, several much bigger ones before she got to Victoria Station. There she intended to get a ticket for the country and live in it for ever. She reached the pillar-box on the corner and looked right, left, right. She put a foot down into the road and sensed something close behind.

'Hullo Rose,' said a familiar voice from overhead, 'going for a walk this fine morning?' It was her father, the Brigadier, in his office suit and tie, his crinkly face all smiley. 'Mind if I come with you? I could do with some exercise before lunch. Or would you prefer to be on your own?' He reached down and stroked the kitten in the special place under its chin and the kitten began to purr.

Rose was surprised to see her father. He did not often come back for lunch. She nearly ran but he did not seem cross with her. She looked at him carefully to make sure, then nodded. They set off side by side, unhurriedly in the direction of Victoria and when they got to the first big road he did not even attempt to take her hand. 'Would you like me to carry puss?' he said just as she began to feel hot and scratchy. Was he going to come with her right to the station, she wondered. Would he try to stop her doing what she wanted? Won't, she thought, and looked up at him, her face set at its crossest to find he was looking down at her with perfect gravity.

'I don't know about you,' he said by and by, 'but I could do with something to wet my whistle. What do you say?' They were passing a café, its windows lined with containers of sandwich filling and squares of cake. They joined a queue of office workers, and when they got to the counter Brigadier Hardy said, 'One cup of tea and the lady here will have …?' Rose planted her legs apart and held her breath for a second. Then she said, 'Coca-Cola, please,' and waited for the rules to come down.

'One Coca-Cola,' said her father in his ringing elegant style, 'and anything to eat? I'm going to have a piece of this chocolate gateau here.' Rose squinted up at him. There was no trace of amusement in his expression so she had herself a sandwich constructed. She simply pointed at dishes as they caught her fancy and the man piled spoonfuls on a square of buttered bread. With every addition the injustices of the morning loosened their grip and, at the final topping of crumbled bacon, they slipped entirely away. Her father held on to his cup of tea and the kitten, and she carried their two plates. They sat on stools at a shelf on the wall and Rose ate using both hands and all her concentration until she was full. She sighed and leaned back. Her father looked at his watch. 'I promised Mum I'd put in an appearance at lunch,' he said. 'Shall we go back together, or have you got things to do?' Rose slid off her stool and found his hand just by her ear where she wanted it. She put hers in it and they strolled back to their square. Her father hummed and whistled and sometimes Rose joined in.

When they got to the house he came upstairs to the playroom. 'Rose has had lunch with me,' he said, looking hard at Chantal. He let go her hand and gave a little push. 'I'll come up and see you before I go back to the office. I've very much enjoyed our outing. We must do it again.' He blew them all kisses and went downstairs to the lunch party in the dining-room.

Years later when Rose's marriage to the Hon. Felix Pitt foundered and failed, she spent a whole summer at her parents' in Wiltshire. She felt shamed and unviable. 'You're so pretty, you should be in films,' so many of her friends had said when she was in her teens. Primed for approval, she became a socialite-starlet. They would not have said it could they have seen her that summer of her divorce, slack and puffy from non-stop eating, hair in lank strings, her grey eyes dull as English sea.

Towards September, she went for some long walks with her father. Breathless with effort she struggled to keep pace with him and by and by the disquiet in her body simmered down. One evening as they came swinging back along the valley, Rose said, 'I'm going to be a teacher, Dad. I've decided. I'm not going to try being an actress any more. I'm going to go to teacher-training college and I'm going to specialise in children with difficulties and psychological problems, the ones that don't fit in.' She looked up at him and grinned.

'That's my girl,' he said. 'I knew you'd sort it out. You always had a way with small animals. You'll make a fine teacher.'

'Like you,' said Rose, and took his arm.

'We can't make any exceptions,' she hears Mrs Upjohn's harsh voice proclaim as she passes the welfare room now. '*What* do you think would happen if everyone came to school in nasty dirty boots like that? You've been warned often enough.' Inside, Sam is sitting on a moulded plastic chair, a sliver of skin and bone in its black ungenerous curve as Mrs Upjohn, her hands in rubber gloves, pulls the boots from his feet. He whistles a monotonous non-tune.

'Stop that,' says Mrs Upjohn. She drops the boots into a plastic bag, and Sam, deprived of alternative means of expression, gathers saliva in his mouth and spits.

'That does it,' says Mrs Upjohn, tight-lipped, 'You're not fit to be in a decent school like this. We'll have to call in Social Services.'

Unaware of the precise nature of the confrontation within, Rose goes on her way. Mr Lovejoy passes, walking with uncharacteristic despatch and they exchange good-mornings. Filled with unease, she reaches the staffroom.

She steps in and down, as into the basement of a department store where the circulation of air is slower, the penetration of light more laborious, the transactions more mundane than on the livelier storeys above. Smoke, from the cigarettes of the one or two members of staff that use them, hangs motionless at intervals above the circle of chairs. Conversational overtures peter out. The elderly Welsh speakers, seasoned campaigners, keep up a neighbourly exchange and, over by the window, Mr Foster in a posture of intense agitation murmurs urgently in the ear of young Miss Bunting.

Rose gives a generalised nod – it's the first time she's seen most of them that morning since she teaches through Assembly – and goes to the kettle where her pale-blue mug on its own remains. She drops her four pence into the tin.

'We're out of milk, I'm afraid, Mrs Pitt,' calls the white-haired Welsh speaker, Mrs Jenkins.

'Black's fine.'

'Pop down to the kitchen. They'll probably let you have a drop.'

'No really. It's perfectly all right. I quite like it like this. Thanks.' Rose smiles again, takes a sip to confirm it and burns her lips. The only chair she feels she has any claim to is occupied, so she leans against the wall.

'Have a biccy. It's my birthday,' says Mr Woolf. He grins and indicates an opened packet on the central table.

'Many happy returns,' says Rose. She steps out and bends to take one.

'I hope you like chocolate digestive. They're my favourite.' Mr Woolf leans forward in his chair.

'Mine too. I always had them on my birthday,' and a brief picture of the dining-room table, the boys and girls in party clothes round it, the cake, the candles, the crackers, and the plates of crustless sandwiches cut into triangles by her mother and Ela, occupies Rose's mind for a moment.

'I like the way the chocolate melts when you dip them in your cuppa,' says Mr Woolf.

'Exactly.' Rose goes back to her station by the wall and dips the biscuit into her mug. The chocolate smears on her fingers and she tries to lick them. The door opens abruptly and Mrs Upjohn comes in. She hurries across to Mr Foster and speaks to him. 'Excuse me, Miss Bunting,' says Mr Foster. Together, he and Mrs Upjohn leave the room.

Rose decides to go to the lavatory. She can sit down there on her own until the bell goes. She empties her coffee down the sink, rinses out her mug and bites off a chunk of biscuit. It goes round and round in her mouth before she can get it down. 'Try to be here on time, dear,' says a voice at her side. 'They never send up enough milk. It's a shame.'

'It's all right,' says Rose, 'but thanks, I will.' She turns to go.

Teachers are getting up from their chairs, brushing down their skirts, stubbing out cigarettes. Outside the door two sixth-year girls are waiting to wash up.

'Can we go in yet, Miss?'

'I'm not sure. Perhaps you'd better wait till everyone comes out.' By the time Rose gets to the staff toilet on a half landing down the back stairs, the bell goes and she comes back. She still has not thanked Mr Woolf for the Plasticine. As she gets to the landing she sees his back going down the front stairs: his class is in a prefab to one side of the playground.

'Mr Woolf,' she calls, and hurries after him.

He turns. His tie, a bright and bouncy one, is knotted tight round his collar today and he's wearing a blue Oxford shirt under his usual patterned pullover.

'Yes, Mrs Pitt?'

'I wanted to thank you – it was you, wasn't it? – for the Plasticine.'

'Pleasure. I hope it's useful.' He has a rather ugly face with a wide nose and a lot of dark springy hair.

'Oh yes. Already. It's been tremendously useful already.'

'Glad to hear it. And by the way, Mrs Pitt, my name's Nathan – Nat for short.'

'And my name's Rose,' says Rose, 'or Miss.' She hesitates and then smiles at him. She has become circumspect with her smiling. It seems foreign currency on school premises. But Mr Woolf smiles back in an open friendly way. She almost laughs with relief and gets back to her place with seconds in which to compose herself before the fifth years swarm in.

They come down on her, a wild and disunited horde, headed by Simon. He takes a flying skid, crashes into the table and sends a battered toy car careering across its surface towards her.

'Look at this, Miss, look!' he shouts and hurls it into the air. There's a bruise on his temple, partially covered by a ragged plaster.

'Wheee!' Gary leaps on to a chair and rides it like a skateboard. 'I took Susie Smith's knickers down in the playground. Wheee. Miss. Can I take down yours?' He jumps off the chair and sits on a table. 'Come on Si. We're going to see Miss's knickers. Come on. It'll be good.'

Wendy sits on the chair next to Rose and scrapes it back and forth. Her bitten nails are pocked with fragments of pink varnish. 'I'll tell Mr Foster,' she squeals, and sits on her hands. James Potterton backs in, grunting and muttering. He's making elaborate feinting movements with his arms. He takes a quick glance over his shoulder, adjusts his course in the direction of Selma and bumps into her with some force. Selma rocks and sits heavily down on the floor. Her head jerks sideways and stays there. Under the dark hairs on her upper lip are beads of sweat, seed-pearl size.

Rose flinches, resists the urge to spring, shouting, to her own feet and puts out a hand to field Simon's car.

'Hullo Simon. Thanks for bringing this. I'll put it on the shelf. It'll be safe there.'

'I want it. Give it back.'

'It's resting. That's its garage. You can have it back after. I'm in charge for now.'

Simon begins talking in a flat rapid tone: '... Sister killed in a car crash ... all our family in hospital ... policeman ... prison ... house fell down when we were out ...' Rose catches some of the words, but he's comparatively static. She takes her eye off him.

'Hullo,' she says to Wendy, 'you've got your pink socks on. Can you write down all the pink things you can think of, in your book?'

'Knickers,' says Wendy, sniggering.

'Knickers, right.'

Wendy puts a pencil in her mouth and sucks, looking up at Rose with round eyes. 'Ooh, Miss!' She lets the pencil fall, puts both hands up to her face and titters relentlessly behind them.

'James,' calls Rose, 'what's happening?' and, breathless, he replies, 'I've got a war on my hands. They're coming at me from all sides. It's all I can do to keep them at bay.'

'Well, you've wounded someone,' says Rose, glaring. 'They won't come in here. Leave your weapons by the window and attend to the injured. *Now.*' Peering stagily round him, James creeps over to the window and backs towards Selma, on all fours.

'Gary, get down and come and sit here.'

'You haven't said good-morning or hullo,' says Gary. '*Dah-dah de-da-dah.* You said we was always to do that when we came in.'

'Good morning, Gary. I'm sorry.'

'Morning, *Miss.*' Gary is swinging his sinewy legs like violent pendulums which strike and topple everything in their trajectory.

'Miss, how do you spell knickers, Miss?' comes Wendy's voice.

'K ...' starts Rose.

'Nah. Miss can't spell. Knickers. Knickers.' Gary swings his legs harder and a chair goes flying.

'Mi-iss, mi-ss,' wails James. 'Mi-iss. She punched me. I'm trying to bandage her and she punched me.'

'Well, that's what happens if you start a war. People hit back,' says Rose. She gets up and bends over Selma. 'Are you all right?' She puts her hands under the child's arms and lifts her, a dead weight, to her feet. Then she propels her to the table and sits her down, stiff, on a chair.

'James. Apologise.' James bows. 'I beg your pardon, madam,' he says, and then, in a loud whisper, 'I kept a revolver just in case.' He pats the side of his grey school pullover which is rucked up and twisted over his grey school shirt in the most improbable way.

'Keep it there. It'll be confiscated if you don't. And sit down.

That's an order.' Rose can see no further than getting them all sitting round the table and three of them, the majority, are. She looks at Simon, on his feet and muttering convulsively, 'Dead … suicide … broken … crash …' She hears the words and decides to leave him, turning to Gary. 'Sit down, here, this instant.'

'Nah. Not until you show me your knickers.'

'You mean, if I were to show you my knickers, you would come and sit down?'

'Ooh, Miss, you wouldn't,' squeaks Wendy.

'No I wouldn't,' says Rose.

'Look, Miss. Look what I've done – lots of knickers,' says Wendy, and indeed, there are: pink, blue, striped, spotted, hanging on a washing line, blowing in the wind and drawn very small in the corner of a page in her exercise book.

'Why, Wendy, that's lovely. What a wonderful picture – good enough for a prize. Whose are they?' says Rose.

'A prize. What?' shouts Gary. 'Can I have a prize? I want a prize.'

'Well, that's me Mum's and that's me sister's and that,' she giggles, 'that's me Dad's …'

Gary comes over to the table and shakes it. 'I wanna prize. Give me a prize. I'm the biggest.'

'Sit down,' says Rose, 'we're going to play a game. The winner will get a prize. I'll draw it in their book and they'll be given out at the end of term.' Slowly, slowly, Rose finds her ways through the Blackboard Jungle of Meadowbrook School – though Simon, now, is beating his head on the bookcase.

10

Rose spent that weekend alone in her flat. She side-stepped invitations, did her washing and ironing, made a game of 'Snap' based on the twelve commonest words in the English language, but in truth the time was filled with waiting. The call came on Sunday morning when she was still muffled in slumber. She scrabbled for the receiver, her heart jerked uncomfortably fast into activity as her limbs were still slurred with sleep.

'Darling,' said his voice in her ear.

'Oh, darling,' said Rose. She cuddled herself and the telephone back under the bedclothes. 'Where are you?'

'In a telephone box. The one on the top of the moor by the crossroads. It's a lovely morning and I'm walking into the village for the papers. They're all fast asleep in their beds.'

'Missing the glory.'

'Darling.'

'How's it going?'

'Swimmingly. The Frogs are amazed by everything – too funny for words. I wish you could see them. We'd have such a laugh together. And their clothes. Perfection. You should have seen the get-up she arrived in. The whole of York station stopped to stare; even the trains halted in their tracks.'

'Darling,' said Rose, 'tell me ...'

'I miss you so,' said Frank, and there was a catch in his voice that evoked a reciprocal surge of tenderness in Rose, quite overwhelmed with yearning already. 'Darling,' she whispered, 'you're here beside me. I feel you.'

'Where are you?' said Frank, his voice now thick and low.

'In bed.'

'What are you wearing?'

'Nothing of course.' She heard him draw in his breath and for a while, neither of them spoke. Then he said, on a plaintive note and quite briskly, 'I've got to go. My money's run out. Too wretched, my darling. Love you, love you …'

'Love you too,' said Rose, but she spoke into an empty purr.

Up in Grassdale, the Wetherbys were entertaining the de la Vignes for the weekend. 'I'm afraid you're going to be awfully bored. There's absolutely nothing here to do,' Frank had said as he drove them up the dale in the dying light on Friday. Rocks, streams, waterfalls and soft grassy patches by running pools surrounded them, glinting where the sun slipping down the sky between clouds struck the brown surfaces with pale brilliance. At the end, where the hills either side met in an encircling curve, lay the house; a stone farm built in the eighteenth century, its comfortable outline honeycombed with squares of yellow light. The air was fresh and sharp and as the de la Vignes gazed briefly round, they did indeed feel a tremor of intimidation at the prospect of two nights and two days in such grave and uncompromising surroundings. But with soft firelight, skilled banter and first-class claret their apprehensions, like shadows at noon, vanished.

'We are very happy with you, dear friends,' said Chloë on Saturday afternoon. She was lying back, a dun-coloured parabola with apricot silk and pearls, against the cretonne, and had flicked off her shoes. With the utmost offhandedness, an elaborately planned day had unrolled itself, casually, as it went along: a walk up to the waterfall behind the house; a drive to the ruined Abbey; lunch in a pub on the banks of the Swale; shopping for postcards and parkin in the village, and back for tea in front of the fire.

'We've asked a few people in for dinner,' said Frank as he closed the doors into the garden. 'Just neighbours, and old Connie Goodall. She's been opening something or other at the University in Leeds.'

'How amusing,' said Chloë. 'You remember, J-B, the Scout lady? We met her at the Vanes.'

Frank laughed. 'That's it; you've got it exactly, only they're Girl Guides here. Now, would you like a nap, or shall I take you up to watch the sun setting on the top of the moor?'

The de la Vignes went up to their rooms. Tamarisk went to hers to lie on her board, and Frank thought of making a quick call to Rose – he ached for her sweet presence – but from where? He would get up early next morning. He put on an ancient silk shirt and saw to the claret instead. As he pottered round straightening silver, stoking fires, lighting candles, a car drew up outside. When the de la Vignes came down half an hour later, they found Lady Goodall cheerfully installed before the fire, a glass of whisky in her hand. Frank, in frayed shirt with a pink scarf tucked perfunctorily into its collar, was lying back in an armchair. He opened a bottle of champagne.

'Poor Connie's had the most frightful day at the University,' he said. 'She's been inaugurating the new Science and Technology building and has had to listen to dreary speeches all day long.'

'To say nothing of the one I had to make,' said Constance. 'I'm quite at sea when it comes to science. Had to rely completely on my PPS, damnfool. He put in a lot of words I hardly knew how to pronounce. You must tell me how you do these things in France, Ambassador. I'd dearly like to know.'

'*Grandes écoles; Science-Po*,' murmured Jean-Baptiste. He took a step towards Connie, 'What can I tell you, dear Madame?'

At eight o'clock precisely Ted Ainsworth parked his Rolls-Royce on the grass outside and Tamarisk, fluttering in one of her off-the-shoulder blouses, ushered him in, to be followed a few minutes later by the Duke of Middlesbrough in his Ford Escort with some of the house guests from his shooting box, a small castle, nearby.

At dinner, Frank kept the most unobtrusive of hands on the social tiller. Again and again, he steered conversation in the direction of industrial architecture, Brunel, science and technology, education. It was nice work: he had to allow just the right amount of slack for idle gossip, but he had many salient interests dispersed among the company to assist him in this most meticulously conceived of weekends.

'I know!' cried Connie, shaking her head at blackberry ice. Her voice rang through the swirl of chatter. 'I've got it! What we need is some kind of an institution, a Royal School of Agriculture to celebrate and conserve the great traditions of British farming, of British farm building. Our great pioneers and inventors! Tractors! Combine harvesters! Mills and breweries, train sheds, canals! HRH himself might be interested!'

'Bravo!' said Jean-Baptiste. 'The father of Brunel was a Frenchman. I am sure we would be happy to co-operate. This kind of enterprise is in the European spirit. A Louvre for the great works of agriculture!' He almost laughed, feeling stylistically quite seduced by this British mode of fun.

'Indeed,' said the Duke, 'indeed. We have a great many ancient farm implements lying around up here and at Tees. Perfectly preserved. Some of 'em we still use.' He looked around, pink with enthusiasm and almost clapped his hands.

'Hmph,' said Ted Ainsworth. He took in the possibilities: instant alliance with a member of the government, an imprimatur of philanthropy, a starring role for Ainsworth Agridustrial, a few million set off against tax, export licences on demand. He had wondered why he had been asked. 'I'd be all in favour,' he said quietly and wiped his lips with his napkin.

Frank said: 'What a brilliant notion, Connie. Out of the blue – pure genius.' He beamed at her through the candlelight. 'Here's to my favourite Minister,' and raised his glass. Then he sat back in his chair and removed his spectacles, misted over with emotion, to rub them with the loose end of his scarf. And in that instant, a loose end that had been oscillating at the back of Ted Ainsworth's mind for several weeks snapped into place. He glanced sharply at Frank, a gleam of recognition in his eyes, and lowered them swiftly to his plate. He placed his spoon and fork together on it, a small insignificant man of limited interest, included in the company for reasons of good neighbourliness alone. Frank caught the look and felt quite unclothed by it. The skin on the back of his neck contracted and his heart gave a hiccup. He replaced his spectacles and turned, as far away as he could, towards Chloë on his right. 'All this talk,' he said languidly, 'you must be stunned with boredom. But I'm told you had quite a hand in the Exhibition of Polynesian Costume that's at the Petit Palais just now. It must be fascinating ...'

The focus splintered, shifted and re-formed. At eleven o'clock Ted Ainsworth got to his feet and Frank rose to let him out into the night. 'I'll back you, Lord Wetherby,' he said, and one side of his mouth curled down into a grim half smile. He shook his hand. 'Don't wait, I'll be letting the dog out for a bit of a run before we drive back. I hope that's convenient.'

Frank watched as he walked over to his car in the starlight and opened the door. A black Labrador jumped out wagging its tail and bounded off, joyously sniffing, beside the stream. Frank's heart gave another hiccup. 'Good night,' he called. Ted Ainsworth raised his hand and gave a curt nod.

Frank closed the door, put his face in his hands and then went back to the dining-room. A few minutes later he heard the engine of the Rolls start up and purr, insulated in precision engineering, away up the rough track.

'You must have just a touch of this Poire William,' said Frank to Chloë. Fear was draining the blood from his bones. He filled a glass for himself and swallowed it in one.

'I'll help myself to whisky, if I may,' said Connie, and reached for the decanter. She felt quite at home. Government was no more than an extension of school, college, university. Running things, public service, suited her.

'*Attention,*' said Jean-Baptiste to Chloë upstairs in her room that night, 'this Lord Wetherby is more than he seems.' But Chloë laughed. 'I adore England,' she said, and held out her arms to her husband of many years.

11

'For what we have just received, may the Lord make us truly thankful,' Rose shouts. 'And the pudding is ...' She leans backwards over the lunch counter, and the head dinner lady, her hair tied up in a white turban, whispers in her ear.

'The pudding is – pear slice and custard.'

'Ugh,' says a voice from the body of the hall. There's a clatter and scraping of chairs. 'You can all talk now – QUIETLY,' yells Rose, 'except for that table, *there!*' She points to where Gary sits, gawkily cramped at a child-sized table for ten which he is jerking up and down on his knees.

'Oh, Miss,' he wails.

'Oh, Miss,' wail nine other voices. Rose paces solemnly over, past the milling line of children now forming, plates in hand, down either side of the hall. She's sometimes alarmed at the ease with which she slips into the role of martinet and how bolstered she feels in it.

'Oh, Miss, it's not fay-yer,' Gary howls when she gets there.

'Be quiet,' she snaps, fixing him with a glare and then, sternly before anyone can protest, 'You are to sit in silence until everyone has got their pudding. Then you can get yours and if no one says a single word, you can talk quietly.' She turns and walks back to her place in front of the hatch, smiling rather graciously at other children as she goes. She sees James Potterton twirling his unfilled plate on one finger and averts her eyes; she sees Selma, empty-faced, sleepwalking back to her table, her plate strangely held in both hands before her;

she sees Elaine and a clutch of other little girls jigging and whispering; she sees Wendy hopping from foot to foot; she sees Simon zigzag through the throng and crash into Mr Foster who seizes his arm and shakes him, but she can't see Sam anywhere.

'Where's Sam Clark?' she asks Miss Bunting in the staffroom after. Sam's in Miss Bunting's class and Miss Bunting, an English graduate with a year's teacher training battles uncomprehendingly to transmit fragments of reading, writing, geography, history, English, mathematics, science, RE, PE, painting and swimming to the likes of Sam, Gary, Simon, Selma – as well as all the other children in 5B – as she has been taught.

'Sam Clark?' says Miss Bunting, her fine skin reddening as it does when anyone speaks to her. 'He's in detention. He's not allowed to mix with the others. He has his lunch in the welfare room on his own.'

'What! Why?'

Miss Bunting draws herself up. Something in Rose's tone has made her face contract. 'He has a disruptive effect on others. He attacked a member of staff. He needs to be disciplined. It's for his own good.'

'What did he do?' says Rose, appalled. She moves so she's standing in front of Miss Bunting again. 'Please, let me know what's going on. I teach him too, you know.' Scarlet in the face, Miss Bunting sidesteps. She picks up a pile of writing books: 'Some people have got work to do. It's the Headmaster's decision.' She sits down to mark the books and Rose is left flapping, beached like a fish, gills ineffectually pumping. She hesitates and takes the only course of action that presents itself: she queues up for a cup of coffee. Mr Woolf joins the line behind her. Feeling his presence, Rose looks round and sees that he's quietly laughing. He raises his eyebrows and shakes his head. 'Why don't you sit down, Mrs Pitt? I'll bring your mug over.' He jerks his features to indicate two vacant chairs. Rose sits on the edge of one. 'There's a five-a-side friendly against St Augustine's this afternoon,' he says as he sits beside her, 'It's much too early in the term for matches even if they are only friendlies. But' – he drops his voice – 'it looks good on the records.'

'Yes, probably.'

'We've got a new ball. Special allocation from petty cash. Big deal.'

'Mmn.'

'It's pointless fretting. You're banging your head against a brick wall. Hope for the best, expect the worst, take what comes. I can tell you after school if you like.'

Rose looks at him directly. 'Is Sam still in that room on his own? Could I go and talk to him?' Mr Woolf gives his head the merest of shakes. 'Better not. I'll wander by your corner at three-thirty. You're not in a hurry, are you?'

'No.' Rose had been going to meet Frank, south of the river this time, on Deptford Strand, but early that morning he had telephoned. 'Too disappointing, my darling,' he had said, 'but there's a special conference been called about my museum and you know how close that is to my heart ...'

'Closer than me?' said Rose before she could stop herself.

'Darling,' Frank had said, 'darling, *darling*,' and Rose had been flooded with shame.

Later that afternoon she catches sight of Sam as she walks by the welfare room. He's sitting kicking the radiator in a strange pair of slippers. She waves and all afternoon she's aware of the Plasticine model he made, at her back, on the shelf behind her.

When the bell goes and the children start streaming out of school Mr Woolf strolls by. He's carrying a pile of reading books. 'Hullo, Mrs Pitt. I'm just changing the books for my top readers. Any suggestions?'

'Well,' says Rose, 'I've got this series about Cowboys. People quite seem to like them. But really, I think fairy stories and Greek myths are best. Lots of children really love this one about Hercules.'

Mr Woolf leans his arms on the bookcase. 'Apparently,' he says,

75

'our Sam gave our revered Welfare Assistant a nasty kick on the shin when she caught him coming into school late. There's been one hell of a fuss – how could you have missed it? Persistent offender, out of control, problem family – *and* he wears boots, which aren't allowed. I don't expect the poor little tyke's got anything else, but *they* see it as insubordination. And he *is* a difficult boy. I can't even get him to play football properly.'

'But I think football's the only thing he's interested in.'

Mr Woolf shakes his head. 'Completely disruptive. Impervious to rules. Absolutely antisocial. I gave up long ago.'

'I can imagine,' says Rose. 'I have him one-to-one. So what's happening now?'

'Sits on his own in class: confined to the welfare room at all other times. Can't say I feel comfortable about it but I don't see what else there is. There's talk of special school, even CARE. He's being referred. They're waiting for Social Services to make contact.'

At the end of the landing Mr Lovejoy looms. He makes his way towards them and nods pointedly as he passes.

'Good afternoon, Headmaster,' says Mr Woolf. 'I'm just picking Mrs Pitt's brains about reading matter for my fluent readers.'

Why should he have to? thinks Rose furiously. She stares at Mr Lovejoy.

'She's got some very good ideas,' says Mr Woolf. He frowns and smiles at Rose who forces her mouth into a smile.

'Ah – quite the expert,' says Mr Lovejoy and moves on.

'What about the classics retold for children and that sort of thing?' Mr Woolf says loudly.

'Yuk.'

'Go on,' mouths Mr Woolf.

'You mean *David Copperfield*, *Treasure Island*, that sort of thing? Ah, yes,' says Rose. Mr Lovejoy turns the corner and starts down the stairs. 'Do I have to?' says Rose, her face contorted with distaste.

'You have to.' Mr Woolf looks at her without smiling. 'You're a hopeless mixture of submissive and headstrong. You actually give the impression you're interested in the children; on their side even. *They* won't forgive you for that. You have to conform and get what you want by stealth. You can do it. You were throwing your weight about all right in the dining-hall today. That'll get you some Brownie points.'

'Yes,' says Rose, 'and it scares me. It's so terrifyingly easy to slip into.'

'Come, come. You have to compromise. Why don't you volunteer some cheese straws for harvest festival?'

'But that's not *teaching*. It won't help the children, and my lot are desperate.'

'You could start a club after school …'

'That's an idea. But I've got things to do. Often I have to rush away.'

'One afternoon a week? It'd all be over by four-thirty.' He puts his head on one side and Rose thinks what an ugly face he has.

'I suppose so,' she says, but who knows when Frank will be free for an hour, for a night, for a weekend. Her availability is the rock on which their love is grounded. A sharp sweet pain of unqualified intensity overcomes her. For a second she gazes at Mr Woolf with undefended eyes and he catches a look of such misery that he's halted in his discourse. In his kind paternal way, he holds it and waits.

'I suppose so,' she says again, doubtfully.

'Have a go. It's just a thought. But it goes down well and you can do things with the kids then that you can't in the school day.' He picks up his books. 'Well, cheery-bye. I must be going.'

'Mr Woolf, wait!'

'Nat,' says Mr Woolf. 'Yes?'

'Nat. What should I do about Sam? He's in a terrible state and he's just, just beginning to trust me. I *can't* let him down.'

Mr Woolf shakes his head. 'It's a hard world, Rose,' he says and walks away.

Let out of school, Sam feels strangely numb and dull. He's used to feeling bored but this is different: his legs and arms feel braked from within and inside his head is fuzzy. His feet drag on the asphalt as he goes round to Infants for Maggie. The friction of his boots, restored to him after their day under lock and key, upon the impacted pebbles is mildly interesting and he exaggerates the movement. She's waiting for him, still as ice floating on water, and her eyes light up when she sees him. Sam smiles at her, an uncomplicated smile of pure love. Backing her car out, Rose, by chance, observes the exchange and is drawn into its radiance as by a work of art unexpectedly come upon. Much affected, she drives quietly away. Maggie puts her hand into Sam's and they walk across the playground. When they get to the gates, Sam picks up a stick. He drags it on the pavement and, every time they get to a tree or a lamppost, he hits it. The stick breaks. He lets go Maggie's hand and uses his boots. The encounter between boot and concrete, wood, metal; unyielding, inanimate, impersonal, sets up a tingling in his blood and suddenly his body becomes possessed of electrifying energy. He runs at the trees, at railings, at the pillar-box with a frenzied thirst for activity; kicking, punching, barging, grunting while Maggie squeals and gives a skip. At the corner he zooms round, seizes her hand again and hurtles into the road. On the other side of the zebra crossing the lollipop lady, just packing up, gives a cry and a couple of cars screech to a stop, their tyres slithering painfully on the tarmac. The two drivers put out their heads and yell, and the lollipop lady flings out a white-overalled arm, her face stripped of its usual benign expression. Sam dodges her and charges on dragging Maggie, almost flying, after him. He runs down the street impervious to obstacles, careering into pedestrians, leaving a trail of outrage behind him while, gathered into a knot, the lollipop lady and the car drivers exchange imprecations and tuts of protest.

The more Sam runs, the more the energy wells inside him. He feels unquenchable and his sister's small hand in his lends him further power like an auxiliary engine, midget-sized, unobtrusive and reliable. They run under the motorway, past the supermarket, the video shop and the swimming bath, round corners to where the paving stones are chipped and the houses shabbier. They almost run right past their own front door but Sam wheels and comes to a skidding stop. He punches Maggie gently in the ribs and kicks the gate. The gate flops sideways on its single hinge and the two of them clamber through the triangular space and up the pathway. Maggie skips ahead. There are pink patches on both her cheeks. By the back door a line of milk bottles stand stinking in the sun. She skips up to the last one, upturns it and holds out the key. Sam turns it in the lock. 'You wait, Mags, till you've had your tea before you go out to play,' he says.

12

There was something about the empty flat that made Rose feel tired when she got back that afternoon. The air itself weighed on her arms as she watered the geraniums. She climbed out on to a bit of flat roof and sat in a patch of sunlight, back slumped against the slates, face held up to the sun. The ornate domes and minarets – an improbable London skyline, the museums of South Kensington – hovered in the haze of her lowered lashes. In the mild warmth of the ageing year her body felt overcome with lassitude. When the sun disappeared below the chimney-pots she would have to mobilise herself and prepare for the evening. But before it did so, the telephone rang and she scrambled back through the window. There was always a chance.

'Hullo Rosie,' said her father, 'glad to find you in.' He lived, since his wife had died, in a cottage not far from her eldest married sister. There, he trained sweet peas up beanpoles, played cricket on the green and toyed with his memoirs.

'Dad!' said Rose. She loved her father and wondered what he would say if she suddenly leaned on him, but he would be appalled at her entanglement with a married man and uncomprehending about school. His distinguished career, much of it spent as Military Attaché in Paris, Rome and Bonn, was governed by the strictest of codes and he was waiting for Rose, any day now, to announce her engagement to another well-connected young man whom he could invite to dine at his club: a fellow with a sense of responsibility this time, because he had to face it, the first affair had been a washout.

He was inviting her now. 'Can I give you dinner at the club next week? Sweet Rosie. You do me proud. You know what pleasure it gives me to be seen in the company of a lovely young woman like yourself.'

'Oh Dad,' said Rose, 'and me. You're still the handsomest man I know.'

They arranged to meet and as Rose thumped with the iron at the creases in her silver jeans for this evening, she tried to smooth out the wrinkles of shame on her conscience. Her father, though he never spoke of it, hated his youngest daughter being a divorcée. If he knew she was an adulteress as well, would he even feel able to invite her to his club? But adultery was not an appropriate concept with which to think about the transcending emotion that existed between Frank and herself.

Yearning, an unpleasant sensation of fruitless physical longing, overcame her as it did with unrelenting regularity when they were apart. It would have to be suppressed and accommodated somehow. She dreaded the effort. She ran round the flat putting herself together but every time she collected herself Frank's face shining with love, that quizzical half-smile athwart his lopsided features, materialised in front of her eyes. Pain clamped the muscles in her throat and her skin went blotchy again. She hurried on. The evening ahead might yield some comfort. There would be people there who knew him: facets of his activities might come into the conversation; there could be talk of him personally. She held in her stomach, pulled up the zip and sped down the stairs.

Outside, the peculiar hush that comes with urban nightfall had descended on the busy street, putting a mute on the harsh grind of traffic, the scrape and clatter, the clip of feet. There was a hiatus in the life of the city, a winding up of daytime and a settling down to the business of night. It absorbed Rose with consoling familiarity. She ran across the road to her car and banged the door. She was pretty, she was popular, her work was serious and absorbing, she loved and was loved. She lifted her head proudly and swung her body, fast into the traffic. Who knew what the night had hidden in its folds?

At her dinner party the first person she encountered was Professor Vane. 'Rose, you look ravishing,' he said. 'I adore your trousers. You wear such delicious clothes.' She had him next to her for dinner too. 'Good,' they said to one another as they shook out their napkins. But there was an automatic rhythm to the quality of their exchange. His attention strayed and he scanned the room with emptied eyes. Rose teased him. He roared with laughter. Rose giggled too. She geared herself for more titillation but, quite unexpectedly, balked. Her eyes emptied too. Frank was all she wanted. And if not Frank, school. Surely there was some way she could engage Max's interest in Sam. He knew so much about education. But at that moment she caught the word 'Wetherby'. Across the table, a plain-looking woman decently dressed in a good navy suit was talking about Grassdale. 'Jolly pretty place,' she was saying.

The nerve ends in Rose's heart quickened. 'Who's that?' she said silently to Max.

'Constance Goodall,' said Max out of the corner of his mouth. 'She's the new Secretary of State for Education. You should meet her,' and he called out over the table, 'I say, Connie, you remember Brigadier Hardy? This is his daughter, Rose. She's in education too.'

'My dear,' Constance Goodall called back, 'of course I know your father. We must get together. What line are you in?'

Rose blushed. When she had been an unsuccessful actress she had found people more than willing to tell her what they thought about the theatre. Now, when she said she was a teacher they said 'how interesting' and turned away. 'I teach in a primary school,' she said.

'My dear, how interesting. We must have a natter,' said Lady Goodall and resumed her conversation.

Rose felt humiliated. 'Why did you make me do that?' she said to Max. 'Nobody, not anyone in this country is interested in children; not until they can vote or fight – or until they turn into delinquents.'

She stared angrily at him and Max was startled. He was used to banter from Rose; delightful badinage with flirtatious undertones from an attractive young woman with whose social provenance he was familiar. The tone was out of place. He did not like it. His mouth opened without anything coming out, and when it did, it surprised him. 'Mummy,' he said, and a picture of himself in grey shorts and striped schoolboy cap popped into his mind. He was at the window of the school train, clinging to his mother with his eyes, as it drew away from the platform and she waved him goodbye. The connection was one he did not wish to pursue. He took a draught of sweet dessert wine to wash the taste away. 'Aah!' he said like someone surfacing in a blue summer pool. He held up his glass and circled it in the light. Rose watched, hating him momentarily. 'When did you first learn to read?' she said.

'*King Solomon's Mines*, Umslopogaas. Ah! Capital stuff!' he said, restored.

'And Belloc, and *Struwelpeter*?' said Rose.

'The red-legged Scissor Man!' cried Max. He laughed so loudly that people turned, amused. An animated discussion overtook the table; *Alice in Wonderland*, E. Nesbitt, Arthur Ransome. Rose looked on. She felt puzzled and a long way off.

Upstairs after dinner, she sat down on the bed beside Lady Goodall. 'What kind of school did you go to?' she asked.

'I went to the Girls' High in the town where we lived,' Lady Goodall said. 'Wonderful place. First class education. I was a scholarship pupil, ended up as head girl. Best days of my life.'

'How marvellous,' said Rose. 'And what about your family? Were they supportive?'

'To the hilt,' said Lady Goodall. 'My father had a passionate sense of justice. He was a great believer in education for girls. Your work must be so enjoyable, dear. I almost envy you. Schooldays are such a happy time.'

'Aren't they!' said Rose. 'But there are a lot of unhappy children where I teach. Some of them are in a bad way. Too disturbed to learn anything, and the system doesn't seem to recognise them at all.'

'Family life is not what it was these days, I'm afraid,' said Lady Goodall. She took a comb from her pocket and passed it through her hair without looking in the mirror. 'Now, I must get back to my boxes. Give my regards to your father.' She got up. With a small bow in Rose's direction she made for the stairs. Rose watched the broad blue-suited back and a spurt of fury drove her to her feet. She hurried down the stairs. In the hall Lady Goodall was shaking her host's hand. Rose hovered as the ritual phrases were exchanged. She nipped round and stood before the front door. 'Lady Goodall,' she said, 'I come across lots of neglected children in my school, desperate children no one takes seriously. They're going to cost the State much more money when they start being put in prisons and mental institutions than if they were attended to now. I'd love to talk to you about it ...'

Lady Goodall glanced at her and frowned. She was already in her pyjamas with a whisky and her papers stacked round her. 'I do admire young people like you with the good of the country at heart,' she said. 'Good night to you,' and, accompanied by her host, passed into the night and the government car that awaited her on the other side of the garden wall.

Rose was alone in the hall. She stood and dug her teeth into her bottom lip. She chewed on it so hard, she tasted blood. Her host, returning, took her by the elbow. 'I'm so glad you had a little chat with Connie,' he said. 'She's a splendid appointment – all the right qualities. Now, let me get you some coffee. And you'll have some Armagnac, won't you?'

Arriving back in his London house after a London evening, Frank kissed his wife at the bottom of the stairs. 'You go on up, darling,' he said. I'm going to give myself a nightcap.' He went into the kitchen, fiddled at the fridge and let himself out by the back door. Acting stargazer, he wandered out into the street and strolled to the next turning where, around the corner, was a telephone box, an old friend by now. He dialled Rose's number and his cock hardened inside the black trousers of his dinner jacket. He counted twelve rings, put the receiver down and collected his 10p. What risks he took. He slipped a hand inside his waistband – there were braces on his evening trousers – and fingered his balls apologetically. Then he sauntered back towards his house. He would have a whisky after all.

From the window of their bedroom, Tamarisk watched him. She changed quickly into her most virginal nightgown, dotted Swiss voile, its broderie anglaise frills all threaded with satin baby ribbon. From underneath the bed, she drew out her back board and lay down upon it flat, an expression of suffering on her pale face.

13

Rose awoke unrested. She had driven home the night before on a high of expectation, polishing her tales of the evening to fine pointed anecdotes that would make Frank crow with delight. The stories were flat now, stale and commonplace. The telephone was the most significant object in her flat. It ruled her thoughts, silent on the floor like an idol invested with the power of life. Her preparations became slower. And slower. When she could delay them no longer she lifted the receiver and dialled his number. A woman's voice answered and she replaced it immediately. She found she was shaking with fright.

On the way to school she stopped by a telephone box and tried again. This time he answered and she said his name. 'Wrong number, I'm afraid,' said his voice courteously. She held on to the receiver, paralysed with warring emotions, and crept back to her car. She got to school as the bell was ringing and raced up the back stairs. Five B was already there. 'Morning. Sorry I'm late.' They were all sitting in their places. 'Well done!'

'Mr Foster said we was to get on with our reading till you came, Miss,' said Wendy. 'He said he'd keep an eye on us.' She lowered her eyes to her reading book. They all still came with their reading books. Oh God, thought Rose, she would have to thank him at break. She sat down. The sound of the hymn came from the hall. Something was missing, an abrasive element.

'Where's Simon?'

James Potterton, who had rolled up his reading book and had it to his eye like a telescope, turned it on her. 'At death's door,' he said in a sepulchral voice.

'Ssh,' said Wendy. 'Be quiet, James. We're not to talk about it. Mr Foster said. Didn't you know, Miss?' She gave Rose a sly look, fluttered her eyelashes and sat on her hands, swinging her legs.

'I'll miss him,' said Rose, shortly. 'Close up your books. We're going to play Snap. It's Friday.'

Gary gave a loud wail. 'Oh, no. You said you was going to show us your knickers. I'm not going to do nuffink till you do.'

Rose smiled at him. 'You're the biggest. Perhaps you'd like to deal the cards for us. Do you know how?'

'Course I know how to deal cards,' said Gary. 'Here, gimme.'

The cards were the ones Rose had made of the commonest words in the language – 'and', 'at', 'for' … The game involved reading, writing, concentration, shouting and getting a bigger pile of cards than anyone else. All the children won it sometimes, except Selma, and Simon won it most. 'I'm gonna win today,' said Gary as he dealt, surprisingly inept. Rose went over and knelt by Selma. As the little girl picked each card up, very slowly, she dropped the others.

'Oh, don't let her play, Miss,' said James, 'she'll spoil it.' He gave her a shove and Selma dropped the one card she was still holding. Rose moved an arm quickly between them before Selma could reach out and fasten into whichever part of James presented itself. They were all getting better at the game.

As Wendy, James and Gary all screamed 'and!' Mr Foster's head appeared over the bookcase. 'Ah, there you are, Mrs Pitt,' he said.

'Wendy's!' said Rose.

'Fucking hell,' said Gary.

Rose flinched. 'Good morning Mr Foster,' she said loudly. 'Thank you for settling 5b down for me,' and turned back to the game. Gary's pile got bigger and bigger.

'I'm winning,' said James.

'Don't tell fibs, James Potterton,' said Wendy.

'All!' yelled Gary, slapping his hand over Wendy's pile and raking them across the table towards him.

'Oh Miss,' wailed Wendy, 'it's not fay-er. Tell him. He's taken my cards.'

'Look out. It'll happen again,' said Rose.

Wendy screwed up her face, a housewife in a Saturday street market, and perched on the edge of her chair. Soon her pile was as big as Gary's.

From under Rose's armpit came an unexpected sound, a boom, flat and toneless as a ship's hooter in fog: 'All!' It was Selma and she was right. No one ever bothered to watch the cards she turned up.

'Selma's,' called Rose.

Everyone waited while Selma, unexpectedly prompt, reached out and fumbled the appropriate cards back into her pile. 'That's very good, Selma,' said James in a fatherly voice.

Rose closed her eyes and took a deep breath: these were the moments, rare and pure, to which all her efforts were directed. And what was more extraordinary, they were recognised by the children themselves. 'Well done, Selma,' she said as matter-of-factly as she could.

Later that day, on duty in the playground, she caught sight of Selma crouched in a corner with three other little girls, playing intently. They caught one another's eye and smiled.

At lunchtime, Rose marked time outside the staffroom door, waiting for Mr Woolf. As he arrived, she stepped up to him. 'What's happened to Simon, Nathan?' she said. 'You know, that tall accident-prone boy in 5b.'

'Concussion,' said Nat, 'suspected fracture of the skull. He ran straight into a wall after school the day before yesterday. It was very strange, looked almost deliberate. We sent for an ambulance. The whole school saw. It must have been one of the afternoons you had to rush off.' He raised an eyebrow.

'Thanks,' said Rose.

Nat grinned. 'Well, what do *you* make of it, then?' So Rose told him about the boy's violent disjointed behaviour, his black drawings, his attachment to damaged toys, his constant references to disasters in the family.

'I don't know,' said Nat, 'you may be right. But no one's going to take any notice of that sort of evidence here. There have to be clear infringements of the rules, test results, expert opinions from people with acronyms. That's what counts. Everything else gets lumped under lazy, dull or plain bad. Come and have a cuppa.'

'Come and see his drawings,' said Rose, 'you'd understand then.'

He shook his head. 'Must put in an appearance. It would be better if you did too. I'll come and look after school.'

Rose thought, for the first time since nine o'clock, of Frank. Pangs, like flames, sprang up and criss-crossed round her heart. They activated a familiar ache. At the same time an admonitory balloon floated in front of her eyes. In it were some words: 'Damn him' they said. She wavered and Nat watched her, his shaggy head on one side

'I ca ... all right,' she said.

'Good,' said Nat, 'you go in and sit down. I'll bring you your tea. It's the pale-blue mug, isn't it?'

Rose sat down preoccupied with thoughts of Frank – no, Simon. To whom was her anxiety directed? Selma popped into her mind and she smiled to herself. Could she tell Mr Woolf – Nat – about Selma? Probably not. Probably no one in the world except herself and the children would ever know about the small miracle that had occurred that morning on the landing at Meadowbrook Primary.

She battled her way through the afternoon. There was a terrible session with the fourth-years among whom the class teacher had included, without warning and without explanation, a newcomer who spoke no English at all. The newcomer was a brown boy, clean and well-dressed. Rose tried to give him some words and pictures to copy: fighting broke out among the others as she did so. Her last session, with Elaine, was so dense and confusing that she found herself falling asleep. Elaine fell asleep too. She had just dictated a story, with many long silences, through the medium of the green-haired rubber doll that she often brought along with her. 'Oink, oink ...' She shook the doll and sat looking at it for several minutes. 'Oink ...' Her voice trailed away, then she said, 'That means, "What would you like to say. It is very cold."' She yawned. Her eyelids dropped and she said in a dreamy voice, 'My father and mother were slaughtered in the slaughterhouse.' There was a gap, then she said, 'No ...' Rose sat motionless, pencil poised, fighting sleep herself. Elaine said, 'You're falling asleep, Miss.'

'We're both falling asleep,' said Rose.

'I'm making you fall asleep,' said Elaine.

'You're making me fall asleep,' said Rose. She gave the words equal emphasis. Her function was to acknowledge the words without influencing them in any way.

'I'm a witch,' said Elaine.

'You're a witch,' said Rose. She felt wide awake.

'I'm a witch but I can't do any spells,' said Elaine.

Spell! Aha! thought Rose and said, 'You can't do any spells.' She saw that Elaine's face had gone fat and red. The little girl looked at her and said quickly. 'I can't do spells any more because my mother cut off my nose.'

Baffled, but intrigued, Rose was repeating the words when Elaine stood up and leaned against her. 'My mother doesn't like you,' she said. And there she stayed, staring out of the window for a full five minutes until the bell went when she gathered up her things, gave Rose an empty kiss and walked demurely away.

Alone in the corner, Rose put her hands to her head and tried to ward off the chaos. She felt unbearably irritated. The little bits of information she had been left with were too many, too disparate and too confusing to make sense of. Nothing added up. She wished more than ever she could go to sleep. She opened her file and forced herself to begin writing down the events of the session in detail. A pattern would no doubt emerge, maybe not immediately but later when she read them through. She felt too tired to think. It was a horrible sensation.

She was grappling thus with the darker aspects of disorder when Nathan Woolf hove to beside her, a stocky tug with a pilot very much on the bridge. 'Hullo, there,' he said, 'I've come to inspect the works of art. Remember?'

Rose looked up at him with a face full of distress. His arms were piled with books. 'What's up?' he said. 'You look as if you'd seen a ghost.'

'I have. Whole cupboards full of skeletons.' She tried to smile.

'Well, don't let them spook you. Now, let's have a look at these pictures.' He put the books down on top of the shelves and stood with his arms folded across his broad chest, an expression of kindly interest on his face.

Rose laid down her pen. She could not possibly rope him into Elaine too. She found Simon's folder. 'It's very kind of you,' she murmured.

'Don't be so bloody diffident. It's insulting. We're professionals discussing a problem of mutual interest. Now, what do you want to show me?' He sat down, his thick body curiously adept and contained on the child-size chair beside her. Rose's senses tightened. She showed him the black drawings, positioned haphazardly on the paper; a head here, an arm there, the circular marks of the pen standing for head, body, themselves not joined up, and the features, when there were any, outside the circles. She explained to him that in the course of normal development, children from the age of two were making whole round circles to stand for the human figure and starting to put eyes, nose and mouth inside them and that, by the age of three they were making bodies and heads. As she talked, her own head cleared and as it cleared, she made a connection. She saw how alike, in their fragmentation, were Simon and Elaine; only Simon reflected his state of mind in his behaviour, whereas Elaine kept hers

91

contained, neatly, within a wholesome exterior. Both had an intolerable effect on others. She sighed with relief and smiled at Nathan. 'You do see, a bit, don't you?' she said, seeing, herself.

'Of course I see,' said Nat. 'You make it all perfectly convincing and it's very worrying, but I don't see what the hell we can do about it.' Rose heard the 'we' and it slipped in like oil. She felt so much better, she began wondering what she looked like. It was hours since she had done her hair. Suddenly, she wanted to get home. The telephone might be ringing, or Frank might be waiting outside the flat in his car. It had happened before. Once.

'I keep hoping,' she said, 'that just by expressing what's going on for them to someone who takes it in, these children will be able to make room for some learning.' She looked into his heavy face already shadowed with bristle, and added cheerfully, 'I'm teaching lots of them, you know.' Now he had heard her, she longed to get out and away.

'I'll think,' he said. 'I've got a friend from college who's in special education. Your little Simon seems to have gone a bit too far for his own safety.' He gathered up his books.

'Thanks,' said Rose, 'thanks awfully.' She jumped up. It was a fine afternoon and the sky was blue behind the few rust and yellow leaves still adhering to the trees. She felt mean as she watched him go back down the stairs to his classroom. He did not look round or wave and Rose, when he got to the top of the stairs, ran after him. She leaned over the banister. 'Thank you, Nat,' she said. He turned and without smiling, nodded.

She drove home. She had thought that teaching, generally so inadequately done, would be easy to be good at. No one had warned her how hard she would find it just to keep order. And of the children she dealt with, every one was a full-time case in its own right. She did not want to be drowned. She wanted to do a worthwhile job well in the day and step out of it at four o'clock, free to dance whichever way and when Frank wished. Love was what mattered in life. She wanted to concentrate on it. But it hurt so.

She put her mind to it and set about recalling all the magic and wonder in the two years of their love. And by and by she felt quite melty.

14

That evening the Wetherbys attended a dinner at the French Embassy. Frank, in fine form, made Tamarisk laugh the whole way there.

Self-intoxicated with dreams of love, Rose found a frilled shirt to put on for dinner with her father. She waltzed as she dressed and piled her hair up on top of her head the way her mother used to wear hers.

Nathan Woolf changed into his tracksuit, jogged round the park three times, telephoned his mother in Hove and went to a local Labour Party meeting. He was in bed by eleven reading Marcuse.

Sam kicked a ball against the wall of the house for several hours. He broke the bathroom window, already cracked. His father cleared up the pieces when he got home and cooked their tea. His mother got up and came downstairs, a wreck hung about with drooping colourless slept-in sails. She shuffled round the kitchen and sat down at the table. Maggie clambered up the unresponsive bluff of her body and settled on the familiar slopes of her lap. Sam and his father grinned at one another over their heads.

James Potterton watched television sitting on his mother's lap. He made her let him stay up until after the news. Elaine watched television too, on her father's lap some of the time. Selma helped her mother in the shop and did not drop anything. 'She's growing up,' said Mrs Patel to her husband as they restocked shelves.

Simon lay twitching in his hospital bed. His face was the colour of frogspawn in water. Bright murals of Noddy, Big Ears and Mr Plod covered the walls of the ward around him but he saw none of them. His mind was entirely taken up with images of death, pursuit and evasion.

Puffing on his pipe, Mr Lovejoy read the latest issue of *Back Track* while his wife and two daughters washed up. Both his girls went to the High and wore dark green uniform with Panama hats in summer and berets with badges in winter.

Mrs Upjohn, even though it was autumn, spring-cleaned the spare room. It had been her son's but he never came home any more. Mr Foster and his friend listened to a recorded performance of *Die Meistersinger* on Radio 3.

At the French Embassy dinner, Ted Ainsworth and Frank circled warily round one another, mostly from a distance. The fact that Ted was there at all indicated that some missiles-for-mangetouts deal must be under way, but no trace of satisfaction showed itself on his face. He looked miserable as ever as he picked his way through the drawing-rooms. He made this journey, three rooms long, twice before dinner was announced. Two liveried footmen drew back the doors. A score of round tables, dressed in stiff pink cloths, glittering with glass and surrounded, each one, with a pattern of gilt chairs, was disclosed. They looked like Sylphides come to rest.

At one of them Tamarisk found herself seated next to Ted Ainsworth. She sighed, squared her sloping shoulders above their shelf of lacy white frills, and turned her blue eyes upon him. On his other side, Millie Vane, disgusted, simply raised her chin and stared coldly ahead. She considered it an act of aggression tantamount to national discrimination that she had been placed with such duds.

Almost on autopilot, Tamarisk said, 'It was so kind of you to come over to Grassdale the other weekend. You *must* come over lots more – if you can bear the squalor.' Beyond him she could see her husband flirting with a chic young woman – French, obviously – in a breathlessly cut black dress (and beyond that, too immaculate in his *habit*, Jean-Baptiste exchanging stiff phrases with his neighbours). Ted

Ainsworth received her remark in silence. He was picking over the food on his plate with his fork which he laid down to take something from his pocket. 'I can't be doing with this mush,' he said and popped a big white pill in his mouth.

'What's that?' said Tamarisk, her attention engaged.

'Bismuth,' said Ted Ainsworth. 'Always carry them with me.'

'Poor you,' said Tamarisk, 'I do hope you didn't need them when you came to dinner with us.'

'Oh no,' said Ted Ainsworth, 'could see what I was eating there. Good plain cooking.'

'But you must eat something,' said Tamarisk.

'I'll stick to bread,' said Ted and added, 'No, I enjoyed myself at your place.' He thought it a shame that this dainty gentlewoman should be being deceived by her husband. He resolved to make an effort.

'I never could be doing with fancy food,' he offered.

'Not brought up to it?' said Tamarisk sympathetically.

'No, indeed,' said Ted Ainsworth, 'when I was a boy ...' As Tamarisk listened to his clipped monotone her back began to hurt. He went through it all; the stern father, the grim unloving mother, the ice on the ewer in winter, the curtailed schooldays – 'You'll learn nowt at school you won't learn on factory floor', his young man's vow to be beholden to no one, his faithful dog, his devotion to the mother country, the family firm now a vast conglomerate; 'We still have a section turning out tractors and farm machinery. The finest in the world. You'll have seen them on display at airports.'

'I've had to travel abroad a good deal in my time,' he went on. 'Can't say I think much of it. You can't trust foreigners.' He bent towards Tamarisk, now squirming in pain. He could not remember when he had talked at such length. Even his boardroom speeches were pared to the minimum essential figures. 'In my opinion,' he said, 'the sooner the lot of them blow themselves to smithereens, the better.'

'Smithereens, ah yes,' said Tamarisk. There was no way she could get comfortable on the thin crimson cushion tied on to the seat of her little gilt chair and the ache in her lumbar region was becoming unendurable. Ted Ainsworth was leaning forward, his eyes narrowed. Tamarisk gave him a wan smile. 'D'you mind if I tell you a secret?' she said. Ted Ainsworth was startled. He shut down. Tamarisk went ahead anyhow. 'You'll think I'm pathetic after telling me about all the fearful things you've had to overcome,' she said, 'but I've got a bad back and it's hurting terribly now. I don't know what to do. What do you think I should do?' She shut her eyes and drew her brows together in an expression of wordless distress. Relieved not to have to consider any other part of her, Ted gave a short snort. 'You've overindulged,' he said, 'that's my diagnosis. Take one of these. It'll put you right in no time, and you may as well have one of these too ...' From the upper inside pocket of his dinner jacket he drew a silvered sheet of tiny yellow pills each housed in its own plastic bubble. 'We've got our pharmaceuticals division,' he said. 'World leaders Ainsworth Agriceuticals – *Xantoxin* – you'll be the first member of the public ... Anything to do with your insides.' He depressed one of the plastic bubbles at which one of the little yellow pills dropped beside the larger white one on to the pink tablecloth, and as he did so he felt an unaccustomed onset of protectiveness such as he generally experienced for his black Labrador, Betsy, alone.

'But it's my back,' said Tamarisk. She felt quite weak.

'Waiter!' said Ted Ainsworth with penetrating authority, and a passing extra stopped in his tracks. 'A glass of water for the lady.'

Tamarisk was aware that, from many pink circles away, the eyes of the Ambassador were upon her. She perked up and fluttered her eyelashes on whose long curling tips she always brushed a trace of blue Meltonian shoecream. Leaning towards Ted Ainsworth she gave a childlike sigh and swallowed the pills. 'You're so kind,' she murmured.

Ted Ainsworth thought that if he were that no-good husband of hers he'd see to it that she went straight home to bed with a back-rub of Sloan's Embrocation and a warm milk drink. No dependent of his would be allowed late nights and overexcitement when her health was in question. But the thought of warm milk brought him down to earth, reminding him of the 400 million tons of Horlicks sold each year in India. Ainsworth Agriceuticals was developing its own food beverage containing a secret hint of cardamom – a commodity he was obtaining at cut-price in the present deal with the French Antilles – and would enter the market shortly on fiercely competitive terms. There was business to be attended to that night.

Tamarisk wondered at his retreat. She fluttered her eyelashes some more. 'I feel so much better already,' she said brightly. 'Glad to hear it, young lady,' said Ted. He patted his mouth with his napkin and his face closed along its customary pinched lines. He was a no-nonsense man who kept himself to himself and he did not hold much with other people. Silence fell on the table.

Millie Vane, who had said little during the course of the dinner, felt ill-humoured and ill-used. Soon it would be time to move into the reception rooms again and, shortly, filter into the night to pick one's way through the press of cars and murmuring chauffeurs to one's own car. From nearby a great burst of laughter rocked the table where Max sat with Frank Wetherby and Connie Goodall. Millie felt corroded with dissatisfaction. Max saw her face. He seemed about to rise and come over when the Ambassador stood up. Glasses were raised and sipped, coffee served, chairs pushed back. Like mishoused press studs, a number of guests homed in on one another and locked: Millie with the Home Secretary, the Ambassador with Tamarisk, Frank with the chic Frenchwoman from whom his attention had been disengaged when talk at his table veered museumward, Ted Ainsworth with his contact in Aid and Development. Other guests drifted uncomplainingly downhill and via the great reception rooms to the great marbled hall and the great doors out into the ordinary night. It was not yet eleven and although the evening had been intangibly unsatisfying, they were used to it and would not have been left out for the world.

15

At Meadowbrook uproar and turmoil of a suppressed kind seethe throughout the day. The staff are on edge; the children excited and frustrated. Breaks have been extended and there are a great many collisions and scuffles in the playground. At dinner the whole sitting is put on silence (as a precautionary measure). Today's the day towards which the life of the school has been directed for all the weeks of that half term. Today's the day of the Harvest Festival.

Classes are constantly disrupted. Dishevelled children, plimsolled and breathless burst through doors with urgent messages.

'Please, Miss, Miss says can she have 5b in the hall for hymn practice now?'

Please, Sir, Mrs Jenkins says please can she have the littlest ones for trying on their bunny costumes?'

'Please Miss, Mr Lovejoy says the marchers are to be in the play-ground in five minutes.'

The sound of hymns, the same phrases rising to a crescendo, dying away and the teacher's voice, bellowing and shshshing above; a constant pattering of feet on the stairs; the incomprehensible boom-ing and squeaking of Mr Lovejoy's megaphone as he directs the senior boys in their demonstration of ornamental marching; a howl of outrage: 'James Potterton – *what* are you doing!' By midday the line outside the Headmaster's office, faces in to the wall, is five boys long and one girl.

Alone in ignominy, chipmunk-fronted slippers on his feet, Sam leaves the chair to which he is bound by threats and constant surveillance, and begins exploring the welfare room. No one's been in to look at him since first thing, not even Miss Bunting with sums. He goes to the window first and stands on a chair to look out. The windows are the metal-framed kind, like at home, that open with a handle halfway up and have bars with holes that fit over a peg in the frame to keep them open. These ones only open so far, for some reason Sam can't work out, and they're very stiff to get undone at all. But he manages, using both hands, which then smell of rusty tin. The smell is one he knows and likes. By lying on the sharp sill and wriggling sideways, he can see down to the ground below which is bare and hard, drifting with papers, plastic shreds and last year's damp and crumbly leaves. It's the unconsidered narrow sort of place grown-ups never go.

He worms back inside the room and hugs his arms into his tummy, now scored with red lines which hurt. He looks around and drops to his knees. Under the radiator, all muddled up with soft strings of dust, he finds a broken pencil, one of the green-painted expensive kind with six sides, and several pennies. He puts 1p in his pocket and sits against the radiator chewing the rubber at the top of the pencil and spitting the bits out. From the end of his legs four felt chipmunk eyes stare at him sightlessly. If he could find a razor blade he could sharpen the pencil and scribble out the eyes. On all fours, he goes on. In the wastepaper-basket he finds cigarette ends. He slits one open with his fingernail and shakes the tobacco on to a bit of paper but it's not very interesting. Later he'll collect enough to take back to his Mum.

He wonders what Maggie's doing down in the distant thrum, alive with pitfalls, trip-wires, and pouncing teachers. It's quite nice under the table with the wastepaper-basket. He looks round to see what else he can pull in with him. He can see the legs of a small chair that children sit on when the doctor examines them or Mrs Upjohn sticks on plasters. He reaches out and draws it in. It fences him in on two sides and he sits there for a bit trying it out. What else? He crawls round between the back of the chair and the wall and reaches for three telephone directories on the top of the table. They fall all at once with a fat thump and he drags them in too. Now he's got things all round him and he can recline with his elbow on a telephone directory looking out, or sit with his back against the wall and his legs stretched out between the legs of the chair, or he can curl up small facing the wall. He needs another thing: on the top of the table is one of those extra bright lamps with a movable head on a tall, hinged metal stick. He crawls out the proper way between the chair and the wall, lifts the lamp on to the floor and adjusts its head so it'll shine straight into his place under the table. He switches it on and goes back, but it's not quite right. He goes out again and fiddles so the beam shines exactly where he wants it. Then he goes back in and settles himself against the wall. The light shines full on his face. He gives a sigh. It feels fine. He's special and he sits there looking out on the world from his world.

Downstairs, in Mr Woolf's prefab classroom outside the main school, the little ones are trying on their bunny costumes. All the leftover children from Infants and first-years who can't manage singing or even triangles, are being rabbits for the final tableau. Squirrels were what the Headmaster had wanted, but Mrs Jenkins had said that would be beyond her – 'Too costly, the tails, you know' was how she'd put it. She had a line in rabbits and there were quite a few bits and pieces in the stockroom from other years. The little ones have got tremendously excited jostling around, squeaking and scuffling in lines where they're meant to keep quiet, and Mrs Jenkins keeps shouting at them. A number are in tears. 'Cry-babies,' says Mrs Jenkins severely. 'I'd expect it from the Nursery, but not from children in proper school.'

Maggie stands so quietly, left behind at the back of the classroom, that she almost gets missed out. 'Why, bless my soul, there's another one,' says Mrs Jenkins. 'Come over here, child.' But Maggie doesn't move. She just looks at the teacher, her brown eyes so big they seem to take up the whole of her white face. 'What's your name, child?' says Mrs Jenkins, but she knows better than to insist on an answer. She goes briskly over and takes Maggie by the hand. And she's surprised, with all her experience, how easily the little girl comes, like a thread with no end. She pushes and pulls her unresistant limbs into the brown stretchy body stocking, sticks on the cotton-wool tail and pops the mask over her head. It's quicker to do it herself. Through the eyeholes she catches a spark of delight shining from Maggie's eyes. 'You look lovely, dear – a proper little bunny,' she says and gives her a pat on the tail.

Rasping round the school on clacking heels Mrs Upjohn shoos the bunnies into the hall for rehearsal. She has a thousand things to attend to and her throat feels quite parched for want of a cup of tea. On the way they pass Mr Woolf and his team of boys bluetacking and drawing-pinning peeled off corners and last-minute notices to the walls. Particles of her straggling troupe fall away and get muddled in with the boys. She takes a whistle from her overall pocket and blows a sharp blast, but Mr Woolf good-humouredly disentangles the bunnies and redirects them. He looks much too relaxed to be pulling his weight properly. 'Cheery-bye,' he says as they move on.

In the hall, the last bars of the harvest hymn are being punched out for the umpteenth time. Hand-in-hand with Tracy in the third row, her golden hair in businesslike plaits, Elaine joins in with all her might. She makes such precise and obliging movements of her mouth that no one ever realises she can't sing the words. She looks the picture of a model schoolgirl in her neat pleated skirt, its hem slightly higher at the front than the back due to the convexity of the stomach beneath. Selma, on the other hand, standing in the front row with her mouth agape and her tongue lolling uselessly between her teeth, looks a perfect fright.

'Move that child to the back!' Mr Foster hurries by with his clipboard. He takes hold of her hand and hauls her, a dead weight, to the last row but one where she stands mute and submerged in taller children.

'Quite right, Mr Foster,' says Mrs Upjohn. 'I'm thinking of making a cup of tea in the welfare room. Pop in, I'm sure you need one.'

'Tzt, tzt. Thank you Mrs Upjohn.' Mr Foster bustles on.

Rose is setting out cups on trestle tables by the front door. She's given up waiting for her groups to turn up. 'I could do with a hand for the parents' teas,' Mrs Jenkins had said. Now, assisted by four older girls who giggle whenever she addresses them, she is wiping thick white cups with a teacloth. From outside the plate glass, much too tall for his shorts, Gary leers in on them. He gives a quick look round, opens the door, sticks his head in, gives a wolf-whistle and scarpers. The girls giggle so hard one drops a cup. They giggle harder. But the cup only bounces.

James Potterton hobbles past, loudly boo-hooing. When he sees Rose, he puts in some groans and slows down.

'What is it, James? Why aren't you with the rest of your class?'

James lets out a roaring wail. 'Mr Lovejoy gave me the slipper,' he gasps, hiccuping between syllables. 'I'm in agony. Oh, Miss.'

Rose wonders what she ought to do. It seems pretty much free for all that day, so she says, 'Would you like to help us here? You could be our waiter.'

James stops wailing. 'Can I have an apron?'

Rose ties a teacloth round his waist.

'And a pencil?'

Rose gives him one and he puts it behind his ear. He takes a cup and sits on the floor with his back to them a little way off, muttering and making elaborate movements of his head and arms. Every now and again he gets up, comes over and, taking the pencil from behind his ear, says to one of the girls or to Rose: 'Can I take your order now, madam?'

By now, Mrs Upjohn's gasping and her bunion is playing up. She feels well justified in giving herself a break. Without slackening the urgency of her pace or of her expression, she hurries towards the welfare room. 'George,' she says, putting her head round the Headmaster's door, 'I'll be making a cup of tea. I'm sure you need one.' Mr Lovejoy, perspiring from his exertions with the megaphone and the marchers, looks up from the lists he's making. 'Thank you, Joyce. That's most considerate. I could certainly do with one.' In the welfare room, Mrs Upjohn makes straight for the kettle which stands on a paper towel by the basin. She fills it, switches it on and – is struck by a thought. She looks around. Sam's nowhere to be seen. There's something odd about the room. Then she sees a piece of paper on the floor. On it are some crumbled cigarette ends and a few specks of tobacco. She puts her hand to her flat breast. Then she puts her head up and sniffs.

At that moment Mr Foster peers in and slips round the door. 'Tea?' he mouths, putting a finger to his lips. Mrs Upjohn takes him by the elbow. 'Mr Foster, do you see anything?' She points to the paper on the floor and draws herself up stiffly. 'That child's been smoking!'

'But where is he?' says Mr Foster. 'Tzt, tzt, tzt.'

Steam is rising from the kettle. Shaking her head, Mrs Upjohn hurries to it. She makes tea with teabags in three mugs and stirs a spoon of powdered milk into each. One, she takes towards Mr Foster and on the way she knocks her shin on the lamp.

'Good gracious me!' she cries, looking down.

Mr Foster takes his tea. 'Good gracious me!' he cries.

The lamp is on. It shines full under the table. There in the lair of his own making, cool as you please, sits Sam Clark.

'Come out of there, you wicked boy!' Mrs Upjohn bends and seizes hold of his ankles.

'Dreadful child,' says Mr Foster. They haul him out.

'You've been smoking, don't deny it!' says Mrs Upjohn as Sam stumbles to his feet. She puts her nose into the palm of his hand and gives a long sniff. There is indeed a trace of stale tobacco to be detected among the nondescript odours of metal and grime coming off his blackish hands.

'Headmaster!' says Mrs Upjohn as Mr Lovejoy enters, 'this child's been smoking.'

'Smoking …' Mr Lovejoy rolls the word around at length through several registers. 'Smoking at Meadowbrook?' He glares down at Sam then he points to the wall. 'Stand there. Nose touching, feet touching. And don't dare to move. I'll deal with you later.' Mrs Upjohn bends and picks up the piece of paper with its few cigarette ends and particles of tobacco from the floor. 'You'll be needing this, George,' she says.

'I'd be obliged if you'd keep it for me, Joyce,' says Mr Lovejoy. For a few minutes the three of them stand, somewhat constrained by Sam's presence, drinking tea. Then Mr Lovejoy puts his mug down. 'Very nice, Joyce,' he says, 'thank you. I must be getting on.' He leaves the room.

Mr Foster and Mrs Upjohn stand looking at each other, the surreptitious interlude in tatters.

'What a disgrace,' says Mr Foster.

'No more than you'd expect from a child with his background,' says Mrs Upjohn.

'Don't you say nuffink …' mutters Sam soundlessly and spits on the wall.

The two teachers make for the door. 'After you,' says Mr Foster.

'I'll be back,' says Mrs Upjohn before she slams it shut, 'so don't you be getting up to any of your tricks, young man.' And stiffened with outrage as much as tea, the two of them hurry back to stir the fray.

As soon as they have left the room, Sam makes for the window. On the way he takes a running kick at the wastepaper-basket. Some of its contents roll on to the floor. He pulls himself on to the windowsill and wriggles through the narrow opening. The metal frame scrapes him painfully, digging through the thin flesh to his bones. Braking with his knees against the brick, he lets himself down until he hangs full length from his hands. Then he gives a push and springs, backwards, into the air.

School dispersed early that afternoon. The children were to go home and come back at five in clean white shirts and Meadowbrook ties, green with wavy blue lines. Mrs Upjohn had been to considerable lengths to make sure every child had one. On arrival parents and grandees were to be served tea in the entrance hall where they would linger admiring the displays. At half past five the service was to start and at half past six, the grandees alone would be led to the Headmaster's office where they would be offered a glass of sherry and variously shaped cheesy biscuits.

Those of the teachers who lived far afield stayed in the staffroom and changed in the staff toilet. Humming to himself, Mr Woolf shaved and put his head through the loop of one of his jazzy ties. He never undid ties; just loosened them and they hung, ready for action, over the handles either side of his bedroom door in Finsbury Park.

Rose drove home, picking up her black velvet suit from the cleaners on the way. She was to help Mrs Jenkins with the teas and, afterwards, with the bunnies and the marshalling of children in and out of the hall. She liked being part of the event in this menial way and she liked Mrs Jenkins: a salt-of-the-earth old pro. She hummed, too, as she did her eyes in the looking-glass.

Outside the door into Infants, Maggie waited for Sam. The last children left the playground. She stood so quietly that the school caretaker, sweeping up leaves, never saw her at all. As the minutes, slow grey bubbles in an unending chain, passed by she became less and less, the animation within confined to autonomic activity alone. A police car drove into the playground and right up to the door. A policewoman and two policemen got out and went into the school. One of them had a dog. They came out again. The policewoman was carrying a boot. It looked like one of Sam's. They walked round the playground with the dog then they got into the car and drove away again. Children started dribbling back into the playground. The girls had ribbons instead of rubber bands in their hair. They stood outside the door into Juniors, more and more of them, until there was a big crowd standing like cows round a gate waiting to be milked. Mrs Upjohn came out. She was wearing a powder-blue coat and skirt and red shoes with heels. The children all went in. Some of them had mothers and fathers with them and were holding hands. More children arrived, running, in ones and twos and went straight into school. Maggie detached herself from her unmarked post and went running in after the last of them. She wanted to be a bunny, no doubt about that. Inside the entrance hall she stood in her plimsolls and dirty blouse hardly breathing at all.

Standing behind the teacups, Rose saw her and smiled. Presently she came over. 'You're Sam's sister, aren't you?' she said. Maggie said nothing but she turned her face up to Rose's and looked at her. 'Whose class are you in?' said Rose, but she knew it was a silly question. She looked at the little girl, all straggling smelly hair and greyish white skin and clothing. 'I expect you're a rabbit,' she said. Maggie uttered not a sound but her face cracked, first into a faint widening of the mouth, then into a slight upturning of the lips and thence into the full sun of a huge grin, ear to ear. Rose dared not leave her post. The urn would be upon it at any moment and her helpers were forbidden utterly to approach it. Nevertheless, 'Run,' she said and held out her hand. Together they flew up the stairs and across the landing into the classroom where Mrs Jenkins was stuffing small children into brown stockinette packages. A row of them was already sitting, fully furred, on a bench.

'Another one for you, I think, Mrs Jenkins.'

'Thank you, Mrs Pitt. Mrs Jenkins glanced at Maggie and raised her eyebrows with distaste in Rose's direction. 'Run along and wash your hands, dear,' she told Maggie. 'I'll do you next.'

Rose closed the door and saw that Maggie, light as thistledown as she vanished down the corridor to the cloakrooms, was skipping.

Very much weighted down with pedestrian considerations, Mr Lovejoy closed the door on to the passage down which Maggie skipped. He had summoned Mrs Upjohn and Mr Foster from their manifold preoccupations for a brief conference. A course of action had to be agreed regarding Sam Clark, who had so inconsiderately taken it upon himself to abscond on that day of all days. Mr Lovejoy sat behind his desk rapping the surface with his pen. The sound gave a disciplinary note to the proceedings. Mrs Upjohn, upright and thin-lipped, sat on the edge of her chair while Mr Foster, his face working, twitched upon his. Should an announcement of some sort be made from the platform or should the evening go ahead without interruption.

'Joyce?' said Mr Lovejoy.

'We've got quite enough on our hands as it is, Headmaster,' said Mrs Upjohn with a sniff.

'Yes, indeed. Quite enough,' said Mr Foster. He shook his head and looked at his watch. He could hardly bring himself to stay still on his chair.

'I incline to that view myself,' said Mr Lovejoy. 'And his class teacher?' They discussed Miss Bunting, a young and inexperienced member of staff, but promising, and decided she should be told but not until the end of the evening.

'And the parents? The police will already have visited the home.' At this, Mrs Upjohn gave a double sniff. 'The parents, as you know, Headmaster, are thoroughly unco-operative. They have never been known to put in an appearance at any school function. They should be left to the police, in my opinion.'

'There's a younger sibling, a sister, is there not?' said Mr Foster. 'I could prepare a note for her to take home to them afterwards.'

'Thank you, Derek,' said Mr Lovejoy, 'I think that covers every aspect that we need to consider for the moment.' He put his pen into his breast pocket and stood up, an unflappable figure if not quite majestic, behind his desk. 'And now, I think we all have plenty to occupy us for the next hour or two,' he said. 'I count myself fortunate to number among my staff two such right-minded members.' He nodded as they stood up and moved to hold the door for Mrs

Upjohn. As she passed through he said, 'And might I mention, Joyce, how much blue becomes you?'

From outside the window watching them, Sam could see but not hear. A concatenation of drainpipes at that point on the wall gave him a purchase of relative stability so that he could lean round and peer in from the extreme corner. Shivering and extremely hungry, his eye was held by a white-covered table on which were laid plates of little biscuits with paper flags on top. The headmaster's office was a room with which he was familiar enough and the table was not usually there. Today it was placed directly under the window which was closed. However, a half window above the main one was open, held by one of the little bars with holes on a peg in the frame. It was beyond his reach. To get there, he would have to jump round a corner, cling, pull himself up by his arms and wriggle through.

He leaned back against the drainpipe. His fingers were very sore. He had had a lot of leaping and clinging and bumping and jolting that day and much of the skin on the exposed parts of his body was raw. An aeroplane went by in the dulled grey sky above. It was a Concorde with a winking light. It flew right across from one side to the other and another one flew across soon after. The playground below, which had been filled with people and noise all day long was completely empty. He could feel the silence and it made him uncomfortable. He could just hear the sound of singing coming from the hall. It seemed contained and far off and it increased his unease. He jumped.

One hand only caught the sill. It dug into his palm. He struggled with his tired muscles to pull himself up, making convulsive movements with the rest of his body against the glass. He got the other hand on to the sill and gave a desperate heave. His head hit the inside of the little window and he butted it up. He wriggled with his shoulders, got both armpits over the frame and hung there. His heart was thumping horribly but he knew he could do it now. A few more heaves and he was in through the narrow space, nose-diving towards the table. He tried to break his slither with his knees and feet. Both the chipmunk-fronted slippers got scraped off by the sharp sill. He fell amid the plates, flipped sideways and rolled off and under the table to the space, concealed by the hang of the tablecloth, beneath. He felt trembly and sick and there was a roaring noise in his head. One day they had all been to the seaside and his mother had found a shell which she held to his ear. The noise was like that. It died away and he heard percussion, very faint, from the hall instead.

He poked his head out from under the tablecloth and there, in front of his nose, was a biscuit. He hoovered it into his mouth and consumed it, crumbly, crunchy and delicious. There were several more near by upon the carpet, together with some broken-off bits and crumbs. Using his snout like an anteater in the zoo, he polished off the lot. There was a plate on the floor and one of the round pieces of paper his class had been folding and cutting into patterns. Sam had quite liked opening up the paper and finding the pattern there, but the cutting was impossible with the round-pointed scissors which were the only ones he was allowed to use. He had got fed up and made paper planes instead. He crawled out from under the table, took a handful of biscuits from on top and went back under to eat them.

He began to feel fine again. The biscuits tasted as good as crisps. He put one in his pocket for Maggie and, crouching, loped for the door. When he opened it he could hear the sing-songy boom of Mr Lovejoy's voice quite clearly. There was no one about in the rest of the school at all. He decided to get out while he could and find somewhere to hide. Then he could meet his sister when she came out and take her home. He knew she would not know what to do if he was not there. Keeping close to the wall, he made his way down the stairs and into the playground. It was getting dark out there. He found a good place by the big dustbins round the back and settled to wait. He could always get in if someone came.

They were singing again in the hall. He licked his knee. The raw bits had a cool tinny taste compared to the unbroken skin round. Black bits of grit and earth got into his mouth and he spat them out.

16

Frank said, 'Rosebud?'

In spite of himself, the voice came out hoarse with excitement. Leaning against the side of the telephone box he tenderly fingered the front of his trousers but first, he looked round to see if he was being watched. The dark outside heightened his sense of thrill. Oh, why was everything one had ever wanted out of bounds? Rose's voice came soft through the receiver into his ear. 'Oh, darling ...'

'Are you in bed?' he said. He thought of her long lashes, the dark sweep against the apricot curve of her sleeping cheek. Emotion swelled up.

I'm going to drown, he thought.

In his most languid voice he said, 'Darling, this is your dirty old man in a long mackintosh on the blower, pestering you from a run-down telephone box in seediest Paddington – crazed with passion. Say something sexy.'

'I love you,' said Rose.

'What are you wearing?' said Frank as nonchalantly as he could.

Lying on the bed in her flat, Rose told him. 'Why don't you come round?' she said.

'Impossible,' said Frank. He spoke lightly, playfully. 'I'm much too late already. My darling. I just thought you might be missing me. I've driven miles out of my way ...'

Rose adjusted instantaneously to the edge on the words. She put her mind to thinking of his white flanks and imagined her hand moving down the long slow curve of them. She said, 'You're here. Beside me now. And I'm loving you all over.'

Frank gave a long sigh. For a moment he thought of taking a room in one of the station hotels opposite and sending for Rose in a taxi. Instead he said, 'I feel it, my beloved. Have you ever thought? We're never apart. A magic link, a golden thread connects us. For ever.'

'Mmnn,' said Rose, trying, 'so there is.' There was silence between them. And then, in a small voice, she said something she never said. 'When am I going to see you?'

'With a love like ours ...' said Frank. 'Oh darling, I'm so afraid you're going to hate me one of these days.'

Rose was shocked, 'Oh darling, never.'

'Trust me,' said Frank.

'I do,' said Rose. Anguished and remorseful she added, 'Our golden thread ... Forever.'

'Forever,' said Frank. And presently, with many a lingering verbal caress they cut the electronic link between them, replacing the receivers upon their rests.

Frank got into his car and put his foot down on the accelerator. It was past midnight. What if he got caught for speeding? The thought of the consequences, of the whole intricate structure of his life crashing round his ears, chilled him. This game was getting too dangerous, this delicious game to which he was held in thrall.

Ah, Rose, he thought, my little love, my soft white sexy dove. He shook his head and slowed the car down to 40 mph.

Rose lay back on the pillows and punched them into a more satisfactory shape under her neck. She felt itchy and rigid and by and by, she let out a howl ... This will never do, Rose Pitt, she told herself and got up to make a cup of tea. With the hot mug in her hands she wandered round the flat. She put up the ironing board and started to press her clothes for the morning. Thump, drag, wriggle, pull; the iron was her friend. She thought of Nathan Woolf, solid and blue-chinned. They had had a drink together, in a pub after Harvest Festival was over. She hated pubs and the fact she hated them was one of the reasons she had felt obliged to accept.

After the teas, after the singing, the speeches and the recitations; the prayers and the poems, Mr Woolf and his team of trusties had gone round the school picking up litter. The governors and the visitors from the Local Education Authority had been discreetly siphoned off and directed towards the Headmaster's office, and Rose had helped Mrs Jenkins fold the fancy dresses and pack them away. In the almost empty building, Mr Woolf approached, 'Coming for a noggin? Mrs Jenkins? Rose?'

'Oh no, Mr Woolf, thank you ever so much,' Mrs Jenkins had said. 'Mr Jenkins will be waiting for me. Besides, I never touch a drop in the week.'

'Just a quick one,' said Rose. They went down to the front hall together and out into the playground. There was a definite chill on the darkening air and a few children still dawdled on the asphalt. All three noticed Sam Clark slip out of the shadows and take his sister by the hand. Maggie skipped but Sam seemed to be limping.

'The child's got no shoes on, for heaven's sakes,' said Mrs Jenkins.

'Oh dear, poor Sam,' said Rose.

'Little blighter,' said Nat. 'We could go to The Crown. It's nearer, but the Black Prince's nicer.'

'Shall I take my car?' said Rose.

They walked down the street together, awkwardly in the outside world. Whatever am I doing, he's not my sort at all, thought Rose. She smiled at him.

I wonder what it's like under those frills, thought Nat. Hang on lad, you're only going for a drink.

In the Black Prince, dark, plush and fusty, Rose asked for plain tonic. Nat leaned against the bar. It was easier to think of him as a Christian name outside school. He came back to where she sat carrying a dimpled tankard in one hand and her see-through tipple in the other. Dotted lines of bubbles fizzed through it and a half slice of lemon on a toothpick listed on its surface.

'I thought you'd like ice,' he said.

'Lovely,' said Rose.

'Chin-chin,' said Nat. He sat down beside her and loosened the tie round his neck. He was wearing a dark blue shirt and the thought of the darker blue patches that might be under his armpits flitted across her mind and lodged in it.

'I thought it went off rather well,' he said.

'It was fun, wasn't it?' said Rose. They both looked round the room. Nothing that presented itself seemed worthy of comment.

'That's all over then,' said Nat. 'Ah well ...'

'What made you be a teacher?' said Rose, wishing for Frank. Tears prickled the backs of her eyeballs. She picked up her glass and took a medicinal sip. Watching her, Nat thought how composed she looked, an exotic from a different world, slim black legs crossed, thigh upon thigh under the black skirt, white ruffles curving from the open front of her jacket.

'It seemed the only thing,' he said. 'I spent some time in Latin America. Ended up in Nicaragua. Education is important in those parts: they take it really seriously. I did a bit to help out. Found I could work with kids ...' He stopped. What could he hope to get across to this well-insulated young woman. What was she doing in a state school anyway? 'What made you go in for teaching then?' he said abruptly.

'It just seemed to be ... the most important thing one could do,' said Rose. 'Children ... I mean, making new people. I don't think any system can work unless the people in it are sound and whole and can think for themselves. My life had got so pointless. I wanted to get out and do what I believed in. But it's so confusing now I'm in it. I thought it would be easy to do well and that everybody would be on the side of the children and of education. But I'm beginning to think they're not. Their agendas are quite other. Except yours, perhaps?'

She looked at him, troubled and tentative.

Nathan Woolf thought he could see a hint of nipple showing through her cotton shirt, or was it a shadow? He wanted to put his finger on it. He wanted to put his whole hand over her breast and hold it … He cleared his throat. Such thoughts were against his principles. 'What did you do before?' he said.

'Oh, nothing much,' said Rose. 'I tried to be an actress in a hopeless sort of way, and I was married for a bit.'

'Married!' said Nathan before he could stop himself. 'Yes of course.' He felt acutely disturbed and, swiftly, annoyed with himself.

'I'm afraid I wasn't much good at that either. It didn't last very long. But I was rather good at acting. I just couldn't take it that seriously and I wanted to be serious. I still do.' She looked down at the semicircle of lemon beached at the bottom of her glass, picked it up, still on its toothpick and ate it, pith, rind and all. It was the first time Nathan had seen anyone eat lemon neat like that except at rugby matches and even there, these days, one got oranges. And she did it with such aplomb! He felt himself slipping and braked hard. They both looked at their watches.

'Goodness, I must fly,' said Rose.

'Time to put my skates on,' said Nat.

They got to their feet, bumped into one another, apologised and walked to the door. Nat let Rose precede him. The top of her head was as high as his cheek and her shoulder would have fitted nicely under his.

'Well, cheery-bye,' he said in the street.

'Thank you,' said Rose, 'it was lovely.' They turned their backs to each other and walked in opposite directions along the pavement; Rose to her car at the end of the road: Nat, away from the station he was aiming for.

The streets were tired and dusty as Rose drove home and there was a flat airlessness upon them. Outside the Tube the flower vendor had nothing but chrysanthemums. She put her foot down and sped by.

She thought of Sam, shoeless, on the hard pavement and her mind shied away. Maybe she had taken on more than she could handle. Maybe she was making a mistake somewhere. She set about constructing a vision of herself and her lover in bed for the evening, nested in pillows, reading to each other, her head on his shoulder, his head on her breast, bathed in the light of the bedside lamp and the blaze from their two hearts. She stopped and bought some sliced bread for toast just in case.

Nathan Woolf walked round the block from the Black Prince and headed back to the station. As soon as he got home he would go for a run, a good pound through the night streets. He wondered briefly what that little blighter Sam Clark was doing out without shoes. It was none of his business. On the flower stall outside the station he noticed some big brown chrysanthemums, beautiful blooms with a rich autumny smell. Rose would like those, he thought, imagining their mutual delight as he handed her a great bunch of them. He fingered the coins in his pocket and bought an evening paper. Capitalist rubbish, he thought, as he scanned the front page and turned to the sport at the back.

Sam, meanwhile, was dawdling home; dawdling because it hurt too much to run. He felt lessened by the absence of his boots, as much part of himself as his legs themselves. Besides, he felt tired in an unsleepy trembly way. Maggie held on to his hand.

'I was a bunny,' she said as soon as they got out of the playground, and gave a hop or two. Sam fished in the pocket of his shorts and brought out a few lumps and fragments of biscuit mixed in with shreds of tobacco and some grit. He emptied them on to her small palm and she put them in her mouth. A scrumpled piece of paper drifted on to the pavement. Her eyes sparkled as she munched, spitting out specks of grit and tobacco as she came to them. She hopped some more until Sam gave her hand a jerk and she fell into step beside him. She rubbed her face against his grey sleeve. They went slower and slower. The lollipop lady had long since left the crossing and all the shops were shut but light spilled out from the pubs. Sam shut his eyes as they passed through the neon glare of the fish and chip shop. The sharp smell of vinegar on the still fumes of fat made the inside of his cheeks contract. They turned into their own street. A police-car was parked outside the house, the light on top still flashing. Sam wriggled through the open triangle between the gate and the gatepost pulling Maggie after him. The back door was half open and there was something unfamiliar about the feeling that came out of it with the weak yellow light. It caused Sam's senses to prick up and he hesitated a second before he went in.

A policewoman was sitting at the table and a policeman stood behind her listening to a two-way radio that crackled and gabbled in his ear. The policeman was holding his flat cap under one arm but the policewoman had hers on her head crisply tilted over the forehead. They took up a lot of room against the cluttered outlines of the kitchen. On the other side of the table, blurred into the generalised mess, sat their mother in her nightdress and cardigan, silently crying. Maggie let go Sam's hand and made straight for her.

'I was a bunny,' she said and began hauling and scrabbling up on to her lap. She put her thumb in her mouth and lay against her mother's body until a rasping sob unseated her and she slithered off again. On the floor she crouched by her skirt giving an occasional springing bob and holding a finger upright on each side of her head.

Sam flattened himself against the wall and wondered if it was the police who were making his mother cry. He hoped the cigarette ends might still be on the floor of the welfare room tomorrow. He wished his Dad were here, now. The policeman spoke first. He muttered something into the radio close to his lips and looked at Sam. Sam looked at the floor. 'Are you Sam Clark, young man?' he said. His voice, so loud and unequivocal, sent a shock wave through the room, setting the knives and cups ashiver in their sluggish repose. Sam said nothing but started to hack the floor with one foot to which a sock, now in tatters, still adhered in some places. His feet were very sore and kicking hurt, so he slid to the floor and sat there, not looking. The policewoman bent down and round the table leg. She put a finger up on either side of her hat and waggled them at Maggie. 'Is that your brother, Sam Clark?' she said almost soundlessly and wrinkled her nose up and down, putting her top teeth over her bottom lip. Maggie nodded, waggling back. The policewoman sat back in her chair patting her hat and the policeman said, 'You've caused a great deal of trouble, young man. A lot of people have been very worried about you. I must ask you to inform us what you have been up to between the hours of two and seven-thirty this afternoon.'

'You don't want to come down to the station now, do you?' said the policewoman.

'I wasn't doing nuffink,' muttered Sam.

His mother got unsteadily to her feet. She wiped her nose on the baggy sleeve of her cardigan and in her high refined voice began to speak. 'This is a well-brought up family,' she said, 'my children would never do anything that infringed the law. Please leave us alone. We don't need you any more.' Her voice grew shrill. She lurched toward the sink and began to tug at a pan handle that poked above the stagnant surface. Her face started to slip and a maenad-like quality overtook her person. With her wild uncombed hair standing out from her head and her white working face she presented an alarming appearance.

The policewoman stood up, so did Sam who edged over to his mother as Maggie, under the table, contracted almost to transparency.

'No offence, ma'am,' said the policeman attempting a smile. He looked at the policewoman and they raised their eyebrows. 'If everything's in order, we'll be going. But I must caution you, young man. Any more complaints and we'll have to take proceedings.' He took a step towards the door.

Mrs Clark gave an ululating shriek. The pan came free and she lifted it, dripping, above her head. 'Mum,' said Sam, 'don't, Mum.' He took a step to stand in front of her, his face whiter than the monochrome of her garments behind him. The policeman drew himself up and with his chin doubled back into his neck, opened his mouth to speak, but the policewoman shook her head. 'Well, now that you're all safe together again,' she said cheerfully, 'we'll be getting back to the station. You know where to find us if you need us. Good evening,' and she nudged her colleague in the direction of the door. With great deliberation, he took his hat from under his arm and adjusted it on his head. Giving Sam an admonitory glare, he departed to pace the short length of pebbled path, following the policewoman to the car. In a shadowless flurry, Maggie flew after and the policewoman was surprised to find a tiny cold hand clutching her fingers. The little girl said nothing. The three of them negotiated the broken gate and the policewoman disengaged her fingers to get into the car. 'Bye-bye, love,' she said. 'Be good.' Maggie stood on the pavement and lifted her skirt to flap farewell then she turned and hopped back, pausing to make nibbling motions at the wisps of greenery that straggled out of the earth beside the path.

Inside the kitchen, Sam's mother made ineffectual swipes at her son's head. She moaned and screeched as she did so, a wordless lament of frustration and fright. The saucepan went clattering to the floor. Sam slithered and dodged on the greasy lino. He made a dart for the cupboard under the sink, squeezed in among the stiffened dishcloths and empty Vim tins and pulled the door to. Not for the first time that day, he put his head on his knees drawn close into his chest and sat there shivering in a limbo of his own making.

17

There were some awkwardnesses at school next day ... It was Friday
and the following week was half term. Rose and Nathan skirted
round one another, though each hailed the other cheerfully enough
at first sight. 'Morning, Rose!'

'Morning, Nat,' thereafter avoiding eye-contact The staff felt
jaded; the children slack and disposed to silliness. At every turn
Elaine and Tracy hand-in-hand were to be found in corners, giggling.
James Potterton kept himself sullenly and egregiously apart, resistant
to cajolery and coercion alike. His chunky person, absorbed in furious mutterings, managed to trip up and annoy almost everyone in
his class, and he finished the day facing the wall outside the
Headmaster's office. Gary tweaked and pinched the girls, provoking
scuffles and skirmishes and sending them shrieking in droves across
the playground. Selma fell among them like a nerveless log, cutting
her knee so badly she had to be sent to hospital for stitches.

'I shan't be sorry to see the back of this half of the term,' said Mrs
Jenkins over her mug at break.

Mr Lovejoy spent the morning on the telephone to head office
trying to procure some emergency order that would take Sam Clark
off his hands and into Social Services, Special Education or CARE.
The memory of his ruined office, the wrecked table, the cheese
roundies and straws scattered over the carpet, the bottle of sherry he
was convinced had been illicitly broached, lay heavy on his chest. He
was determined to rid himself of this pernicious presence in his

school – and punish the boy into the bargain. He felt fully justified, moreover, that it was in the child's best interests for him to do so. Mrs Upjohn, at frequent intervals, popped her head discreetly round the door proffering tea and coffee. She felt energised with outrage and bustled round the school in her white overall and Dr Scholl sandals, the very arbiter of right and wrong. Mr Foster, poor Mr Foster, had a headache bordering on migraine. He felt wrung out. The noise from corridors and other classrooms twanged unbearably inside his head: he kept his own class in silence the whole day long.

Rose struggled through the day. Her midnight call from Frank had left her bereft; she had no immediate hope, no foreseeable future, nothing to fix her sights on. She wished to be alone to nurse her desolation, picking it through for crumbs of comfort with uninterrupted concentration. In this state of mind she missed any number of signals; her pupils turned boring and wilfully contrary as she tried to force them into reading and writing.

'Don't like you any more,' said James, sitting on his hands and turning his back, 'My mother doesn't like you either.'

'Phew – you smell,' said Gary. 'Miss smells, just like my Nan,' and he leered at her before jumping on to a distant chair and stamping there holding his nose. Selma, her bandaged knee held stiff before her, bared her teeth and snarled as Rose patted her shoulder with unfelt friendliness. And Elaine sat for a full half hour without speaking as her rosy cheeks went geranium pink and her eyelids fell lower and lower over her dulled blue eyes. 'I'm going to follow my father,' she said brightly as she picked up her belongings to go. 'He's got big thighs like me. I'm going to follow my father.' Utterly mystified, Rose put her head down on the table and closed her eyes.

Then Sam turned up, at the exact hour on which he was timetabled to do so. Somehow, she had not expected him. Vague unspoken buffers surrounded the thought of him in the staffroom; she had not seen him that day through the door into the welfare room, and her last sighting as he limped shoeless with his sister the evening before from the playground had had a valedictory quality.

He stood without speaking and she lifted her head. 'Why Sam!' she said. 'Hullo.' He was in such a state of raggedness and filth that her lethargy fell away like an invisible cloak. She smiled at him. He still wore no shoes. Alert to every nuance, she took his folder from the shelf behind her, and his Plasticine model of the bear and the boot. Then she put her hands on her lap, relaxing them consciously and waited with her eyes on his face. He sat down, by and by, and the principal smell that came off him was the one Rose knew as the smell from washing left damp and impacted too long.

'Would you like to do some reading?'

Sam said nothing but sat there, and Rose gained an impression that grew stronger as they sat, that he needed to rest. She said, 'Maybe you just need to have a rest.' Sam laid his head on his arms and his eyes slowly closed. Through the dank curls she could see a number of grazes on which the blood had clotted as well as some fearsome bumps and bruises. She wondered if he had been fighting or if, perhaps, he had been beaten up. At any rate, he made her feel sad; very differently from the frantic irritation evoked by Elaine's sleepiness. After a quarter of an hour he sat up. 'Little fella,' he said, giving the Plasticine bear a pat and drew his folder towards him. He took out his exercise book. 'I'm gonna write a story,' he said. Grasping a pencil in his fist and pressing hard he began to write, laboriously, with his head down on the table beside the exercise book. There was no sound in the fenced-off corner of the landing but for the scrape of the pencil and the wheeze of his breathing. He sat up, pushed away from the table and leaned his chair back on two legs. He kicked at the legs with his feet and, bootless, Rose found the muffled drumming sound to be unnervingly meek.

'Finished?' Sam nodded. 'Would you like to read it out to me?' He shook his head. 'Shall I read it?' He nodded. 'Aloud?' He nodded, so Rose read what he had written in scrawling irregular script:

Wuns upon a time the children and the dad went down the pub and the van krased and the mum was ded and she skreemd and skreemd and blood evrywere. The weels was brok and the engn. The boy and his sistr went to see the mum in hosptl and sum flors and she was happy and the dad said I have bort a new van. The end.

'Oh Sam,' said Rose when she had finished and then, 'Well done. That's a good piece of work. Would you like to do a picture?' Sam looked at her, 'Nah,' he said cheerfully. She offered him Plasticine and then said, 'What about tape-recording it?' Sam shook his head. 'You do it, Miss. I'll be the machine man.' Soon after they had finished recording, but before there was time to play it back, the bell went for break. Sam sighed and leaned back. He balanced his chair on two legs again and said, 'Time goes fast when you're havin' fun. See you, Miss,' and ran. Rose watched him skedaddle down the corridor. He dashed down the stairs and disappeared. She held her breath and prayed for him to go unremarked. She felt warmed and, in some way, blessed.

Sam made for the dustbins. He tore round the back as fast as he could, hoping to make them in the few seconds before teachers and children came pouring out of their classrooms. As he slithered the last few feet and squeezed himself into a space between the four great wheeled containers, he heard the familiar stampede and roar of children bursting into the playground. His head felt swimmy and his heart was thumping. There was only an hour or so of the day left to sit out before the Infants finished and he could creep out, seize Maggie by the hand and flee across the playground into the anonymous street. He was very hungry. He wriggled upright, jumped to grasp the rim of one of the bins and shinned up it. There among the fetid remnants, he seized a handful of apple peelings and slid down again. Everything hurt: the new scabs on his grazed knees had reopened and his sore feet throbbed. Blood mixed with pus trickled down his legs. He crouched down pushing apple skin and bits of core into his mouth and swallowing them almost whole. When his father came home the night before, he had opened a tin of soup. The children had eaten it with slices of bread while their parents drank cups of tea which Sam's mother held delicately, her little finger crooked. None of them spoke. Only Maggie said, 'The police lady was a bunny too,' as she licked the bowl clean.

Now, among the dustbins, Sam burped and presently fell into a half sleep to dream of giant rabbits and bears chasing him across the roof-tops. He missed his footing, slipped and woke with a start. Footsteps were approaching and he saw the blunt toecaps of the school caretaker's boots. He was singing softly in his deep voice: *John Brown's body lies a-mouldring in the grave, John Brown's body …'* Grunting and blowing, he emptied slops and rubbish on to the tops of the overfilled bins. 'Drat those cussed dustmen,' Sam heard him mutter as he trudged away. In the silence of the grey afternoon, he could not tell if the absence of activity in the playground meant school was still going on or that everyone had gone home. He flattened himself and crawled out. No one was about so he crept to the corner of the school buildings and peeped round. There on the far side of the playground in the shadow of the Infants entrance was a darker shadow, Maggie-shaped. He waved, looked round and sped across to her. They began the long trail home.

During the week of half-term, Sam went out on several jobs with his Dad. He handed him tools, fetched and carried lengths of pipe, valves and washers while Maggie sat in the van and made a burrow into the horsehair and springs on the back seat which she furnished with bits of grass and earth. One evening they all went down to the swimming baths where they spent a couple of hours jumping in and out of the warm chlorinated water and pretending they could swim. Sam's father rigged up an old pair of his own shoes with string so they would stay on Sam's feet. He asked no questions. Possessions came and, mostly, went and at the end of the week he found a perfectly good pair of boy's lace-up shoes in a plastic bag by the dustbin of one of the larger houses where he had been called in to unblock a drain. Towards the end of the week, their mother began getting out of bed and, twice, went down to the shops. She bought jam, a tin of rhubarb in syrup and a jumbo packet of Cornflakes as well as several bottles of scented body lotion which she rubbed on to her unwashed hands and up her arms. Maggie put a thick layer on to her own face where it dried and made her cheeks feel stiff.

On Monday when school started again they set off, running hand-in-hand. But after the motorway it became clear to Sam that he was not going to go back to school and he slowed down. When they got into the road where the school was he held back, chucking stones and kicking lampposts until he saw there were no more children going in through the gates. Then he ran, let go of Maggie at the entrance and gave her a push. 'Go on,' he said, and ran back the way they had come and round the corner the other way. There, he slowed down, picked up a stick and loitered, running the stick along gates and whacking hedges. He wondered how he would know when it was time to go back for Maggie and he kept the school more or less in sight most of the day.

Meanwhile, Mr Lovejoy had exhausted his contacts at head office. Each section manager, even those who had enjoyed his school's sherry two weeks before, referred him to another. To get Sam statemented, let alone accommodated would take months, possibly years. Only the Deputy Director of Education, a fellow railway enthusiast, had promised to lean on Child Guidance and get them to assess the case. 'We should be able to get an educational psychologist round before Christmas, old boy,' he had said, 'but keep it under your hat.' Mr Lovejoy resolved to take matters into his own hands. He would advise the parents, informally of course, that it was in their child's interest that he be excluded from school for a week or two pending further investigation and proper classification. He would send the letter by post. He leaned back in his chair and folded his hands over his stomach. 'Ah, Joyce,' he said when Mrs Upjohn next popped her head round the door, 'I think I will have a cup of tea just now, if you're making one.'

Mrs Upjohn noted his lightened demeanour and put it down to her own frequent ministrations. She brought the Headmaster his mug on a small tray with the milk and sugar separately. 'I thought you'd like to know, George,' she said with a sniff as she put it on the desk, 'that Sam Clark has failed to put in an appearance at school today.'

'Excellent,' said Mr Lovejoy before he could stop himself. The boy was falling in with his plans as if by prior arrangement.

'I know what you mean, Headmaster,' said Mrs Upjohn, taken aback. She had been looking forward to several censorious minutes of tutting and head-shaking.

'I might as well take you into my confidence, Joyce,' said Mr Lovejoy. 'I have decided to exclude the boy from school temporarily. Would you be so good as to ask Miss Bunting if she can spare me a moment or two?'

Miss Bunting had just led her class back from PE in the hall. They had swept past her at the door into the classroom with a suppressed roar and were milling about now at desk level.

'Settle down, 5b,' screamed Miss Bunting, the fine fair skin of her neck flushed deep red. 'Get out your maths books.' She had long since jettisoned the principles of liberal education imparted at College. As Mrs Upjohn stepped up to her, she reddened to the roots of her hair.

'The Headmaster would like a word with you, Miss Bunting,' said Mrs Upjohn.

'Now? Oh dear,' said Miss Bunting. 'We were just going to do maths. I ...'

Mrs Upjohn looked at the watch pinned to the lapel of her white overall and stepped in front of the dithering Miss Bunting. 'We mustn't keep the Headmaster waiting,' she said. She took the whistle from her pocket and blew a sharp blast. The class froze, took in her presence and deflated with a palpable hiss. 'James Potterton, stand in the corner,' Miss Bunting heard her say, and the ice in the voice sent a shiver through her spine as she hurried down the corridor.

At the Headmaster's door she smoothed down her hair and knocked.

'Ah, Miss Bunting. Have a seat,' said Mr Lovejoy. 'How are you getting on with Sam Clark these days?'

'I haven't seen him today, Headmaster,' said Miss Bunting. 'I've marked him absent on the register.'

Mr Lovejoy shook his head. 'Now, confidentially, Miss Bunting,' he said, 'how would you describe his conduct?'

'I find him – rather unco-operative,' said Miss Bunting and she paled internally as she thought of the many fruitless skirmishes with Sam.

'Hmmn,' said Mr Lovejoy. 'And educationally? How would you assess his progress?'

'I'm afraid I can't say he's made any progress at all this term, so far,' said Miss Bunting.

'Quite so,' said Mr Lovejoy. 'Well, Miss Bunting, I have decided to exclude him from school temporarily. I am in touch with the schools' psychological service and Social Services and they will look into the case at the first opportunity. Meanwhile I hope you agree with me that it's for the best. There are standards at Meadowbrook, Miss Bunting, and they must be maintained.'

Miss Bunting was not sure for a moment how to respond. What would he do all day, she wondered, thinking of Sam. His absence would certainly make her life easier, but was that the point? 'Yes, Headmaster,' she said, and waited for further instruction. 'Excellent,' said Mr Lovejoy, 'and how are you finding life at Meadowbrook, Miss Bunting? The first term can be quite trying for young teachers, but I'm sure you're doing splendidly.'

'Yes, thank you, Headmaster.' She looked down at her hands clasped on her lap and felt her ears grow warm.

'We're certainly very happy to have you with us. Thank you, Miss Bunting. That will be all.'

Mr Lovejoy nodded and drew some papers towards him. Miss Bunting closed the door softly behind her. As she walked back to her class she almost thought she caught the flash of a familiar ragged figure disappearing down the end of a corridor. She wondered briefly whether to pursue it and put the thought out of her mind. Imagination, she told herself sternly, you're overwrought, and resolved to buy herself a soothing bedtime drink on the way home.

18

Sam's days took on a terrible monotony. It was October now and the air had a definite bite in it. Sometimes it was wet and windy as well. He never went far from the school but circled it, more or less, approaching to look in from outside when there was activity in the playground. The other children saw him but never the staff. He had the odd exchange with Gary through the railings. Gary would say, 'You lucky bugger,' and Sam would put on a swagger and whistle through his teeth. When the playground emptied he sometimes crept inside to raid the dustbins or just sit there in the smelly crevasse between the four giant wheeled containers. The school caretaker thought it was a fox. Sam heard him grumbling and swearing as he gathered up spilled peelings and vowing to call in the rodent officer. On occasion, when it rained, he even went into the school itself to lurk in the corridors, slithering round corners when he heard footsteps and hiding in the boys' toilets where he found it quite easy to get in and out of the high, frosted window. In that first week he kept his appointments with Rose, appearing in an increasing state of dilapidation as soon as the previous child or group had gone and vanishing as his half hour ended. Rose, needless to say, was unaware he'd been excluded from school.

Most of the time he wandered round the immediate neighbourhood, kicking things and bashing hedges with a stick. He threw stones at lampposts and cats, made faces at himself in windows and shinned up trees. He grew increasingly bold and took to going into people's gardens to do this as the trees in the street were pollarded to well above climbing level, with only blunt bosses hideously sprouting twigs like hairy boils where branches should have been. He picked unripe apples which he threw away after one sour bite and once hit a baby in a pram. The baby woke with a start and began to bawl. Its mother hurried out, mop in hand, to rock the pram. She caught sight of Sam, chased him and got him on the shoulder with a swipe of her mop. He began nicking pints from the milk van.

A letter addressed to his parents came one day and lay on the mat inside the front door which no one ever used. His mother found it later in the week and threw it away along with the bills which were all the postman ever brought. She was getting dressed in the afternoons these days and even took a broom to the floor now and then. Strange wavery marks streaked the ground floor in some places. The dust, collected in little heaps, soon blew back over them but everyone felt better. One evening over a pot of tea she took some snaps from her bag and passed them round. The snaps of Sam as a baby and a very little boy were ones they had all seen before but they pored over them none the less. 'Go on, Mum. And then what did I do?' said Sam over and over again.

At his sessions with Rose he listened to the tape-recording they had made of his story about the crashed van over and over again as well. Though touchy, uncommunicative and defensive, he appeared to be entranced by it. He got Rose to move the furniture so that he was walled up in a tiny corner of her corner on the landing. He sat in it, directed her to turn on the light, and listened some more, switching the tape-recorder on and off himself. 'It's nice when you feel special, Miss,' he said and gave her one of his rare grins. There was an intensity about his behaviour that made Rose feel she was on a razor edge: one false move and they would be catapulted over a precipice from which there would be no coming back. She was aware time was passing and that in a few minutes she must warn him that it would soon be up, but she ceased to heed anything but the process before

130

her. And in this way she failed to protect Sam, for which she was to blame herself ever after.

As the hands of the clock near three-fifteen, the end of the school day, on the Friday of the first week after half-term, Mr Lovejoy strolls by. Things have been proceeding satisfactorily enough and he thinks he'll just give Mrs Pitt the benefit of his good-afternoon. He perceives from a few paces away that something is out of alignment but proceeds unperturbed. He slows down, his head and shoulders appear above the bookcases, he opens his mouth. 'Good afternoon, Mrs Pitt,' he's about to say when he takes in the scene on the other side. For a moment he stands open-mouthed, winded by its enormity. Confounded. The Clark boy, the scourge of his school, evacuated from the system on his orders, is on the premises and apparently enjoying the attention of a member of his staff. What's more, school furniture appears to have been rearranged in a most unsuitable way. A strange gurgling grunt, as of someone pushed under protest into a swimming pool, issues from his throat. Rose hears it and, startled, looks up to see looming above her the lowering countenance and raging eyes of the Headmaster. Her heart makes a dive for the soles of her feet. She pulls herself together and takes the initiative.

'Good afternoon, Mr Lovejoy,' she says quickly and stares at him before turning back to Sam. Sam's face, so lately warmed with frail interest has tautened into blank whiteness; his posture has hardened, poised for flight. She can feel him receding.

Mr Lovejoy breathes in and his voice comes out in a low roar. 'Sam Clark, how dare you set foot on school premises without my permission, and Mrs Pitt ...' He begins to splutter, 'Mrs Pitt, why has the school furniture been so dangerously interfered with?' The chair on which Sam's sitting, walled in by other child-sized chairs piled upon one another, is actually on top of a low table. Rose quivers, half in fury half in despair. All the regulations covering safety and responsibility can legitimately be invoked against her. She takes her eyes off Sam: 'Mr Lovejoy, I'm teaching. Perhaps we could discuss it later.'

'This boy,' thunders Mr Lovejoy, 'this boy has been excluded from school for a very good reason; excluded from school on my authority. He has no right to be on school premises at all, and you, Mrs Pitt, have no right to be teaching him.'

'Excluded from school? What does that mean, "excluded from school"?' She turns distressed towards Sam.

But Sam has gone. As the bell for the end of school begins to sound he's streaked, less tangible than the shadows, down the corridor – not for the stairs already seething with the first exodus of children – but to the boys' toilets. There, convulsively kicking, he levers himself through the window, slithers headfirst down the abrasive surface of the brick wall, braking himself against the soil pipe, and lands on the flinty earth beneath. He picks himself up, possessed with one thought, and hares towards the back entrance. He squeezes through the railings and runs, away from the school, in the opposite direction from home: runs and runs.

When he reaches the motorway leading west out of the city, he slows down and begins to walk, limping; a bedraggled wraith as the traffic in an unending stream thunders by.

Tight-lipped on the landing, Rose and Mr Lovejoy stare at one another in wordless confrontation. Then Rose pushes back her chair and runs for the stairs. She has to reach Sam. Mr Lovejoy draws himself up and strides after her. 'Mrs Pitt,' he calls in a voice that years of teaching have deepened to an instrument of rare projective capacity. The sea of children sweeping waist-high towards the doors part at its sound leaving Rose exposed nearly at the bottom. She feels herself caught in the beam. Mr Lovejoy speaks again in a lowered but resounding tone. 'Mrs Pitt, I wonder if you would mind delaying your departure for a moment or two. I'd like to have a word with you in my office.' He turns, an imposing figure on his own patch, and strolls in the direction of his room pausing to pat the heads of a favoured pupil or two in his path. Rose cranes for a glimpse of Sam and then runs back up the stairs. She follows Mr Lovejoy to his office and stands inside the door. She's out of breath.

'We've got to get Sam. You caught him at a very vulnerable moment – I can explain later. He might do anything now. We've got to find him and look after him.'

Mr Lovejoy, bent over his desk, does not reply. He looks up and says with an abstracted air, 'Ah, Mrs Pitt – I wonder if you would wait outside. I have some important matters of administration to see to just now. And Mrs Pitt, it is customary for staff at Meadowbrook to knock and wait for an answer before entering the Headmaster's office.'

'But Mr Lovejoy ...' begins Rose, and leaves. She hurries to one of the windows looking out on the playground and scours it with her eyes. The crowd is thinning and she knows that Sam, long practised at making himself scarce, is unlikely to be in it. She sees Nat in a tracksuit come out of his prefab. He has a football under his arm and a cluster of small boys round him. She signals wildly. He looks up and waves. She makes desperate gestures. He makes a drinking motion with one hand and holds up four fingers before walking off, surrounded by jumping boys on course for the park. Rose leans against the window with her back to it. She rocks backwards and forwards hugging herself. Sam might be miles away by now; he certainly is miles away so far as reclaiming him for education goes, out of touch; beyond reach. The word 'excluded' comes to mind. Down the corridor she spies Mrs Jenkins, raincoated, come out of her classroom and lock it behind her. 'Mrs Jenkins, Mrs Jenkins!' she calls, hurrying to her.

'All set for the weekend, Mrs Pitt?' says Mrs Jenkins, as Rose catches up with her.

'Mrs Jenkins, please, can you tell me. What does 'excluded from school' mean?' She walks alongside.

'It means that the Headmaster can ask a child's parents to keep him at home for a few days, a week or two at most, if he's making a real nuisance of himself,' says Mrs Jenkins. 'On an informal basis of course. It's not like expulsion. You need an order from head office for that. Now, put it all behind you, dear, and enjoy the weekend. You look tired.' She nods kindly and goes on her way. Rose stands alone and wondering: so Sam has been coming into school just for his sessions with her! She begins to feel indignant as well as deeply touched.

At this moment one of the school cleaners, a big black woman in a hat and overall, comes towards her. She seems agitated. 'I can't get on with my work,' she says, 'they've left it dreadful over there on the landing. We're not meant to clear up after the teachers.'

'Oh dear,' says Rose. 'I'm afraid that's my fault. I'll put it away. I'm so sorry.'

'There won't be no time,' says the cleaner, 'I've got my work to get through. You teachers never consider us cleaners. You'd be surprised the things we have to clear up. And where would you be without us?'

'I'll do it straightaway,' says Rose.

Mr Lovejoy puts his head round the door. 'Mrs Pitt?' His voice sounds pained. 'I've been expecting you for some minutes now. Could you come in rightaway and postpone gossiping with the cleaners until some other time?'

Rose looks helplessly from one to the other, hating both. The cleaner stands hands on hips glaring and grumbling under her breath. Mr Lovejoy, just within his door, glares too but with an expression of stony exasperation on his face. Like Sam, Rose wants to run. Instead, she smiles resignedly at the cleaner and follows Mr Lovejoy into his room. He does not ask her to sit but addresses her from behind his desk with a litany of regulations, procedural obligations and hierarchical expectations, delivered in a numbing boom. Shifting from foot to foot, her thoughts stray. She summons them and interrupts. 'Headmaster. That boy is in urgent need. Lots of the children I teach are in urgent need. I'd like to consult you about them. I'd like to consult you about Sam. He's clearly got awful problems. I'm not quite sure why yet. But he's just starting to let them out. You interrupted us at a crucial moment. He may do anything

134

now. I'm really worried for his safety. I ...'

'Mrs Pitt,' says Mr Lovejoy, and she sees his face is working in a most unusual manner. He stands up. 'Mrs Pitt, are you suggesting that I have no right of access in my own school? I find that unacceptable. You are a junior member of the staff here at Meadowbrook. The boy Sam Clark is not to come to you any more for tuition under any circumstances. I act in the child's best interests which are for me to judge. That will be all.' He nods and waits for her to go.

But Rose, valiant for truth in her father's words, hangs on to her end of the bone. 'Mr Lovejoy, you can't do that,' she says and lifts her chin. 'Sam's beginning to trust me. If that trust's broken he'll get pushed even further out. He can't be let down. It would be disastrous for him.'

'*That will be all,*' says Mr Lovejoy. He comes out from behind his desk and holds the door open.

'But Mr Lovejoy, we must help him. It's our duty.' Rose is ramrod-straight by now.

'That will be all, Mrs Pitt,' says Mr Lovejoy, and his eyes are directed to the middle distance. 'There are other school matters which need my attention. Good afternoon.'

At a loss, Rose takes a step towards the door. Nothing seems to be working as it ought. Mr Lovejoy moves behind her, edging her out. His large form blocks re-entry and his attention is ostentatiously elsewhere. Rose walks slowly out and the door closes behind her so promptly and so forcefully that it grazes her skirts. She wants to batter it down. She wants to set fire to the school. She thinks of running out to the staff parking place and letting down the tyres of his car. She gives the nearest bookcase a kick and visualises herself smashing glass fronts and hurling books all down the corridor. She goes back to her corner and begins deconstructing Sam's 'special' place. Chairs have to be placed upside down on tables so the cleaners can get underneath. She tidies up and packs her school bag, putting Sam's exercise book and her tape-recorder in it. Then she leaves by the back stairs and gets into her car, remembering as she does so Nathan Woolf's gesture seen through the window. It's after four. She drives to the pub to meet him.

In the Black Prince, Nat said, 'Have a brandy. I'll go and get it. You sit down.' He folded his copy of the *Guardian*. Watching his back, thickset, solid and covered in royal blue cotton jersey, Rose felt her eyes go blurry. Now she had a chance to let go, it was herself she felt sorry for. She swallowed hard.

'Oh, Nat,' she said, turning a tragic face up to him as he returned.

'Drink up,' he said, and sat down beside her. Male warmth and a sweaty smell came through his tracksuit. Rose, who would normally have cringed from the colour alone, found the combination curiously reassuring. She drank the brandy, coughed and felt it hit the massed-up emotion inside to send wires of heat worming through. Nat watched her: she reminded him of a cornered deer, eyes big with fright, quivering and soft. 'Tell me,' he said, 'if you'd like.' He looked into her face and did not smile.

So Rose talked and Nat listened and when she had finished, he groaned. 'You miss so much, working in breaks.'

'Why, did you know Sam had been excluded, or whatever it is?'

'Of course.'

'How?'

'I heard Miss Bunting telling Mrs Jenkins. We all picked it up, one way or another.'

'But what difference would it have made to me? I couldn't not have given him his sessions if he came in specially for them. It makes it even worse. I *couldn't* not have.'

Nat groaned again. 'I don't suppose you know about all the things he did that led up to it either.'

Rose shook her head and Nat told her about Sam's attack on Mrs Upjohn, his disappearance from the welfare room and the cigarette ends on the floor; about the havoc in Mr Lovejoy's room, the stolen cheese straws and the broached bottle of sherry; about the unanswered notes and letters sent to his parents. 'As a matter of fact, now I tell you, it all sounds pretty minor stuff,' he said, 'but that's not how it's seen in school. I can assure you. It's become a major crime and Sam, a sort of gangster – practically Al Capone.'

Rose stared at him. 'How terrifying,' she said. 'How terrifyingly easy to demonise someone. And he's only a child. What can you expect if you shut a small boy up in a room with nothing to do day after day? He was obviously famished. He always looks half-starved anyway. He seems to me to have shown great initiative and resource. It's the sort of thing that would get him an extra pip in the army. He could be a brilliant gymnast. He ...'

'Rose!' said Nat, 'Calm down. The point is, what can we do about it now? And you simply must learn not to get on the wrong side of Mr Lovejoy.'

'I can't. I won't,' said Rose, much heartened by the 'we'. 'Mr Lovejoy's a monstrous bully. He's not fit to be within ten miles of a school. I'll expose him. I'll fight him. It's the children that count.'

As she spoke, Nat glanced anxiously round him. 'Ssh,' he said and then, curtly, 'You'll lose.'

Rose sat straight and leaned towards him. Her cheeks were pink, her eyes were bright, pretty tendrils of hair, escaped from their French knot, waved round her face, the skirt of her yellow wool suit had ridden quite far up above her black stockinged knees and her white shirt pulled slightly on the pearl button at breast level. It's the brandy, thought Nat hopefully. He wondered if he could ask her to come for a pizza.

'What about Sam *now*?' said Rose.

Nat shook his head slowly. 'We can't go to his home. That would be quite outside our brief as teachers.'

'I agree,' said Rose, 'it would be outside my role as I define it, too.'

'If you've got your car, we could drive around and see if we can see him.'

'Good idea,' said Rose, seeing Sam's figure, in her mind's eye, trailing forlornly on the bleak pavement.

In Rose's old Morris Minor they drove round and round the streets of the vicinity, stopping to peer down alleyways and over high hedges. Nat got out to inspect the park. Twice they passed Sam by, skulking from shadow to shadow as he got nearer the school to fetch his little sister home. When it got too dark to see any more, Nat said, 'How about a pizza. There's a Spaghetti House down the High Street.'

In the Spaghetti House they drank a bottle of wine rather fast and Rose found that Nat made her laugh surprisingly often while Nat found himself being so funny he felt like three Marx Brothers at once. He went down the stairs to the Tube walking like Groucho but the ticket collector did not laugh.

Rose drove home troubled. Nothing in her repertory fitted the present situation with Sam. She could not think of a way through it and she badly wanted to continue her work with him. Her bed, so often sensuous container of passionate embrace, felt rucked and inhospitable beneath her skin. Her body yearned for Frank in an arid yawning way and she fell into fitful sleep only as the sun rose palely behind the chimneys and the mail vans sped snorting from the sorting offices.

19

A shivering fit seizes Sam as he nears the school. Fingers of cold walk down his spine and his legs shake. A zone of repulsion that he finds difficult to breach surrounds the area but breach it he must – for Maggie. He circles, flitting between the shadowy parts of the street. On the bypass, he had been apprehended by a police car whose occupants had questioned him and transported him off the motorway. The car returns from time to time, picking him up in its headlights, to check his progress back to the domestic streets.

He finds it easier, eventually, to draw in on the school somewhere round the back. He scales a wall, drops down and crouches in its unlit lea. Every inch, though deserted at this hour, feels electrified with peril to his raw senses. He worms through the laurel bushes in the narrow space to one side of the school and reaches the corner where the playground begins. The Infants' entrance is away across the bald brick face of the building. He makes it in a series of dashes from one bluff or indentation to another.

'Mags,' he whispers, 'Mags. Come on.' She's curled up, a darker shadow, scarcely opaque, on the dark ground to which she has subsided during the shapeless hours of waiting. She puts her hand – it's very cold – in his and they run, keeping to the edges of the playground. At every rustle and creak in the night, Sam flattens them to the wall. They steal through the gates and run again. Not until they've crossed the main road, which is the first part of the motorway along which Sam has limped earlier, does the grip of terror on the back of his neck slacken and he slows them down to a walk.

At the end of their street, their father, come to look for them in the van, sees them. 'Hop in kids,' he says, opening the door, and they drive the last few yards back to the house.

There's nothing much to say. He warms up baked beans. They eat ravenously in the accepting silence that is home. Their mother's in bed.

'How's school?' says their father, once.

'All right,' says Sam.

Maggie says nothing. Tomato sauce has got in the ends of her hair and all round her mouth. Sam's head droops on to the table and he falls asleep. His father carries him up the stairs and lays him on his bed. Maggie, in vest and knickers, climbs on to hers and worms a way in through the covers. Her father bending over feels her arms creep round his neck. He hugs her. 'Night-night, Maggie girl,' he says and, leaving the door ajar, goes to his own bed where he slips quietly between the sour sheets alongside the body of his wife, who is snoring mindlessly in Valium-induced slumber.

On Monday, Sam was expected back at school. According to Mr Lovejoy's calculations, the exclusion order was up and he needed to confront the boy face to face before issuing the family with another. Mrs Upjohn kept the front entrance under surveillance. When the boy failed to turn up, she sniffed round the corridor and toilets, poked her head over the bookcases in Rose's corner, checked with Miss Bunting in 5b and hurried to the Headmaster's office.

'Be so good as to notify the Education Welfare Officer if you would, Joyce,' said Mr Lovejoy.

'Certainly, Headmaster,' said Mrs Upjohn.

Outside in the windswept streets, Sam kicked about in the leaves. An unattended bicycle leaned by a gate. He mounted and rode around for a while enjoying occasional flying moments but it was much too big to manage comfortably and he dropped it in a gutter and wandered on. He went into an empty church and looked at the pictures. They were spooky and the silence frightened him, but the candles smelled nice. He took one and ran out making for the shops where there were people. The candle was too long to go in his pocket, so he broke it.

Round the shops he watched the women go in and out. He found it quite easy to nick apples and plums. He grew more daring and took a packet of biscuits off a supermarket trolley while the woman was paying. He stuffed it up his shirt and scooted; plums and apples bulging, biscuits bobbing and scratching, down the alleyways and back streets, under the wire fencing secured by concrete posts, to the bit of wasteland by the canal just before it went under the tunnel. He slithered down the bank and lay there, sprawled and panting. Then he looked around him and began gathering stones and debris. He hauled some quite large slabs of rusted metal and a bicycle wheel from the water, arranged them in a rough circle, got inside and placed the apples, the plums, the packet of biscuits and one half of the candle round about him on stones. It took some time and when he had positioned them to his satisfaction he crouched in the centre and surveyed his camp.

It had begun to drizzle. He would have liked to light the candle. He gave a big sigh and opened the biscuits. He took a bite of apple, a bite of plum and munched on them all at once, whacking the stones now and then with a stick he had found. Before long he put his hand on his stomach and belched. He felt quite full. He put a biscuit in his pocket for Maggie and scrabbled in the scrubby grass-pocked earth to bury the rest. He threw stones into the canal, jumped in and out of his enclosure and decided to make a gateway. It looked great. 'Sam's Place', he christened it in his mind. Later, in the afternoon, he went back up the shops and stole an umbrella which he did quite simply by unhooking it from a pram handle. It was perfect. The more it rained, the more perfect it was.

Thus his second week at large in the community passed. He took comics, matches, crisps, buns and cans of Tango and 7-Up. The empty tins made shiny patches in the stone and junk walls of his 'place'. Maggie got used to waiting until after dark to be fetched. She began to look forward to the sweets and hair slides he handed her. Once he brought her down to show her. 'You're not to tell no one. Not ever,' he told her and Maggie shook her head and shivered.

On Friday, the Education Welfare Officer called on their house. She pressed the bell, knocked on the knocker, walked round the house, banged on the back door, pushed her card through the letter-box and wrote 'Failed to gain access' on her report. Inside, Sam's mother heard the sounds and put a pillow over her head. She did not stir until her husband came up with a cup of tea after seven.

'Come down, Sammy, love,' he said, and she did, stumbling in high-heeled shoes under her trailing nightie.

Sam, hurtling round the kitchen, full of beans, felt a surge of power. An idea had been born in his head: he would get them a telly. He started leaping against the walls and pushing himself off with one leg. His parents sat at the kitchen table; Maggie, under her mother's skirts on the floor, and Sam went round and round. The rain seeped through the wall in places and wind whistled in through the cracks under the doors for it was a wild night and in Sam's Place down by the canal many of the stones got dislodged or washed away. He was dismayed when he went back after the weekend and set about building it up again.

In her corner on the landing, Rose kept his sessions free. She had not been able to work out what to do if he turned up for one. Mr Lovejoy asked for a copy of her timetable. 'But you've got one,' said Rose. Mr Lovejoy frowned and stared at her. She copied out another and he returned it with 'swimming' written across the spaces which had Sam Clark in them. She knocked on the door of his office and protested. 'I've got to be there for Sam if he turns up. Even if I bring him straight to you, I've got to be there for him.'

'That is for me to judge, Mrs Pitt,' said Mr Lovejoy, barely glancing up from his desk. 'One or two of the larger classes could do with assistance on swimming days. Kindly report to the appropriate teachers.'

'But I'll be late for the children,' said Rose, and added, 'You wouldn't want me to be late for class, Headmaster?'

'There is nothing more to discuss,' said Mr Lovejoy.

She sought out Nat in his classroom. 'You'd better do it, Rosie,' he said. 'Show willing. I doubt we'll see the little blighter again. Now come along to the staffroom and pretend you watched *Neighbours* last night.' He laid an arm briefly across her shoulders and gave one of them a squeeze.

Outside the window Gary, peering in, sneaked away. 'Mr Woolf loves Mrs Pitt,' he shouted, elbowing his way into an illicit football game. 'I seen 'em snoggin' in his classroom.'

At the end of the week there was a staff meeting. Rose had already been to the swimming baths twice. She was relieved to find she was not required to swim herself but only to patrol the pool's edge and harry the children in the changing room. Damp little girls smelling of chlorine hung on to her arms and stood jigging before her as she fastened their pony tails. Little boys belaboured each other with wet trunks and she had to shout at them. Natural exuberance had to be muted down at all stages but she tried not to be subversive.

Now, as the teachers settled in their chairs round the room, waiting for Mr Lovejoy, she geared herself to speak out. She tried to do it the right way and caught Mr Foster as he scurried towards the staffroom. 'Is there an agenda, Mr Foster, because there's something I'd like to bring up?'

Mr Foster paused and stared at her. He looked uncomprehending, astonished even. Rose repeated the question. 'Tzt, tzt,' said Mr Foster. He rustled the papers on his clipboard and hurried on.

The staff meeting began. A veteran by now, Rose had secured a seat well in time and sat there with her mug like everyone else. It took its customary course; the Headmaster, an exhortatory pastor with fire and brimstone up his sleeve led an obedient congregation in a series of murmured responses. How like Ian Paisley he looks, thought Rose. The same old topics came up. At every conjunction Rose took a deep breath, leaned forward, heart thumping, and opened her mouth. Time passed. She grew more and more agitated. Mr Lovejoy rubbed his large white palms together, fingers curved like uncooked sausages. 'I think we've covered everything,' he said, raising his chin with his eyelids lowered before doubling it back into his collar. Rose took a deeper breath. Her heart was knocking in her throat. 'There's something I'd like to bring up, Headmaster,' she said. Her voice came out a squeak which frightened her even more. Silence fell on the room; leaden silence not of expectation but of witting uninterest. No one looked at her. In the absence of any sign she forced herself to go on. 'I'd like to bring up the question of Sam Clark,' she said, ever further from shore. 'I'd like to know what the situation is exactly, first, and second, I don't think he should be cut off from his sessions with me. I've established a certain kind of link with him. It's very tenuous, but it exists. I feel a great deal of responsibility towards him. It would be very damaging for him if I were suddenly to be not there for him.' She looked round. Not an eye met hers. Blood sang in her ears. Pins dropped.

'Mrs Pitt,' boomed Mr Lovejoy. He fixed her with a burning glare. 'You are aware of my decision on the subject, made in the boy's best interests. There is no more to be said.' He gathered his papers and made to rise.

Rose felt very cold.

'I don't agree with you, Mr Lovejoy. I work with Sam. I know it would be bad for him if his sessions with me were to be suddenly discontinued with no preparation at all.'

Mr Lovejoy stood. His face was red and his ears stood out from his head. He banged on the table. 'This is my school. I will have obedience. What I say goes,' he shouted and strode from the room. Mr

Foster and Mrs Upjohn got up and followed. Around the room, the other teachers turned to one another and began to converse in low voices. Thus engaged, they gathered their belongings and, as the bell rang, left the room. The last to leave, Nathan Woolf gave her a quick smile and she was alone.

Ostracised and disempowered, she stood up. The very walls seemed to be watching her with disapproval. Outside, she noted, the sky was glassy blue with tattered wisps of cloud scudding across; one of those bright-faced autumn interludes between bouts of rain. She wished she could burst out from the hateful constrictions confining her, but she picked up her books and hurried to her next lesson. On the way she passed Mrs Upjohn who brushed by without acknowledgement.

A terrible racket was coming from her corner. James Potterton charged out and seized her hand. 'Come on, Mith,' he lisped winsomely, 'where've you been? I've done a picture of you. It's a present – or maybe I'll give it to my mother. Come and see.' He put down his head, a chunky engine, and dragged her faster. 'She's here,' he shouted as they rounded the corner. There was much scuffling and Rose beheld the group, all five, at their places round the table drawing in their exercise books.

'It's a surprise, Miss. D'you like it?' shouted Gary. He jumped up and stood on his chair.

'Sit down, Gary, you'll spoil it,' said Wendy. They turned beaming faces to her and even Selma delivered a vapid lopsided leer.

Rose was enchanted. She smiled and smiled. 'Look at mine first,' shouted Simon, now back at school with a black patch over one eye. He could not wait to get to her but hurled his book across the table. Uproar prevailed and soon deteriorated to a savage struggle for primacy. She sat down with her hands over her ears and watched. When the children, expecting intervention, began to look at her she said, 'The first person sitting down in silence gets their work looked at first. Anyone who speaks or stands up after that goes to the bottom of the queue,' and turned quickly to Selma who had not moved.

Ten minutes later, Mr Lovejoy patrolling by, still seething inwardly, marked nothing but bent heads and the scratch of pencils. Rose heard his tread but did not look up. As it passed by, she experienced a few warming pinpricks of triumph. She felt very close to her pupils and Gary lifted his head to give her a wink of hideous complicity.

'My dear,' murmured Mrs Jenkins, passing Rose in the corridor later, 'I do so agree with you. Poor little soul ...'

Down by the canal, Sam squats on the bank fishing. He has rigged himself up with a stick and a piece of string. A bit of bun's tied to the end. He sits in the brief sunshine waiting for a bite. He's given up hanging round the school. His days are full of activity conducted at his own pace. The canal is a constant source of treasure. He hauled an old pair of wheels from it that very morning. They might be just what's needed for transporting the telly when he finds the right one. He's become quite bold at nicking; at going right up to the counter for a Wimpey and running off without paying. It's better at lunchtime when the place is crowded and much more exciting than school; it makes sense too in a way school never did. The shopkeepers in the High Street are beginning to look out for him. One or two of the softer-hearted give him blemished fruits and stale rolls; mostly they come out from behind their counters and chase him off. The supermarket has him on video. He starts roaming farther afield.

The Education Welfare Officer steps up her visits to his home. On one of them she catches sight of his mother taking a few wobbly steps towards the dustbin. She darts up the side calling, 'Mrs Clark!'

Mrs Clark looks up in fright, a worrying sight with her wild hair, bagged nightdress, shapeless cardigan and high-heeled shoes. The Education Welfare Officer gets to her just as the door closes and succeeds in thrusting a letter into her hand. Mrs Clark, her heart palpitating horribly, sits down at the kitchen table. She stares at the envelope in her hand. Intrusions mean trouble and the family keeps them at bay. She opens it slowly and the words surrounded by dots and haloes, mill in front of her eyes. She tries to catch a few of them before they slide into the blur and makes out something of the drift. There's a meeting about Sam: they have to go to it. She makes for the stairs and totters up them. In bed, she gropes for obliteration, pushes a handful of pills into her mouth and lets the swirling mist take her. Sam finds her there when he gets back with Maggie, not dead but in a familiar state of drug-induced oblivion. He puts the lipstick he's stolen for her on the bed where she'll see it when she opens her eyes, and goes to sit against the wall facing the bed. By and by, Maggie climbs the stairs to join him and they sit side by side in the half dark where they most want to be at that time.

20

Frank had had a narrow squeak. Driving back from his night with Rose the week before he had found himself, divided only by two squares of toughened glass, shoulder to shoulder with Ted Ainsworth at the lights. They were at the gates into Hyde Park. Ted Ainsworth, chauffeur-driven, sat upright in the back with his dog. It was seven in the morning and he was already dressed for the office but with a tweed cap on his head. Frank, tieless and in his dinner jacket with the collar turned up, was as yet unshaven and carolling merrily: *'You're the sail in my love boat / You're my captain and crew / You will always be my necessity / I'd be lost without you-hoo-ooo ...'*

Frank saw first and tried to duck but Ted Ainsworth caught his eye and gave a stiff nod. There was no evading him. That Monday he had stayed on in Yorkshire for a works' tour of Ainsworth Agridustrials. Ted had shown him some marvellous old machines in tiptop condition. He leaned across and rolled down the window. 'Lovely morning,' he called. 'Just been walking by the river. Best time of day.' Ted Ainsworth nodded again and his car slid on. Disreputable rapscallion, he thought. The acid rose in his oesophagus. He took a Xantoxin from the pill box in his breast pocket and let it dissolve on his tongue. He would make the twister pay a high price for co-operation in his project. The black Labrador, Betsy, put her muzzle on his knee and looked up at him with brown eyes. A peerage at least, he thought, with sour satisfaction and put a hand on her sleek head.

Frank too felt his stomach give a nasty blip. How could he have been so careless? There were many more roundabout ways to get back to Regent's Park. But why should he *have* to bother in his pure joy? It was not fair to be saddled with such pressures and precautions. Then his stomach gave another blip as he thought of the consequences if he were not; of the wreckage and recriminations he would have to face. He was sailing much too close to the vortex. He would have to pull out, and soon. Maybe he and Tamarisk should take a trip abroad; new pastures might revive some of that first flush of feeling for her. He could surely fix some semi-official mission for them to go on.

But the unspoken words 'flush' and 'feeling' were too much for his resolution. He got no further than halfway before the craving of his body for Rose's overwhelmed him. The light of his life – he could not give her up. He parked his car and sauntered into a newsagent's, sauntered out again and into a telephone box. Hunched against the fixture he dialled her number. 'Just checking in,' he said, delighted at the surprise and gratitude in her voice. 'You see, I can't live without you even for an hour.' But he opened his mail soberly after he had bathed and shaved back at his house.

The sun danced on the polished surface of the Hepplewhite table, a little-used piece from Tamarisk's family home; the fumes from his coffee, scalding hot in the fine Leeds cup, black and white in his hand, expanded his nostrils; the old silk curtains looped at the windows; the Aubusson rug on the Norfolk rush matting, all objects assembled over the years by the two of them, enclosed him in undemanding perfection and the shell-pink sow in the George Morland, one of his most prized possessions, drowsed in her sty, one eye open, over the fireplace.

His breakfast finished and his letters read, he telephoned his wife in Yorkshire. 'Darling,' he said, 'how's your poor back? I'm going to take you away. As soon as you're strong enough, we sail for sunnier climes. So do your exercises and get better soon. *Darling.*' He was the victim of addiction, he told himself as he closed his front door behind him, and addictions were subject to the exercise of willpower.

Would the clean break be the best method for him? It held a certain drama, an asceticism that appealed to him.

Damp leaves, yellowy-brown, lay all over the garden path. He inhaled their scent indescribably redolent of autumn, of childhood tumbles in mushroomy-smelling drifts, of bonfires and berries. There was so much sensual pleasure to be gleaned from the everyday world roundabout. Mellow nostalgia engulfed him and the phrase 'close-bosom' floated up in his mind. It brought him back to Rose. Before he could check himself, his head was between her breasts, his mouth over her nipples and the familiar wires were trilling in his blood. He shook himself like a wet dog and drew sternly upright. Graduated detoxification, a period of decompression might be easier to manage and probably more absolute in the long run. Besides, it fitted in with his principles about organic growth and change. He would set himself goals of deprivation, both in thought and reality, for each day and the days would become weeks, the weeks months: a year would pass and he would be cured. He would need to build in compensations, alternative treats for his senses; a bout of opera-going, weekend expeditions across the Channel to Normandy; some expensive claret. It would cost money. He would spend it.

Ah, '*Goldengrove unleaving*', he thought and tried to replace Rose's presence at his side with his wife's girlish form. He could not quite get her hand into his, but he managed to take her arm, just. Work was the answer. His museum, an engrossing objective, would be off the ground and on the drawing board, an officially sanctioned project, this day twelve months. All his activities would be directed towards its realisation; and its forms, its vaulted roof and rounded girders, its slender iron columns and rehabilitated turnstiles; its complement of ancient agricultural tools, hoes, threshers, winnowers and ploughs, shapes of truth and beauty in which form and function were perfectly balanced, would absorb his mental life, his waking days and his dreams.

It was all perfectly feasible. He went through the components in his mind, assets first. He ticked them off: old Constance Goodall, the Secretary of State for Education herself. He had her in the palm of his hand, but she might not last long. He had to get a move on there. Max Vane, rising fast in the establishment but still at the stage where he would welcome further appointments, and ever-obliging by nature. He had already mentioned lending one, maybe two, industrial scientists from his department. An industrial historian would be more to the point. He must get the posts established and funded forthwith. The Duke of Middlesbrough: pots of money there and a storehouse, no doubt, of potential exhibits among his many estates. He had nothing whatever to do. He could be co-opted and given a job, unpaid, paternalistic; honorary chairman or director-in-chief would fit the bill. Then there were the de la Vignes. A touch of Europe would give the project no end of extra clout. And Ted Ainsworth – a problem. But Tamarisk would come in handy. No question he fancied her in his pinched way, and another reason for reinstalling her to a more central position in his life. Moreover, Ainsworth craved acceptance. He could be bought with honours. He must drop a few hints, less tentatively, vigorously indeed. A committee was what was wanted, a face and a name. He would take the first steps in forming a provisional committee that day. It could meet in the newly renovated offices above St Pancras Station overlooking the site of his dreams. A newspaper diarist's paragraph on its own!

Walking past the shops now on his way to the Underground, his stride lengthened to a springing lope. He swung his briefcase, an honourable object scarred and battered, that had once belonged to his wife's father when he was ambassador in Paris. Going down the escalator he avoided the posters gliding by to the right and left. Hitherto, he would have allowed his eye to dwell on the girlier ones. His eyes were firmly on the future, ahead. How much of his creative power had been locked up in Rose these past few years!

Rose, of course, knew nothing of this conversion. Sustained by his last words hoarsely whispered over the telephone she coasted on them through the trying week at school, consoled and reassured. As the hours became days and the days nearly a week they became less and less substantial. She turned them over and over, examining them and re-examining them; the timing, the tone, the inflexion. By the eve of the weekend she felt intolerably edgy. Round and round went the needle of her recall, stuck in its groove. There was nowhere else for it to go.

'Doing anything Saturday night?' asked Nathan Woolf. He had waited for her at the bottom of the stairs. She stared at him miserably. 'Cheer up. It's not the end of the world,' he said. 'We'll sort it out.'

'It's not only school. There are other things,' she muttered, and thought, hating herself, 'other things!' what a traduction. But what words could carry the vastness of the love she and Frank had for each other across into the outside world? None existed. It was unique. She must cherish it within. 'Trust me,' said Frank on so many occasions. He must be suffering too.

'No good brooding,' said Nat. 'What are you doing on Saturday night?'

'I don't know,' said Rose. She wished he would leave her alone.

'Well, come to a bash with me,' he said. 'That friend I told you about, the one in special education, it's his birthday. He's asked some friends round. It's a nice crowd. You might enjoy it. Take you out of yourself.'

I don't want to be taken out of myself, thought Rose furiously. He was so clumsy. She looked up at him glowering but found he was smiling at her with such a kindly expression that she was obliged to smile back. The smile reached her eyes in spite of herself and a flake of her customary gaiety surfaced. 'All right,' she said.

He took the bulging school bag from her hand – 'God, what a weight!' – and walked with her to her car.

'Shall I come and pick you up?' he said as he handed her in.

'No, of course not,' said Rose.

'I'd like to,' he said. 'I'll just ring the bell and you can come down when you're ready.' He waited for her to say yes.

What a quaint way to behave, thought Rose, he'll have to cross half London and he hasn't even got a car. She felt a little uncomfortable. 'Okay,' she said, 'where is it?' Maybe he wanted a lift.

'Near me, up in Wood Green,' said Nat.

'Wood Green! Where's that?' said Rose.

'Not so far.' His smile broadened. He looked solid, trustworthy and male; at ease with himself in his own skin. Rose reddened. She looked away and settled herself behind the wheel. Nat stopped smiling. He touched her shoulder. 'Take care,' he said, and gravely closed the door.

Rose shut her mind on him and drove home, but she found the words 'take care' sometimes muddling themselves in with 'can't live without you even for an hour'.

There was a letter from Frank lying on the mat when she got home. She carried it upstairs unopened and deposited her coat and her belongings before settling on the windowsill to open it. One thin sheet was covered with his wavery handwriting and the first two lines said, 'Darling, darling, darling, darling ...' Her heart lurched at each one. He missed her, he loved her, a golden thread connected them, his week had been too ghastly buried in inescapable obligations. He touched on some of them. 'Love you, love you ...' went the last few lines followed by a slanting block of Os and Xs. She laid her cheek against it, read it and reread it, put it under her pillow and went to write a letter back to him. It took her three hours and included a poem. She put it in a double envelope, addressed it to the box number to which she was allowed to send urgent communications and went out to post it. The letter would not reach him until Monday, but the partial discharge of feeling, its conversion into phrases of intimacy and innuendo took the edge off her torment. It was a beautiful letter. She made herself a nutritious pap of leaves, seeds and nuts tamped down with yoghurt and went to bed not uncontent. She almost forgot the thin sheet of paper under her pillow.

On Saturday, she dressed reluctantly for her excursion with Nat Woolf, not quite sure where to pitch her outfit. In the end she wore a light blue cotton jersey dress with a white collar like a rugby shirt slit quite far up the sides, and little lace-up boots. She walked down the stairs when the bell rang, wanting to make him wait. Frank's letter which she had fingered in her pocket all day, lay behind on the pillow with a geranium flower beside it.

Nat stood on the pavement outside. 'Hullo there,' he said rather too quickly when she opened the door. In the light from the hall, his new-shaven face was ruddy and he looked, to Rose's eye, perfectly ghastly in a fiercely blue checked jacket with right angled shoulders. He smiled. She had never realised quite how big his teeth were.

'Hullo,' she said in a weak voice. Above his head, the sky, fretted along either side with the dark outlines of roofs, spires and trees, was the deep blue of delphiniums. She kept her eyes on it as they walked to her car.

'Had a nice rest?' said Nat as he sat in the seat beside her. He held a bottle wrapped in paper on his lap.

'Rest?' said Rose, 'how d'you mean, *rest*?' She glared straight ahead, so irritated that she failed to stop at a red light.

Nat said nothing. She smelled delicious and he was touched by her petulance. He gave her time, then said, 'I had a game of football this afternoon. Do you play any sport?'

Sport! thought Rose, and said, inaccurately, 'I played squash, if that's what you mean. I only just got back in time.' She felt better when she had said it and a little remorseful. She turned to him and smiled. He smiled back and said just what she wanted, 'Wow, that's a tough game. You've probably had more exercise than me. I bet you're good at it and you must look wonderful darting round the court.' He could see her, all leg in short shorts, the line of her breasts wobbling as she reached for the ball.

'I'm not really much good,' said Rose, 'but I love playing.' The colour of his jacket hardly noticed in the dark.

'Left here,' said Nat. They drove along streets that unwound mile after mile, finally through a desert of small houses and drew up before one of them. Light and a generalised blare beat out of the downstairs windows. None of Rose's customary zest for conviviality rose to meet it. The front door was open and a couple turned into it from the street.

'Here we are,' said Nat. He looked at Rose's unresponsive profile in the dark beside him and said, 'Or shall we give it a miss and go to the pub?'

'Come on,' said Rose and stepped from the car. Faced by an alien hullabaloo and with Nat behind her, she wished to be associated with neither.

They crossed the threshold from the crisp night into the steamy throng. A pile of coats blocked the stairway and a gravy-like smell of body heat underlaid with cooking fat and cigarette smoke thickened the air. Men, many bearded, flourished glasses and shouted enthusiastically at women dressed in skirts and blouses or in caftans with earrings. Some held tins of beer in their hands.

Nat took Rose's elbow and steered her. In the kitchen, a small man with a pointed beard and a bottle in either hand was refilling glasses. His forehead was wet and beads of sweat twinkled in his beard.

'This is Gerry,' shouted Nat, 'Gerry, this is Rose.'

'Pleased to meet you,' shouted Gerry. 'Grab a glass.'

'Happy birthday,' mouthed Rose.

Gerry nodded and smiled. 'Have you eaten?' he shouted. His lips, under the bristling hairs, had an oyster-like texture. He jerked his head to a table on which were crammed pudding bowls of crisps and coleslaw; plates of sausages, quiche, and a whole round Brie, its skin yellowed and crusty at the cut edges where rubbery pools leaked on to the thin wood on which it stood.

Nat gave Rose a cardboard plate and a glass. He smiled at her encouragingly. Rose put some peanuts and a piece of celery on the plate and edged away. Insinuating herself between packed backs she shouldered a way towards the wall. There was some comfort to be had from the feel of it behind her but little from the peanuts as she nibbled them on her front teeth between sips. She marvelled at her fellow guests' capacity for sustained conversation in circumstances where she herself found it impossible to distinguish more than one word in a dozen.

'I like your dress,' shouted a man coming up to stand beside her.

'Thanks,' shouted Rose. What could she say?

'How d'you know Gerry?' shouted the man.

He was wearing a suit, one of the few – grey flannel, and a silk tie. She must hang on to him. 'I don't,' she shouted. 'I came with some-one who was at college with him.'

The man came close and spoke in her ear. 'Are you a teacher too, then?' His face was narrow and dark, good-looking as a cigarette advertisement.

'Yes. And you?'

The man shook his head. 'I'm a nurse.'

'A nurse! In a hospital?'

'Yup,' said the man. 'St Thomas's. Come and dance,' and he guided her through the crowd, nodding at the many who hailed him. 'Hi, Tony!'; 'How're you doing, Tony?'

In the hall he let her go. 'Phew. Some journey. You all right?' Rose nodded and heard for the first time the beat of music from below.

'Ready for the next stage?'

'Yup,' said Rose and smiled. He took her hand again and led her to the basement. There, by candlelight where the air was clearer, were three musicians: a bespectacled man with a series of wooden drums and tubes which he struck with extreme dexterity; a black-eyed man with high flat cheekbones blowing on some lashed-together bamboo pipes, and a girl with long black hair and a fiddle tucked under her chin. A few people sat on cushions round the walls and three or four couples were dancing with fluid and rhythmic precision, rapt expressions on their faces. One in particular caught her attention.

The man who was tall and straight wore a hat tilted at a steep angle over his forehead and his rounded bottom tightly encased by sharply cut pants rolled and swivelled as he tapped and stamped. His partner who was black had red flowers in her hair and her short skirt, below a bare midriff, stood out round her waist flat as a plate as she spun. Despite the compressed energy of their footwork they moved with sublime nonchalance and aplomb.

'Cubans,' said Tony. 'Aren't they marvellous? Come ...' He stepped back and held out his arms. The pipes breathed out their catchy heart-breaking airs; the drums, incessant insistent, beat the rhythm, and the fiddle lacing and looping between told the tune. Rose stepped into the music and stumbled. She tripped and faltered. Confusion quickened her heart. She felt monstrous in her ineptitude. 'Tap, *one* two three; tap, *one* two three,' sang Tony into her hair. She heard him by and by and her feet fell into time. She found herself twirling, spinning out and returning. The beat entered her blood. It aerated her like pure oxygen. She found herself taken over by an alternative system. She moved within it, entranced, her face bisected by a grin of pure delight.

Time passed without meaning. The girl let go her fiddle and sang. She sang slightly off beat in a harsh voice. The two men backed her up with cries and warbles. Their song increased the tension. Tony threw off his jacket. There were dark patches on his back and chest. Like a garden sprinkler beads of sweat showered out from Rose's head as she swung. And then they all stopped. Everyone clapped. Nat was standing against the wall watching. Rose noticed him with dismay. He clapped too. He and Tony clasped one another. They kissed cheeks and patted each other's back. Panting, Rose looked on. She felt thrown. They drew apart and both put an arm round Rose.

'Introduce me to your friend,' said Tony.

'I must sit down,' said Rose. But Satchmo was singing. *'For the shark has/pearly teeth dear ...'* and Nat was rolling his weight from foot to foot. 'D'you really want to sit down?' he said.

So he shed his dreadful jacket and they danced, rocking their way inside a different kind of rhythm, equally impelling. Though his movements appeared to be minimal, Rose was flung wide and caught again, always within control. She heard herself laughing aloud. Whenever she felt her lungs would fail he pulled her in and she rested against his stocky chest, now drenched with sweat as his feet kept the pulse going. Where were her refinement, her fastidiousness, her distaste? Subsumed, it seemed, under a greater imperative. There were no thoughts whatever inside her head.

One good old tune succeeded another and when at last they stopped, Rose still in their thrall, sank to the floor speechless. Nat and Tony talked above her head. I must say something, she thought. But there was no need because their host, the diminutive Gerry, was playing a guitar and he seemed to Rose to be playing it rather well. In a sweet surprising bass, he began to sing and soon she was humming and swaying, Nat's arm loosely round her shoulders. The Indian pipe player took a wooden whistle from his pocket and joined in. After a while, Gerry laid down his guitar and came across to them.

'One of Rose's kids at school is in trouble,' said Nat. 'She's having a bad time because of him. Gerry's deputy at a special unit for difficult kids. It's got a great reputation. Maybe you've heard of it, The Pear Tree, in Harrow …'

Gerry shook his head. 'Not for long,' he said, 'it's being closed.' He waved down the protests and faced Rose, cross-legged. 'What is it?' he said quietly. 'Tell me.' So Rose began to speak and the more he listened the more she found there was to say. She stopped looking out for the cinders of uninterest to which she was, by habit, finely attuned.

'It's a difficult one,' he said when she had finished, 'but absolutely run-of-the-mill. It happens all the time. Hundreds of thousands of pounds – millions – are spent every year on adolescents and young adults who've been pushed out so far they're pretty well irreclaimable when just a bit of input at the primary stage would have done the trick. But why am I telling you this?'

'So what can I do?' said Rose.

'Dunno,' said Gerry.

They were both silent. Then he said, 'You've got to get the staff to respect *you* and to do that you've got to bolster up your Headmaster. You've got to make him feel worthwhile somehow.'

'I *couldn't!*'

'Then you'll get thrown out,' said Gerry. Rose sighed, filling her cheeks with air and blowing it out with a brrr. 'That's what Nat said.'

'What you need is support,' said Gerry, 'and a course of instruction in co-operation and management. There's lots of ways of doing it – just the order in which you put things can help. Come and spend a day with us at the Pear Tree before it closes and we'll do what we can to help.'

Rose stared at him. 'You are nice,' she said. They were alone in the basement.

Gerry stood. 'Let's go up to the kitchen and make some tea. I expect that's what the others are doing anyway.'

Upstairs a few people were sitting round the table. It was cold. The front door was open and chilled threads of night air stalked through the sour and vinous clutter. Rose looked on it with an affectionate eye. 'What time is it?' she asked. It was after four. Arm-in-arm she and Nat left the house. Tony came with them. 'Can I give you a lift?' said Rose. 'Thanks, but I've got my motor-bike,' said Tony. He kissed her on both cheeks. Rose and Nat got into her car. Gerry and the girl with long black hair waved to them from the doorway. They had their arms round one another.

'Where shall I take you?' said Rose to Nat.

'I'll see you to your front door,' said Nat.

Rose stiffened. 'How will you get home?'

'I'll walk. Dawn over the sleeping city. It's perfect.'

'You can't. It's much too far.'

'That's for me to decide. Drive on. Left here and right at the lights.' He started to sing.

When they got to her street the sky was paling and the lamps shone feeble and redundant against it. She put her key in the front door and turned to face him. 'It was lovely. Thank you so much,' she said. Would he try to come in? Was he going to kiss her? Dread and gratitude battled inside her. She avoided his eyes. Nat put his hand behind her head and brought it down to rest on his chest. He stroked the back of her neck and let his cheek rest against her hair. 'It was good,' he said and let her go. 'Cheery-bye.' And he swung off into the morning. Rose watched his back grow smaller and fainter in the grey light. She walked up the stairs. What did she feel? She was not sure: grey and soft and still, like the morning but also deliciously tired. She dropped her clothes on the floor and got straight into bed. A piece of thin paper crackled against her cheek. She tucked it underneath the pillow along with a wilted flower. Ah yes, she thought sleepily, and whispered, 'Darling, darling, I wish you were here.'

21

Up in Grassdale mist encloses the old stone house where Frank and Tamarisk sleep in twin beds, side by side. Opening the door to let the pugs out Frank holds his hand out in front of him and can barely see the fingers. He shivers, still in his dressing-gown, and goes to riddle the Aga. No question of an early morning walk today. The mist, thick as phlegm against the windows, yellows the light inside the house giving it a discouragingly dead and static tinge. He makes tea and takes it up to the bedroom. It's Sunday. 'Coo-ee,' he sings on the threshold, 'tea-ee.' He sits on the end of the bed where his wife lies flat on her board. 'Terrible day. Can't see the nose in front of one's face. I wonder if old Ted'll be able to make it?'

'I expect it'll lift by midday. It usually does. Darling, would you be too sweet, and put the little pillow behind my head? I'm so sorry to be such a drag. It's too stupid of me.' Tamarisk's voice is faint, her expression wistful and the blue eyes in her pale face round as saucers. As Frank pokes a frilled pillow beneath her neck and plumps up the rest she gives him a brave smile.

'It's too wretched,' says Frank. He pours tea and holds the cup to her mouth. 'I'll telephone Ted and put him off.'

'No, no,' says Tamarisk. 'Ah, that's better. I'll do my breathing and have a hot bath. But you may have to put the casserole in the oven.'

'My poor lamb.' Frank kisses her forehead and takes his tea to the window. The tops of trees nearest the house hang smudged in space. The world is devoid of colour: it is impossible to judge distance except by rote and the taste of skin on his lips has opened a sickening emptiness inside. Afraid that it shows in his eyes, he looks into the nothingness outside. He feels shocked and vulnerable, as though a lift bearing him upward has dropped three floors: he can actually see Rose tousled in her Sunday morning bed, feel the length of her body dissolve into his own as she reaches sleepily up to him. He sniffs at his fingers but smells only the mere antiseptic whiff of Pears Transparent soap, barely discernible. For a giddy moment he feels himself falling. But the pugs are yelping, the sound muffled in mist.

'The doggies!' says Tamarisk.

'Withdrawal symptoms,' says Frank under his breath.

'What was that?' says Tamarisk.

'I said "Sybil and Trish". I'll go and let them in – poor girlies. They must be frozen.' He leaves the room, tightening the cord of his dressing gown in exaggerated anticipation of the rigours ahead, for he can't bring himself to look towards the bed.

Soon after eleven the mist, thinning in patches, begins to lift at the corners. By midday, a glassy disc glinting in the sky discloses an outer firmament within which vapours mass and drift while shapes of boulders, streams and walls sketch themselves in, infused here and there with muted colour. The outlines of hilltops appear shining weakly in the chilled light of a silver sun.

'He still may not be able to make it over the moor,' calls Frank, busy in a butcher's apron at the oven door.

'Of course he will,' says Tamarisk, busy with her powder puff in the bathroom. Once her limbs are smoothed and whitened with the scent of violets, she's going to slip into one of her nightdress and negligée sets and arrange herself on the chintz downstairs before the fire. She'll need Ted's arm to get thence to the dining-room table for lunch.

'Coo-ee,' calls Frank, 'do I need to put the apple crumble in now or should it wait for later?' He pours cream into a silver jug, thick unpasteurised cream from the farm down the dale and directs his mind to dwell on byres, stalls and styes, on ancient stone troughs and mangers, and on stout iron rings and hinges.

'My dear fellow, you made it,' he calls, going out to greet Ted Ainsworth when he hears the Rolls draw up on the track outside.

'No trouble at all,' says Ted. He climbs stiffly down and Betsy bounds after him. There's a flurry of yapping pugs at Frank's ankles.

'Down girl,' calls Ted. He holds open the door of the car and the dog leaps back in and settles on her blanket. He walks up the path to the house rubbing his ungloved hands before him.

'Wretched weather,' says Frank at his side, 'we were so afraid you wouldn't be able to get across the moor.'

A dourness that repels small talk comes off Ted. He makes no response to this overture and Frank wonders how the three of them are going to get through lunch. 'Poor Tamarisk's back's been playing up,' he says with redoubled affability. 'She's spent most of the week-end in bed. But she was determined to come down for lunch. We've been so looking forward to your visit.'

Ted grunts. Slimy bastard, he thinks, but he's shaken when he sees Tamarisk, so frail on the sofa in her floating muslin and lacy wool. She holds up a white hand and the sleeve of the negligee falls back from her arm. 'Mr Ainsworth,' she cries, 'how wonderful to see you! How brave of you to come! And just for us!' Her face clouds. 'It *is* just us, you know, but you're such a close neighbour. We would so like to get to know you – I can't think why we haven't before. We thought it would be so cosy – formal gatherings are such a bore. But you're such a busy man …' She rattles on, letting her hand rest in his all the while until Ted feels himself thaw.

'Thanks, I'll have a sherry,' he says and takes it to stand in front of the fire whereupon Tamarisk cries out: 'Oh Mr Ainsworth, I can't see you there. My back's so stiff. It's too stupid!' And she pats the sofa by her feet, a shallow hump under a drift of mohair. The pugs jump up and snuffle round. One of them puts a cold nose against Ted's hand and Tamarisk exclaims in delight: 'She likes you! I can't tell you what a doggy compliment that is. You must have a very special way with dogs.'

Frank leaves them discussing the local veterinary practice and goes to pull the dishes from the oven. He and Tamarisk make a good team, one has to hand it to her. He makes quite sure to call 'Luncheon!' from well away, leaving Ted to offer her his arm.

As he picks his way to the next room acutely sensible of the fragility of the burden so light upon his sleeve, Ted smells violets. The scent so disturbs his senses that he fears for his digestion. With his free hand he feels in his pocket for his pill box. In the dining-room a bright fire burns in the grate, to Ted's way of thinking, a reckless indulgence. He takes his seat at the table, pours himself a glass of water and pops a Xantoxin into his mouth.

'Did you know, darling, that Mr Ainsworth's company is doing the cleverest things with pills and medicines?' says Tamarisk to her husband.

'Aye. Ainsworth Agriceuticals. Fast becoming a world leader,' says Ted. It's the first independent contribution he has made to the discourse. Frank seizes on it. 'Well, I had heard something. Tell me, does that mean you're moving away from farm machinery and – er – armaments, then?'

'Not a bit of it,' says Ted. 'It just means we're growing, that's all.' He compresses his mouth and looks down at his plate upon which he's placed three or four cubes of meat carefully withdrawn from the rich gravy in which they've been simmering for numberless hours. Frank signals at Tamarisk with his eyebrows. 'Turnips, Mr Ainsworth?' she says. 'They're our own, you know, fresh from the ground. We had them dug up with you in mind. I adore turnips, don't you?'

'Can't say I do,' says Ted. 'Don't hold with vegetables as a rule. But I'll take one not to give offence.' He reaches out his hand for the dish and then raises his eyes. 'Anything to oblige a pretty lady.' The words quite go to his head. He's never said anything like it in his life before. He turns to Frank. 'We're expanding in every sector, you know, all over the world, manufacturing under licence, entering new markets.' He puts a small piece of meat into his mouth and chews on it, shifting it from cheek to cheek before swallowing. In the silence Tamarisk says, 'How wonderful. What a clever man you are!' and Frank pours a small amount of burgundy into his glass. Ted takes a sip and goes on talking. The newest factory, manufacturing tactical weapons and spare parts for tractors in exchange for long-term credit plus a certain quantity of spices, cereals and medicinal plants will start functioning in the New Year. He speaks mechanically in fits and starts as if writing in a cramped unpractised hand. 'Can't say I enjoy doing business with any of these dagoes,' he says. 'They'd be better off up in the trees where they belong and letting us run their countries for them.'

There's a choking sound from Frank. He takes a swift draught of burgundy and fills Ted's glass, but Tamarisk says brightly, 'Oh, I do so sympathise, Mr Ainsworth. England's the best place in the world, isn't it? There's grass and cricket and Cox's Orange Pippins and the police don't really carry guns here, do they? It must be awful for you having to be away so much and I don't expect it does your digestion much good either.'

'Don't go abroad myself unless it's essential, you can be sure of that,' says Ted. He feels he's never met such a sensible woman and resolves to send her a whole case of Ainsworth's new maize-based cardamom-flavoured night-food, Nutrinox. He supposes he'll have to do something for that good-for-nothing husband of hers too, though it goes against the grain. 'You must come over to the warehouses again and choose something for that museum of yours,' he says with a downward turn of his lips. 'There's plenty to spare.' Tamarisk claps her hands. 'Oh, Mr Ainsworth, wouldn't it be lovely if there was a whole section named after you! After all, your company's got an historic place in British industrial development, hasn't it? Wouldn't that be exciting? And I'm sure Frank could make you chairman of the trustees or something ...' She turns to her husband then puts a hand over her mouth. 'But you're much too busy. You'd never have time!' She looks at Ted with wide eyes. 'Please don't be cross, Mr Ainsworth, I wasn't thinking ...' She drops her eyes and to his consternation Ted sees, or thinks he sees, a pale tear roll down her cheek like a single drop of dew tumbling from the petal of a flower.

'I daresay something could be managed,' he mutters.

'How's your poor back doing?' says Frank to Tamarisk. He fetches the Stilton from the sideboard and places it, wrapped in a white napkin, before Ted. 'You'll have a drop of port to go with it, won't you?'

'Do you know,' says Tamarisk, 'it's been so fascinating listening to Ted – you won't mind if I call you Ted, will you? – that I'd completely forgotten about my back. It feels much better. And you will try some port, won't you? Just to please me. Frank brought it up specially.'

Half an hour later, when Ted gets up to leave before the light should fail completely, he finds an unfamiliar skittish note introduce itself into his farewells. 'Cheerio!' he says and, 'Toodle-oo!' Down the track and out of sight of the house, he lets Betsy out for a run. 'I've made a fool of myself,' he tells her. But instead of striding silently alongside with his hands in his pockets, he picks up a stick and throws it. She bounds after with barks of joy and brings it back, wagging her tail. So he throws another and after that, another.

Back at the house the bleak November afternoon closes early in on Frank and Tamarisk. Frank clears the table and switches on the electric blanket, then he helps Tamarisk to bed. 'I hate to leave you,' he says, torn between admiration and impatience.

'Must you go?' says Tamarisk. Flat on her back she watches him through narrowed eyelids while he packs a few things.

'Mrs Bumble will be up with your supper,' he says, 'my brave baby. It's too wretched but I'm sure another day or two will do the trick. You'll be right as rain for the American Embassy on Thursday.'

'Don't worry about me, darling,' says Tamarisk. She draws her breath in sharply. 'No, no. Just a twinge. It's nothing.' She lets her head fall sideways then gives herself a little shake. 'Could you be too sweet, darling, and give me my book? I can't quite reach.' She looks up at him, her eyes at their widest, as he bends over and kisses her on the forehead. 'You're a great trouper,' he says truthfully. 'I don't know where I'd be without you,' and runs down the stairs. Tamarisk calls after him, 'Drive carefully. Telephone as soon as you get back.' She hears the front door close and jumps out of bed. *Madame Bovary* falls to the floor with a thud. She runs to the window and watches the big station wagon, its headlights making swirling yellowed pathways in the mist, drive away down the track. The tail lights like angry eyes glow briefly, cloud over and disappear. The two pugs come rushing up the stairs and throw themselves on the bed. 'Darling girlies,' says Tamarisk sitting down beside them. They have a great game together all muddled up in the bedclothes, then Tamarisk picks up the telephone. Swinging her thin white legs, she dials her friend Daisy Middlesbrough over in the shooting lodge on the other side of the moor. They have a delicious chat punctuated with shrieks and screams of laughter. Daisy promises to come over next day provided she can get rid of her guests by lunchtime. Tamarisk skips downstairs and helps herself to a big dollop of apple crumble. She covers it with brown sugar and cream, pours herself a glass of port and takes them back to bed. She climbs in, taking care not to disturb the doggies, piles up the pillows behind her, reaches into her bedside table for *Gone With the Wind* and settles back for an evening of bliss. She feels very satisfied with life.

Nosing his way down the dale, Frank feels not unsatisfied either. He loves the fact that every twist and incline of the road are so well known to him that he can operate the car as confidently as a blind man reading braille. The weekend has gone swimmingly. He feels much relieved and toys with the idea of visiting his jeweller back in London to pick a trinket for Tamarisk; a garnet, or some old paste. By the time he gets off the moors the mist has quite dissolved and the sky is as clear as blue Bristol glass. He depresses the accelerator and feels the big car unleash its full power in response. It's an agreeable sensation. Life, he feels, is full of agreeable sensations if you take hold of it with determination and look on the bright side. He might even be able to award himself a small indulgence and telephone Rose from the next petrol station. But the car's going so well that he finds himself speeding past them, one by one. As the lights of London swallow him up and traffic boxes him in he's obliged to slow down and her presence grows more insistent: but a mile or so away now, in the white attic flat, on the big bed, a cave of soft darkness and salty smells. He feels the golden thread snaking across the congested roof-tops, twining itself round his bones, weakening them with yearning.

He takes the car off the fly-over, choked with traffic, at the next junction. The move is agonisingly slow and his impulse turns to irri-tation. By fits and starts he arrives in the back streets of Kilburn. He pulls up not far from a telephone box outside a pub. First he'll telephone Tamarisk, then Rose. No, first he'll telephone Rose, then Tamarisk. He sits there frowning, fingering his balls. How featureless is the street and how unconvivial the pub. This demi-life of skulking in the city's underskirts has its romantic aspects, its magnetism and thrills which tonight hold unusually little appeal. The rosy rooms of his own house, harmonious, mellow, well-cared-for, beckon. He goes into the pub and buys a packet of small cigars. A non-smoker for some years he'll smoke one, maybe two, open a bottle of good claret and telephone from the comfort of his own armchair. After all, the house is empty. The good soul who looks after it has, no doubt, left some delicious titbit out for him on a tray. He'll play some Brahms and leave his paperwork till morning. He sees himself there in the lamplight ensconced with the new biography of Dickens. He turns on the ignition and hurries towards it before the vision should retreat – or change its form to any other.

22

Sam spent much of that weekend watching television. He went from shop to shop in the High Street and began to haunt the arcades and precincts of the posher localities near by. Sometimes Maggie came with him. They leaned against the plate glass engrossed in the multiple images that repeated themselves in facsimile at many levels. From time to time they got so caught up in the action of one that they pressed their noses to the glass, transfixed. Then the manager or one of his assistants would come out. 'Scram. Buzz off, kids. We'll call the police,' they'd storm and the children would scamper down the road. Sam thought one of the really small ones about the size of a cornflake packet would be just the thing for his Mum. She could carry it downstairs with her whenever she got up, almost like a puppy. A small one would not make too big a hole and there were so many that no one would ever miss it. He decided which: in the corner of a Dixon's, near the front and not too high up in the window.

On Sunday he and Maggie went with their father to the launderette. They left him to go and play. 'Hey kids,' he called from his seat in front of the revolving drums, 'get yourselves an ice-cream.' They were good children. He wished he had time to take them to the park.

Sam and Maggie ran down the quiet street. Outside a newsagent's Sam let go of Maggie's hand, slipped inside, fingered some comics, pocketed two packets of chewing gum and slipped out again. They ran on. It was a grey day, drizzling and misty. The McDonald's on the High Street was open. Sam left Maggie in an alleyway and joined the queue behind a woman with two children. The children kept changing their minds. 'I wanted strawberry. Why can't I have strawberry …' whined the little one when their order came through.

'You take what you've got, Lee. Naughty boy,' said the woman and slapped him.

Puce with rage, the child began to wail. The woman shook him. Sam reached up a hand and snatched one of the big bags with their main order from the counter, wriggled under the railing and fled. He heard uproar behind him as the woman screeched and the children bellowed. Hugging the warm bag to his chest he sped fleet as a swallow and darted into the alley before the lumbering knot of protesters had even reached the shop doorway. He leaned against the brick wall panting and grinned at Maggie. They stole to the end, squeezed through a fence into a back garden, down the path at the side of the house, through the hedge and into the street on the other side. Sam put the bag inside his thin school pullover and squashed it to him. Maggie skipped at his side. They made for the canal. When they got there they slithered down the bank to his camp, found the umbrella and sat at the water's edge. Sam opened the bag and the smell of armpit floated up to them, strong and full, from its interior. He broke open the polystyrene container. Maggie took the first bite. She opened her jaws to their extreme limit, so wide her mouth felt like cracking at the corners, and sank her teeth into the soft white bun. Sam poked a handful of French fries into his mouth. They were limp and cooling and he stuffed so many in that some drooped out like pale stalks from his bulging cheeks. They ate as much as they were able and threw the remains into the canal where they floated for a while on its static surface before sinking to join the riches of its stagnant depths.

Leaning against her brother, Maggie fell into a doze. 'Wake up, Mags,' said Sam. He needed her to work with him on the trolley he was assembling from the wheels recovered out of the water. They mucked about with it all afternoon, fixing a cardboard box on to the axle with bits of wire and tying on string to pull it with. Maggie crouched, wobbling, in the box; Sam dragged her to the top, jumped on and they careered down the bank bumping, braking and throwing themselves off at the canal's edge.

When, in mid-afternoon, night overtook the unmoving grey of day, the sky cleared and a few sparse stars pricked far overhead. Maggie and Sam walked home using the trolley alternately as skateboard and sled. Sam parked it in the recessed doorway of a jewellers off the main High Street. It was a shop no one ever went into, the window dusty and unchanged for years, and there was a grille before the entrance to which he tied the trolley. He larked about with Maggie all the rest of the way zooming in on her, jostling and nudging while she squealed and dodged and hugged herself with excitement.

A line of light was showing under the kitchen door when they reached home, but no one was inside. They went on chasing and swerving sending chairs skidding over the floor and water slopping out of the sink. Presently their parents came down the stairs. They were laughing. It was the first time Sam's mother had come out of the bedroom since the Education Welfare Officer's visit two weeks before. They had sausages round the table all together and by a quarter to ten the lights in the house were out and everyone in bed.

Under the bedclothes Sam was tight with excitement. He had kept his boots on and after what seemed an age he rolled out and crept downstairs. A white moon illuminated the garden path and cast deep shadows to the lee side of the palings. He flitted between them and climbed through the broken gate into the road. No one was about but the cool inhuman light of television sets still flickered on the interiors of many front rooms as he passed them by. At the end of the road the pub was still open. Dim light and beery laughter issued from behind the sand-blasted glass doors. Sam crossed the street to avoid it. He reached the High Street. The space between shops seemed further than in the day, but the street itself shorter and some-how more unapproachable. The windows were unlit and only the mini-cab shop had a running sign in flowing red letters, saying 'Al's taxis twenty-four-hour service'. He watched the letters going round and round, feeling strangely aimless: generally, he took things as they came but the plan in his mind took the edge off each moment's tex-ture as it came along. He felt uncomfortable and even a bit anxious.

Round the corner in the jeweller's his trolley was still tied to the grille. He skateboarded up and down the pavement for a bit but his heart was not in it and he missed his footing once or twice. He thought of his bed and of Maggie sleeping in hers on the other side of the room, and he thought, surprisingly, of Mrs Upjohn and the way she blew the whistle so it gave him a fright. None of the other teachers blew the whistle so it sounded quite like that. He trundled the trolley after him round the corner, dawdling as he neared the television shop. It looked funny all in the dark with the screens grey and glassy and empty.

There was his, nice and near the front. He clenched his fist and punched the glass.

Ow! his knuckle hurt, his wrist hurt, and his arm all the way to the top. He doubled over hugging it. Nothing at all had happened to the window. He looked up and down the street. It was as empty as ever. He took a few paces back and made a run at the window, hitting it with both fists and all the momentum of his body behind them. The plate glass vibrated. He jabbed at it with his knee, jarred all over, then slid to the pavement and sat hunched with his back to the window. He had often broken windows before: there must be something special about this one. He supposed he needed a stick or better still, an iron bar. He had better go and find something to hit it with. But he went on sitting there, not feeling like moving. Once or twice he half scrambled to his feet and flopped back. Then he fell asleep.

He was cold when he woke up and there were pins and needles

in his bottom. His mouth opened itself under the propulsion of a huge yawn. He stood up. He was not quite sure where to go or what to do with the trolley. He left it and ran off in the direction of the canal, but the nearer he got the less he wanted to be there. He turned back to the streets: even the ragged ends that petered out at the edge of the waste land made him feel uneasy and he hurried to where the shops began.

One of the front gardens he passed was surrounded by wedge-shaped hunks of stone. They caught his eye because with no hedge or fence in the way he felt unusually unguarded against the ground floor windows. He squatted on his haunches and started tussling. Maybe, like teeth, one of them would be loose enough to pull out. He got a grip on one and tugged at it with all his might. It wobbled and came free and Sam sat down with a bump. Inside the house a dog barked. It gave him a horrible fright. He picked up the stone and staggered down the road. The dog went on barking and Sam pushed ahead intent on putting as much space between himself and the noise as he could. His heart beat hard against the stone.

Round the first corner he let it drop and raced through the still streets to fetch his trolley. He found it was not possible to go fast with it: pulled, it veered uncontrollably; and scooting, it made too much racket rattling over the paving stones. In the day he had not noticed it make any noise at all. But once he had heaved the stone into the cardboard box it went more smoothly, though he had to strain to get the bare wheels across the cracks and ridges of the pavement. He was actually sweating by the time he reached the television shop again.

He dropped his pullover on the ground and parked the trolley close to the part of the window where his set sat. It looked just right. His mum would be really pleased. He flexed his shoulders and spat on his hands. If Gary could see him now he would be impressed. Grunting from effort, he picked up the stone in his arms and, with a swing of his body, heaved it at the plate glass and let go.

There was a crack like the report of a gun as he fell over and a burst of small fragments and splinters exploded outwards. Simultaneously, a tremendous clanging noise started up, the shrill and raucous clamour of a mechanical bell ripping the night apart. Sam's heart leaped out of its ribcage. He felt it jump and was frozen in a moment of indelible clarity. The moment was filled with glass and bells and blinding light. It passed but the bell shrilled on. He clambered to his feet and saw that there was a hole in the glass about the size of a football with cracks like a crooked spider's web radiating from it. The hole was not quite big enough to get the television through. He put out his hand, saw that it was dark with blood which was funny because it did not hurt at all, and pulled at one of the jagged corners round the hole. It came away too easily, bringing with it a whole unexpected section of spikes and splinters, some of which fell inwards. He staggered back and there was a crunching sound beneath his feet.

The hole looked big enough now. He stepped forward and reached through. He could touch the television set but his arms were not long enough to get a proper grip on it. He backed out and put his head through and then his shoulders, first one, then the other. As more glass showered round him he seized the television and pulled it back with him through the hole and ran. A violent tug pulled him short. It almost jerked the set from his arms. He staggered and fell on one knee. Frightened now, he let out a yelp. The clanging of the bell went on and on. He got up and tried to run but the television would not come and then he saw that a cable at the back was holding it to something inside the window. He tugged and wriggled and the movement of the tautened cable dislodged more glass which crashed down on to the bloody fragments all round his feet. He put the television down on top of them and pulled at the plug with both hands. Blood was making his hands slippery and difficult to feel through, but he got it free after a tussle and picked up the television set again. His arms were shaking and he nearly dropped it. And then a blaze of light caught him full in the face. He heard a screech of tyres and the banging of car doors. He had to get to the trolley. Torches flashed. He struggled on and above his head a man's voice said loudly and clearly, 'Where do you think you're going with that, young laddie?'

Sam did not look up. He simply staggered on and reached the trolley which was only a few paces away.

'What a god-awful mess,' said another voice above him. 'They want stringing up and hanging, the lot of 'em if you ask me.'

With a final heave he got the telly into the cardboard box and as he did so a hand came down on his neck. Hard fingers tightened round it. He turned and bit into one of them. There was a bellow, a grunt and the fingers slackened. Quick as a fish in water, Sam slipped away and grabbed the string of the trolley. With it over his shoulder he ran for his life, the trolley trundling at full speed after. Heavy footsteps rang on the pavement behind but he heard nothing. All his senses were concentrated on flight and when a blow to the side of his head knocked him off his feet he was taken entirely by surprise. Stars and flashes, just like a Tom and Jerry cartoon, whizzed in front of his eyes. He lay stunned then opened his eyes to see two big black-booted feet on the pavement beside him. He aimed a kick at the nearest ankle but a hand caught his leg and held it and he was lifted up from behind, a coat thrown over his head and his arms pinioned under it to his sides.

He fought desperately and in silence with wiry wild animal fury. The two policemen could barely contain him at times as they bundled him towards the squad car. 'This one's a right little bugger,' said one. The second policeman gave Sam a jab and put his knee in the small of his back. Half stifled in the dark Sam gasped. Parts of his body were hurting badly; stabs of pain went through it when he moved his knee and his arm in certain ways and he was bleeding from several wounds.

'It had better be the hospital, pronto,' said the first policeman. He lifted Sam, now limp and unresisting into the back of the car. It was his coat into which blood was soaking. He lowered it round Sam's head and leaned towards him. 'We're taking you to hospital, laddie,' he said. 'You've been quite badly cut. Whatever did you think you were doing?'

Sam stared at him. He said nothing but shrank further into the corner of the seat. There was nothing of him, thought the policeman, and he could not be more than ten. 'Whatever did you do it for?' he said again. He took out his handkerchief and held it to a deep cut under Sam's ear. Sam wanted to be sick. He was shivering. 'It was for Mum,' he whispered so low the policeman barely caught the words, and was sick. 'Oh Christ,' said the policeman, 'step on it, mate.'

Sam came to in a ward full of old men. He opened his eyes and thought he must be in heaven. It was quiet and light and white and opposite him sitting in what seemed to be a kind of bed propped up on pillows was an old gentleman with blue eyes and white hair. On either side of the old gentleman were other old gentlemen wearing loose, striped garments, one of them sitting sideways on and moving very slowly. Sam felt peaceful and somehow airborne: he was probably floating and clouds had got into his head. He liked watching the old gentlemen. The sideways one put a boat-shaped bottle under his robe and brought it out half filled with golden liquid. He became aware that there were bottles round him too, on silver shepherds' crooks. One was clear and one was dark red. He could see them without moving his head which he did not want to do, and there were transparent filaments leading from them into his own body. He was all in white himself and his hands seemed to have disappeared. Where they usually were were big white blobs which he supposed wings would be growing out of, the way butterflies came out of chrysalises. He let his eyelids drop over his eyes and saw bright smooth-moving patterns rainbow-coloured and unending. There would be the old gentlemen to look at when he felt like opening them again.

His breath came and went in slow strokes as though he were being breathed. The last thing he wanted to do was move or to disturb any of it. He opened one eye. The pattern went and the old gentlemen, blurred and haloed in light, swam into each other. He closed it and this time it was dark with threads of green and gold floating up from the corners. Mum, he thought to himself.

While he was watching the threads which only stayed when he kept his mind and his eyeballs still he felt a flutter in one of his arms. It was a nasty feeling like a choke and it broke up the slow flow holding him. The bright threads jangled and disappeared, to his concern because he wanted them back again. A loud voice from close to and very far away said, 'Sam, can you hear me? Sam? It's time to wake up. Come along now.' He could hear the words but they had no meaning. He kept his eyes shut and waited for heaven to settle back round him. He knew he had to keep perfectly still and that some trick of the brain like multiplication or final 'e' would bring it back. But the trick, though he knew it was there, remained just over the rim of his mind.

Something rough like sandpaper pinched his eyelid and yanked it up. The eyelid made a small sucking noise and very bright light sliced into his eye; first one eye then the other, leaving fierce swirling patterns of black and red. While he was trying to keep up with them his mouth was poked open and fingers pressed his wrist. They were minor sensations, unwelcome but unimportant compared to the effort he was making to tame the swirling. They ceased by and by, the swirls quietened down and when they were quite calm he opened his eyes, only for a moment to see the old gentleman, white-haired, blue-eyed, in place across the way – and closed them again. He was balanced exactly, like a feather in windless air.

It was half past two in the morning when the police started banging on the door of Sam's house. Eventually his father disentwined himself from the ropes of sleep. He pulled himself out of the folds of his wife's flaccid form and went downstairs unwillingly in his bare feet and vest, pulling on trousers as he went. He was disbelieving and wary; the police insistent and unbending, and Sam's bed was indeed empty when he went up to look. He came running down the stairs again and got into the squad car with the police. 'He's a good lad,' he kept saying to them over and over again.

At the hospital he was in time to identify his son as he was wheeled back to the ward from the theatre, though the white sliver on the stretcher was as unlike his Sam as a changeling from another world. He sat outside the curtains with his head bowed and his big hands on his knees wondering how it had all happened and what he was going to tell his wife. Things had been going so well lately compared with how they could, and he had been feeling quite cheerful. 'Good lad,' he said and kissed Sam's cold forehead.

He walked back through the hushed streets, grey, the wetted colour of shingle on the beach and getting palpably paler. It was a long way from the hospital and by the time he got back the postmen and the milkmen were whistling up the garden paths in the pearly morning light. He made a cup of tea and took it up to the bedroom. Maggie was still asleep in her bed next to Sam's empty one.

His wife was impossible to rouse. She lay snoring on her back surfacing for a few seconds only and beating him off with clumsy flappings of her fists. He knew she had taken in some of what he had to tell her because of the moans and cries she let out from time to time. 'Don't take on, love,' he said. 'It's not serious, they say. He'll pull through all right.'

His first job was at seven. There might just be time to fit it in before waking Maggie and taking her to school. He would have to give his eight o'clock job a miss. His courage sank as he realised how the fragile fabric of his life and his family's might disintegrate in the face of the strains now upon it.

That afternoon he fetched Maggie from school and they drove to hospital in the van. In the white-coated setting, all long corridors and hushed busyness there seemed to be something wrong about her appearance. He tried to tidy her up, wetting a paper towel in the men's toilet and patting at her hair with his fingers. They bought a bottle of Lucozade and a get-well card in the hospital shop. Maggie chose it. It had a picture of a smiling bear tucked up in bed attended by a nurse-bear with red crosses on the front of her cap and apron.

'Are you sure he'll like that one best?' said her father; he would have chosen one with cars and motor bikes. But Maggie nodded. She seemed quite sure. She shrank close in to his leg as they went up to the ward; William Waitrose on the third floor. It seemed like a huge white church to her and she wondered if Sam had died. She saw him first high up on a bed half way down and she ran to him immediately, past all the old gentlemen still as stones on either side. A black nurse in a mauve dress was bending over him. She had smooth shiny arms. Every time they came by his face Sam thought they were fireman's poles and that he was required to slide up them, but they never stayed quite long enough. He felt sorry and tried to say so.

Maggie clambered straight up on to the bed. She was really excited to be with Sam again. The nurse gave a little shriek and pulled her off and slapped her. To his immense surprise as he came down the ward behind her, their father saw Maggie stamp on the nurse's foot. The nurse gasped and slapped her again. 'Naughty little girl,' she said, 'you'll have to wait outside.' Maggie hid behind her father's leg, clinging to it, and when the nurse had gone, he lifted her up and held her so her face was close to Sam's. Sam saw the face with its fizz of curls come towards him through the haze and smiled. 'Hullo Mags,' he said voicelessly and went on smiling, on and off. Though Maggie was now sitting on her father's lap beside the bed, her face kept coming back to him and he kept smiling at it. How nice that she was there, he thought, floating from time to time.

'Hullo lad,' said his father, 'we've brought you a drink and a card.' He did not know if Sam had heard, nor what else to say, so he sat with Maggie on his knee, soothed by the slowed-down life of the ward and trying to keep his mind on his son. After half an hour he sighed and stood up. 'We'll be off now,' he said. 'I'll come tomorrow. Mum sends love.' He wondered if there was anyone he could talk to and stopped a nurse who was hurrying by with a cloth-covered tray. 'Sister'll see you,' she said, nodding towards the doorway. 'We'll be moving him tomorrow.'

Skipping at his side, Maggie waved to the stone gentlemen. They were immensely old; the oldest people she had ever seen. Sometimes they lifted a hand very slowly and waved back but mostly they stayed unmoving, staring straight ahead, or with their eyes closed. At the door she turned and jumped up and down so Sam could see her then she dropped on to her knees, put her hands together and shut her eyes tight like she had seen people do in pictures of churches and holy places.

Outside, they found a door marked 'Sister'. Inside, a woman in a blue dress with a very tight belt sat at a desk. She had a stiff cap like a small white hen on top of her head and she looked too young to be the sister of the old gentlemen inside. But then probably grown-up people did not have sisters and brothers. A man in a white coat with a stethoscope coming out of his pocket sat on the desk and they were both eating chocolates. Maggie stared at them and her father said, 'Pardon me, I'm Mr Clark. Could you tell me how my boy is getting along?'

The doctor jumped down from the desk. 'See you later, Hugh,' said the sister.

'Ah, yes – Sam Clark. He shouldn't be in here at all of course.' She looked at them severely. 'We'll be moving him tomorrow. There's a bed in Anne Frank. Are you the father?'

Sam's father nodded. 'Yes,' he said. 'Is anything broken? Has he been badly hurt?'

The sister opened a drawer and took out some papers. 'We'll need his things,' she said, 'pyjamas, dressing-gown, his slippers, toilet things, cuddly toy. Would you bring them in as soon as possible? Here's a list.' She handed Sam's father a printed sheet. 'Any queries?'

Sam's father looked from her to the list and back again. 'But my boy,' he said, 'how is he?' The sister made a tzt followed by a brief exhalation of breath. 'We've removed all the glass we can find,' she said. 'He may have to go down to theatre again if there are signs of internal bleeding. No nerves were severed. He's a bit confused at the moment but that's normal after an anaesthetic. No need to worry. Anything else?' She pushed her chair back and it made a muffled scrape upon the high gloss rubberised vinyl. Holding a clipboard to the rounded blue boss of her dress, she looked down at a watch pinned to its upper reach and stood up. 'I'm afraid that's all the time I can spare just now. You should have him home in a week or so. Good-evening.'

Maggie and her father watched as her legs like bottle-shaped black scissors, ate up the shiny floor between her office and the outer corridor. A chocolate-coloured woman wearing rubber gloves and a yellow dress walked by.

'Excuse me, Miss,' said Sam's father, 'but this list …' He held out the piece of paper. 'I don't see how …'

'Ah-ah sweetheart,' said the black woman, 'dat ain't nutting to do wid me. You'll have to see sister. I got me dinners to get.'

In the night things started hurting for Sam. Everything hurt; his arms, his hands, his legs, and his head throbbed. It hurt so much he cried and when he put up his hand to rub the tears a nurse hurried over and put it flat again. 'You're to keep your hands still for me,' she said. 'Lie quite still now and don't disturb the drip.' Sam wondered who she was and had the old gentleman sent her. He tried to ask but was sick instead. He was sick several times and could not be bothered to wonder after that. The hall was dark and he could not see the old gentlemen either but not far from his bed, between him and the other side, was a still pool of light. Outlined against it he could see two women in short cloaks sitting at a table and murmuring to one another. The dark was blacker and softer round them and the cave of light within made Sam think of Christmas. It was the Nativity, he realised without surprise, and tried not to cry too loudly.

The cave of light faded as the hours went by and Sam felt worse and worse. The old gentlemen had gone and in their place were unseeing low mounds. It was frightening without them. His head ached, he felt sick, hot, itchy and in great pain. When would the blobs turn into wings? He tried to hurry them up by shaking them and the nurse came over and told him off. He wanted to hit her, but all he could do was spit. What had she done to the old gentlemen? She might do it to him too. Though it hurt horribly, he twisted and turned. He had to escape. Two nurses came up and put shiny green boards along either side of him so he was imprisoned in a kind of box with no lid. He screamed but only a tiny shrill squeak came out. They had taken his voice as well! He thrashed with all his might but there were too many things to fight against. Through the turmoil he saw a brown face in a white coat looking down at him. A voice, all muddled with the noises in his head said, 'Yes, give him five mil,' and Sam knew it was a spell. He had a moment of white panic more terrifying than anything that had gone before, then he arched his back, spat, screamed and tried to get his teeth into a sleeve that went past his face. He felt the spell bite his bottom as a voice said, 'Just a little prick,' and knew he was lost. His legs and arms went floppy, his head filled up with fuzz like a snowstorm in a glass ball and he slid out of his body down a long colourless slope with nothing to hold on to.

The next thing he knew, he was being lifted. It was daytime. A white ceiling tilted this way and that and strange faces tipped in and out of the corners. They were going to take him apart and, maybe eat him was the thought that came to his mind. He howled and heard the sound hit the air and roll away from him. A face put itself close up to his and said, 'There, there, dear. We're just taking you to the children's ward. You'll feel much better there and you'll have other children to play with.'

'No,' shouted Sam. 'No!' He tried to jerk himself backwards to where he had come from and where it was safe in the quiet white space with the old gentlemen all round, but he was pinned down by heavy hands and put on to a moving table. He lifted his head and jerked it from side to side. There were tall windows with sky in them on one side and on the other, the three old gentlemen sitting just as he had first seen them. The middle one with his white hair swept back from his pink face was looking straight at him with his mild blue eyes. 'They're taking me away. Help me,' shouted Sam. He tried to put out his arms and hold on but the table moved by with him on it. He could only just see the old gentlemen and then they were gone; all there was were walls and window-frames passing by. A wild sadness filled him. It hurt much more than the pains in his arms and legs and went through him in waves each one more breathtaking than the last. 'Take me back,' he shouted, 'I won't go. I won't.'

The table went on through a door and the walls changed colour. They turned yellow, the colour of egg yolk, and they were covered with Noddy and Big Ears/Mickey Mouse and Bugs Bunny. White teeth leered down on him and he cringed. There were balloons, the sound of nursery rhymes being played and he heard children's voices. They were sending him back to school, back to school to Mr Lovejoy and Mrs Upjohn; back to school to be punished. He made himself very small and hard inside. They would never get him. Never.

23

'Nah,' says Gary, '*never.*'

'Not bloody likely,' says James.

'Sss,' says Selma. She moves her head very slowly from one side to the other and back to the middle again.

'Catch me!' Simon jerks his chair backwards so his head hits the bookcase.

Wendy purses her lips and shakes her head. Then she looks round the table. 'Where's Sam?'

'In prison,' says Gary.

'I don't know,' says Rose miserably.

She's been told by Mr Lovejoy to recruit among her groups for the new Keep Meadowbrook Tidy campaign. The collector of most rubbish is to get a certificate of merit and, maybe, along with other regional winners, an appearance on television. She tries to imagine Selma's incompetent claws groping at balls of fluff under radiators and conveying them thence to a plastic bag bafflingly fused at the opening. She smiles at her. It's taken ten minutes to get the group round the table and sitting down.

'Right,' she says, 'sentences today. The subject is – ghosts.'

'I seen 'im,' says Gary, 'last weekend it was. Arrested by the police. Sent down for life ...'

'Life!' says Wendy, and adds primly, 'Serve him right.' At the same time Simon jumps up rocking the table with his knees and shouting, 'My uncle's in prison. He strangled my aunt. There was blood,

blood, lots of blood ...'

'Sit down, Simon,' says Rose.

James Potterton has turned his back on the table. He's making loud staccato grunts and sweeping his arms, held out before him, from side to side across the back of his chair.

'James?' says Rose sharply.

'Don't interrupt,' says James, 'I'm keeping the ghosts off with my ghostbuster. Aargh ...' He falls back against Selma with his eyes closed.

Selma says, 'Sss.' She slowly lifts a fist and brings it towards James's face. Rose reaches out and grabs the hand. She's taken to physical intervention in the last weeks. 'Put it into your sentence, James,' she says. She keeps hold of Selma's fist. The skin's surprisingly rough and the fingers stay clenched.

'Me first. Me first. Can I begin?' shouts Simon. He's actually sitting on his chair but jumping with it up and down. 'Well done,' says Rose. 'Yes, begin.' Simon lets go the chair with a clatter and stands up. The others watch him. He suddenly looks quite small; a thin, white-faced little boy with nothing to say. Then, with his head down he mumbles very fast: 'One night a ghost came and shot me dead.' He sits down and hides his head in his hands. 'Very good,' said Rose. 'A proper sentence about one thing only, with a verb ... Very good.' She's moved by the effort he has made; the risk he has taken.

'He didn't speak up, Miss. He didn't speak clear,' says Wendy.

Nathan Woolf walks by. 'Good morning, Mrs Pitt,' he says amiably and looks at the children. 'Good morning everyone,' he says to them too. In a low aside he says to Rose: 'I've got some news. See you in my classroom,' and passes on.

'Miss and Sir ...' begins Gary.

'You next, Gary,' says Rose quickly. 'Ghosts ...'

'Nah,' says Gary, 'there's no such thing –'

'Is that your sentence?' says Rose. 'Stand up and say it clearly with the verb in the right place.'

'I did! I did!' shouts Simon. 'Go on Gary. Put the verb in the right place.' He's sitting on his hands and knocking at the underside of the table with his knees.'

'Go on Gary,' says Wendy.

'My turn,' says James in his deep voice. He stands up with his chest and stomach pushed out before him. 'I've got a sentence and it's an excellent one.'

'Fuck off,' says Gary. He puts up his fists and stands.

'Miss, Miss,' wails James, 'he's threatening me. Protect me!' He puts one hand on his heart, the other on his forehead.

'You can be next,' says Rose to James. 'Sit down. Carry on Gary, now. Fucking ghosts, yes …?'

'Fuckin' ghosts there ain't no such things,' says Gary, still standing.

'Good,' said Rose, 'not bad at all. You can sit down now. "Fucking ghosts there aren't any such things." James, your turn now.'

Before she can stop him James stands on his chair, bows to left and right and says: 'We've got a ghost in my family. It tries to get in the chimney but my Mum puts paper up. The end.' He bows again and sits down. Wendy says her sentence. 'Wooo, wuhoo, once upon a time Mum put crumbs out for the ghosts and in the morning they was all gone. Whooo, wuhooo,' and Selma says, 'Ssss.' The group breaks up and Rose manages to get some of them drawing pictures of their sentences and others at least choosing books to read. James sits under the table constructing a ghost bunker and Selma makes a few faint marks in her book with a pencil. When the bell goes they all dash away, Selma limping and James weaving from side to side with his arms extended. Rose has to get them all back and make them leave in some sort of order. It's halfway through break when the last of them leaves and she's able to get off to Nat's classroom. She hopes he'll still be there.

He's drawing shapes on the blackboard and filling them with different coloured chalk: square, triangle, rhombus – he has labelled them in big round writing and matching colours.

'See how you influence my teaching day,' he says when she comes in. A very small red-haired boy is sitting at one of the tables sorting pencils into jam jars. 'You can go and play now, Ian,' said Mr Woolf. Transformed from static to projectile, the boy shoots out of the room. The jam jars topple over and the pencils roll out. Rose starts picking them up. 'Sorry I've been so long,' she says.

Keeping his eyes on the blackboard, Nat says: 'Apparently young Sam was picked up by the police last night stealing a television set. He'd smashed a plate glass window and was trying to carry it off. They took him to hospital. He was badly cut. Our noble Headmaster is now collecting information from obliging members of staff so that he can write as black a report as possible for Social Services. They'll get him sent to Devil's Island for life if they have their way. He and Mrs Upjohn are delighted.' He speaks the last sentences in a whisper, looking at Rose who puts her head in her hands.

'Oh, no!'

Nat goes on: 'Mrs Jenkins says the father brought the little girl in this morning. They both looked quite exhausted. That's the side of it that worries me. Sam's okay for the moment, but the family clearly can't cope at all.'

Rose stands. 'I must go and get the report altered. His whole life could be ruined if he gets the wrong sort of handling now. It's a crucial moment.' She almost runs to the door.

'Stop! Oh, Rose, think! What d'you suppose will happen if you go barging in on Mr Lovejoy now giving him your opinion on how to run his school?'

'He doesn't understand,' says Rose. 'I'll explain to him. He's a teacher. He's interested in children and education. He must understand. I just haven't tried hard enough before. I must also let Sam know that I'm keeping his sessions for him and that the others are thinking of him. Could we go and see him in hospital?' Almost at the door, she hears herself say 'we'. She turns her head away. Outside in the playground, the whistle blows and there's an abrupt drop in noise level. Inside the hut there's a moment of tension. Suspended in silence, the 'we' hovers between them, disowned. The first children burst through the door.

'Don't, Mrs Pitt,' says Nat.

'Thank you, Mr Woolf,' says Rose.

Upstairs on the landing Elaine's already waiting. Her face looks fat and red and she's fiddling with her sock. Strands of golden hair, escaped from their headband, fall over her eyes.

'Hullo, Elaine,' says Rose.

'There's an itch in there,' says Elaine. She sits down, hunched and slumped. Rose sits beside her.

After a while, Elaine says, looking straight ahead: 'Miss, everyone calls me a baby. I don't like being called a baby.'

'Are you?'

Minutes pass. Elaine says, 'Yes, because I can't spell.'

Very carefully, keeping her voice even, Rose says, 'Why d'you think it is that you can't spell?'

There's a long silence. 'I get worried.'

'And the worries get in the way?'

Elaine nods and looks at Rose for the first time. 'My mother's worried too,' she says.

'About you?'

'Yes, because I can't spell.'

'Can she spell?'

'I can't do spells,' says Elaine. There's another long silence.

Rose says, 'Is your father worried about you?'

'Oh no.' Elaine shakes her head. 'When he was at school he was just like me. I'm going to follow my father. I'm going to be very tall.' She gets up and stands by Rose. 'I've got big thighs, look,' she pats at her grey skirt. 'I'm going to follow my father.'

'And can your father spell?' asks Rose.

Elaine shakes her head. 'He goes to classes,' she says, 'and my mother tells him words. He asks her and she tells him. Like you tell me.'

They look at one another. Elaine's face is pink and white again, pointy and composed.

Into this crucial moment and from above comes the voice of Mr Lovejoy, startling them both. 'Good morning, Mrs Pitt,' it says, 'I thought you might like to be informed ahead in case it affects your timetable that Sam Clark will not be coming back to school this term. I have timetabled you to take the fifth years swimming for the periods you would be taking him. A note will be going round to all staff later this day. And now, don't let me hold up your – er – lesson any longer. Reading and writing, isn't it? Good morning, Mrs Pitt.'

Rose jumps up – half. Elaine's watching her. She looks after Mr Lovejoy's retreating back and then at the child standing beside her. 'What a shame,' she says, 'I'll really miss Sam. "Like you tell me", you said. What kind of words?'

'Grown-up words. Big words like corry – corry something, and foreign letters.' She sits down on Rose's lap.

Rose is mystified. She feels the solid weight of the little girl upon her upper leg. Physical warmth but no feeling comes from her. 'Would you like to spell big words beginning with "corry"?' she says after a while.

Elaine shakes her head. 'I'm going to follow my father,' she says.

'You mean,' says Rose, 'if you spelled big words you'd be going ahead of your father?'

'I'm going to follow my father,' says Elaine. She stands up and leans against Rose. Very slowly, she begins to rub against her shoulder. All at sea, Rose begins to feel afraid. It's not nice. She doesn't like it. 'Little words are quite all right for you to spell,' she says firmly. 'You don't need to spell big words yet. Not until you're much older. Little words are the right words for you to be thinking about now. Write down the smallest word you can think of in your book before the bell goes.'

Elaine stops rubbing and sits down on her child-sized chair next to Rose. In a businesslike manner she addresses herself to the wide lines of her exercise book. With a firm round hand, she inscribes between two of them a perfect 'b' and shows it to Rose. 'Not quite,' says Rose, 'small and nice writing, but not quite a word.' Elaine looks at her and opens her blue eyes wide. She flutters her eyelashes, turns back to her book and as the bell rings, writes beneath the 'b', an 'a'. 'Very good,' says Rose and ticks it. 'There's a book I've got called *Ant and Bee*. You might like to have a look at it. But it's time to go now. Good-bye.'

Elaine stands up. 'Good-bye Mrs Pitt,' she says and skips away down the corridor.

Watching her, Rose laughs. She feels full of confidence as she makes her way towards Mr Lovejoy's office. There must be some way of getting through to him too. She knocks on his door. Mrs Upjohn opens it. She sniffs when she sees Rose who smiles and says, 'Hullo,' then, as Mrs Upjohn stands there, 'I'd like to speak to Mr Lovejoy.'

Mrs Upjohn shuts the door and as Rose raises her hand to knock again, opens it. 'The Headmaster is very busy today. If you will put the request in writing, he will try to make ten minutes available before the end of the week.' She comes out of the door and shuts it behind her. Rose shrugs and knocks again, louder this time. It occurs to her that Mr Lovejoy might not be there at all. 'Come in,' comes the muffled boom of his voice, and she steps inside.

At his desk, Mr Lovejoy is puffing on his pipe and reading a magazine. The magazine has a photograph of a locomotive on its cover. The pipe trembles on the pink inside of his lip as his mouth falls open and his cheeks flush brick-red.

'Hullo, Mr Lovejoy,' says Rose. 'I'm sorry to disturb you but there's something I really need to talk to you about urgently.' She thinks it rather sweet that Mr Lovejoy should be interested in trains and gives him her most sociable of smiles. Mr Lovejoy's teeth come down on the stem of his pipe and he grips the edge of his desk. 'Would you mind telling me what you are doing in my room, Mrs Pitt? I gave express instructions that you should not enter my room. Would you mind leaving instantly?'

'But Mr Lovejoy …'

'Leave the room!' Mr Lovejoy stands up.

Rose takes a step towards him. 'I can't. I've got something really important to talk to you about. You don't understand how important it is. Mrs Upjohn said something about not until the end of the week. That's too long. It's urgent. I need to talk to you about Sam Clark's state of mind …'

'State of mind!' shouts Mr Lovejoy. He bangs his fist on the desk and comes out from behind it. 'Leave the room. There is nothing more to be said on the subject of this boy. Leave the room.'

Rose takes a step back. 'Well, when can I talk to you if it's inconvenient now? You must consider the well-being of your pupils and Sam Clark is in a very vulnerable state. We must help him.'

'Get out,' says Mr Lovejoy. He's walking steadily forwards and forcing Rose to move backwards. 'When I need your help I will ask for it. I have many more experienced members of staff to consult before you.' They're at the door and Mr Lovejoy holds it open.

'You bully,' says Rose. 'I'm not afraid of you, but you ought to be afraid of what you're doing. It's inhuman – and irresponsible …' but the door has banged to and she's in the corridor, alone. She lifts both fists to batter on the door and kick it too, but turns away. There must be some higher authority to whom she can appeal over Mr Lovejoy's head. Nat will know. It's still lunchtime and she runs towards the staffroom. Two or three people look up as she bursts in. The mugs are almost empty and a thin smell of powdered coffee and cigarette smoke hangs on the air. He's not there.

'Where is Mr Woolf?' she cries.

There's not a quiver of response, but Mr Foster turns with a pained expression and passes a hand across his forehead. He's sitting with a small group of teachers, their chairs pulled close to his, and is filling a sheet on his clipboard. Mrs Jenkins is among them. 'I've saved some milk for you, Mrs Pitt, dear,' she calls. 'You'll find it on the shelf beneath the sink. There'll just be time for a cup before …' Rose hardly hears her. She makes to run out of the room again, stops herself, thanks Mrs Jenkins and hops from foot to foot as the kettle boils. The word 'Clark' catches her ear from the knot of teachers round Mr Foster.

'What was that you were working on? I hope you don't mind me asking,' she says as the bell goes and teachers begin leaving the room.

'Not at all, dear,' says Mrs Jenkins. 'Quite right to keep up with what's going on. It was about that young man of yours, Sam Clark. He's been in trouble with the police, I'm afraid, and some of us have been asked to compile a report on his school performance.' She looks at Rose kindly. 'These things happen, dear. Life is hard for some of these children. You mustn't blame yourself. Now, I must get back to my class.' Walking at her side, Rose begs to know what's in the report. 'Aren't I to be asked? I know more about Sam than anyone.'

'I don't think it's considered you have been a member of staff long enough, Mrs Pitt,' says Mrs Jenkins and walks firmly into her classroom.

That night at home Rose wrote a letter to the Chief Education Officer. In it she frankly laid out her observations of Sam's personality and her fears for his well-being. It was a cogent document by the time she had finished: no one could fail to be convinced by it or moved. She wrote it out with copies for the Schools Psychological Service, the hospital, Lady Goodall and – she was not so sure about this – for Mr Lovejoy. Next morning she got up early and took it round to the Civic Centre. Nobody had yet arrived in the Education Offices, so she left it at the receptionist's desk with 'URGENT' written on the envelope in red.

She got to school in good time to prepare for her first group but they never arrived. She sat waiting at the empty table with the empty chairs round it and watched the latecomers run across the playground. There were no leaves at all on the trees any more. She heard the sound of the day's hymn start up in the hall. Frowning, she went to look for her group in their classroom but there was no one there. She looked through the glass doors of the Hall. Dotted among the lines sitting cross-legged on the floor she saw the children who ought to have been with her. She caught the eye of one of them and beckoned. He half rose, looked towards his class teacher at the end of the row, who shook her head. He sat down again. The boy next door started whispering and nudging. They were both looking at Rose outside the doors. The class teacher leaned across and shook the first boy by his grey pullovered shoulder. Rose's courage ebbed. She went back to her corner. Maybe today's Assembly was special and she had failed to hear about it. If so, maybe she should be in there? She sat down and began to read through her notes. She was still reading when, some minutes into her next session a neat short-haired boy from sixth-years appeared beside her. He was out of breath and held a clutch of envelopes to his chest.

'Morning, Miss,' he said, 'there's a note from Mr Lovejoy for you. Morning, Miss.'

Rose opened the thin beige envelope. On the sheet of paper inside, faintly photocopied, there appeared to be a timetable and it appeared to be hers. A lot of periods seemed to be filled with swimming and deputising for class teachers; a few were still reserved for individual sessions with exceptionally backward children; some were marked 'extra reading in the classroom'. The names of all the teachers and Mrs Upjohn were listed at the bottom and it was initialled in a spiky blue hand, G.O.L.

I wonder what the 'O' is, Rose found herself thinking. She saw that at that very moment she was down for 'extra reading' in Mr Foster's classroom and, sure enough, a stout bespectacled girl presented herself before her. 'Please Miss,' she said, 'Mr Foster says he's expecting you now for reading in our class and please can you come now rightaway because he doesn't want to wait all day.' Magnified under the thick lenses, the girl had astonishing blue eyes with thick dark lashes curling upward. Between blinks she kept them fixed on Rose. 'Please, Miss,' she said, 'he says I'm to wait, Miss, in case you need any help.'

24

Without Sam to help with her shoelaces in the mornings, or make tea, Maggie grew whey-faced and more unkempt. Most of the time at home she spent at the bottom of her mother's bed, against the wall in the half dark. She daydreamed of rabbits, furry brown families hopping in and out of burrows and nibbling blades of grass in the rain. She began pulling at her ears and wished so hard for a tail, that when she got out of bed in the mornings and looked to see, she was quite surprised to find there was nothing there. At school she faded into near see-through invisibility. Her teacher was startled when one day she put up her hand. She leaned right down to hear what she had to say.

'How long does it take for a tail to grow?' she thought she heard.

'Speak up dear,' said the teacher, but Maggie, frightened by the sound of voices so close to her head, simply stared. The teacher tried to keep an eye on her but she was so easy to miss.

In the afternoon she waited for her father outside school. Sometimes he was even later than Sam had been. Then they went to the hospital and sat by Sam's bed for half an hour. Sam had a wild look in his eye, more like a runaway horse than a rabbit and he hardly ever spoke but he always smiled at Maggie.

'That's a tough young man you've got there,' said the head nurse. Her teeth showed in a wide smile, which pushed her red cheeks up into round apple shapes with broken lines in the red like hairs, and her stiff belt cut into her dark blue dress in the middle as if she were a shiny cottage loaf. Sometimes she carried a baby there, clasped to the upper half. 'Little mite,' she would say, joggling it up and down. Sometimes Maggie got under Sam's bed and crouched in the quiet among the paper handkerchiefs and the hairs. 'He's had a lot to put up with and he never complains. In fact, we never get a peep out of him,' she heard the head nurse say. 'We'll be removing the dressings from his hands tomorrow; you should be able to take him home quite soon after that.'

'How are we going to look after him?' her father said. 'His mother's not well and I'm out at work all day.'

'Oh, you'll manage,' said the head nurse. 'He's ever so quiet and the district nurse will be round every day. Your GP'll have all the notes.'

'GP …?' said her father.

Maggie hopped out and climbed on to his lap. She put her fingers into the short lines up and down on his forehead where the flesh was quite hard and rubbery on either side. Sam's forehead had big bumps on it. They had been dark, the colour of sky before thunder, but now they were paler, yellow-brown with bits of mould-green. Sometimes water came out from the sides of his eyes.

When they got back to their house there was almost always a letter pushed under the back door or lying in the front hall where no one ever looked. The letters were from the Education Welfare Officer to say she had called, or from the Children's Department at Social Services, or from the police. Sometimes Maggie's father read them and sighed, sometimes he took them upstairs and read them to his wife and sometimes he threw them away without opening them. The best evenings were when they went to the launderette and sat in the warm with the drums revolving behind thick glass, first one way, then the other, and the smell of hot washing all round them. Maggie hopped among the machines holding her forefingers up on either side of her head and in and out of the red plastic baskets. No one told her off and sometimes she got given a sweet.

A flat feeling of unreality came off those days. They were not made to last. One morning the Education Welfare Officer caught Sam and Maggie's mother by the hem of her skirt. The end of her nightdress got caught in the door as she shut it in the EWO's face. A conference had been called to consider the Clark case: thirty-six workers from across the spectrum including a representative from the police had abandoned their day-to-day work and made their way to Committee Room 9 in the Civic Centre. Mr Lovejoy brought Miss Bunting. Both had been listened to with respect. It was quite an outing. Though nothing had been said, the Education Welfare Officer felt her professional competence in question. For over a month she had failed to make contact with the family. A conscientious woman, she resolved to keep day-long watch until she did. Loitering by the broken gate one chilly November day she caught a glimpse of the back door opening and sped up the garden path. 'Drat that gate,' she said aloud as she clambered through the splintered palings and felt her stockings go.

Like a ghost hulk with barely a soul on board Samantha Clark had come swaying downstairs that morning earlier on. All hung about with drooping remnants she lurched round the kitchen, moving an object here, flapping a cloth there, some vestige of homekeeping astir. She inserted two fingers into the smeary necks of two milk bottles and took them to put out the back door. 'Mrs Clark?' sang out a cheery voice as her head appeared in the open. 'Hang on a moment, dear!'

The links in Mrs Clark's nervous system had become dulled and blunted. Though panic flared within, she was slow to move. She turned clumsily, banged the door to and found herself tethered. She whimpered and fumbled with ineffectual underwater movements. From the pebble-dash path without the Education Welfare Officer called encouragement and advice. 'It's a shame, dear. Your nice nightie caught in the door. There's nothing I can do from this side. You'll have to open up.' She observed the trapped fragment with distaste.

Maddened, Samantha Clark jerked back the door, flipped out her nightdress and pushed it to. But the EWO was an old hand: her foot was already by the jamb. 'So sorry to disturb you, dear. I won't keep you long. My, but it's chilly for the time of year,' she said as she shouldered her way in. Samantha Clark flew at her. 'Get out,' she screeched, her voice ranging through a number of registers from growl to squeak. 'This is private property. You are uninvited. This is a trespass. Get out.' The EWO was taken aback, not by the reception but by the accent – so posh – and the choice of words which suggested a familiarity with civic process unusual for her clients. She fended her off. 'There, there, dear,' she said comfortably. 'Let's just sit down a mo, shall we? No need to be alarmed. I'm sure we're going to get along like a house on fire,' and she drew out a chair, wiped the seat with a corner of her coat and sat down, her face wreathed in motherly smiles. No wonder, she thought to herself, no wonder and if ever there was a family at risk it's this one. She drew in her skirts round her calves and took a form from her bag. 'There are two children aren't there, dear? Samuel, Margaret ...?'

Mrs Clark collapsed on to a chair: her upper torso subsided all in a heap on the kitchen table and rasping sobs racked her body. Above the din, the EWO delivered her message: she had had enough of this. 'Were you aware dear,' she shouted, 'that your boy's not been to school for several weeks before his accident? Please answer yes or no. I've my forms to fill in and you have a statutory obligation to reply.'

The words touched a chord, still intact, in Mrs Clark's mind. She brought up her head, her face all streaked with slobber and tears. 'Statutory obligation!' she hissed in those thin refined tones. 'Don't you statutory obligation me, woman. You have a statutory obligation to leave my house ('hice' was what she said). Now get out.' She stood to advance on the EWO and, mindful of her recent tactic when the police had called, reached out for the frying pan. The EWO sat her ground. 'Now, now, dear,' she said, her eye on her client's face, 'no need to take offence. There's nothing that can't be sorted out over a nice cup of tea. Let me ...' But the rest of the sentence, so mundane in its composition, so mindless in concept, remained unsaid for, in a swoosh of greasy drops centrifugally dispersed, the frying pan came down with a crack upon her head. Breathing hard, Mrs Clark seized her arm and lugged her, half dazed, towards the door. She tugged it open and, with a kick of the knee on the EWO's bottom, shoved her through.

This time, it was the EWO who stumbled on the pebble dash path. 'God bless my soul,' she moaned, both hands to her head. She had never been so insulted in her life. 'They'll get you for assault!' she cried as the clamour in her head slowed down and a throbbing ache replaced it. She was truly shaken. She had a name in the borough for tact and was committed to her constituency. Her unabrasive presence had a mollifying effect on the touchiest of families, and the most unlikely of fathers had been persuaded to accompany sons to school after a visit or two from her. Much distressed she made her way back to the office trying to make head or tail of the whole business.

Inside her seedy kitchen Samantha Clark looked around, heart thumping from exertion. With peeled eyes she saw the room in all its unappetising squalor. Sensation flooded the capillaries of her consciousness, causing acute pain. She drew in her breath and held it trying to keep feeling at bay. But the images intensified as she grew dizzier. She saw her own body grown flabby and alien beyond redemption; her skin, her hair, flaking, greyed, unkempt, irreparable. She saw her children, neglected, ailing, far from reach, and her husband locked into hopeless struggle against insurmountable odds. She saw, with disgust, herself a burden unjustified, unjustifiable, insupportable, and she made a dive for the bread knife. She sawed away at the wrists using first her left hand then her right – needing both at once – and scoring the skin till it was red and sore. She drew a bead or two of blood. With an enraged cry she threw the bread knife against the wall and stumbled for the stairway. She clawed her way up on all fours banging her head against the banisters, leaving spots of blood on the stained paintwork, swaying and bellowing. Despair came down on her with unprecedented ferocity like a great black bull out to gore and crush her. She reached the bed and failed to hoist herself on it. Slumped among the uncapped pill bottles she tilted her head to a bright stream of gaudy capsules. Brilliant yellow, emerald green, shiny red-belted, filled with rainbow coloured grains gay as children's cake decorations. She swallowed and swallowed, retched and swallowed. From the undrunk cups beside her on the floor she poured long draughts of tea and by and by the pills flowed smoothly. The black bull lay down in the shadows at the four corners, her pulse slowed and almost ceased, unfathomable darkness enclosed her and she slipped sideways, half supported by the bed, her limbs oddly deployed, insensible on the undemanding floor.

It was quite quiet. Inside the house, nothing stirred but the drip of a tap at the kitchen sink. From the street, a general air of unkemptness apart, it stood indistinguishable from its neighbours in an area of mediocre council housing, home to a few score low-income families who by and large hung on to their dreams somehow and kept the nightmares shut out.

That night, Maggie and her father slept side by side in her bed. A keen wind whipped up the curtains and whistled through the opened windows of the room next door affording very little protection from the cold. It was the smell that had first struck them when they got home from the hospital. Phil Clark ran up the stairs.

'Stay down, Mags,' he called when he saw what was inside the bedroom. In a way, he was not as shocked as he would have expected and that surprised him. They both went in the ambulance to hospital, the same hospital where Sam was, but a different part of it, fifteen minutes walk away. He lay now sleepless beside his daughter aware that his world was falling to bits about him. Rack his brains as he might, he could see no way of holding the pieces together. It always came back to Sam. He began to see how vital a part the boy had had in the ongoing survival of the family. Towards morning he wept to think of its impending break-up. He shifted his position and reached up to cover Maggie's small hand with his own.

Next day, the police arrived first thing·including the policewoman who had played with Maggie. They wanted to know if it was attempted suicide, or had there been a row. Maggie's father laid his head on the kitchen table and shook it slowly. He did not know how to answer the questions, though he knew it was important to do so; they seemed all out of gear with his family as he knew it. The policewoman gave Maggie a wink and waggled a forefinger on either side of her hat; Maggie hopped over and crouched by her leg. There had been no time to take her to school.

Then a lady and a man came from Social Services. They went all round the house making notes on a form. The lady talked to Maggie, bending close, on one side of the kitchen table and the man to her father on the other. Maggie generally said nothing when people asked her questions and they usually gave up. This one went on and on. She wanted to know if Maggie had any dolls and what time she went to bed and did she ever make tea on her own. In the end Maggie went to sleep. On the other side of the table her father said nothing much either. He did not know what his income was nor whether his wife collected child benefit; he suspected not.

'He's a fine lad,' he said when they asked about Sam. 'We'd be lost without him.'

'So why wasn't he attending school?' said the man. 'You have a statutory obligation to see that he does.'

Mr Clark stood up. Who were these people and what business was it of theirs? He had his own business to attend to. 'There's nothing wrong with my family that a bit of cash wouldn't cure,' he said. 'I've missed my first two jobs of the morning and I can't afford to be missing the third. So if you don't mind I'll be getting on my way.'

'What about the little girl?' said the lady.

'That's my affair,' said Mr Clark. The two social workers exchanged glances and departed. But before he could carry Maggie to the van, the EWO arrived with her supervisor and when they had gone, a visitor from the Social Work Department at the hospital. He lost a day's work and heaven knew what that would lead to. He walked with Maggie to the telephone box and tried to explain things to his angry customers. But the promises he made them were ones he doubted he could keep.

When he and Maggie got to Sam's ward for their visit that evening there were two unknown people sitting by the bed. One of them, Sam's father had seen before. He was a teacher from Meadowbrook, a dark thickset chap who played football with the boys after school. The other was a young woman, very pretty with bright eyes and soft lips. She was wearing a grey dress with a frill round the neck and she was leaning towards Sam, so absorbed she never noticed them arrive. Sam looked more alert than usual. He was sitting up and there was a funny-looking object before him, a kind of model on a piece of cardboard. A packet of Plasticine lay on the sheet.

The man stood up. 'I'm Nathan Woolf from Meadowbrook. We've brought Sam a get-well card signed by some of his mates, and we're extremely sorry to hear what's happened.' He held out his hand. The woman did not get up. She went on looking at Sam. 'Time to leave now,' she said. 'I'll come back the day after tomorrow. Would you like to keep the bear in the boot, or shall I look after it for now?' Sam shook his head. 'You take it, Miss,' he muttered. At the door, they turned and waved. Maggie, who had hopped after, sped back, pink-faced and climbed up on to the bottom of Sam's bed. She crouched there nibbling and, by and by, toppled sideways and dozed off.

Phil Clark tried to tell Sam about his mother. 'Mum's had a bad turn. She's been taken to hospital, lad,' he said. From a white face Sam's eyes held his for a moment or two, then he turned away his head and cried. He made no sound but his shoulders heaved and shuddered. His father patted them with a shaking hand. 'There, lad,' he said, 'there, there.' Sam stopped crying but kept his face turned away. His father wondered if he could leave the two of them there on the bed while he went off to visit their mother.

The hot drinks trolley came trundling down the ward. 'Bedtime drink?' said the black woman in the yellow overall. She stopped at the end of Sam's bed. 'I usually leaves him Ovaltine, nice and nourishin'. But there's a new one they're sending out now. Nutrinox it's called. It's meant to be ever so strengthening. Perhaps he'd like that for a change?' She took the lack of response in her stride and shook some cream-coloured granules into a cup, filled the cup with milk out of a big aluminium jug from which vapour still rose, whisked it about with a plastic spoon and set it on the locker by Sam's head. 'I've given you a new drink to try tonight, Samuel,' she said loudly as to a deaf person, and trundled on.

From the far end of the ward the noise of a hand bell being shaken sounded. Apple cheeks aglow the head nurse came rollicking down. 'Time for all you Mummies and Daddies to go home. It's bye-byes for Anne Frank,' she called. Phil Clark sighed. He would have to take Maggie with him. He picked her up still sleeping and bent over Sam. 'Night-night, lad,' he said. 'Don't take it to heart. I'll be up again tomorrow.' Maggie's little breath warmed the space between his shirt collar and his jacket. He shifted her to a more comfortable position: Lord knows how I'm going to manage, he thought as he trudged through the corridors.

When Rose came to see Sam after school two days later he had gone. A little girl under a plastic tent lay in his bed. She asked a student nurse: 'Samuel Clark? Wasn't he the one with severe lacerations? Discharged yesterday, I think. I've only just come on. You'd better ask at the desk.'

Halfway up the ward was a counter around which nurses congregated, sometimes behind it reading up notes; sometimes against the front gossiping. Two of them were leaning there now, drinking Pepsi-Cola out of cans. They were in no hurry to answer Rose.

'Discharged yesterday,' said one of them over her shoulder.

'Why? Where?' said Rose. She was becoming breathless with

agitation.

'Are you family?' said the nurse.

'No,' said Rose, 'I'm a teacher from his school.'

'There's nothing in the notes about a teacher coming from the school,' said the nurse.

'It's informal,' said Rose. 'You see ...' She started to explain her connection to Sam but stopped. She opened her bag and proffered a tube of Polos, taking one herself. The three of them stood sucking. 'Oh dear,' she said after a bit. 'He's one of the Three Wise Men in our Christmas play. He's ever so keen. I promised I'd help him with his part. I wonder how I can find out where he's gone?'

'It's a shame,' said the first nurse.

'Hasn't he gone to Fiveways?' said the second.

'Fiveways?' said Rose.

'Short term residential for Delicate and Difficult Children. It's out in the country. Somewhere in Surrey, I think. Come to think of it, there was quite a scene when they came for him. He ran away while he was being signed for. They found him hours later in Men's Surgical. He was clinging to the bottom of some old man's bed. Wouldn't let go. They had to sedate him.' She shrugged. 'Kids,' she said, and then, 'Time for the drugs round. Bye now.'

'Bye now,' said the first nurse.

'Bye for now. Thanks awfully,' said Rose. She watched them stroll down the ward, two long-legged Brixton rangers, slightly pigeon toed in their black stockings and flat Oxfords, tight waists and white caps moored like tiny hovercraft atop their springy hair. She tried not to think about Sam. His anguish, the sense of terror and abandonment were too painful to imagine. The exercise simply raised a reciprocal panic in her. She drove home as fast as she could and set about locating Fiveways. She wondered whether to telephone Nat: she did not want to become any more beholden to him than she was. She hesitated and her own telephone rang. 'Darling,' said Frank's voice, 'darling, darling, *darling ...*'

25

He was brimful of joy. A preliminary meeting of his pilot committee had just taken place and in the most entrancing of places: a vault under St Pancras Station. 'What a lark,' he said. 'We're going to have such fun!' His creased face wrinkled with pleasure, as he welcomed his members. Ted Ainsworth, unsmiling, dyspeptic, punctual to the second; the Duke of Middlesbrough, long-bodied, loose-limbed, his face baby-pink with anticipation; Professor Vane, polished toes twinkling, knife creases breaking, rich laugh rolling round the arched brickwork as he ran down the stairs in overdrive; the Cultural Attaché from the French Embassy, 'the Ambassador so regrets he cannot be with you, but the preparations for the State Visit have prevented him from leaving his desk'; the Secretary of State herself striding in just as they began, 'God Bless this Ship ... the best of luck ...' and striding out.

It had gone like a dream. The Duke had accepted honorary chairmanship with a modest shiver of the chin, proposed a study weekend at Tees House some time in the spring and disclosed that the train sheds at King's Cross were built partly on Middlesbrough land. Ted Ainsworth, keeping his eyes on his fingers – he could not quite bring himself to address Lord Wetherby directly – undertook to fund and provide exhibits for an entire section provided it was named after his company. Max Vane reiterated the offer of two industrial scientists from his department and agreed to substitute an industrial historian for one of them. 'I've got just the chap,' he said, rubbing his hands.

The Cultural Attaché shrugged gracefully. 'We might arrange a little word with the President himself while he is here. He, too, is a farmer with some historic lands in the Auvergne.' By the time they emerged an hour later – 'the conspirators' – Frank was bubbling over.

In this elevated mood his thoughts turned naturally to Rose. There were two hours before his next engagement. They would do something perfectly absurd, something intoxicating in its ordinariness, they would go for a ride on a train! They would hold hands and laugh as the gasometers and the sewage works, the water towers and the allotments sped by; they would speculate on the point and date of odd minarets and domes affixed to Victorian and Edwardian buildings; they would pick love nests for themselves glimpsed at the corners of anonymous streets; they would eat railway cake in cling-filmed slabs and her beloved presence close to his would warm him through again.

There was a pause as he held the receiver. 'Darling. Oh, darling,' she said. Her voice was flat with an uneasy edge to it. Where had he been? They had loved each other two years and more but she had never felt so far away. 'I've needed you so,' she said.

Frank breezed on. 'I've got such a lot to tell you,' he cried.

'Have you?' said Rose, and added, 'Oh, darling.' Were they going to see each other?

'Meet me.' He dropped his voice. 'Meet me at South Kensington Station. You'll recognise me because I'll be buying a tin of Balkan Sobranies at the kiosk. We're going on a journey, round the Circle Line to – to Siberia.'

Rose laughed. The old rhythms took over. Her cares dropped away like a grubby carapace round her feet. She stepped out of it and said, 'And you'll recognise me because I'll be wearing a black veil studded with diamonds – and just in case there are too many other people wearing the same, I'll lift my skirt and there'll be a satin garter above my black-stockinged knee.'

'Ten minutes,' said Frank.

'Nine and a half,' said Rose and skipped to the bathroom to squirt herself with scent.

By the time Frank had parked the car, some of his exuberance had abated. South Kensington was a dangerous zone; any number of people might be coming back from Whitehall or the City. He sauntered with his nose in the *Evening Standard*. She would come romping into his arms and he would have to say, 'Madam, I think you must be mistaken.' But she was too well trained. He caught sight of her, sauntering too, behind a paper. She had her coat collar up and a beret tilted deep over her eyes. She did not raise them as she passed him by but swung the skirt of her coat so that a long leg was exposed almost to the thigh. The faint familiar breath of her made him priapic with longing. He jerked his head in the direction of 'Eastbound' and stalked off-handedly for the stairs. In the train they sat on opposite sides of the carriage. After Sloane Square, the most fraught of all stations, Frank lowered his paper and gave her a questioning stare. He leaned forward. 'Haven't we met? A week or two ago wasn't it? At the ... at the ...'

'At the Opera!' said Rose. She looked him full in the eye for the first time, intending to laugh but emotion caught her by the throat and her eyes filled with tears. Frank gave her a steadying look. 'Mind if I come and sit next to you?' he said. 'I've remembered our conversation ever since. I'd so like to continue it.' Rose, speechless, shook her head, or should she be nodding it? She felt quite limp. He sat down beside her and pressed the length of his body slowly closer. They were both too moved to speak. The train, still underground, drew in at St James's Park.

'I do hope you don't have to get out here for cocktails with the Queen,' said Frank.

Rose shook her head, all restraints dispersed. Her face glowed with love. 'No,' she said, 'I'm getting out at ... at ... Siberia.' She smiled at him. 'So tell me,' she said and she stroked the back of his hand with her finger.

Frank embarked on a spirited rendering of developments on the Museum front though he stumbled now and then and Rose listened with faint cries of 'Brilliant!' 'How thrilling!' She tried earnestly to rev up her zeal but a strange indigestion of the heart persisted.

'Now you, my angel,' said Frank. He glanced over his shoulder and put a hand up her thigh. Rose pressed herself against it and wriggled. 'Naughty,' whispered Frank, 'this is just for comfort. Now, tell me. I must know.'

Rose sighed. 'It's been awful,' she said in a small voice.

'I was afraid so,' said Frank, and Rose thought, how odd. She felt slighted. 'It's the villainous Headmaster, isn't it?' said Frank.

Rose nodded. 'Mostly, but it's got much worse than that. It's really bad and I don't know *what* to do.' His hand was causing a pulse to beat in her vagina. Its thumping filled her whole body and she could not think how to tell her tale so it would make him laugh.

'My little one,' said Frank, 'I want to know every detail of what's happened to you since we were last together a thousand years too long ago,' and he raised his eyebrows above his spectacles to regard her with a rapt expression on his face. So Rose began and she felt that she would never get to the end as, station by station, the train got emptier. She would lose his interest. She had lost it.

'Oh, the river!' he cried. 'The dear old Thames. Time for our picnic.' He dug in his pocket and produced a paper bag. 'Guess what's in here,' he said, kind eyes dancing.

'I know,' said Rose, 'you told me. It's railway cake.'

'And to go with it, tarrum …!' He removed his hand from her thigh to dig into his other pocket. 'Navvies rum. You know about navvies building the railway lines, don't you?'

'Absolutely, I do. You've told me,' said Rose. She looked forward to the rum burning a way through the constriction in her chest which caused her spirits to sink when they ought to be fizzing.

'Me first,' she cried.

Frank put an arm round her neck. 'Chin up,' he said encouragingly and poured some into her throat. His face was very close, every well-known fold and crease; his eyes, magnified behind his spectacles held an anxious spark, and hers an unaccustomed melancholy. 'Darling,' he said and gathered her into his arm. But the bottle was still in his hand. Over her shoulder he emptied some into his own mouth and set it down. They huddled close, the lines between them erased while the rum, in cahoots, seared their gullets and emitted rays of heat as it settled on their abdomens below.

'In harbour,' breathed Frank. His eyes were damp and his spectacles all misted up. Rose lay against him. I mustn't put my problems on him, she thought, it's silly. She felt infinitely protective. She wished she could wash his handkerchiefs, sew on his buttons, iron his shirts smooth as smooth.

At Tower Hill he stirred. 'Next time we'll get out here and watch the river from the top of the bridge. I promise,' he said. They fed each other morsels of cake and sipped from the bottle. By Moorgate they were giggling and at Euston Square Frank burst into song. 'Is this the Chatanooga Choo-choo,' he crooned in her ear.

'Will you have music in your museum?' said Rose.

'Of course!' cried Frank. 'What a brilliant idea.' King's Cross had not gone unremarked by either of them.

Rose pressed closer and looked up in his face. 'Maybe I could be a turnstile lady?' she said.

'In uniform. I'd like that,' said Frank. At Edgware Road, he said: 'I'm going to leave you at the next station, darling, though it breaks my heart.'

Her senses deliciously lulled, the words had little meaning for Rose. 'Must you?' she murmured. She fingered the tendons on the inside of his wrist. 'Why?'

'I love you,' said Frank. He had seen a clock. If he went on to South Kensington, collected his car and drove back, he would be late for Tamarisk, whom he was due to pick up at nine. He could telephone and say he was delayed: in the old days he would have telephoned. But this was the new order. He would pick up his car next day. He disengaged himself from Rose and stood up. As the train drew into Edgware Road he performed a little tap dance to cheer her up and slipped out of the doors. They slid to behind him and before she could quite take in what was happening, the train itself slid away from the platform.

At first she was incredulous. They had been so inseparably together with no hint of interruption and five stations to go. Now, without any apparent change of gear, Frank had gone and they were apart. Like an extraction, the pain came after as blood pumped into the wounded tissue. She felt bereft. A dreamlike sensation took hold. She was standing far out from land on an endless expanse of water. A causeway connected her to the shore but her limbs had been deprived of power. I'll never get back, she thought. She closed her eyes and as the feeling died away, an ache of such intensity gripped her that she could scarcely breathe. She tried to force in air and produced a rasp more like a bark than a human sound. Her eyes opened in fright and it was then she noticed there were people in the carriage.

A woman with a child stared at her; the woman averted her eyes but the child went on staring. A man put up his newspaper and rustled the pages. A big black woman in dark green gabardine with a badge on the lapel leaned over and tapped her knee. 'Anything wrong dear?'

Rose backed into the prickly patterned plush. She shook her head and turned to look out of the window where, against the black of the tunnel outside, slices of herself distorted by concavity reflected themselves back to her. She concentrated on them. What was I doing before this – this jaunt? she thought, and started to cry.

At Gloucester Road she got out and walked. The movement made some space in her head. She must mobilise herself and do something about Sam. Whom could she summon? Not Nat. That would be marking time. Someone with clout, a name to impress. Of course, Max!

As she ran up her own stairs, the more she thought about it the more evident it seemed. A pillar of the educational establishment and an old friend, he could not but respond in an emergency like this. She had already opened the subject with him. There was no need to be formal. She threw her beret on the bed and dialled the Vanes' number before removing her coat.

Millie answered in a high toneless voice. 'We're just going out,' she said. 'It's too trying having to put on one's tight-buttoned boots at this hour.' She gave a short exasperated sigh.

'I've got to speak to Max. It's really urgent,' said Rose.

With a moan Millie let the telephone drop and Rose heard her voice, thin with irritation calling: 'Oh, do come on. You know we have to be there before HRH.'

Shaking off the last few drops and buttoning his flies, Max came bustling down the hall. 'Rose, my dear,' he said. 'Can we give you a lift? We'd be only too delighted.'

'Oh, Max,' said Rose, 'I need your help. It's urgent. Please can you advise me?' Now she had him there she did not know how to tell him, or what.

'Absolutely anything. Yours to command ...' said Max. But he was on his guard. An abrasive undertone struck him as untoward. He made a silent kissing motion of his lips in Millie's direction.

'There's an emergency with one of the children I teach,' began Rose. Words tumbled forth. She sounded breathless and upset. Max, who was not at all partial to emotion in its untreated state, looked at his watch. 'My dear,' he said, 'how too appalling. I'll do what I can of course. Have a word with my secretary in the morning. You'll make your own way to the Palace, I take it then? What a splendid girl you are. We'll see you later,' and put the telephone down. He lifted his shoulders up and down like a large young bird learning to fly and took Millie's arm. She was clearly in a filthy mood by now and he felt put out by Rose's untimely intrusion. They were in for a rough ride, though mercifully of limited duration. He patted Millie's bottom.

What if HRH had decided to have the whole do at Hampton Court!

Where were they all going? thought Rose. She imagined Frank in his tails and herself all in white and gold on his arm. But she did not even know when she was going to see him again. She ignored the stabs of pain striking her in the solar plexus and set to, writing down her thoughts on Sam as if making out a report for an informed and well-disposed readership. She must practise presenting him convincingly. She would make copies and give them round.

It was after one when she got into bed. She wondered if Frank was yet in bed and with Tamarisk beside him, or did they sleep, like her own parents, hygienically, in adjacent beds. Sam's whereabouts were beyond imagination. All she could see was his white face, receding as it grew tighter and harder, farther and farther out of reach. The faces of all the children she taught jostled in her head: 'Me first!', 'Miss, can I see your knickers?', 'Miss, why don't we come to you any more?', 'Save me, Miss, save me!' The tumult went on, the din and the clatter and all just beyond reach. She would never get to sleep. She saw Nathan Woolf watching her and grinning. 'Come and have a noggin at the pub,' he said and walked away between a long line of trees until the neon blaze of his jacket was nothing but a cornflower-blue blur.

Frank, meanwhile had flagged down a taxi. Determined to by-pass the ache round his heart, he jumped aboard and sang out the address.

'Full of the joys of spring, are we, mate?' remarked the taxi driver.

Frank took the hint. He must watch it. 'Would you mind waiting a few moments while I go in and fetch my wife,' he said flattening his voice and elongating the vowel sounds.

'Take your time, mate,' said the taxi driver. He drew a paperback from beside his seat and opened it. By swivelling his eyeballs to their limit Frank could see it was called *How to Heal your Life*. He was delighted with this titbit. He took it as an affirmation of his faith in the boundless diversity and resourcefulness of his fellow men.

People like Professor Vane and the Duke of Middlesbrough did not somehow fit into the category of 'fellow men'. What were they then, he wondered and paused as he bounded up the garden path. But Tamarisk was at the door.

'Coo-ee,' he called. She was all fluffy in Cambridge blue, some arrangement of ruffles and ribbon unfamiliar to him.

'Where's the car?' she called back, and, 'Oh, dearest, you *can't* go like that.'

Frank kissed her forehead. 'How pretty you look,' he said. 'I haven't seen that before.' He took her arm. 'Come on. We mustn't be late.'

Tamarisk withdrew it. 'You simply cannot go like that,' she said, and added, 'Poppet.'

'Why not?' said Frank. 'It's not black tie.' In his elevated mood he simply could not be bothered to fiddle about with buttons and knots. But maybe there was a spattering of cake crumbs strewn about his person. 'Oh, all right,' he said.

'Good boy,' said Tamarisk. She began to make her way haltingly towards the street.

In front of the glass in his dressing-room wardrobe he saw that indeed a few squashed currants and a gingery crumb or two were clinging to the surface of his pullover. He whipped it off, battled his way into a clean shirt without undoing any but the top button, seized the nearest tie – he left them hanging by the loosened noose over the door handle – and ran down the stairs tightening it.

Tamarisk was just mounting the cab. She had the driver holding the door. 'You want to take a positive attitude to your body,' he was saying, 'like your old man back there. I don't expect he has much trouble with aches and pains.' Tamarisk gave a steely look from between the corn-yellow fronds that curled downwards like reversed horns on her forehead. 'I don't expect he does,' she replied.

At the reception, Frank settled her in the corner of a hard brocaded sofa and went to look for champagne. He ran into Max Vane.

'My dear fellow,' said Max.

'My dear fellow,' said Frank.

'You must come to the Opera again soon,' said Max.

'We'd adore to,' said Frank. 'Talk it over with Tamarisk. It'll cheer her up. She's still a bit unsteady on her pins.'

He glanced back to where he had left her alone on the sofa and saw that she had been joined by Daisy Middlesbrough and, of all people, Ted Ainsworth. She was speaking with some animation and the three of them had their heads quite close together. Every now and then they threw them back and trilled with laughter, even, to an extent, Ted. What could the joke be? wondered Frank. He blew his wife a kiss but she failed to see and he strolled on, disconcerted, in search of champagne.

Driving home past midnight, Max Vane put a hand on his wife's knee. 'Not too bored, my pussycat?' he said. Millie was twisting the feathers of her boa between fingertips. The long nails were painted black pearl. She gave a tight, closed smile. 'Just passable,' she said and flexed her hands. Even by her own standards, she had had an ace evening. Amateur painters both, HRH had spent some time with her, tête à tête, and had come over especially to say goodbye. Millie knew that she curtsied well. She was thankful that she had put on her sleek side-split Jean Muir which allowed a suggestion of the contours beneath to ripple as she swept her leg to one side and genuflected deeply.

'I suppose we couldn't ask him to the Opera,' she said in a high disinterested tone.

'Not impossible,' said Max. 'What would you think? Verdi? Mozart? Not Wagner.'

'*Andrea Chénier*,' said Millie promptly. 'He'd be flattered.'

Max took his eyes off the road. It was raining and the windscreen wipers blurred the bright light-holding drops into streaks that were sometimes even more difficult to see through than straight rain.

'Spot on,' he said, looking at her with admiration. 'You really do get it right, pussykins. There's even a new production coming up in six months. I'll look into it.' Millie gave a tiny sigh. Max judged the moment right to approach one or two other domestic matters requiring joint decisions. 'Consider for a moment, my pussy,' he said. 'Whom shall we have for *Fidelio*? I've already mentioned it to the Wetherbys.'

'I do wish you wouldn't pussy me,' said Millie. Max growled through his teeth. 'All right then – Tiger,' he said.

Millie pouted at him through the feathers. 'All right. Tiger,' she said and gave a long, despairing sigh. 'Come on then. Whom do we owe? How about Rose?'

'*Not* Rose,' said Max with unaccustomed vehemence. Millie looked at him with interest. 'Not Rose? Why not Rose? I always thought you thought she was the near-perfect young woman. You can't say she's losing her looks ...'

'She's become a bit of a bore lately,' said Max. 'She's getting serious about her work, or something. Oh, I don't know – let's ask her. It's not for a month. She'll probably be back to normal by then.'

'Certainly not,' said Millie, 'nuff said. Women who talk about their work are insufferable.'

'Quite,' said Max, 'then there's Connie Goodall. I've got to keep in with her so long as she's where she is. And she'd enjoy the cross-dressing – Gwynneth Jones' thighs, all that. D'you think she's a bit ...? I've always wondered.'

'Oh, of *course* she is,' said Millie. 'All right, Connie Goodall, plain but harmless. Who else?'

Keeping the ball thus offhandedly in play, the Vanes cast several essential social functions before they drew up outside their house in the upper part of Highgate.

'You've been so good, my tiger-baby,' said Max. He growled and nosed her nipple, shrouded but evident through the Jean Muir. Considering its start, the evening had gone extremely smoothly.

'Don't be tiresome,' snapped Millie. She held her skirt high and walked on up the long flagged pathway, shiny with rain, taking hobbled steps in her high-heeled shoes. Max watched her. An owl hooted. He put the car in the garage and ran after her up the stairs.

In the bedroom they settled, in their black pyjamas, into their twin beds, reached for their earplugs and turned out their lights. Max, soon, was asleep and strolling through marble halls full of laboratory technicians, androgynous in white coats, who presented their bottoms to him for pinching – all part of the experiment. Millie tossed and wriggled a little longer. Dissatisfaction, like crumbs under the skin, kept her dry and wakeful. It was a condition she was accustomed to.

26

Sam had a crutch. He hung on to it tenaciously at all times and took it into bed at nights. His bed was made of black iron and there were three others in the room. Each had two red blankets and the boys were meant to make them in the mornings. At home nobody ever interfered with the beds. They stayed undisturbed year in, year out in the same cocoon-like conformation of sheets and blankets to be wormed into at night and burst out of in the morning. He and Maggie often picked the pinhead-sized grey balls off the blankets. They were like snot to look at but quite different to feel and endless in number. They never knew who made them but it must have been when they were out or asleep, because they never caught anyone doing it. Maggie thought it was curls for dolls, but Sam said, 'Nah – somefink's laying eggs.' He was planning to run away, back to his real bed, as soon as he got some shoes, but he was not going to let them have the crutch back: he knew he would be needing it.

The first two days he had spent in the room alone, at first half-conscious and fogged-in from the injection at the hospital; then mute and wary as he tried to work out where he was. His foot hurt badly but his hands and arms were more or less as they had been: no wings, though he had examined them minutely when the bandages came off in hospital. A doctor and a nurse came in to look at him and ask him questions and sometimes the nurse came in on her own. She sat on the bed and chatted, or just sat. It was not difficult to ignore them both, though it made a change to have them there. He was worried: he knew his Dad would not be able to manage without him. He had to get home.

The other boys did not give him much trouble. They were a goofy-looking lot. One of them came over to look at him. He stood by the bed with a weird smile on his face and poked with a finger. He dribbled and Sam was glad when he went away. He put up his fists and stared hard and the boy shuffled away, making whimpering noises. But he kept coming back. At night one or two of them made noises in their sleep and cried out, loud enough, occasionally, to waken Sam, who wondered at that point how Maggie was getting on without him before going back to sleep. On the third day he was given clothes. A lady in a blue overall with a brooch on the lapel saying 'Eleanor' put them on the bottom of the bed and said, 'You can come down to breakfast today, Sam. We'll run through your timetable when you've finished and one of the boys will show you round.'

The clothes were OK: jeans and a pair of track shoes, but he wondered where his own had gone. He waited until the other boys had left before he put them on. Tears squeezed out of his eyes it hurt so much getting the shoe on his worst foot. He took his crutch and went into the corridor outside. It was a large one and high, with doors opening off either side and big windows at each end. The windows were not square like the windows at home but pattern-shaped with round bits and points. There were exterior iron stairways leading from both, but none of the windows would open. Outside there was grass and trees, big fir trees, one with low-sweeping branches that touched the ground. It looked more like the country than garden. He found a landing and some stairs. The stairs were made of stone and the banisters had patterned iron supports and the whole thing was huge, about the size of the old baths that were closed now that the new Leisure Centre had been built.

Sam ran his crutch along the banister rails and then leaned on the banisters themselves and scooted down to the bottom. Voices and the clatter of cutlery came from one direction. He went in the other.

Some of the doors he opened led into classrooms, some into offices and one into a big room with armchairs and a rocking-horse. None of the windows opened nor did any of the doors to outside. He put his nose right up to the glass in one and stared. The crutch slithered to the floor. He placed a foot on it and went on staring. There seemed to be no way through the trees, no path, no road, nothing. If he could lean out he might see something. He thought of breaking the glass and then that it might be better to leave it for later. What was on the other side? How long would it take him to walk home?

While he was thinking in this quiet place a whole lot of children surged in. Sam did not stir. A voice shouted above the noise. 'Line up, Crusaders'; 'Get your swimming things, Explorers'; 'Off to woodwork, Pioneers' – familiar teacher-like orders. Sam stayed absolutely still and by and by found himself alone again.

'Oh, there you are,' said a voice behind him. 'We've been looking for you everywhere. You've missed breakfast. You've got to do your tests now. Maybe we can get something from the kitchen on the way.' It was Eleanor. She sighed when he said nothing. 'Sam,' she enquired, 'can you hear me?' She took hold of his arm. Sam hardened his flesh, and she tugged. 'Maybe you need this,' she said and bent to pick up his crutch. But Sam reached down swiftly and picked it up before her. She backed away and looked at him. 'Follow me, then,' she said, 'if you can manage on your own.' She left the room without looking behind and Sam went after.

They went down passages, through swing doors into other passages, up and down short flights of stone steps and into a big kitchen. Eleanor said, 'This is a new patient – Sam Clark. He's missed breakfast. Can you oblige, please cook?'

The cook who wore a white apron and white hat had a brown face. He said, 'How do you expect me to do my work faced with such irregularities, please?' but he went away and came back with a plate and a mug on a tray. 'Sign here, please,' he said, producing an exercise book from which a pencil dangled on a string. Behind his back on

218

the far side of the room Sam could see a door. The door led into another room, smaller and darker. And in that room was another door, an open door, giving out on to a paved yard.

Eleanor led the way to a small room with a desk in it. She put the tray on the desk and drew up a chair. She waved at the chair. 'You must be hungry. Tuck in,' she said. Sam sat on the chair holding on to his crutch and thought about the door. Eleanor stood at the window with her back to him looking out. Every now and then she turned round as if they were playing Grandmother's Footsteps and turned away again with a sigh. Finally she said, looking at her watch, 'That's it Sam, I'm afraid. Time to go. You'll have to wait till lunchtime now.'

All morning he was taken to see different people who asked him different questions and put different things in front of him to do. He began to recognise bits of corridor and stairway. It was not difficult to pick up the lie of the land. At twelve o'clock Eleanor left him at the dining-room door. 'I'm going to leave you now, Sam,' she said. 'Mr Watkins – Steve – will take you this afternoon for physical exercise and assessment. He'll come and get you. You're a Pioneer. Have your lunch over at that table with the other Pioneers.' She pointed to a table at which Sam could see all the boys from his bedroom plus a dozen more. There was one empty chair. He stood in the lee of the doorway quite still until lunch was over. As soon as the room emptied he darted in and put two pieces of jam slice in his pocket, then he limped upstairs and ate them under the bed. It was there that Mr Watkins, come in search of him for 'activities', found him drowsing with his head on his crutch.

Though he did not know it, Sam was getting near the end of his tether. Prolonged exile was making him tetchy. He began to feel fractious at all times and uncharacteristically ill-disposed towards living things, animals included. 'Vicious' was a word that appeared in his reports. He lay awake in the night tearing at his flesh and wheezing, and on his irregular diet – crusts, remnants and hunks snatched from serving trolleys or hatches and consumed in secret places – he rapidly became not only spectre thin but ghoul-like in appearance. The general deterioration was spectacular and Rose, when she paid a visit on Saturday afternoon, was appalled. 'Oh Nat,' she said as they drove back. She stopped the car and wept and he put her head on his shoulder and patted her hair. He, too, was shocked and they completed the journey in silence.

But Sam's foot was healing. It no longer hurt to get shoes on and he could shin up trees quite easily especially with the aid of his crutch which he used to hurl up and hook over branches. In public, however, he kept up his limp. He became, as he had never been before, devious and crafty. After two weeks, driven by a yearning for home that was uncontainable, he concealed himself outside the kitchen for a whole half day. Round about two when no one was there but the cook, sitting with his back to him at the table and snoozing over his accounts, he stole in. The cook, reacting to some flutter in the atmosphere, stirred and looked up. He caught sight of Sam: 'Dacoit!' he cried and jumped to his feet. Sam thrust his crutch at him and dashed for the door. The cook, his feet entangled, tripped and crashed to the floor hitting his head on the table as he fell. He lay there, dazed, then sat himself shakily upright. He leaned against a table leg and put his fingers to his temples. They were red and wet. His head spun. 'Assassin,' he moaned and clambered to his feet to raise the alarm.

The yard where Sam found himself was paved and surrounded with small buildings all joined together. On one side there was an archway below a small tower with a clock in it. The arch had big wooden gates in it, closed, but with plenty of space, top and bottom. Sam rolled under and out into a driveway that led across the open grass and down into.the trees. The sound of carols came from behind him, the drone of many tuneless voices aimed at *Away In a Manger* on the long run-up to Christmas. He heard the sound break, bells ring, footsteps running, and sped, crouched low, for the sheltering tree whose branches swept the grass. He knew it well and was soon among the top branches, scratched, out of breath and with the bitter dusty taste of bark in his mouth and nostrils. It was cold up there now he had stopped running and sway-y like a swing. He wedged himself into a slim fork and watched Mr Watkins like a wind-up toy, running round and round on the grass shouting, 'Sam,' and other words he could not make out. He longed, suddenly, for Maggie.

It was dusk before the police arrived. Sam saw them get out of their car. They had a dog with them and he knew it was time to move on. The lights came on in the windows and he thought it was proba- bly teatime. Baked beans, bread and tea. He wondered if that was what they were having at home without him and started to slide, recklessly, down the tree. But it was too late. Before he got even to the widest part of the trunk but after the branches were too thick for him to see through, the dog was whining and pawing at its foot. He froze and climbed rapidly back up again and sat in the gathering dark observing the stars come out one by one and then, magically, all at once, all over the heavens.

By ten o'clock at night the police and the staff had pretty well set up camp down there round the foot of the tree. There was a tea urn, an ambulance and, by and by, a searchlight. A man kept shouting up at him through a megaphone and Mr Watkins made several attempts, with the aid of a ladder, to get up the tree himself. At first, Sam felt quite comfortable with all the attention but it got cold and the searchlight was much too bright (unlike the lamp in the welfare room at school). It burned right through him and, though he shut himself down as tight as he was able, the unrelenting beam made his head swim.

Wakeful and shivering he watched the slow hours of the night pass imperceptibly one into the next. Now and again, though his eyes never closed, his limbs slackened and his grip loosened. He wobbled and lurched before tensing himself back into position. It was at one of these moments that he focused his eyes to a disturbance in the branches beneath and saw a face arising, a helmeted face, hard-eyed and unsmiling. He kicked out at it with all his might, seized his crutch and brought it down on the head which slowly rose disclosing a body harnessed to some kind of contraption. He struggled to insert the crutch and lever the body off but the man lunged, wrapped his arms round Sam and dislodged him with a single heave. He was pinioned, wriggling, kicking, biting, butting, and lowered in the hard blaze of the searchlight to the ground and the encircling watchers below. There was a murmur of voices.

'Careful now,' said the man in whose arms he was trapped, 'This one bites!'

'Sam,' said the voice of Mr Watkins, 'thank God you're safe. Whatever ...' But Sam had gone.

In the instant of adaptation between above-reach to ground level, as the emergency changed gear, Sam espied a gap. Like a bullet he made for it and the blackness beyond. He knew where to go. From the treetop, the topography was imprinted under his skull and he had seen the dog depart many hours gone by. Before the hue and cry could get under way he had reached the trees. He plunged straight into the thicket and, having no superfluous matter on his mind or frame, bored through the undergrowth at a surprising rate. Where the plantation was at its narrowest and most dense the stout surrounding wall gave way to a shallow ditch filled with barbed wire, held to be impenetrable. Sam tore his way through close to the ground, wielding his crutch before him like a snout. Whenever the thud of boots and the flashing of torchlight drew near he lay still, no more remarkable than a collection of broken twigs.

Beyond the ditch was a strip of scruffed roadside wood and beyond that, motorway. Sam came upon it from the top of a bank and stood, watching the sweep and curve of it to either side, the perforations of light twinkling like Christmas strings at intersections far away, and the dazzling whizz of passing traffic intermittent at that time of night. For a few seconds he hesitated. Which way was home?

Then he noticed there was a reddish haze low in the sky in one direction only. He slid down the bank and started walking towards it, taking great care to conceal himself whenever he was able.

Some time in the late afternoon next day he reached his own street. A funny feeling overcame him when he turned into it. It started in his chest which felt as if it was growing bigger. Then the insides of his elbows, the tops of his legs, his arms and knees went floppy. His throat started to wobble and he stumbled. He had to force his feet to put themselves one in front of the other; the more he forced them, the farther the front gate slipped away. The air went round and round in front of his eyes and his head was as floaty as a balloon. He stumbled up the garden path and found the key in the milk bottle. Its unwashed smell filled his nostrils with such relief he could scarcely breathe. He unlocked the door with hands that shook and stepped inside his own home. He felt warm all over, wave after wave of warmth filled him up from top to toe. He lay down on the old linoleum with his head under the table and went to sleep.

Maggie saw him first. They had come back from visiting her mother, now transferred to the hospital's psychiatric wing, an ornate brick building in an outlying reach of the borough. It was a long trek. Before that, her father had spent the hours of the afternoon in the Council Offices, stalled between one desk and the next. They were going down to Fiveways to see Sam at last. It was all arranged. But his work was collapsing: the goodwill his customers allowed him was paper-thin and his earnings were becoming frighteningly few.

Maggie was not surprised to see Sam. She let go her father's hand, scudded over the floor and lay down with her head close up to his, looking into his eyes. Sam opened his. He and Maggie smiled at one another. Their father, after his first start of astonishment, let out a cry, strode over and, crouched on his haunches beside them, gathered both children to him and sat holding them close. All three were welded by intense emotion for some minutes. Then Sam spoke. 'I couldn't make it any quicker, Dad,' he said and slid off his father's lap to light the gas for tea. He felt right as rain as he filled the kettle and stood on a chair to unhook the mugs. Maggie skipped round him and they had a pretend fight. He warmed the pot from the kettle, feeling strong enough to lift a cauldron to the sky, and while he busied himself with these household tasks he could not prevent his lips from grinning all over his face. When he carried his mother's thin china cup and saucer carefully across, his father put out a hand. 'Mum's away, lad,' he said, 'she's still in hospital. They've moved her to St Bernard's. We're just back.' He looked Sam steadily in the eye. Sam looked back: he knew now for sure he should not have let them keep him away so long. He nodded at his father and gave Maggie a little punch on the cheek.

That night they all slept in the same room together. Sam's father lit the geyser. It leaped out at them with a flash and a juddering reverberation which made them all squeal and hug each other. Sam and Maggie had a bath. The steam was so dense it ran down the walls in quick rivulets as the children played at ghosts, foghorns and whales, and the water cooled turning murky and the skin on their fingers puckered into ridges.

'I hid in a van, Dad,' said Sam. He felt very sleepy, so sleepy he could hardly be bothered to nest himself into the blankets properly. Maggie was already asleep between them.

'Did you, lad?' said his father. He patted his son's damp locks and prepared himself for a watchful night on the edge of the bed. Little by little, however, he too dropped off and slipped into seamless sleep as deep and smooth as the night between stars.

Next day, Sam was out when the police came for him. He took Maggie to school, his father went to work on time for his first job and for a few hours life was back running on its familiar rails. He revisited his territory systematically. Nothing had changed except there were Christmas trees and old-fashioned writing with snowflakes in most of the shop windows. Little was left of his camp by the canal. He spent a good hour or two restoring it but it was colder now. He nicked a Big Mac in the usual way when he needed it and kicked stones around and threw sticks and minded his own business in his own way, which was fine by him. He wondered whether to set out for St Bernard's but then he thought he would leave it until next day. He would nick something nice for Mum and take it over tomorrow. It was good being back.

Meanwhile, the police paid a call on Meadowbrook school. Mrs Upjohn led them round into Infants. Maggie was withdrawn from class and questioned. 'When Did You Last See Your Brother?' She kept her eyes on the policeman's face and said nothing. They got stiller and larger as he blustered and bribed. 'She's a quiet one,' said her teacher, come to fetch her back. 'It's not often we get a word out of Maggie.'

Mrs Upjohn reported back. She tapped her forehead and shook her head with a significant look. 'Something wrong with the whole family, if you ask me,' she told Mr Lovejoy.

Mr Lovejoy put it about that Sam was on the run, that the whole family was in trouble. There were darker undertones implicit in the rumours as they seeped through the school. Any sighting of Sam and he was to be immediately informed. Rose, out at the swimming-pool most of the morning, buried at the back of classrooms 'hearing' children read from reading books, floundering and thoroughly miserable in her work, got the word from Nat at lunchtime. 'I'm not surprised,' she said. She half-wondered whether to dash out to a telephone box and try to get hold of Lady Goodall, but her bravado was wearing thin. She and Nathan simply looked at one another in wordless distress and walked back to their classrooms. That morning she had received a letter in answer to hers from the Director of Education's office. It said that the Director of Education was in receipt of her letter and would be looking into the matter further on his return.

The spectre of Sam, feral and at bay in the recreation room at Fiveways, nagged at her heart; urgent, restless and unappeased.

The police went back in their car and sat in it outside Sam's home for an hour or two. Though they lounged and bantered, fiddling with the radio and exchanging mild insults with the WPC on duty at the station, they were on the alert. This was no run-of-the-mill local truancy case but a hardened young delinquent of Houdini-like cunning and with a growing reputation for violence from an unnaturally unco-operative family. There was no knowing what bad blood would get up to.

Not long after five Sam and Maggie skidded sideways into the street. They were playing a game of barging, striking shoulders in mid-run. It was surprising how accurate and stable an opponent Maggie could be. They were both grunting with effort and shouting with laughter. Beneath his clothing, its white icing hairy with wool from the underside of his pullover, Sam was carrying a Chelsea bun. He saw the police car and froze. 'Go home, Mags,' he said giving her a push and melted away. The police, reacting a fraction of a second later to a flutter in the driving mirror, saw a scrap of a girl walking slowly down the street with her head down, scuffing the toes of her shoes on the pavement. 'That's her,' they said to each other and watched as she drew abreast and turned to clamber through the broken gate and hop up the path on her haunches. One of the police-men strolled over. Maggie, still on her haunches and making nibbling movements with her mouth, shook a key out of a milk bottle.

'Hullo, there,' said the policeman in a friendly voice.

Reaching up, Maggie unlocked the back door, hopped over the threshold and looked at the policeman through the crack. She gave a squeak and shut it in his face.

'Hold on there!' said the policeman. 'There's a few questions I want to ask you, young lady.' He banged on the door. 'Open up,' he said sternly. He drew himself up and waited for the weight of his words to take effect. 'Open up! Police here.' But Maggie had scuttled up the stairs and was burrowed deep under the bedclothes where she was holding an imaginary conversation with the naughty baby bunnies she had left at home all day.

Sam kicked his heels for an hour or so. He kept himself well concealed and off the public thoroughfares. He eventually re-entered his own home through the bathroom window. His father was still out working. Maggie was conducting her own world, deeply absorbed in a realm with logic and structure of its own. Sam slipped into it, the boundaries shifted to accommodate him and they played without friction for another hour or two. Then as enigmatically as it had begun, the game finished. They found some food, ate it and went to bed. Sam left tea in the pot and wrote a note: 'Der Dad, Good Night, Love from Sam.' He felt fulfilled.

Next day when he had taken Maggie to school, he set out for St Bernard's. He left his crutch safe at home. On the way he picked up a magazine with a picture of a lady in a red dress and high-heeled red shoes on the cover. The lady had cherry-red lips and Sam reckoned his Mum would like it best. He jumped on a bus at the traffic lights and off it before the conductor came round. He travelled thus on a series of buses hanging on by the chromium pole on the platform, swinging along the hand holds inside and crocodiling over seat backs on the top deck. Furious conductors caught him at it from time to time and chased him off. He had a great time.

St Bernard's was a purpose-built institution constructed by the Victorians who believed that light, loftiness and outdoor occupation were beneficial to sick minds. It was huge, with an unbroken red wall all round the grounds. As his bus sped the length of one side Sam leaned out into the rush of air and let himself off. Back on board women shoppers clutched their plastic bags and pensioners gasped while Sam's legs went faster than ever before in his life. As he slowed down his breath came in rib-cracking gulps and his heart thumped at speed, but he was still upright. He whistled between his teeth as he squeezed in through a side door, so missing the police-car waiting for him at the main gate.

Once inside it took several hours to find his Mum. He went

through every ward, inspected every bed and looked behind every closed door. He found her finally at the end of a ground floor ward sitting in a wheelchair with a blanket over her knees, like a passenger in an observation car, staring through the windows with flat eyes. He was so pleased his heart bopped with delight. He stood by her chair, put the magazine in her lap and smiled. She smiled back and put out a hand to touch his head. The shadows that drifted through her tranquillised world were without substance or affect. The touch brought feeling and slow tears rolled out of her eyes, over her slack cheeks and dripped down on them both. Sam leaned against the chair. He put his head on her knee and would have climbed into her lap but something made him feel shy. They stayed like that for some time, close but quiet. Neither action nor words were required, just the rhythms of one another's presence which soon smoothed into one.

A voice broke into this reverie: 'No visitors before six on Wednesdays,' it said. 'You can come and see mother later. She's got to have her injection now,' and Sam was shepherded out of the ward, into the corridor outside. There, a young man in blue uniform with a flat cap under his arm pushed himself off the wall against which he had been leaning and barred the way. 'You Sam Clark?' he said. Sam, elsewhere, nodded as he walked round him. It was only when the policeman gripped him by the upper arm and he heard the crackle of the walkie-talkie that fright seized him and he tried to spring away.

Although Sam went through the motions, flailing, punching and even spitting, the struggle he put up was muted. He was dazed from the reunion with his mother and his fighting spirit had lost its edge. He experienced an unfamiliar change in mood which became sullen and resentful. He stumbled along in the policeman's grip, trying to kick him round the ankles and trip him up. When two other policemen, summoned from the squad car, came pacing down the corridor to help subdue him they simply fell in beside their colleague.

Sam went slack and let himself be dragged. It felt horrible. As they bundled him into the car, Maggie and their father arriving in good time for visiting hours, passed by quite close, anonymised among the relatives and friends converging on the hospital in ones and twos. The squad-car nosed its way through and Maggie tugged her father's hand. 'Mhm, mhm,' she squeaked, rising on to tiptoe. Inside the car, Sam's face, moth-pale, glimmered, barely visible. His eyes picked up Maggie's without animation; a single frame and the moment was gone. Maggie hid her face in her father's hand and he, seeing only the police car, brushed away a presentiment of unease and proceeded stoically on his way to visit his deranged wife.

27

When Rose drives into school next morning she finds James Potterton waiting at the staff entrance. He runs in after her car, a strictly illegal move, and stands puffing as she steps out. A large sheet of paper flaps in his hand and his chubby frame, well muffled for it's a frosty morning, seems about to burst with importance.

'Oh, James,' says Rose, 'Hullo, Good Morning, but *what* are you doing coming in this way? You *know* it's against the rules.'

'I've got something,' says James with extreme gravity. 'You'll like it. It's for you.'

All round them staff are getting out of cars, hoicking bicycles into concrete slots, hurrying up from Underground and bus stop. One or two give James a disapproving glance and Rose catches sight of Mrs Upjohn's sharp nose behind a window pane.

'Come on, let's go round to the boys' entrance.'

James's mouth tightens. He plants his feet more firmly on the asphalt.

'I'm dying to see it,' says Rose and starts for the gate. There's a pause before she hears his footsteps behind her, running.

'Slow down,' he says with some indignation. 'It's fragile.'

'What can it be?' says Rose.

Inside the boys' entrance they stop to one side of the stream, and Rose looks down at James.

'For what you are about to see may the Lord make you truly thankful,' says James and, with a flourish, turns the sheet of paper around. He keeps a close watch on her face. Rose sees an expanse of colour and movement. He's drawn a boat bucking on serpentine waves of blue; the waves are full of fish, smiling, and the boat, of people, shouting, waving, trailing pennants and scarves, in stripes, spots, checks – all the primary colours under the sun; flags fly from the funnels out of which steam loops into a blue sky. There are birds in the sky and from the top corner a yellow sun smiles. It makes Rose laugh aloud.

'Do you like it?' demands James.

'Yes. I like it very much. I think it's marvellous.'

'Do you think it's very good?'

'Very good? What do you think?'

'I think it's very, very good. It's my best work. It took hours and hours and hours.'

'Tell me about it.'

James spreads the drawing on the ground and they kneel at each corner. Behind them a few children are still arriving and inside the school the bell rings for Assembly. 'Guess which one's me,' says James. On top of the superstructure, orange and purple striped, is a figure drawn much larger than the rest, waving a top hat in one hand and a Union Jack in the other.

'You tell me. Which is you?'

'That's me. And this is my Mum. She's driving the boat and I'm telling her where to go.'

'How does that feel?' Rose ignores the voice in her head, almost visible like a balloon in a cartoon saying 'You're going to be late', and the decision is to cost her, ultimately, her job.

'Great,' says James. 'I'm a bit frightened of sharks but my Mum knows where they are.'

'Your Mum knows where the sharks are. That's good. Which one is she?'

For the next five minutes they crouch side by side going through the picture.

'It's a present,' says James.

'Thank you,' says Rose.

'I might give it to my Mum,' says James.

'We must go in now. Why not give it to me for today and you can take it back and give it to your Mum after school?'

They run across the empty playground. In the school, no one's about and the boom of Mr Lovejoy's voice, rising and falling, sounds from the hall.

'Where shall I go?' says James, suddenly deflating. He shrinks against her. 'I don't know what to do.' The sheet of paper trails from his hand on the floor. As Rose wonders too, Mrs Upjohn comes running down the stairs, clackety-clack on the wooden soles of her Dr Scholl sandals. She takes hold of James's hand. 'Where have you been, James Potterton? You're late.'

James lets out a screech. 'You're hurting me,' he yowls. 'Oh, Miss, save me.'

Mrs Upjohn gives his hand a jerk. 'Be quiet. You're to come with me. And as for you -' she turns to Rose, 'poor Miss Bunting, as if she didn't have enough to do, has had to leave her class and take the second years swimming ...'

'Oh, dear,' says Rose, 'I'll dash after her. She'll be back before the end of Assembly.' She watches Mrs Upjohn, her back quivering with disapproval, drag James towards the stairs. At the bottom step James turns, screws one side of his face into an outsize wink and lets the sheet of paper drop from his hand.

For the rest of the day Rose toils, against the grain of her inclination, to do what's required of her. She's begun to see why no one in the staffroom ever talks about the children they're teaching. There's nothing to say from an authoritarian perspective: to consider them as individuals of interest or concern in their own right would undermine that perspective. They have to be dehumanised.

Confined at the back of Mr Foster's classroom to the most mechanical aspects of literacy and obliged to stifle her curiosity, she feels half alive. The children, she knows, must be bored stiff. The knowledge that she has betrayed them makes her keep to the staffroom at breaks where there's no fear of meeting their eyes. Most of those who had been in her groups avoid her anyway. James's offering of that morning is an earnest of the work they've done together. She finds it infinitely consoling and it's at the back of her mind most of the day. As it is in James's.

At every possible moment he waylays her. 'Are you looking after it properly?'; 'My mother'll be cross if you don't.' There are other manifests to be seen about the place. Selma now has regular company in the playground. She walks round and round it, hand-in-hand with two other little girls from her class and often crouches in a corner with them rapt in some mysterious game. Whenever she passes Rose by she smiles at her shyly. One or two of the others she had taught seem more integrated with their peers, but Simon looks desperate, forever bandaged and scabbed in some new area of his body, while Gary and Wendy shoulder past her with scorn. She still sees Elaine.

'There's not much harm she can do to that poppet,' said Mr Lovejoy to himself, as he initialled the new timetable. Pink-cheeked Elaine skipped primly into her sessions, grey cardigan buttoned over the stout curve of her stomach, clean socks neatly turned down. Her behaviour was as complex and foxing as ever. It seemed each time to be on the verge of adding up but remained perpetually just beyond comprehension. Except at moments, she was almost totally illiterate.

One bright November morning as sun poured through the plate glass she came dancing in and, without sitting down, dictated a story: 'One day there was a witch a very nasty witch,' she said. 'She had lots of things to wear, long dresses, small dresses and flat dresses and thin dresses, very thin. She dressed up like a human being but she had one problem and that was her nose. It stuck out like an elephant's. So she had to have her nose amputated. When she came home she said, "Oh, can I do some spells? – Your nose! the mother said. Why, you can't do your spells without your nose ..."' Elaine stopped speaking. She looked acutely unhappy. Her cheeks were geranium-red. She stared out of the window. After a long time she said dreamily, 'That's the end of the witch because she died.' She sat down and turned to Rose. 'I don't like you,' she said brightly.

At the end of the session she kissed Rose and skipped away. Rose stared after her. She sometimes felt her pupils had read a chapter on symbol formation or the meaning of fairytales before they came to her, but it was all so scrambled in Elaine's case. What scrambled it? She pummelled her temples. An ominous noise swelled up from the hall below. She was meant to be taking the fifth-years swimming and fetching the fourth-years back. She jumped up and ran – straight into Mr Lovejoy. She tried to hurry on but he blocked her way. 'Might I have a word with you after school, Mrs Pitt? – *if* you can spare the time,' he said.

At the end of the afternoon she knocked on his door. 'Wait for me, Nat,' she said, before she went in, 'please. I'm sure it's going to be something awful.'

Mr Lovejoy was standing behind his desk; his pipe smouldered in a tin ashtray on it. He did not sit down. He said, 'Mrs Pitt, it has come to my attention that you have been in correspondence with the – Director of Education in this authority (his voice dropped as he spoke the words) and ... and ... the *Minister of Education* herself ... about matters concerning' – he paused and breathed in – '*this school* ...' He swayed like an inflated balloon on cardboard feet.

'But Mr Lovejoy,' said Rose. She had to squeeze the words in with an effort for the room was so filled with outrage, 'Mr Lovejoy – I sent you a copy ...'

'Mrs Pitt,' said Mr Lovejoy, 'I am speaking.' He turned a colour approaching dull plum and raised his voice. 'Naturally, the correspondence has been passed to me for my comment. I ...'

'But Mr Lovejoy,' shouted Rose, 'you've got it. Why didn't you do anything about it then?'

She began to feel frightened. He was quivering. It was all mad and there was no one to help her. Wherever she turned, people turned away. At a loss for words, she hung her head and, just in time, a picture, dazzling in purple and orange, flashed through her mind. Flags flew, bands played, the sun smiled out of blue sky. There was Sam's little bear in its boot; Elaine's witch with no nose. She raised her eyes and stood her ground. He shouted back: 'The proper procedures have been followed. They have nothing whatever to do with you. I must insist that you withdraw your accusations in writing.' He thumped the desk and the pipe jumped in its tin ashtray. 'This is my school. I will be obeyed.' He sat, suddenly.

'I haven't accused anyone of anything,' said Rose. 'I simply ...'

'Mrs Pitt,' Lovejoy's voice trembled, 'Are you arguing with me?' He came out from behind the desk. 'I shall expect your withdrawal in writing by the end of the week. And Mrs Pitt –' he bore down on her, a cross-Channel ferry on a sailing dinghy, and Rose was forced to step back. 'I must insist on punctuality in my staff members. Not only did you cause severe disruption by your own unpunctuality this morning but you also wilfully caused a pupil to be late. Mrs Pitt, your conduct is far from satisfactory.'

By now, Rose had her back to the door and Mr Lovejoy's voice had reached thunder pitch, reverberating round the room and setting up a hubbub among the particles. He reached round behind her back and wrenched the door open, so close upon her she could feel the zigzag lines of anger radiating from him. She tried to take a step forward but was obliged to retreat. She found herself, once again, alone in the corridor outside with the door shut behind her.

It's open war now, was the thought that came to mind, as she walked slowly away and her senses adjusted to the absence of commotion.

'What!' said Nat. 'You didn't even insist he showed you the letters? Oh, Rose.'

It was very quiet in the pub. Shafts of dusty light from the low winter sun slanted through the coloured glass and hit the patterned carpet in twinkling patches filled with slow-moving haze. Rose stared at them. She's looking a bit dusty herself, thought Nat; not quite so spanking fresh and crisp these days. There were even a few hairs on the back of her jacket. Grubby satin bra straps, unmade beds, his mouth filled with saliva and he swallowed several times.

'Perhaps I could request copies direct from the offices that sent them,' said Rose. 'I'd have the right, wouldn't I?'

Nat shook his head. 'I shouldn't think so. Really they should send you copies as a matter of form. You haven't had any replies yet, have you?'

'Not unless they've come today. I leave before the postman. Oh, Nat. Sam … I don't know what to do.'

Nat watched her. Tears were drizzling over her cheekbones. He fished a handkerchief from his pocket and pressed it into her hand. 'Wipe your eyes, Princess,' he said and he was laughing. Rose shot him a furious glance. She blew her nose hard, a rich multi-stage trumpet. If he was laughing, it couldn't be so bad. She gave him a cautious flicker of a smile. Her hair was a mess, her nose shone like a strawberry and eye make-up smudged her cheeks. 'It occurs to me,' she said in a shaky voice, 'that I could fight this better from outside. Should I resign? But the children – oh! You don't *know* what James Potterton did today and Elaine. They mustn't be let down; I won't, I can't,' and she started crying again. This time, Nat put his arm round her.

'There are channels,' he said, 'but they're dreadfully slow. I don't know whether you should resign, you might lose your foothold. Perhaps we could discuss it with Gerry.' He got up. 'I've got to go. It's my weight-lifting night. I'll come home with you first if you like.' He held out his hands and Rose took them. She hardly noticed what she was doing, but Nat had never held her hands in his. The sensation unsettled him. He withdrew his and put them in his pockets. They walked back to the school, Rose, painfully preoccupied; Nat, battling to cleanse his thoughts, and drove to South Kensington without speaking. 'It's nice of you to be there,' said Rose, turning a blotched face towards him.

Among the letters on her mat were four in thin biscuit-coloured envelopes. One was franked OHMS, the others THAMESFORD THE BOROUGH THAT CARES. There was also a thick blue one emblazoned with Frank's faint runaway script. Rose snatched at it. Nat, school, the children were flushed from her mind. She put it in the pocket of her skirt and fingered it like a miser. Then she looked guiltily back and held up the brown letters. 'Look, this might be them,' she said. Nat, on the pavement, nodded. 'Looks like it,' he said and half turned. 'Oh, won't you wait while I open them?' cried Rose. She ran back and took his arm. 'Come up and have a cup of coffee. It'd be lovely to have you there when I read them. Nat's upper arm made contact with the wool-covered curve of her breast. He felt his arm flush. 'Why not?' he said, 'the gym's this end of town.'

They climbed the stairs. At the top, Rose, slightly breathless, unlocked the door. Nat followed her in.

'What a lovely room!'

The white attic was golden with light. With its wicker chairs and board floor it reminded Nat of a famous picture. A wicker chair by a dormer window, he could not quite place it. He walked over to look out and saw the London roofscape, hazy in all its diverse improbability, streaked with occasional bars of liquid gold where the dying sun picked up a reflection, pricked with the first lamps twinkling on the streets and spread out like an elaborate carpet that covered the earth as far as the eye could see. He gave a silent whistle and leaned out. A pigeon took off from the parapet below with a wooden flapping of its lavender wings. He turned in again. Rose was on the other side of the room in an alcove. The windows there were fringed on the outside with geraniums standing stiffly against the paling lemon sky.

'What a nice place,' he said again.

'Coffee?' called Rose, 'or I think there's gin? What would you like?' She could not bear his being there, a thickset alien on her territory. She made her movements deliberately jaunty and lightened her voice. She was not going to give anything away.

'Coffee, if you're making some. White with two sugars,' said Nat. Rose ignored the 'if you're making some', and prepared a single cup.

She opened the OHMS letter first. It was from the Secretary of State's own office and said that Rose's complaint had been passed to the relevant authority for further investigation.

Of the three from THE BOROUGH THAT CARES, two were from deputies in the Director of Education's office. Both said that the Director of Education had received her complaint and was passing it on to the appropriate department and to the headmaster of Meadowbrook Junior School for further investigation.

The third was from Customer Services, THAMESFORD THE BOROUGH THAT CARES and was on thicker whiter paper. The paper had embossed shiny lettering on it and a logo hinting at blue water, green meadow and white seagull. It addressed itself to *Dear Rose*, covered two pages describing services available within THAMESFORD THE BOROUGH THAT CARES and was signed, *Sandra* in a backward sloping hand. 'For your convenience,' said the letter, 'you have been allocated a personal reference number and if you would like a further chat about things don't hesitate to contact me on the above.' A number of leaflets, quasi-cartoon in style plus an offer, FREE, for airmiles, were included. Rose gathered up the lot and took them over to the wastepaper-basket.

'Don't do that!' said Nat.

'What d'you mean, don't do that?' said Rose. She looked at him, so square, in one of her lovingly collected old wicker chairs. He was exactly the stodgy, law-abiding sort of person bureaucracy fed on. She crumpled some sheets and flung them into the basket.

Nat stood. 'Seriously Rosie,' he said, 'you may need those. It could be important.' He went over to the basket and took them out.

Rosie! thought Rose. He was no good. All very well at school, but not here. She must get rid of him. He was smoothing out the papers on her scrubbed deal table top. She gave a little laugh, as offhand as she could make it, and pulled them from under his fingertips. 'This really is rubbish. You must see that,' she said and tore them into little bits. She looked up at him. 'I've got to change now, and won't you be late for your boxing, or whatever it is?'

Nat looked down into her face. There was very little make-up left on it but smudges beneath the eyes. Her lips were quite white and he could smell her hair. She looked like a pert gypsy girl; Eliza Dolittle. 'You're being very provocative,' he said. His voice was thick. He put his arms round her and pulled her to him, crushed so tight she was immobilised by the pressure. He brought his mouth down on hers covering it right over and his hard blunt tongue in a succession of little stabs, forced a way through her lips, which he prised open with his. He felt Rose struggle, squeak and blow, flutter and grow soft. He felt her kiss him back and the absolute sweetness of the moment was so intense that he drew back from it aware that he had broken his own code. He dropped his arms and stepped back. 'I'm sorry,' he said, 'I find you extraordinarily attractive. But I also think you're a good teacher and a good woman up against a rotten system. I mustn't let the two get mixed. It won't happen again. I'll speak to you tomorrow.' He walked away from her and out of the flat. Rose felt the vibration of the stairs as he ran down them and the bang of the door as he reached the street.

She stood where he had left her for some time. She put up the fingers of her left hand and touched them all round her mouth, then she went to the wastepaper-basket and picked out the pieces. She spread them over the table and began fitting them together, all except the thick white bits from Customer Services. She thought that maybe the state of being in love was one of heightened receptivity and could account for the unexpected warmth of her response to Nat, rather as drunkards needed little more than a thimbleful to make them, apparently, drunk from cold sober. The more you practise any sport, she thought, the easier you can do it well anywhere with anyone. The thought tickled her fancy and made her feel quite giggly. It could be rather fun to have two lovers, a reserve to fill in the aching blanks that Frank left. It would be positively good for her and she could manage Nat: he would be astounded by the things she knew how to do.

She began to imagine some of them and stopped herself, shocked. How could she have forgotten Sam? What could she do? Short of kidnapping him, what could she do. She played around inside that fantasy for a while: a sunny upland, Sam and Maggie, laughing, hand-in-hand, tumbling with the other children in the grass, painting, acting, reading stories and writing them, blossoming. And Nat, running a football game in an adjacent meadow; she could hear the happy shouts. But where would Frank be? She tried to imagine him, benign, amused, admiring, at her elbow, for ever – and remembered the letter in her pocket. She took it out and kissed the scrawly writing. It gave her an idea: when she had finished reading it, she would write a long letter to Lady Goodall, not as Minister but woman to woman and deliver it to her house. She sat on the bed and opened the letter. It was postmarked Yorkshire. What was he doing up there in the middle of the week?

There were the '*darlings*' sloped across the page, a dozen, and the '*love yous*', only ten. It said, besides, that he had been having a too funny time at Tees House going round the old dairies and pigsties. They had found a mechanical pig feeder and, even more exciting, an early milking machine, maybe the first, dated 1891. Rubber-cushioned cows' horns were affixed to the teats and thence, via a series of tubes, to a suction pump. When the udders emptied the horns fell off. Too mad. Oh, darling he missed her so. Now he was in Grassdale, all alone for the night and going over to Ted Ainsworth's tomorrow. There were three pages. Rose read them again and again leaving the final paragraph till last. She expected endearments, suggestive ones that would make her tingle and yearn. Instead, she read: 'Too boring, my angel, I've got to go away, far, far away over the silver crawling sea to, of all places, Oronada.

How I hate having to miss Proper English Christmas, but these things have to be done, O my darling, sometimes. We'll see each other lots before. There's at least three more weeks.'

The import of the lines was more than Rose could bear. She fended it off and went to look for a drink. There was nothing in the flat. She took her purse and ran to the nearby Wine Merchants, bought a quarter bottle of brandy; brandy was good for emergencies, and ran back up with it. She looked at the letter again. It still said the same. She read it over very slowly to make sure she had got all the words right. They began to hurt. She swallowed some brandy. It burned but the words hurt through it. They were going to hurt much more if she did not do something about it. Questions started knocking on her mind, each one so painful she flinched. Was she going to lose him? Was his – his – wife going with him? Christmas. She must be. Could he steal a few days for them to be together on some island in the Caribbean? She would fly anywhere to be near him, any time. Her craving was so great she would go now. She would find out where he was and wait for him outside the door. Their bodies would touch and the world would stop screaming. And she would put it to him and he could plan it and they could escape for a timeless slice of paradise such as they had often dreamed of. If she had that to hold on to, a jewel in her fantasy, she could survive.

So Rose seized the first outdoor garment that came to hand, a black trenchcoat, flung it round her shoulders and put the brandy in the pocket. Outside it was nearly dark and had begun to rain. She put her arms through the sleeves and took a draught of brandy. There was no moon, no stars, no light but the fuzzed halo round the street lamps hatched with lines of driving rain. She set her car on course for St Pancras. The letter had been posted yesterday: he might well come down tonight after spending the day with Ainsworth Agridustrials.

A train from Edinburgh via York was just due. She got to the barrier as it drew in. Doors started flapping open down the length of it and the bare platform came alive with passengers all making for her, at differing speeds. The first of them, hurrying with briefcases, drew up and passed on. Frank was not one for scurrying. She pocketed her hands, kept her head high and raised one eyebrow in a look of casual anticipation. They were crowding through the barrier now, an unheeding clutch of bundles empty-eyed with suitcases on casters. Far down at the end of the line a solitary door opened and a long figure stepped out. The movement of the heart from its customary position at such moments is very like a foetal kick. Rose's heart gave just such a kick. She slipped round the barrier and ran along the platform, but long before she remembered that strolling would be more appropriate, she had slowed down. It was not he. She walked right to the end of the train looking into the empty compartments and back again. Her mouth was trembling at the corners.

Austere at the best of times, the station had a peculiarly derelict air. It was a place to hurry home from. Rose walked back to her car. She swallowed some brandy and wiped the tears from under her eyes. She must get to Frank. She drove to his house and parked a little way off on the opposite side of the street. The house was full of light seeping from behind drawn curtains and the street, of unlit parked cars, one or two of them, she observed, with chauffeurs snoozing at the wheel. She sat tight, shivering a little, and trying not to blink as she watched the front door. There was a blast of light and laughter. It opened and across the driving rain she saw Frank's form, inclined to its most affable degree as he saw a second tall figure out. There seemed to be some sort of party going on inside. A chauffeur hurried up the path with a big umbrella and the door closed again. A limousine with blackened windows and a sheathed flag on the bonnet swept past.

Next time the door opened, Rose stepped immediately out and ran across the wet road. She opened the garden gate and slipped up the path dodging the departing guests as they came down it. She got to the door just as Frank was about to close it. 'Darling!' she said. He looked at her and without breaking the rhythm of his movement, shut the door. Against the dark street, he must not have seen me, thought Rose. She rang the bell. He opened it. 'I'm so sorry,' he said in ringing tones, 'you've made a mistake, I'm afraid. That's farther down the road. What a wretched night to miss the way,' and closed the door.

Rose had no memory of what happened then. She found herself walking fast along unknown streets. The rain had stopped, leaving glinting puddles, the pavements had turned shiny anthracite and the carriageway held a mosaic of light beneath its gleaming black surface. There was no one about. She walked faster. She would walk all night and literally wear out her heartache and the sense of shame now so unpleasantly coming down on her in sickening waves. She reached the canal and walked along the bank. She could always jump in. It looked very black and even by this light the water had a treacly aspect. She pulled up her sleeve and tested it out. It was icy. Not until her arm was numb did she withdraw it and leave the canal behind. It was always there. She should not be so far from Frank's. He would probably come out to find her when his last guest had gone. That was what he must have meant when he said 'further down the road'. She had to get back there quickly.

She hurried through the cold streets. Every corner, in passable resemblance to the one she sought, egged her on. Round each, she conjured his figure, beloved, known from every angle and no more improbable now than at any of the other manifestations of pure magic that had characterised their relationship from the start. O my darling, she thought. I'll explain. You'll understand. We'll make it up. She turned into his street and walked the length of it, looking into every front garden. Then she came back and stood outside his house. There was not a crack of light. Only the suffused roar and hiss of traffic moving in incessant streams on the main road over the tarmac hill broke into the stillness. She walked up the path to press herself against the front door. There was peculiarly little comfort she found, though she tried, in the thought of how many times his hands had touched it.

Very damp, she went back to her car and had the last of the brandy, hunched behind the wheel. She yawned, a maximum yawn that strained the hinges of her jaw. Almost without knowing she switched on the ignition, and drove away. Her limbs felt shaky and stiff. She drove down Park Lane and through the Mall, the still untouched throughways of London whose monumental character was in keeping with her sombre mood. On Westminster Bridge she got out and watched the steady flow of water, muscular as thick snakes, sweep under. She looked down at it from both sides and then took in the building to one side: the Houses of Parliament. The night was almost gone and she had not written to Lady Goodall!

She drove quickly back through the dirty grey dawn and composed an impassioned letter. In it she set out with great clarity and eloquence the facts of Sam's case, his history so far as she knew it and her understanding of both. 'We are colluding in pushing a young boy beyond the boundaries of society and into delinquency to which he will be irrevocably condemned for the rest of his life. It would not cost anything at this stage, anything but care, to recall him,' she wrote, and appealed to Lady Goodall, woman to woman, to exercise her humanity, her duty, her responsibility as well as her powers as a member of the government to save him. 'There are many other children to my knowledge who will cost the state hundreds of thousands of pounds in legal, medical and penal fees later in life when a little informed attention to their needs before the onset of puberty could nudge them back into the mainstream.'

She read the letter through and found it irresistible. With hope renewed, she ran down the stairs again and drove at top speed to the other side of South Kensington. The front door was painted no-nonsense red. It was opened almost as soon as she rang by a woman in an overall. She gave Rose an unfriendly stare. 'If you have anything to deliver, kindly ...' she began but Rose thrust the envelope at her.

'Please,' she said, 'would you give this to Lady Goodall? It's terribly urgent.'

'I can't think where the constable has gone,' she heard the woman say as she ran back down the front door steps and into her car.

She drove back at top speed, rubbed herself with a loofah in the bath, dressed herself in canary yellow, had some hot coffee and set off for school. As long as she kept going, she felt, she would be all right. She nodded brightly at everyone she met when she got there. Apart from a faint fuzziness in the head and a sensation of its not being quite tethered to her body she felt fine.

'That's her, that's Mrs Pitt!' said James Potterton, clutching his mother's hand. 'Isn't she lovely. Just like a chicken.'

Along the corridor she almost bumped into Nat whom she had quite forgotten and smiled brightly at him too. At her table on the landing, still her base, she saw there was an envelope addressed to her, a meagre brown envelope of the thinnest sort. She picked it up, turned it over, put it in her pocket. If she moved fast, she would be well on time for her first readers in Mr Foster's classroom. She was beating the odds: she felt rather pleased with herself. At break, she put a lot of milk and two spoonfuls of sugar in her coffee. She settled on a staffroom chair and drew the half-remembered letter from her pocket. Inside was a single sheet, the texture of hard lavatory paper. It was from Thamesford Local Education Office and the writing on it was faint as if the Borough were deliberately reminding its employees of the need to economise. It said: Dear Madam, As you are on short-term contract you are advised that this contract will not be renewed. Your employment will terminate at the end of the month. Please detach the form of acknowledgement and return it to this office with your signature. Yours faithfully ...'

28

Rose was so startled when she read the letter that she went red. She wondered who else knew and wished to hide. She kept her head down and suffered the physical discomfort as the hateful heat spread over her scalp and the palms of her hands went sticky. She covered the letter with her hand and edged it across her skirt so it could fall in her bag. She scrabbled in the bag to conceal the manoeuvre and came up with a pocket mirror. From behind it she looked round the room. The staff were engaged in the usual murmured conversational exchanges. She hated the lot of them and the whole place too. They were spineless toadies operating a corrupt system out to defraud the nation's children of genuine education. Subjugation was more like it. She shut her pocket mirror with a snap. She would walk out there and then.

'Mrs Pitt,' said Mrs Jenkins' voice, 'there's a young man out here asking for you.' She smiled at Rose in a motherly way. 'He says it's urgent. Should I tell him to come back another time?' Rose turned to her and Mrs Jenkins caught the look of desperation on her face. 'Everything all right, dear?' she said. 'I'll tell him you're busy.'

'No, no,' said Rose, 'I'll come. Thank you very much, Mrs Jenkins.

Out in the corridor James Potterton was shifting from foot to foot. He had another drawing. This time it was of a woman with round blue eyes and curling eyelashes in a striped dress of many colours. Each one was carefully delineated and filled in. There was some writing underneath and this was something that James had steadfastly refused to do. It said: 'By James. My teacher. Cum bake'.

'Do you like it, do you like it?' he said, holding on to his crotch. 'Guess how many stripes there are.'

'I think it's wonderful,' said Rose. 'I like it very much and I'm impressed by the writing. Well done.'

'Well, will you?' said James. He picked up the drawing and glared at her. 'If you don't come back I won't give it to you. It's a present. I did it specially for you.'

They faced one another in the corridor and Rose said, 'I don't think I'm going to be able to. I'm sorry James. I'd really like to.'

'Bloody bitch,' said James. He stuck his chin out. 'I hate you.' He snatched the drawing and ran away just as the staffroom door opened and the movement back to the classrooms began. Head down, he charged straight into Mrs Jenkins, barged her out of his way and came up against Mr Foster.

'I beg your pardon ...!' Mr Foster began, but the phrase modulated to a yelp as James butted him in the groin and kneed him on the shins. In horror Rose watched as James, all fists and knees and fury was overpowered and dragged off.

'Mr Foster,' she said, stepping out, 'I can explain ...'

'Out of my way, Mrs Pitt,' panted Mr Foster. 'I am in an emergency.'

As the knot of agitated teachers surrounding the struggling boy moved round the corner at the end of the corridor, James poked his head out and shot Rose a furious look. He crumpled the paper in his hand and stepped on it. Rose picked it up and smoothed it out. She felt rooted: every pathway led to a pitfall. Eventually she started moving in the direction of the school office. She could at least divert some of the wrath directed at James on to herself. Footsteps approached and Nathan overtook her. 'Morning, Rosie,' he said, 'what's all the rumpus?' He had never seen her look so wan. He slowed down, although he was late for his own class.

'It's all my fault,' said Rose. 'James Potterton kicked Mr Foster, but it was because he was upset with me. I must rescue him somehow … and it's all worse than that because … because I've been given the sack.' She looked so white he thought she might faint. He put a hand on her arm. She reminded him of a newly hatched chick with no chirp in it.

'I'll get James out,' he said, 'I'll think of an errand. You keep your head down. Go and do what you're meant to be doing. We'll discuss it after school.' He gave Rose a little push and went the other way.

Rose drifted to her class in a daze. She was beginning to feel as if several sheets of plastic separated her from the rest of the world. Through the haze she noticed James Potterton buzzing round the playground picking up bits of paper and putting them into a bag. He had a red armband and swaggered occasionally as if to a triumphal band. He looked quite cheerful. At the end of afternoon school she went straight down the back stairs to her car and fell asleep. Nat found her there and left a note on the windscreen. Shortly after, the school caretaker woke her. Hers was the only car in the car park. 'I'd be obliged if you'd move on, Miss,' he said. 'I go in for me tea at four o'clock.' He stood by, a monolith of righteousness, as she surfaced and fumbled with the keys. She parked directly outside and read the note under the windscreen wiper. Then she drove to the Black Prince.

Nat was already there. She saw him from the door, behind his newspaper; the backs of his hands all hairy, the big watch on its tank track metal strap, the dense dark head, the brown suede shoes. If I take another step, she thought, I'm going to get in much deeper than I ought. He looked up and made no attempt to smile. Instead he put down the paper and came over.

'You go and sit down,' he said, 'I'll get a drink. What would you like?'

'Water,' said Rose. She felt relieved that she did not have to smile.

When he came back she had her letter of dismissal out. He took a long time reading it. 'Disgusting,' he said when he had finished.

'We'll have to get the Union on to it. Tell me what happened if you'd like, but before you start, let me tell you what I suggest. I thought we might talk it over with Gerry. I've telephoned him. He can be free by half seven. We can meet up in a Turkish restaurant by his place. How do you feel about that?'

Pop, pop, pop, went off the objections in Rose's head.

She had to reach Frank and explain.

Maybe there was a letter from him

Maybe there was a letter from Lady Goodall.

She must go home and change.

Each was too weak to do more than ruffle the surface of her mind. 'Thank you,' she said, 'I'd love to,' and began to recount the events of that morning and the second half of the night before, including Frank under the heading of 'upsetting personal news'. She was interested that such anguish as she had experienced for so many dark hours could be telescoped into so few sentences. 'I didn't feel like going to bed'; 'I walked by the canal for a bit'.

'Perhaps you'd rather go home and get a good night's sleep,' said Nat.

'I couldn't,' said Rose.

Gerry was already waiting in the restaurant when they got there, barely discernible against an artificial vine at the back of a dim, pink-lit room. He was older than Rose remembered and smaller, boy-sized but bearded. She held out her hand and he gave her a look of such understanding that it cut through the formal preliminaries she had been preparing.

'I don't know what to do,' she said and began to shake. Both men watched her. 'I'm sorry,' she stuttered.

'It's okay,' they replied as one.

A waiter poured wine. Rose took a deep breath and tried some. It was strong with an aftertaste of iron, more medicinal than sensuous. Gerry started talking.

'As I see it, this little fellow Sam is the priority. There are procedures for getting him out and better places for him to be. Fiveways has not got a very good reputation. I can help with all that but it's a long drawn-out process. In the meanwhile I suggest you keep in touch with him. Write regularly. He mustn't feel you've abandoned him.'

Hot pitta steaming like piles of poultices appeared before them, and tiny quails stuffed with cracked wheat and sultanas. Gerry did the ordering. Nat loosened his tie. The three of them sat, heads together, their faces illuminated in the pink glow of the table lamp.

'Cut your losses,' said Gerry. 'Establish exactly with this Head-master when you have to leave. Try and extend it to the end of term and then tell all the children you work with exactly what's happening in writing. Word'll get round – even if they can't read it all. Send copies of everything to the Local Education Office and to the Head-master and, maybe, the staff. What do you think, Nat? You must bring it all out into the open. This kind of thing flourishes on veiled threats and innuendo, unspoken fear and evasion. You're going to have to leave and you're going to have to leave the children, but you can do it cleanly. At least, they'll have the experience of an adult who's straight with them.'

'You're right,' said Rose. 'And I suppose I can be bolder now the worst has happened. It'll be a relief. Oh, how kind you are! I could never have thought this all out on my own.'

'It's the middle of November,' Gerry warned, 'only two weeks till the end of the month. Five or so if you manage to hang on till the end of term.'

'I must write all the letters over the weekend so everyone gets them on Monday. But what should I say to the children about when I'm leaving. Would "very soon" be all right?'

'No,' said Nathan and Gerry.

'Tell them the truth,' said Nathan, 'either, or ...'

'But won't that confuse them?' said Rose.

'Not as much as "very soon",' said Nathan. 'Come on, Rosie,

think what it means to children when adults say "in a minute". It means anything from ten minutes to a day to never.' He pushed back his chair. 'The gap between words and meaning – it's where all the trouble starts. It gets filled with fantasy and mistrust. You must say what you mean – especially to children.'

'You do,' said Rose. 'You said you'd think of something to get James Potterton out this morning and you did. Come to think of it, you always seem to say what you mean – or is it, do what you say? I've got used to translating what people say and even then, I'm not sure what language is being used.'

I love you. Trust me. Darling. Was that the same language as *very soon?*

'The language of evasion has many dialects,' she said and surprised herself. She tried not to think what the words she had just said might mean. They swung about, all fragmented, like titles on a black screen. The blackness was frightening.

'If Rose is going to distribute these letters on Monday, we'd better help her draft them now,' said Gerry. 'Are you up to it?'

'I am if you are,' said Rose. The last thing she wanted was to be left alone with the blackness.

'We can go to my place,' said Nat. He stood. 'Rose can drive Gerry. I need a run. See you – very soon.' He grinned, tucked up his arms like chickens' wings and trotted out of the door.

Nat's house was one of a heavily ornamented Edwardian terrace facing a park and his were the ground floor rooms. A ginger cat came running down the front steps and rubbed against his legs. He picked it up. 'Hullo Barnet.' Inside, he lit lamps and a gas fire. Rose sat in the armchair nearest. She tucked up her legs and the cat sprang up and pushed its nose against her hand, purring. 'Now,' said Gerry, 'where shall we start?'

They worked for some hours, composing letters to the Director of Education, to Mr Lovejoy, to the teachers at Meadowbrook, to Social Services, the police, Fiveways, to the children, to Sam.

'I don't think that one's for us,' said Gerry. 'Rose can handle it on her own. If you're not sure about anything, give me a ring over the weekend, okay, Rosie?'

But Rose had fallen asleep. Her yellow skirt rucked high over her thighs, her black legs shoeless, her whole body was slumped sideways in the armchair.

'Rose?' said Nat.

'She can't drive home now,' said Gerry. The two men lifted her legs on to a chair. They put cushions behind her head and covered her with a blanket. Nathan let Gerry out and came back into the room. He kept his eyes away from his old armchair and lay down on the divan. The cat padded its claws in his shoulder and settled to sleep across his face. 'Fuck off, Barnet,' said Nathan. He felt itchy from lack of sleep and restless to an extreme degree beyond that. He shut out the soft sound of breathing coming from the room and tried to remember his mantra. *Parashna*, he said to himself determinedly, *parashna, parashna, parashna.* By and by, he too fell asleep.

Weak sunlight playing on her face wakened Rose in the morning. Bare branches tapped against the glass mediating the watery beam. It was a windy day outside. There was a weight on her chest. She squinted down and met the narrowed eyes of a ginger cat. It was making a hollow purring sound. Why was she still in her clothes? She moved her head. There was a terrible crick in her neck.

'Good morning,' said Nat from the kitchen end of the room. 'Don't bother to move. I'm making some coffee. I'll bring it across.' He felt terribly pleased she was there. He had run round the park at twice the usual speed and there was a lift in his heart as he let himself in.

Oh God, thought Rose, what have I done? She gave a little moan.

'It's all right,' said Nat, 'you fell asleep. Gerry and I tucked you up. You've had a good sleep.' He was wearing the royal blue track suit with trainers and his face, for once, was smooth.

'What time is it?' said Rose.

'Almost eleven,' said Nathan.

'Oh, no!' said Rose.

'D'you want to make a 'phone call? The box is in the hall.' His voice, so uncensorious, rang true as a bell in her head. She looked down at her crumpled clothes and lay back. 'It's all right,' she said. 'It's much too much trouble to move.' He came across with a tin tray, an old percolator with a glass-bubble top, and a plate of toast. 'Shall I butter you a piece?' he said.

Rose looked at his face. The lines in it reminded her of the adults in her childhood: the gas fire, the cat before it, hot-buttered toast; she was in the nursery, safe, at home. 'Yes, please,' she said.

He reached behind him for the paper. 'Which bit would you like?' he said.

'Which bit would you?' said she.

'Sport for me.'

'Then I'll have Arts.'

She settled back. There was no sound in the room save the muted roar of the gas burning in the meringue-like cylinders of the fire, the purring of the cat and the occasional rustle of a page turning. Rain slanted across the window panes and the wet black branches of the tree creaked and scratched against them. Peace came down on the room like quiet snow, immaculate, with not a splinter of dissonance to wrinkle it. Rose felt her limbs slacken and her thoughts steady down. Nathan felt his heart expand. He looked over the top of the paper and smiled to see her all ruffled and undefended in his chair by his fire. He put up the paper again. Queens Park Rangers were bound to win that afternoon.

'I'm going now,' said Rose with a sigh. She swung her legs off the chair and stood up, stretching and scratching herself as if she were alone. She bent down and shook out her hair. Nathan opened a drawer filled with plastic and string. He put the notes from last night into a Tesco bag. 'Here,' he said, 'there's quite a bit of work. Ring up if you have a problem.' They went into the hall.

'You've been so kind,' said Rose at the door. She hesitated then put up her hand and touched his face, 'Thank you.' She ran down the steps in the rain. The wind slapped her in the face and whipped up her hair. She laughed and turned to wave. Nat watched till she got to her car then he turned back into the room. The place she had touched on his cheek felt creamy as Devon fudge.

29

The rain, which had started as a few whirling drops earlier that morning, settled into driving downpour. It slanted across the windows of the Rover as it sped along the Mall under the tall trees whose bare branches tossed helplessly in high wind. The windscreen wipers made their brief semicircular run back and forth at top speed and Tomlinson, his chauffeur's cap seemingly supported by pink jug-ears alone, bent forward to peer through the watery blur.

'Any word of the flight being cancelled?' Lady Goodall called through to him.

'No word yet, Secretary of State,' Tomlinson replied. 'I'll check with airport police.'

Connie sighed. Two polytechnics converting to university status, a purpose-built area comprehensive swallowing up half a dozen local schools, *Any Questions* and Divine Service in the Minster lay between her and Sunday lunch with the Wetherbys next day. She placed her briefcase firmly upon her knees and began to commit to memory the facts her officials had set out for her in the first brief, concerning the newly-styled University of Middlesbrough (lately Tees Poly). And as she did so, it crossed her mind that it might be more appropriate for someone of her persuasions to be converting universities to polytechnics.

The car jolted unexpectedly to a halt and the briefcase shot off her knees, scattering papers all over the floor. 'Beg pardon, ma'am,' said Tomlinson, 'small boy ran out straight in front of us. Came from nowhere. Only just missed him.'

'No harm done, Tomlinson,' said Connie, gathering up papers. 'I'm sure you did your best.' She spread them out alongside and a rather superior Manila envelope, woven in texture, caught her eye. It was addressed in a bold black hand to her personally, at home. Its egregiousness among the mass of memos and notices held her attention: could it perhaps contain an incendiary device? It was exceptionally thick. She dismissed the namby-pamby notion and reached out to open it. Inside was nothing but some sheets of good white paper covered with the same black writing, rhythmic and readable.

'Dear Lady Goodall, I know you are a good and serious woman,' it went, 'an old friend and trusted colleague of my father, a valued friend to many of my own friends and a staunch friend, I am sure, to the millions of children that now come under your ministry ...' She looked through the pages to the signature: *Rose Pitt (Hardy)*. Brigadier Hardy's girl that must be: a distinguished record of service to the nation there. She read on: some tale of victimisation in an outer London primary school, a direct appeal to the Commander-in-Chief. The account grew positively Dickensian. The writer certainly had a way with words, accompanied no doubt by an economical use of fact. Lady Goodall sniffed. She had little respect for speculation and the letter was becoming hysterical.

'Intractable problem', 'Irrevocably condemned for the rest of his life ...' What tosh. She knew perfectly well the carefully designed checks and procedures in place at every level to ensure that just the kind of occurrence the writer was describing never took place. Childhood had its ups and downs of course, and some children were born bad – not a fashionable view but facts were facts. She found herself becoming increasingly uncomfortable, none the less, and, with a sickening loop through the dark passage of time, saw herself in scratchy stockings and hated pinafore, unjustly punished and beside herself with rage, attacking the window of her schoolroom with the thick end of the blackboard cue. One had been so helpless, she began to remember and pushed the thought away. It led to so many others.

As she read on, '... driven to extremes of physical effort ...' another memory, even more painful, surfaced of her first period coming upon her in a history exam. Ah, the shame of that moment – and of the hours that ensued. She shuddered. Thank God all that was behind her. Childhood was a messy business, an affliction to be gone through before one attained its upper reaches and had learned to handle tent pegs and hockey sticks with confidence. She skimmed the remainder with distaste and returned the letter to its envelope. 'Inspectorate. Non-urgent' she wrote on top, initialled it and placed it in the file for one of her junior private secretaries, the one with responsibility for primary schools.

Something about the quality of light made her look up. They were in the tunnel approaching Heathrow already and not a stroke of work had she done. Damn that young woman – the impudence! And it all came back to her: a London dinner, old friends, agreeable conversation and then a very fancy young woman taking advantage of the nose-powdering hiatus after dinner and importuning her in the most inappropriate way. She snorted and Tomlinson opened the door. 'Beg pardon, ma'am,' he said.

A police constable stood discreetly at his back and behind him, a manager bearing a huge checkered umbrella, red, white and blue, with the words *Albion Airways All-executive* spiralling round it. They posed briefly beneath while a photographer took a picture before the manager accompanied her directly to her seat on the plane.

As she lowered herself into it, he bent over. 'Is there anything you'd like, Secretary of State? A little champagne, perhaps, with our compliments?' He had a smooth pink skin and a strongish smell came off him, sweet, geranium-based with a hint of petrol.

Connie, who felt beguiled enough to allow herself a whisky thought better of it. Something lighter might be more suitable for mid-morning. 'I'll have a gin and tonic, please,' she said, 'and would you ask your people not to disturb me. I have a great deal of work to do.'

Many hours and one night later Frank, in his old donkey jacket and Land-Rover, picked her up after Morning Service outside York Minster. A diffident silvery light shone out between the clouds and, from time to time sailed into a patch of blue. It was a long drive out to Grassdale. They stopped at a riverside pub for a pint. Connie, grasping her tankard, rocked back and forth on her feet. She enjoyed the way Frank pulled her leg. He made her feel outrageously skittish. It was not until they were back in the car, swinging up the short curves to the high moors that the Hardy girl entered her mind again. Frank was telling her of his forthcoming trip over Christmas. 'We'll be hanging up our stockings under a banana tree. It's going to be too odd. I don't think I've ever spent Christmas out of England. But Tamarisk needs a break, poor girl,' he was saying, 'and I've got a little semi-official oiling of wheels to do.'

'Of course,' said Connie, 'your services in that area are much appreciated by us all.' She wagged her head and at the back of her mind a little picture about the size of a postage stamp appeared. It was so bright it compelled her attention for a second or two: Brigadier Hardy's girl again engaged in intense and abrupt confrontation with herself towards the end of that perfectly civilised private dinner party. She almost snorted, 'Unlike Brigadier Hardy's girl,' she said, half to herself. 'I must say, she's a troublesome young woman – taking her duties as a schoolteacher altogether too much to heart.' She pursed her lips and shook her head.

Frank's grip on the steering wheel intensified so the bones showed white through the knuckles. He experienced a moment of suffocating fear followed by one of such acute yearning, he thought he might be in danger of fainting. 'Look! A lark,' he said and, indeed, there were two or three tossing overhead under the rain-washed pearl-coloured skies. 'I do adore this bit of the moor,' he went on, 'they call it Hangman's Mile. I don't know why. Stark. Absolute. It goes straight to my heart.' He looked at Connie with a grave face and, extreme situations called for extreme measures, let his hand rest on her knee. It had been a close shave. He must distance himself from Rose, erase all traces of their liaison. It was imperative. Maybe his foreign travel could be advanced by a few days. But no, HRH had promised to inaugurate the site of the new museum. He replaced his hand on the steering wheel and his face resumed its customary lopsided expression, amused and affectionate. 'Off the record, for your ears only ...?' he said.

Connie blew down her nostrils, 'You can depend on me,' she said, 'I know how to keep a secret.'

'Well,' said Frank. He leaned a little in her direction, 'HRH came round the other night and – you know how keen he is on this sort of thing – offered his services. He's going to launch works on the museum at the end of the month. And – this is priceless – we've found an absolutely darling old mechanical digger in the vast edifice they call 'the potting shed' at Tees House and HRH is going to sit on that and turn the first sod.' He turned a beaming face to her. 'Isn't that fun?'

At that moment the sun came right out and infused the world around them with colour. The heather became enriched with a full spectrum of browns from peat to purple and every quivering raindrop for miles around flashed in response. 'He's just a boy,' thought Connie, looking at his excited face. She saw the Hornby train set laid out on the schoolroom floor and her father on all fours beside it while she and her boy-cousins manipulated the points.

'Bravo,' she said, warmly.

30

That inhospitable Saturday morning Maggie and her father set out for the Surrey hinterland and its network of asylums, positioned like a moat round London to mop up its misfits. Phil Clark, who now passed most of the hours between eight-thirty and four in a no-man's-land between one local government functionary and another, had been handed a number of vouchers to cover the cost of the journey by public transport. He wondered if these bits of paper meant he was obliged to take the bus, but it was so wild and wet that the two of them just hopped in the van. He had two or three Sunday jobs which should cover the petrol: he looked no further ahead these days than the morrow. Maggie, wearing a garment awarded her by Social Services, sat by him drumming her heels against the tin plinth of the seat. He glanced at her, his Maggie submerged within an emerald green anorak quartered in mustard and fuchsia. She was humming inside it and turned to give him a delighted grin. He grinned back. It was an outing, after all, and they were going to see Sam.

The van put-putted its way in fits and starts through the crammed streets clenched ten miles deep like clogged intestines at the verges of the big city. On the short stretches where the road opened up Phil Clark knew better than to depress the accelerator: he nursed the van, 'Come on, old lady,' until, juddering, it attained 50 mph when the sensation of effort and speed caused Maggie to hug herself tight.

They nearly missed Fiveways on one of these stretches. It was Maggie whose eye caught sight of a noticeboard by a half-concealed entrance plunging into dark evergreens. They turned round at the next fly-over and back to the preceding roundabout before locating it again.

'It's coming. It's coming,' squeaked Maggie, her nose squashed to the window, and they swung into the drive. She was filled with pure joy, intense and undiluted. For as long as she could remember the arbiter of her life had been her brother. Much of it she had lived through him. In his absence it had closed down to a dismal trickle. She missed him physically and all the time. She was accustomed to waiting for him but the monotony of this wait had almost snuffed her out. As they bumped through the sunless plantation, the long wait was almost at an end.

For her father, the spark of joy flared intermittently, alloyed with sorrow and apprehension. His boy had taken a terrible beating. Without him the family's frail ecology had collapsed. He knew there would be no miraculous reprieve at the end of the day and that his son would be thrice betrayed when they left again without him. He knew it and grieved as they drew up on the thin gravel in front of the big bare house. But Maggie pulled back the door and jumped out. She ran round to tug his hand with both of hers and he had to smile.

High above, Sam watched from the attic room to which he was mostly confined. There were bars outside the windows which were unopenable and made of unbreakable glass. The room was bare, there were no sheets on the bed and whenever he went outside, even to the toilet, Eleanor or Mr Watkins accompanied him. He felt nothing when he saw the old van round the bend, nothing when he saw Maggie jump out, but a sharp pain yanked a buried nerve when he saw her walk round the bonnet hand-in-hand with his Dad. He battened it down. Not much got through his defences nowadays and the spirit within was well nigh atrophied. Only his hand picked at a splinter of the frame as he stood at the window, motionless and impassive, seeing the bare branches of the big tree as they creaked painfully in the wind.

The door was unlocked, the handle, outside only, turned and Eleanor's voice said, 'Your Dad's come to visit, Sam, and your little sister. Come along now. Put on a smile for them.' Cheerful impersonality was her mode. She had cultivated it to an implacable degree. Not many of the young gentlemen as she called them got a rise out of her. Sam hardened his muscles. He looked past Eleanor at the corridor outside and spat. 'Now, now,' said Eleanor. She pinioned his arms behind him, took a comb from her pocket and passed it through his short-back-and-sides. The comb scraped Sam's scalp. Such manifold indignities were intrinsic to day-to-day life but the scalp was an area he had not yet learned how to harden. Far, far away at the end of a tunnel a boy screamed with rage.

Keeping a firm hand on his upper arm Eleanor trundled him along the passages and stairways. Sam stayed inert, dragging his feet. He looked dreadful, greyed with the slack snotty look that overcomes small children within a week or two of institutionalisation. They came down by the main staircase into the hall and Maggie sensed his approach before they had turned the bend on the half landing. She let go her father's hand, darted to him and flung herself at the first part of him that presented itself. Clutching on to the grey sock surrounding the sharp bone of his ankle she went flop, flop, light as a rag doll, down the stairs beside him. She tuned into his mood, melting with it like a shadow. And she stayed like that, grey, insubstantial, transparent, an aspect of him attached to an ankle on the cold uncarpeted floor.

His father was not quite sure who was there, coming down the stairs in the grip of a blue-overalled woman. It was not so much the altered externals as the vacated interior that failed to stir his sense of recognition. He faltered as he stepped towards him. 'Hullo lad,' he said. Sam neither moved nor spoke. His gaze was fixed on some indefinable spot in the air, a little way past, or through, his father. Phil Clark put up a hand and touched the strange, close-cropped cranium. 'We've brought you your paper, lad,' he said, 'and some sweets.' He held out the *Beano* and three tubes of Refreshers.

Eleanor intervened. 'We'll take those,' she said, 'Home policy. All gifts to be pooled except on birthdays. It's only fair.' As she said the word 'fair' Sam's free foot came out and he kicked her hard on the shin. Eleanor tightened her mouth so there were no lips to be seen. 'That'll go down in the order book young man,' she said and then yelped, dropping the comic and the sweets, as Maggie's little white milk teeth nipped into her leg. Worming forward, Maggie grabbed at the dropped offerings. She slithered across the floor and wriggled into the small space under a hard armchair on the other side of the hall. Eleanor slapped Sam on both sides of his head. 'That's enough of that,' she said and called out 'Steve!' Mr Watkins came out of the playroom leading a trouserless boy of about twelve by the hand. 'Naughty Jason,' he said, 'never put on his Paddi-pants this morning. I'll be with you in a tic.'

Sam stood taut and sullen, still gripped by the upper arm; his father watched, dazed and distressed. The pressure in his chest became suffocating. He stepped forward and picked up Sam. 'There, there,' he said and held him close. Sam's bony body gave no sign of response. It stayed rigid as wood. Only his breathing set up a faint fanning of the warm air below his father's ear. Eleanor looked at them. She was a kind girl at heart: why else would she have gone into welfare when she could have taken up hairdressing? She decided to skirt the rules for a bit. She sat down on a stair and rubbed her shin. The four occupants of the hall remained locked in their separate postures for some minutes and might have remained so indefinitely had not Mr Watkins hurried back, the boy Jason, now in pyjama-bottoms, at his heels.

'Take over here for a mo' would you, Steve?' said Eleanor. 'Interaction situation needs reframing.'

'Bin in the wars, have you?' said Mr Watkins.

'Not half,' said Eleanor and limped away.

'Now, Sam,' said Mr Watkins cheerfully, 'glad to see your family, are you? Been some time, has it …?'

Down in the dusty space between the sack-cloth and the flag-stones Maggie sneezed. She held herself still and, when nothing happened, opened her eyes and peered out. She saw that the lady who had tried to steal Sam's present was gone so she wormed out and went to stand by her father's leg. One of Sam's feet dangled by her head so she held on to it too.

Mr Watkins said, 'I'm afraid Sam's on Special Supervision Order, so we can't leave him alone with you. Perhaps you'd like to continue the visit in the visiting room?' He lowered his voice, 'I expect we can rustle up a cup of tea for you there.' He gave the big boy in the pyjama-bottoms' hand a tweak and led the way through passages and corridors to the back of the house. The visiting room was next to the kitchen. A hatch led through, and there was a table in the middle with cretonne-covered chairs round the walls. Piles of colour supplements and some boxes of board games lay on the top of an upright piano and the room felt un-used to human presence. At its threshold Phil Clark made to set Sam down on the floor, but Sam gave a convulsive squirm and dug his head into his father's neck. An arm came up and hooked itself on like a wire claw. Mr Watkins knocked on the hatch and a brown face in a white chef's hat looked through.

'Oh, no, no, no, no. No,' said the face, seeing Sam.

'It's all right,' said Mr Watkins, 'he's off all privileges, but could you let us have a cup of tea for this gentleman and his little girl? They've had a long journey.'

The small group stood awkwardly then Mr Watkins said, 'Do make yourselves comfortable, please.' Raising his voice he addressed Sam's back. 'How about a game of Ludo, Sam? Jason and I will take you three on.'

Phil Clark sat down carefully on the edge of a chair. Maggie leaned on the arm. Mr Watkins set up the Ludo board. 'What colour, Sam? You can choose first,' he said. Smiling gamely, he turned to the big boy in pyjama-bottoms. 'You and I'll have a game then. I'll teach you, the others can join in later,' he said.

There were few sounds in the room after that: the click and rattle of the dice shaking in their cardboard cylinder, grunts and snuffles from Jason as he laboured to count his move, the unsynchronised breathing of Sam and his father, and a tiny rustle of paper as Maggie tore a Refresher packet and started stuffing the sweets, one by one, into a hole she had found in the armchair. Hanging over his father's shoulder, Sam watched her. She stuffed one into his mouth. It felt no more alive than the hole in the sofa. She went back to stuffing that, but next time she looked up his mouth was opened and shaped into an 'O'. He put out his tongue and Maggie placed a sweet upon it. He flicked it in and closed his eyes but Maggie could see a faint movement of cheeks and jaw, skull thin, as he sucked and swallowed.

Outside in the yard the clock in the arch struck twelve. 'I'll have to take Sam now. It's his dinner time,' said Mr Watkins. 'I'll bring him back after. You can stay or get yourselves a bite outside. Locking-up time's at four.' He came for Sam. 'Come along now. The quicker you eat up the quicker you'll be able to get back.' The statement was nominal because Sam had not been seen to eat in the dining-room since his return. He sat over his plate long into the afternoons and occasionally members of staff, one holding his nose, another the spoon, attempted to force-feed him. But one never knew: on this occasion … Mr Watkins waited. Sam stayed clamped to his father. Mr Watkins tried to prise him off. Sam contracted every muscle. He clung as if suctioned. Red in the face Mr Watkins retreated.

'Go and get your dinner. We won't move. I'll guarantee you that,' said Sam's father. He stroked Sam's head very slowly. Mr Watkins, dragging Jason by the hand, left the room. Maggie climbed up beside Sam. She put her thumb in her mouth and leaned back. First she, then Sam and then their father fell asleep. Ten minutes later Mr Watkins came back with a tray. He ate his dinner at the table and then his head fell forward on to his chest. He jerked it up again but it lolled sideways. He pinched the backs of his hands but, despite the pain, it flopped forward again and he too slept.

The slow minutes of the afternoon ticked by. In their armchair the three members of the Clark family settled into one another, their movements adjusting as if to the music of a pavane. Phil Clark went in and out of sleep. He was aware of his son's body growing slacker. The weight and warmth of it felt integral to his own. He experienced an immense responsibility, oceanic in its boundlessness, towards the two children in his arms. Mr Watkins stretched, yawned and took out his Filofax. He began to note points in it for the Home meeting tomorrow. Sam dreamed of rabbits and so did Maggie. At quarter to four Mr Watkins coughed. He got up and banged about a bit. Maggie burrowed further into her father's chest and he looked up, blinking. The realities of the situation swam back into hard-edged focus.

'Time to say good-bye everyone,' said Mr Watkins. He used a jolly tone as if he were announcing raffle winners at a fête, 'Lock-up and roll-call before tea.'

Phil Clark, still in the chair, looked at him helplessly. Mr Watkins met his gaze with a hearty matter-of-fact air, and averted his eyes. 'Come along now, please,' he said and began aligning chairs.

'It's time to go, Sam, lad,' Phil Clark said in his son's ear. 'Get up Maggie, there's a good girl.' Maggie slid off her father's lap straight on to her haunches. She put two fingers up on either side of her head and hopped under the table. Sam made no response. His body against his father's stiffened, though there was no visible alteration of its position. His father stroked his head. 'Come along lad. Maggie and I have got to go home now.'

'No,' said Sam in a loud toneless voice in his ear.

'There,' said his father. Still holding him he struggled on to his feet.

'Come along now, please,' said Mr Watkins. He looked at his watch. It was already nearly five to. He ushered Sam and his father out of the room and shooed Maggie from under the table. He locked the door of the visiting room behind him and beckoned as he hurried through the passageways.

In the entrance boys were shuffling towards the dining-hall. Some element of homogeneity was missing from them as a group and they made a displaced, ill-assorted impression. Two or three green-over-alled women were stationed at intervals to shepherd them, more cow- than boy-like, on their way. The small band from the visiting room came to a halt at their rear as the last stragglers loitered by.

'Get down now, Sam, we'll only just make roll-call,' said Mr Watkins. He was clearly on edge. But Sam clung to his father. He was attached as the boys who had preceded him into the dining-hall were not.

'Adrian, Albany, Apu …' came a male voice from the dining-hall.

'Sam!' said Mr Watkins sharply. He took hold of him by the elbow. He felt the bone beneath the sleeve. He tugged, but he could have been tugging at a chunk of masonry. 'Get down, Sam,' he said again. He took hold of both his shoulders and gave a mighty heave.

The wiry desperation with which Sam braced himself against this onslaught made his father's heart turn over. 'No,' he cried out, 'don't take him away.'

Mr Watkins, out of breath, gave a startled look and hurried to the dining hall. He came back with Eleanor and a tall man with a ruddy face. The tall man was older than the others. He wore a dark blue suit and a tie. He walked straight up to Sam and his father. 'Leave go!' he said. He took Sam by the arms and pulled him backwards. Sam's knees dug into his father's sides, he crossed his ankles round the back of him but his top half was dislodged. His face showed, white with such fear that the tall man let go, shocked.

'Oh, Sam, lad,' said his father, 'you'll have to do what the gentleman says. Maggie and me, we'll be back …' He looked into his son's eyes and saw there such a depth of despair that he clasped his head again and cradled it back to his shoulder. He closed his eyes.

'One, two, three …' came the voice of the tall man. He advanced, flanked by Eleanor and Mr Watkins. Each laid their hands on a section of Sam's person. 'Now,' said the tall man and Sam came away.

And as his body was torn from his father's he gave a wild inhuman scream, a scream of such primitive terror that there was a scraping of chairs from the dining-hall and a number of gaping faces peered round the door. The two men held on to Sam who crouched between them, feral and snarling. His father faced him, shaking.

Eleanor bustled up. She took Maggie by the hand, 'Come along, little girl,' she said and pushed with some force against her father's elbow. 'Not to worry. It's all for the best. Time to hit the road now.'

Sam stopped struggling and stood still. His face went dead and he looked his father in the eye, then he gathered the saliva in his mouth and spat at him. The spittle landed at his father's feet. It lay on the flagstones, a gob the colour of ice rinks. The two men half lifted him off his feet and dragged him away. Maggie ran after him. 'Oh, no you don't,' said Eleanor. She made a dive and scooped her up light as a soap bubble. She set her down by her father and stood in front of them blocking the view of the door through which Sam had gone. 'Bye now,' she said.

At the end of the drive Phil Clark turned left on to the dual carriageway and drove for some time without knowing which way he was going. He made a harsh barking sound and stopped the van. He hid his face in his hands. His shoulders shook. Up and down they went, heaving and quivering, up and down. Maggie sat beside him. She was very frightened. She dared not move for fear of breaking something more. She was hungry and she wanted to pee. She sat on her hands. Her bladder burned and prickled, worse and worse. She let go and the hot urine trickled out and made a warm pool round her. She stopped thinking about Sam and began to pick her nose.

31

On Monday, James Potterton brought his letter home from school. 'It's not for you. See? It says "James",' he said, showing his mother the envelope.

'So it does,' said his mother. 'Well, aren't you going to open it and see what it says?'

James tucked the letter inside the V of his pullover as if it were a breast pocket and strutted round the room patting his chest. 'It may be something important, I could need to use the telephone. Please keep it free, Mother.'

'Is it from Mrs Upjohn?' asked his mother and wrinkled up her freckled nose.

'No.'

'Who?'

'Not going to tell you.'

His mother sighed and went back to the forms she was filling in: supplementary benefit, child benefit ... as if divorce were not enough on its own. She could never quite make up her mind whether to handle James would be easier or more difficult with a man in the house, or not. The right man, of course. Certainly not his father.

'I think I'll have some breakfast now,' said James.

'But it's afternoon,' said his mother. 'Oh, I see. Of course. To read your letter with. Certainly. Full breakfast or Continental?'

'Don't be silly,' said James. He stamped his foot. 'I hate you when you're like that. I'll have egg and chips.' He walked over to his mother and stuck his chin out.

'One egg and chips. Right,' said his mother. 'Now, just let me put the kettle on and then we'll have a look and see what this letter's all about.'

They settled into the kitchen table, James on his mother's lap, his pink thighs flattened into chubby triangles across her jeans. From his pullover he withdrew the envelope and tore open the flap with his teeth.

'Dear James,' he read out, 'Your turn now ...'

His mother read on:

> 'I would like to let you know that I am leaving Meadow-brook, either at the end of the month (Thursday, 30th November) or at the end of term. This is because my contract with the Local Education Authority has not been renewed. I am very sorry about this. I have enjoyed teaching you and I will miss you.
>
> 'I will still be at school for another two weeks at least. I have written to tell all the other children I have been teaching. All the best. Yours sincerely, Rose Pitt.'

'Mrs Pitt!' said his mother.

'She can't,' said James. 'I've given her two pictures. My best work. She can't go. I'll kill her.'

'But that's terrible,' said his mother. 'She's the only teacher you've ever got on with, isn't she? And you did seem to be making some headway at last. Poor thing. She must have been sacked. It's nice of her to let you know.'

James slid off her lap. He stamped his foot. 'Not poor. Not nice. Horrible.' He stumped out and came back dragging the telephone on its cord. 'Telephone her, Mother! Now. She's not to go.' He stood glowering.

'I can't Jamesy,' said his mother, 'I haven't got her number and besides ...'

'You're horrible too,' said James. His brow was furrowed and his lips puckered into a down-turning crescent. He dropped the telephone and made for the bathroom. Back he came with a bottle of lavatory bleach and some shampoo. He stood on a chair at the sink and began unscrewing the caps. 'I'm going to poison her,' he muttered and repeated the words, louder, in his mother's direction.

'Oh James,' she said, 'poor woman.' She picked the telephone off the floor, thanking heavens that both economy-size bottles were no more than a quarter full. 'Here,' she said, 'if you're using bleach you'll need these,' and handed him some rubber gloves.

'I need bowls,' he said, 'and empty bottles.'

For the next fifty minutes there was absence of conflict in the Potterton kitchen. James mixed and stirred; bleach, shampoo, washing up liquid, cream-cleaner, vinegar, a shake of scouring powder, a sprinkle of pepper. He fetched his felt tips and made labels, copying off their bottles of origin; Quosh, Lime Juice Cordial, Fanta. 'That's not how you spell Ribena,' he said indignantly. His mother finished her forms and put her feet up with a magazine; *For women who juggle their lives* it said on the cover, and *'Christmas without tears'*. It was bliss when James was occupied.

'I shall offer her a choice,' he said, 'but there's some left over. I'll give it to you. You can poison anyone you don't like at work. Free of charge.'

'Oh, I could never do that,' she said half-listening. She laid the magazine down. 'I'm going to get supper now.'

James arranged a row of bottles on the draining-board. He looked critically and brought them over to the table; jam jars, sauce bottles, clear plastic containers. 'I need some colour,' he said, 'I tried felt-tip juice but it didn't work.'

'How about food-colouring?' said his mother. 'There's the stuff we use for icing.'

'Food ...?' said James, 'that'll take the poison off.'

'No, it won't,' said his mother.

By the time she brought their supper to the table the row of bottles with their coloured labels looked very pretty, winking in the electric light. 'Mmn,' she said, 'they look good enough to drink.'

'Mmn,' said James. 'Let's have a party instead. A Christmas party with proper drinks to drink. What colour are cocktails?'

'A farewell party for Mrs Pitt! What a good idea,' said his mother. 'We could start doing invitations after supper.'

'We can start doing invitations *now*,' said James.

Next day as Elaine skipped to the end of her road with Tracy she remembered something. They were having a skipping-race. She slowed down. 'You win,' she said. Tracy was miles ahead anyway. She strolled back towards Elaine. 'I always win,' she said, 'I've got longer legs.'

'I've got big thighs,' said Elaine. She lifted her skirt and twisted her head this way and that, inspecting the wide areas of rosy skin, slightly chapped in front, that stretched from her knickers to her knees. 'I've got a secret,' she said. Tracy hurled a pebble, overarm, at a lamppost. 'Tell,' she said. The pebble missed the lamppost and dropped on to a passing car. Both girls clapped their hands to their mouths and tee-heed behind their fingers. They resumed walking.

D'you want to hear?' said Elaine. Tracy bent her head and Elaine whispered into her ear. She loved telling secrets. It made her feel tremendously important, almost grown-up.

'*Every*one knows *that*,' said Tracy. 'Mrs Pitt told Mr Woolf in the corridor on Friday. Then they went for a drink in the Black Prince. They're always going for a drink in the Black Prince.' She hooked a stone from under a front gate and dribbled it along the pavement.

Puffed and put out, Elaine scurried to keep up. 'Course I know that too,' she said, 'but I've got a letter …'

'A note from Mrs Upjohn? Pooh. Everyone has those,' said Tracy.

'No, no,' said Elaine, 'a proper letter from Mrs Pitt to me. It's mine. I've got one for her, wanna see?'

'I don't mind,' said Tracy. They had reached the school gates and slowed down as they converged into a single stream, congesting the narrow entrance. Through the other side, Elaine beckoned Tracy and they huddled over the letter.

'*Dear Elaine*,' read Tracy. 'Go on. Then what does it say?'

'It says,' said Elaine, and she tried to remember the words her mother had read out yesterday evening to her – sitting on her father's knee after tea. Her mother, in her spotless pinnie had smoothed the paper down and taken her blue-winged spectacles out of their case. Her father, who had been jigging her up and down in that special way of his, had both big red hands over the little knobs on her chest. Elaine tried to listen but so many other things kept coming in. She had shown the letter to her father first and they had looked at it together. 'Your mother will read it after tea, Poppet,' he had said and patted her bum.

'It says . . .' said Elaine, '. . . all about bums,' and both girls fell about.

'It never,' said Tracy.

'I haven't got time to read it to you now,' said Elaine, 'but it's about Mrs Pitt's not going to teach me any more and she's very sorry, and my letter to her says not to leave, please, and I'll try harder and I'm making her a present. I copied the words off my Mum.'

'What present?' said Tracy.

'Well, my Mum said a tea-cosy, but I'm going to make a cake. I'm going to buy a packet on the way home. Look,' said Elaine and showed Tracy inside her pocket where three pound coins chinked.

'My!' said Tracy. They held hands and went into the school.

'There she is!' said Tracy. Elaine let go and pushed her way towards Rose, a little way ahead of them up the stairs. She tugged at her jacket and handed her the letter she had written. Rose stopped to receive it and a pile-up of children began bumping into one another on the lower reaches of the stairs: 'Oh, thank you, Elaine. What pretty paper – and is that your writing on the envelope?'

At the same time, James Potterton, who had been jumping up and down on the landing above since long before the bell, pushed his way down, against the tide, to reach her. He elbowed Elaine out of the way and planted himself between her and Rose. 'I've got something for you. Something you're going to like,' he said.

Elaine who had gone very red gave him a shove of her sturdy hip and thigh. ''Scuse me,' she said.

James glowered. He put his hands round one of her golden plaits and hung on it.

At the bottom of the stairs Simon, who had just arrived shouted, 'Miss! Miss Pitt!' He made a jerky unco-ordinated leap and hurled himself at the clogged mass of children now almost come to a halt on the stairway. He began to battle a way through with no apparent awareness of the parts of body he was displacing.

'Come,' said Rose. She took the hands of the two children and pulled, 'let's talk upstairs.'

'Mrs Pitt!' said a voice from above. 'Surely you can choose a more suitable time and place to pass the time of day with pupils.' It was Mr Lovejoy. He stood like a bollard in rising sea at the head of the stairs. His voice stilled it with a single boom: 'Halt.' The chattering ceased and the children stood, all except Simon thrashing on and up regardless. Still booming, Mr Lovejoy addressed Rose: 'Mrs Pitt, if you wouldn't mind making your way up here I am sure we can find you a more suitable place to converse.'

Holding on to James and Elaine – she was not going to let them down again at this stage – Rose moved forward through a pathway that opened up at every step. When she reached the top Mr Lovejoy ignored her but boomed on: 'Children on the first two stairs, move,' as Simon, now tunnelling, arrived on the landing.

'Miss,' he yelled, 'I've got something,' and hurled a small hard paper-wrapped object in the air.

Rose picked it up, a battered car came loose from its wrapping. A week ago her mind would have fragmented and gone soft. This morning, she said, 'Thank you Simon. Perhaps you'd like to come to my place on the landing and we can talk there.' She spoke loudly and clearly and smiled at him as she moved unhurriedly on.

Behind her Mr Lovejoy, booming and swaggering, cleared the stairway by numbers. Nat, who had been standing by, raised his eyebrows at Mrs Jenkins and they nodded to each other. Rose crossed the landing. Behind her barrier of bookshelves she and the children were alone.

'Me first!', 'I was first!' they shouted.

A paper aeroplane sailed overhead and Gary's face peered above the books: 'Nah, na-na-na-nah,' he jeered, 'Miss has got the sa-ack.' He pranced round and handed the aeroplane to Rose. 'It's for you,' he said and turned his back. The aeroplane was made out of her letter to him. It was coloured with a scribble of blue and red and on the body was written, 'Miss from Gary'.

Selma edged, crablike, round the corner. 'Ssss,' she said. The sound had a curiously penetrating effect. It cut through the contesting voices and all the children watched as Selma handed Rose a tin of poppadums and then leaned heavily against her. Rose smelled a smell, a musty smell of unwashed hair, coconut oil and garlic underlaid with – was it betel-nut? She put her arm round the little girl, touched.

'Mr Foster says ...' said Wendy.

'Who cares,' said Gary.

'Don't interrupt,' said James.

'Oh, all right,' said Wendy. She giggled and bit her bottom lip. Looking at Rose she unclipped the pink slide from her hair and held it out: 'It's for you, Miss,' she said, 'but don't go,' and she traced along the grain of the wood floor with the toe of her plastic patent shoe.

'Everybody listen. You're to listen to *me*,' shouted James. He stamped his foot. 'There's going to be a party.' He handed Rose an envelope entirely covered on both sides with a dense mosaic of colour. 'Open it, open it.'

Inside was one of James's crowd scenes: pennants, streamers, paper hats, smiles, stars, ice-cream cones and a Union Jack. '*Invitation*' it said in an adult hand. '*You are cordially invited to a Party, Cocktails*' and in James's writing, 'dy James'.

The bell had long since gone and a hush fallen on the corridors and classrooms of Meadowbrook school. Only Rose's corner, a satellite of conviviality, glowed and pulsed with life. The children, without intervention, talked loudly and excitedly among themselves. Rose sat at the centre of it, at home in the din. Nat, concerned, walked by, his heart sinking as the noise increased. He looked in and grinned. He was about to walk on when James saw him. 'Mr Woolf, Mr Woolf,' he shouted, 'we're having a party. Come and do the writing.' Wendy and Elaine darted round the bookcases and grabbed his hands. They pulled him in and pushed him into a chair.

'What a good idea,' said Nat. He pulled a sheet of paper towards him. 'What do you want me to write?'

'It was my idea. Mine! Mine!' shouted James.

'And a very good one too,' said Nat. 'Where are you going to have it and when? Or is this it?'

'Silly,' said Wendy.

'Nah,' said Gary.

'Course not,' said James, 'there's going to be cocktails on the day.'

Rose was laughing. Nat caught her eye and soon he began laughing too.

32

'Angel,' said Frank. He glanced at his watch and saw that he had a good five minutes in hand. 'I adore you.' It was the old hairy-faced watch whose numerals were so difficult to discern. For a moment he saw it with piercing clarity on a green turf among the tiny rioting pimpernels, attending while he and Rose, entwined on the grass near by, were assumed into the heavens on a peal of silver trumpet calls. His indrawn breath was involuntary, approaching a rasp of pain.

'What darling? What is it?' said Rose.

Frank flexed his back further into the wooden corner: these House of Lords telephone boxes were the safest as well as the cosiest of all public telephone points in the entire capital. One was completely unobservable and if, as he emerged, anyone passing by were to ask themselves why he was not availing himself of a proper Peers' office telephone, well, that was what these were for. The old boys were always tottering in and out, eyes agleam, to make assignations with their girl friends. He longed to put his hand down inside his trousers.

'Darling,' said Rose's sweet voice again in his ear, 'what is it? Tell me.'

Frank held himself back. The effort brought tears to his eyes. 'I just wanted to hear you speak,' he said. 'Just wanted to activate the golden thread' – careful now – 'just wanted to tell you that we – I'm – off to Oronada at the end of next week and ... and ... well, I won't be seeing you for a while.' There, he had said it. It was not difficult. There seemed so little to say. He braced himself to deflect Rose's pain. He did love her. He would always love her. She would be for ever a bright jewel, maybe the brightest, in his chain of experience. But that was not what he had implied nor she had understood. He knew that as he stood there, one of the Establishment's many flawed pillars, in this insulated red-carpeted womb. But Rose said nothing and perhaps she wouldn't. Perhaps all she would say was, '*Bon voyage*', '*Kalo taxidi*', '*Buenviaje*', or even 'Have fun'. He waited. He was good at female timing. Then, in a small, cool voice from far away on the other side of London, she said: 'What do you mean, "for a while", and who? Who's off to Oronada and why?'

'Too boring,' Frank tried to say with the old cryptic nonchalance, but he could not get it out. He sighed. 'Oh, my darling,' he said, and could go no further.

'Are you crying?' said Rose.

Frank nodded. A sob scraped up his throat and lingered painfully on the wires between them. He waited for her soft affectionate laugh, the loving sign of their intimacy and her unqualified indulgence. He waited unusually long.

'You shit,' said Rose, 'you fucking deceiver. You ought to be castrated. You self-indulgent hypocrite. You toady.' Her voice was clear and hard. The delicious tickle in his balls died away and his sex contracted to a faraway pellet. 'Tut, tut,' he was about to say. 'I *am* surprised. Such lack of style,' but she put down the telephone and there was no one to hear. He was cut off and there was no one to hear.

He stumbled a little in the padded box and emerged feeling naked and exposed. He patted his hands up and down his body, confirming the material of his suit. Then, as was his way with trying moments, he assumed an air of exaggerated languor and strolled towards the bar. He would have a small brandy and watch the slow flow of the river as it rolled by the great bastions of Westminster. All is vanity, he told himself. He must calm down for there was a great deal to be done. He settled at a table by the windows and the waitress, midway between buxom barmaid and nanny, brought him his drink.

'That'll be one pound, thank you, My Lord,' she said.

What nice short words, what certainties. He put an extra 20p on the tray and waved her away with a confiding look over the top of his spectacles.

'That's a nice gentleman, that Lord Wetherby,' she said to her sister as they polished glasses behind the bar. But Frank failed to convince himself. There was something stale about his gestures and responses. They felt see-through and tawdry. He put his back to the room and tried to get the rhythms of the great river to carry him along with them. Alas, his attention was caught and held by the bright eye of a seagull bobbing on the choppy wavelets, cocky as you please. How he and Rose, watching it, would have laughed together. He waited for the sweet swell of nostalgia to rise up, a melancholy air like *Danny Boy*, or *La Vie en rose*, but what caught him by the throat and stuck in it had too many awkward corners for comfort. It was quite unfamiliar, too, in his repertory of bodily sensations. He pushed himself away from the table, tossed down the brandy and strode from the room. There were demons abroad that day and he would have his work cut out to dodge them. The pace at which he made for the car park was nearer a run than a walk and most unlike his customary leisured gait. He slammed the door, grated the gears, omitted to greet the policeman at the barrier and erupted straight out into the moving traffic. And instead of drawing up in front of the arches under St Pancras where a meeting of his museum committee was to take place, he found himself driving up and down the streets surrounding Rose's flat. It gave him quite a turn to see what he was doing. He would make an appointment with his doctor the very next day and, for now, maybe ask Ted Ainsworth at the meeting for a few of those magic pills everybody seemed to be swallowing these days, Xantoxin, he believed they were called.

Aware that her husband was under a strain, Tamarisk minimised her own ailments in a most accommodating way. It was ten days later.

She had bought the sweetest droopy blouse for the Inauguration. It was sprigged silk, tiny blue pimpernels and he loved wildflowers, she knew. She was to mount the earth mover, 'Thor' and get up on the seat beside HRH after he had cast the first sod and they were to ride round the site together. She applied a second layer of Meltonian blue to her eyelashes and studied the relationship between her skirt and her legs quite carefully in the looking-glass. Frank would be calling for her soon.

'Coo-eee,' she heard him call and the door slammed. 'Where's my best bib and tucker?'

'Coo-ee,' she sang back, 'all laid out on the bed in the dressing-room.'

'How sweet you look,' he said as she limped in. 'I do like your hat.' The hat, a halo with a half veil, showed her broad pale forehead and made an outer frame for the inner frame of babysoft curls. He saw her face in the looking-glass over his shoulder and the sight of it acted on his organism as a squeeze of lemon on an oyster. He dropped his eyes. He had elected to wear a bow tie and was struggling with the ends.

'You'll have to help me with the wretched thing,' he laughed. 'The ultimate humiliation for a grown man, you'll have to do a Mrs Darling on me.'

He kept his eyes shut and held his breath as she fiddled under his chin. The sweet powdery smell that came off her, more fragrance than scent, made him feel sick. Ah well, he thought to himself, let's hope the Trade Winds blow it all away. He saw palm trees waving, blue, blue skies and Tamarisk swathed in pale muslin lying, etiolated, in the shade. 'Come along,' he said quite sharply and preceded her to the car.

They drove in silence to King's Cross. There, the traffic was being diverted and first a few, then dozens and finally scores of unsuspecting motorists found themselves tooting and fuming in stasis down the seedy side streets. 'Ah! Lord Wetherby,' said the policeman at the checkpoint. He stuck a purple spot on the windscreen and waved him through. They drove up the broad sweep of York Way entirely on their own for a bit and then spied a big airforce-blue BMW coming towards them from the other direction. 'It's Max and Millie,' said Tamarisk. She stuck a suede-gloved hand out of the window to wave.

'All very well for *her*,' said Millie and raised a pencilled eyebrow. Eleven o'clock in the morning was an impossible time to get oneself dressed up for, and what was one supposed to do with oneself for the rest of the day? She felt thoroughly put upon in her black Rykiel suit to which she had added a fox fur and a beret tilted well down over the right eye. Max put a hand on the black-stockinged leg beside him: through the 15 denier the white skin over his wife's knee glimmered all ghostly. 'The smartest pussykins in the whole wicked metropolis,' he said, and gave it a squeeze. The red jewel in his cuff glowed against the stripes, emerald green and whiter than white. With her painter's eye, Millie registered the appositional relationships and sniffed. 'Don't,' she said in her high, small voice and nodded at Tamarisk and Frank.

A stand had been erected in the wide space in front of the train sheds and, before it, a carpet of false grass, bright green, of the kind sometimes to be seen on greengrocers' stalls, was laid out. Upon this grass, in the centre, was a small pyramid of earth and beside it, its brass all burnished, its decorative ironwork newly picked out in red and green, the 'Thor' with two little shovels suspended before it from a double armed prong. One or two officials stood by, among them the Duke of Middlesbrough's farm manager who wore a bowler hat and a suit with rounded fronts. Frank slowed the car and wound the window down. The man came over and lifted his hat. 'How d'you think she's looking, sir?' he said. 'Perfectly beautiful,' said Frank. He got out of the car to shake hands and Tamarisk watched as they went over to inspect the 'Thor'.

Max Vane strolled over to join them. He threw back his head and chortled and all three smiled or laughed. There was something off-key about Frank's bearing, as if he had a metaphorical pebble in his shoe somewhere, but Tamarisk could not quite put her finger on it. He came back to the car with a beam spread all over his face and eyes that were as dead as currants.

They drove to the space reserved for them and parked next to a chauffeur-driven Rolls-Royce. The Duke of Middlesbrough sat in the dove-grey interior holding the *Racing Times* in front of his face. He threw the paper down and came eagerly out, holding a silver mug in one hand and a quarter bottle of Bollinger in the other. 'My dears, my dears,' he said, 'what a thrilling occasion,' and handed Tamarisk a foaming fluted mug. He dived into the back for more and let out a series of hoots as fat corks shot high into the sky. A fine drizzle was starting to fall from it, or rather, hung in the air for there was no wind and the dying year sent a December chill out from the ground itself. The Duke's chauffeur got down from the car and held a giant umbrella over Millie and Tamarisk who fluttered her rich blue eyelashes and murmured, 'You're too sweet.'

A large Peugeot drew up and the de la Vignes got out, followed by their own chauffeur with two umbrellas. Jean-Baptiste went straight over to Frank. 'I 'ave good news,' he said, 'our *Musée de la Vie Rurale de Languedoc* has agreed to a permanent loan. We must arrange a visit for you to choose some pieces.'

'A picnic! How charming!' cried Chloë. She was wearing a redingote of grey Mongolian lamb, extravagantly skirted with a long lean body and a collar that was turned up round her chic, chignoned head. They kissed hands and cheeks all round the company.

Another Rolls-Royce, this one a Silver Cloud, glided silently into place at the end of the row. Ted Ainsworth got out and looked at his watch. He stood tight-lipped and close to his car. 'We're over here, Mr Ainsworth,' called Tamarisk. He came across, taking short jerky steps and gave a few brisk nods of his head. 'No, thanks. I never touch the stuff,' he said. The very proximity made him reach inside his waistcoat for his pill box and he popped a Xantoxin under his tongue. Tamarisk moved to stand beside him. 'Is that your dear doggie in the back?' she said. 'Do let him out. I'm sure no one would mind.'

The stand was filling up with the few dozen guests: social historians, museum curators, engineers, landowners, who had been invited. The officials looked at their watches and up at the sky. 'Perhaps we'd better move over,' said Frank. He was nervous and excited in a way he remembered well from childhood. It made him want to pee and he looked round at the wide tarmacadam field in fruitless quest for a bush.

Lady Goodall dismounted from her car. She was puffing rather and came over to join them. The Duke of Middlesbrough fetched a thin silver flask, shaped to the curve of his hip, from his pocket. 'A little whisky, Secretary of State?' He unscrewed the cap and poured out a measure. Though his hands shook – he was as highly strung as one of his own racehorses – not a drip missed its destination.

The group moved over to the stand and sat down in the front row. Borne along for the moment by Bollinger, they chattered among themselves, or leaned back to hail acquaintances in the rows behind. Tamarisk was relieved to see that the Duke's man had opened an umbrella over the 'Thor'.

'He's late,' said Frank, looking at his watch. He was not sure how much longer he could hang on.

There was a tremendous clattering roar and the red helicopter sailed slowly over the pink brick and green slate turrets of St Pancras. The false grass was blown flat and Millie and Tamarisk gasped as they held on to their hats. Briefed by the social secretary, Chloë de la Vigne's head was hatless, and Connie never wore one. The helicopter came to rest, the door was opened and HRH ran down the steps and straight over. 'I'm so sorry to keep you all waiting,' he said. Real concern furrowed his brow.

Frank stepped out. 'It's quite all right, Sir. Good of you to come. I expect you remember Tamarisk, my wife.'

'Ah yes,' said HRH, 'my hostess of the other evening and the gallant lady who's to be my passenger. I hope you've made your will.' He looked quizzically expectant, hopeful that his joke might be understood but resigned to its falling flat.

Presentations were made – most people knew one another, and the party moved over to the central set. Tail down, Betsy, the black Labrador, padded at her master's heels. HRH paused and held back. 'What a sweet dog,' he said and bent to stroke her. At that moment an idea oscillating at the back of Ted Ainsworth's mind jelled to a plan: he would invite HRH up to see over Ainsworth Agridustrials, present him with a million or so for his Heritage Trust and make two workplaces available for his Youth Training Scheme. His heart fluttered like a pennant in summer breeze, but so unused was he to agreeable sensations that he felt for another Xantoxin. The Duke's man was introduced. He led HRH round the 'Thor' and explained its workings. HRH climbed aboard and with a clunk and a hiss the 'Thor' trundled forward, its two arms clanking up and down alternately.

Trying hard to look carefree as a boy, though he had clearly never been one, HRH bent forward manipulating the levers. He trundled the 'Thor' to the pile of earth. The action of its two-armed prong had a hit-or-miss ineptitude, much like that of a claw-grab slot machine on a pier. At the third essay it shovelled up a scoop of dirt and a sub-dued cheer went up. He manoeuvred the machine backwards and brought it to a halt, panting and creaking. Tamarisk stepped out, the Duke's man handed her aboard, she arranged her legs becomingly sideways and HRH tucked her small gloved hand through his arm. 'Hang on,' he said and the 'Thor' clanked forward bearing its shovel-ful of dirt aloft.

The small crowd clapped.

Betsy growled.

'How charming!' cried Chloë de la Vigne.

'Bitch,' hissed Millie under her breath.

Right round the site and along the canal's edge went the 'Thor' like a strange ungainly insect but curiously more at home in its setting against the iron girders and arched brickwork of the old train workings than the two-legged creatures herded in the stand. 'What a triumph, old boy. I do congratulate you,' said Max Vane into Frank's ear. The 'Thor' approached. Betsy bounded out to meet it and backed, wagging her tail as HRH jumped out and ran round to assist Tamarisk back to earth. She stepped down, damp and breathless, her halo a little askew. 'What a fright she looks,' said Millie Vane in a perfectly audible small voice amid the claps and cheers. Frank stepped forward and put his hand on Tamarisk's shoulder.

'Thank you so much, Sir,' he said. Emotion thickened his voice and misted up his spectacles. He took them off and wiped them. What a dear man. His heart's really in it, thought the majority of onlookers, in particular, HRH and Connie.

'Cherished dream, what?' said HRH, shaking his hand. He patted him on the back. 'Must say, I've enjoyed it. Haven't had such fun for ages.' He waved and was gone, this time to the royal Vauxhall for his next appointment at the Crafts Council near by before lunch at the RIBA.

'I've got my table at Claridges,' said the Duke. 'Would anyone care to join me there? I'd be delighted if you'd keep me company.'

Frank went over to the 'Thor'. He climbed into the seat and waggled the steering wheel. He felt the kind of stirring and churning of emotion he associated with great ceremonies, say, in the Abbey; coronations, marriages, or was it funerals he was thinking of?

33

The minibus careers down Regent Street. Above it, huge red bows and yellow bells made from hundreds of light bulbs flanking Father Christmases in sleighs are slung across the road. The children rush from side to side craning their heads, throwing streamers out of the windows, shouting at passers-by. 'Hey mister, your trousers are coming down,' yells Gary at a policeman and they all duck, gripped by wave after wave of terrified, delicious giggles. Some of the boys lurch over to join him. With their heads just above window-level, they egg each other on.

'You've dropped your false teeth!'

'Lookout! Your knickers are falling off!'

'Have a banana ...'

Wendy hangs on to Rose's arm. 'Oh, Miss,' she breathes, 'isn't that lovely. Just like fairyland.' They round the curve and come upon Piccadilly Circus, a universe dazzling with lights; flowing, flashing, winking, all colours. No longer a member of staff, Rose puts an arm round her shoulders. 'It's magic, isn't it?'

'Anyone for fudge?' calls Mrs Jenkins. She sits with Maggie, nose pressed to the window, on her lap, looking the good soul she is. As she bends to rummage in her bag she tethers Maggie with a protective arm. 'It's like having a bubble on one's knee, dearie,' she says, 'there's no knowing when you'll float away.'

She brings out a round Christmas tin filled with layers of home-made fudge, a clean paper handkerchief between each. 'Plenty for everyone,' she says as the children crowd round.

James stomps up: 'I'm in charge.' He snatches the tin away.

'Nah, you're never,' says Gary, leaving his post by the windows. He seizes the tin, jams two pieces into his mouth and hands it back to Mrs Jenkins. James butts him in the stomach and they fall to the floor, punching and scuffling in the aisle.

'Silly boys,' says Wendy, stepping over them. Her chipped pink fingernails hover above the tin.

'Take that one, dear, it's the biggest,' says Mrs Jenkins.

'What about the driver?' asks Nat through the dense sugary mass now melting in his mouth. Looking in the driving mirror, Mr Clark gives a thumbs-up. Selma slithers off her seat and clasps the tin to her chest. She makes her way unsteadily to the front. 'Ta, ever so,' says Mr Clark. He's wearing a peaked cap pushed to the back of his head. James had insisted. *'Bright clothes and dressing up will be worn'* the invitations had said. He himself has a giant Mickey Mouse down the front of his T-shirt (a night-shirt of his mother's) and he wears green jelly sandals, red socks and a yellow sou'wester with it.

'Look at that tree, Simon. Simon, look!' says Elaine. Spanking clean in her red tartan party dress, she's sitting next to Simon, bandaged and grubby as always. She's taken the red ribbons out of her hair to knot round his neck like a tie and is holding on to his hand. Simon seems mesmerised by the lights and the motion. He leans back against the seat and partly against Elaine with his mouth open and he looks smaller than usual.

The minibus drives round Trafalgar Square and the children run to the side nearest the Christmas Tree.

'Is it as high as the sky? I want to see,' shouts James. Mr Clark draws the bus to a halt and they all scramble out and charge across the square. Round the base they stare up into the velvet sky. 'Nearly. I'd say, nearly, wouldn't you, Mr Woolf?' says James, 'If God leaned out of the sky he could probably touch it.' He turns and runs off towards the fountains and the lions. The children stream after.

287

Wendy lingers, her attention held by the National Gallery. 'Is that where Princess Di lives and the Queen, Miss?' she says. She's wearing high-heeled shoes, red ones and spotted pink socks. She clings on to Rose for the heels skeeter, frequently, sideways from under her. 'Shall I give you a piggyback?' asks Nat and canters off, the red shoes wobbling by his ears.

Rose gives a leap and runs zigzagging after them with her arms out like an aeroplane. The wind rushes in her ears and the cold air stings her eyes with a keen zing like the driest of Martinis. Selma, of all people, is already in the fountain giggling, with her skirts held up. Simon and Elaine jump up and down, on and off the parapet, shouting encouragement.

'Ooh, isn't she brave, Miss. I couldn't ever,' says Simon.

'Isn't she!' Rose rolls up her own trouser leg and takes off her shoe. 'It's freezing,' she calls as the icy water creeps up her calf. 'Well done, Selma.'

The little girl comes splashing back towards the parapet. She's subsumed by giggles. Mrs Jenkins takes a big towel out of her bag and wraps her up like a mummy. She pats her and hugs her and feeds her fresh fudge. 'I think they're enjoying themselves, dear, don't you?' she says to Rose.

James and Gary are floundering on the slippery sides of the lions. 'Give us a leg-up, Sir,' shouts Gary. 'Me too, Me too,' shout the others. One by one Nat shoulders them up on to the lions until all four are full of yippee-ing children. Rose and Nat climb up behind Selma. They throw their heads back.

'Yippee,' they shout up at the stars.

'Yippee, up there!' calls Mrs Jenkins, patrolling from lion to lion and throwing streamers while Maggie hops at her heels. Coloured streamers are draped all over her and she pretend-nibbles them from time to time.

When they get back to the minibus Mr Clark has put a present on every seat. Small ones, all the same size, they look like large shiny sweets. He watches as the paper's torn off, chuckling with pleasure but sick at heart for Sam. He's made each person a wooden whistle. The noise of the engine, as he starts it up, is obliterated by the jubilant din as all at once everyone blows, hangs out of the windows and blows some more.

'Sir, mine won't work, Sir,' whines Gary. 'I've got a dud.' His cheeks are puffed out and his eyes start from his head as he blows with all his might.

Nat removes the whistle from his own mouth. 'You're overdoing it,' he says, 'it needs less power than you're giving it, not more, for optimum functioning.'

'Nah,' says Gary, but he tries an ordinary blast and produces a piercing note of penetrating timbre. 'Yeah!' And he blows a harsh squawk in Wendy's ear. Wendy gives as good as she gets if not better. She kicks off her shoes and the two of them march up and down, outdoing one another in length and variety of note.

Pulsating with noise and light the minibus approaches Waterloo Bridge. Along the Strand, the vagrants in doorways unfurl their sleeping-bags and flourish them aloft: theatre-goers in Aldwych turn to wave.

'Catch!' calls a rigidly coiffed lady in a fur coat. She throws her box of chocolates, handmade in Golders Green, at a window. The box sails in and lands on Simon's lap. He starts, spooked, relaxes with a grin and feels in his pocket for his dilapidated toy car.

'Merry Christmas,' he yells as he hurls it back at her.

Now the children rush from side to side. 'Merry Christmas, merry Christmas,' they yell and whistle to the drivers of cars alongside.

'Merry Christmas,' the drivers hoot back.

On either side of the bridge the black waters of the Thames swim with myriad reflected lights, shivering like silver apricots. Along the banks as far as the eye can see in every direction, gardens of illumination curve into the far distance, a miraculous spectacle in which every building is crowned, necklaced, outlined and bathed in glorious manifestation of electricity, exultant in the dark. James briefly notes the display. 'It looks like fireworks frozen quiet,' he says. 'I like that blue one far away best.' He leans back in his seat sucking and blowing on his whistle. For a few minutes soft silence fills the bus. It swings round the end of the bridge and down on to the embankment where it pulls up on a grassy space between trees. Coloured lights, strung from the branches and between lampposts along the embankment wall, sway in the night air touching it with friendly pallor.

'We're going to have cocktails now,' says James, 'and I'm in charge.' In his sou'wester and sandals he marches up and down giving out tickets. The tickets say: 'Pink Lady', 'Tango Sour', 'Coke Fizz', and so on. Mr Clark stretches, lets a little air in under his cap and pulls a crate out from beneath his seat. The crate's packed with bottles filled with coloured drink that wink wickedly at the lights in the trees. On the bottles are labels corresponding to the tickets. 'It doesn't matter what you have. The tickets are for looking nice. Roll up. Roll up,' says James. He passes from seat to seat, taking orders. Rose and Mrs Jenkins pour the drinks into glasses and Mr Clark pops a couple of bendy-straws into each. They're delicious, warming and cooling, as well as covering all the tastes from pink to purple. Nat, refreshed, gets out and starts spreading rugs on the grass. Similarly refreshed, the rest storm out and over to the riverside.

The tide is out and the strand, pocked with stones and bits of rock, gleams all slimy with mud. The children find a break in the wall and a stone stairway. They tumble down it, carolling with glee. They slosh and flounder, slapping their hands on the thin veils of water lying on the sand, trailing strings of seaweed and slime and skimming stones at the water. A Port of London Authority launch buzzes by and then a pleasure steamer, all lit up. The children run shrieking from the rush of waves and chase them back, feinting and squealing as the incoming and outgoing swells collide, swirl, recede and are overtaken by the next oily-surfaced influx. Rose and Mrs Jenkins sit on the embankment wall enjoying the night air and the cries of excitement and enthusiasm floating up from the muddy riverbed. Mrs Jenkins hums, familiar tunes like *Rock of Ages*. She lifts her head. Her voice grows stronger. It rings across the water, a clear quavering soprano; hymns and songs from the valleys. Rose lies back on the parapet with her hands behind her head. Nat strolls across. He joins in with Mrs Jenkins and he has a pleasant working voice, steady and true as one of the lesser planets shining lower down in the sky.

The children straggle back up the stairs, smelling of wet river water and rotten eggs. They see a circle of candles glowing on the grass. There are dozens of them, a swimming pool of light circled by rugs and casting the dark around into deeper black. They run across, a little awed and the warmth eats up the damp from their limbs and their clothes as they stare, spellbound. On the far side, white-faced, sits Mr Clark with Maggie in his arms. Simon creeps round and leans against them. Between them and the light, pyramids of sausages, crisps, twiglets, pizzas and Penguins are piled on plates interspersed with bottles of tomato ketchup. By and by the children plunge in. 'Tea, Mrs Pitt?' says Mrs Jenkins, unscrewing a Thermos.

James jumps up, his mouth so crammed with twiglets that some stick out like straws from a scarecrow. He adjusts the tilt of his sou'wester, leaving tomato ketchup smudges on its brim. 'Ladies and Gentlemen,' he says, 'all be quiet and listen to me.'

'Shush,' says Gary, unnecessarily.

'Pass me a sausage,' says James. With one reassuringly in each hand he begins to speak. 'This is an important speech, and I am making it. Hip hooray for Mrs Pitt. Here's your present. 'He takes a bite from each hand, bows, and stands, feet apart, arms akimbo. Mrs Jenkins brings a scroll out of her bag. It's as long as a magic wand and all twined round with shiny ribbons. Rose takes it and begins to unroll it as the others watch from the circle of light. It goes on and on. One by one the children crawl over and hold it down.

'This is me!'

'I did that bit!'

'D'you like it? D'you like it?' they shout.

It's a bus, rather like the 'Jesus loves me' buses of Africa and the Caribbean, exuberantly decorated, swarming and crammed with people. It bowls along a road lined with palm trees, Christmas trees, apple trees and all manner of birds fly in the blue sky overhead from which flowers in garlands, bunches and one by one rain down. On the ground are cats, dogs, worms, monkeys, some in hats and ties and some without. The people waving from the bus all have balloons coming out of their mouths. 'Good luck', 'I love you', 'Happy Christmas' and along the top, in giant writing, striped and spotted, it says 'To Mrs Pitt', followed by all their names, ending with Nathan, Gwynneth, Phil and Maggie.

'Thank you,' says Rose. 'Thank you very, very much. I think it's wonderful. The best present, truly, I've ever had in my life.' She goes and stands by Mr Clark and puts her arm round him. Then she kneels on the grass by the picture and goes through it, bit by bit, with each participant.

The candles sputter and die out, one by one. Nat replaces some, maintaining a lesser source of softness and radiance. They all settle comfortably round making pillows and armrests of each other. Mrs Jenkins takes some packets of sweets from her bag and passes them round. Then she tells a story. As she finishes –

'The prince got on to the white horse and lifted the princess up behind him. Leaving the dragon dead in a lake of black blood, the horse spread its wings and they flew over the mountains –'

Big Ben, clearly visible above the bare branches and the strings of swinging lights, strikes midnight. Everyone climbs back into the minibus which rolls them, smooth as an ambulance, through the streets of London to their own front doors.

James Potterton, his cheeks bulging with bull's-eyes, leans back on the close-cropped fawn prickles of his seat. 'I wonder how long it would take to colour in the stars,' he says.

Epilogue

There was no light at all in Sam's room but for some peripheral refractions from the big searchlights directed on the front and the back of the house. It was a harsh light, unnaturally bleached, and the searchlights had been installed as a direct result of Sam's incessant attempts to run away. He crouched where no light could touch him in a corner of the room, unmoving, hour after hour, more like an animal at bay than a child of ten. By and by, his head might drop on his chest but his sense of danger was never at rest. He dug himself further into the corner. Angles and hard surfaces shored up his body; mistrust and hate filled his heart. Instinctively, he avoided even the thin mattress and blankets on his bed, just as he refused any form of human contact and blocked all feeling from his mind.

'It's not natural, I've never come across a child like him,' Eleanor was saying even now to Mr Watkins over bedtime cocoa. 'He must of been born bad.'

Sam prised up splinters from the floor with his fingernail. He selected the longest and jabbed it into the outside corner of his eye. Without much difficulty he stifled his reactions; the cry of pain, the closing of the lid. Though the eye reddened and watered, his face remained impassive. He began banging his head, experimenting with different surfaces: wood, stone and iron. He hated his head now stripped of its own rank mass of matted curls. He smashed both fists into it. His fists were as hard and sharp as two flints as was his whole whip-thin body, scarred and bruised the entire four feet of its length.

However, the sudden screech of a night owl caused him to start. He went over to the window and pressed his nose to the toughened glass. As he stared into the black, a spike of longing pricked its way through the pith beneath the skin. It was for night air; fresh, clean, cool, as high as the sky, as wide as the world. He wished to breathe. He was going to suffocate in here like the princes in the Tower, a story his mother used to read them along with *Joan of Arc* and *Romulus and Remus* from her own *Child's Book of Stories from History*. The memory came unbidden. He screamed in panic and clapped his hands over his ears. His eyes started from his head and his mouth opened in terror, a black hole, a silent scream. Needles of fear showered round him. He ran to his corner and curled into a tight ball, hugging and rocking himself.

Under the board on which he sat were his precious things, a secret cache located outside himself beneath the floor. Using his teeth and his nails he prised up the board and felt around among the dusty timbers not knowing when his hand would be bitten off by whatever lived there. He brought them out, a few letters, a get-well card, the wrapping of a Refresher packet, a brightly coloured picture from some of the children at his old school with all their names on it. He held them to his cheek for a moment or two. Then very carefully he arranged them round him in a thin line so that a small cone-shaped section of the room was marked off from the rest. He kept one letter back, laid his head down upon it and went to sleep.